THE REDEEMER

A SHANNA REGAN MURDER MYSTERY

VICTORIA GOLDMAN

THREE CROWNS PUBLISHING

First published in the United Kingdom by Three Crowns Publishing UK in 2022
www.threecrownspublishing.com
www.vgoldmanbooks.com
Twitter: @VictoriaGoldma2 & @3CPublishingUK

Cover design by Design for Writers
Crown icons created by Freepik – Flaticon

Paperback ISBN: 978-1-7396954-1-5
eBook ISBN: 978-1-7396954-0-8

THE REDEEMER

CHAPTER ONE

She scurries across the rain-drenched grass. Stone missiles bounce off her shiny black boots, spattering mud on her burgundy coat. One hits the side of her head, knocking her grey beret askew.

I shift on the wooden bench under the sycamore trees and lean forwards. Willing someone, anyone, to help her.

Anyone but me.

'Pig. Ham. Bacon butty,' yell the two youths behind her. Whipping up the grass with their trainers, they close in on her like two wolves targeting their prey.

A man saunters on a nearby path. 'He's the one, for sure,' I whisper. Young. Fit. Hopefully fearless. But he keeps his head down. Pulls his navy baseball cap low over his eyes and murmurs into his phone as he heads for the park gate.

I want to chase him, shake him, beg him to step in. But instead I watch a woman with frizzy blonde hair shoving two little girls towards the swings. She shakes her head when one runs towards the mud-splattered slide. As she glances around, her eyes meet mine. She gives me a half-hearted shrug and a weak smile.

If she thinks it's easier to turn a blind eye, she's right. Getting involved often leads to trouble – I should know.

This is the first time I've noticed signs of tension in this Hertfordshire town so I'm hoping it's a one-off. Two bored yobs looking for mischief on this chilly Saturday morning, creating havoc wherever they go.

The woman with the beret is just here at the wrong time.

Me too.

One of the youths pauses and reaches down for more ammunition, scrambling around for anything he can find.

'Ya stuck up Jewish bitch!' he shouts, as he stands up and flings pellets of stones and turf and mud towards her.

The woman holds up her head in defiance. But her clenched hands tell me a different story. Her mouth flinches at each word thrown at her, every dig at her Jewish faith. Pig, ham, bacon butty ... Not just random words. Not just random foods. Not just a random target.

I stand up and grab my tatty, red rucksack. My shoulder throbs in protest when my heart somersaults at the familiar routine. But I can't wait any longer. Someone has to do something. And I guess that someone will be me.

I sprint across the grass, my black jeans scuffing against my hips and my grubby white trainers squelching into the mud, reminding myself I've been involved in worse.

'Hey. Get the fuck back to your holes, you toads!' I hope the yobs can't hear the tremor in my voice. 'Get outta here,' I add, more loudly this time.

But still they don't give up. Stampeding across the grass like African bull elephants.

'Die in the gas chamber, yer fuckin' Yid,' the taller one yells at the woman, flicking a long strand of blond fringe away from his eyes. 'Yer ain't wanted here.' He stops and picks up a fistful of rocks. Flings them towards her feet.

The woman comes to a sudden halt. A big mistake when you're running on slippery grass. One of her boot heels slides. She loses her balance and falls back, landing on her rear, her arms outstretched behind her to break her fall. Her beret lands on the ground beside her.

I reach her and drop my rucksack to the ground. Stand in front of her like a lioness protecting her cub, a rush of adrenaline surging through my limbs. My fight or flight response is kicking in. I'm ready for battle, even though my head warns me otherwise.

Don't get involved. This is not your fight.

'Fuckin' Yids. Fuckin' Yids.'

A stone flies towards me. My face stings as it clips my cheek. When I press my hand against my skin, my fingers feel wet and sticky. When I pull them away, a thin stream of blood trickles down.

'Leave her alone, you racist shits.' I reach into my jeans back pocket to pull out my phone. 'Or I'll call the police.' My heart pounds and my breath snakes away from me like puffs of dragon smoke.

The taller youth flinches at my words. Maybe he's been in trouble with the law before.

Close up, they're younger than I thought. Adolescent acne with little sign of stubble. In their teens, but not much older than fourteen or fifteen, sixteen at a push.

The smaller one lifts two fingers spread apart. Points to his piercing blue eyes, then at me.

'Be afraid,' he mouths.

Maybe he's been brought up on old gangster movies, thinks he can intimidate me, but I don't scare that easily.

'Calling them now.' I press some random keys on my mobile and throw him my strongest glare.

It's not easy being intimidating when you're only five foot five. But I clearly do something right as he shouts at the other youth and then they run off, heading back across the grass, laughing and nudging each other. They grab two mountain bikes propped up against a nearby oak tree, swing themselves onto the saddles and cycle off at high speed, shouting 'Fuckin' Yids, Fuckin' Yids' as they go.

I slide my mobile back into my jeans pocket. Take a deep breath.

Never show weakness, I'd been taught early on, pounded into me by my grandad. Never let the bullies win.

'Your cheek...' The woman is gazing up at me, a worried expression spreading across her face.

'I'll be fine. I've had worse.' I ignore the twinge in my shoulder and hold my hand out towards her.

She grasps it with a trembling hand. Her grip is weak but she manages to pull herself up, then grabs her beret and clutches it to her chest.

'Are you sure ... are you sure you're okay?' She speaks so quietly that I have to concentrate hard to hear her. 'You're bleeding.' She clears her throat with a gentle cough. 'I'm so sorry. It's all my fault. If it wasn't for me, you—'

'Their fault. Not yours.' My cheek stings with each word. 'And I'll be fine. But what about you? They had no right to—'

'I'm...' She pauses, looks me up and down. 'Come back to my place so I can sort out your cheek.'

Black smudges of mascara frame her tear-stained eyes, with crow's feet strutting around the corners. She has a good twenty years on me, maybe in her early fifties.

'I live over there.' She points to a brown-roofed bungalow that backs onto the park, next to the gate.

I glance down at my rucksack, check the time on my watch. As if I have somewhere to be. As if someone is waiting for me at my destination.

Even though I don't and there isn't.

'Please.' She takes my hand, clasps it in hers. 'I'm good at first aid. It's the least I can do.'

I'm not sure if her pallid skin is a sign of shock or her natural complexion. Maybe she needs more medical attention than I do. I feel a sudden urge to see her home, make sure she's safe. Plus, never knock back an opportunity that comes your way. Years of experience have taught me that. And I can visualise my headline already: 'Jewish woman terrorised by racist louts in Hillsbury Park.'

'Sure.' I ignore the bulging first aid kit in my rucksack. 'I'm Shanna.'

She gives the hint of a smile, flushing a glimmer of light back into her hazel eyes. 'I'm Valerie.'

I pick up my bag and follow her across the grass to the gravel path.

CHAPTER TWO

Excitement flutters in my chest like a cluster of dragonflies when I see the blue commemorative plaque embedded into the wall by Valerie's white front door. Maybe those youths have done me a favour. I smile at the irony, then wince with pain. Pressing my hand against my injured cheek reminds me they haven't.

Though I'm desperate to find more historical plaques.

'It's a straightforward feature,' said David Black, editor of *Hillsbury Living*, the magazine I've been working on for over a month. 'Research our local artists online and include pictures of paintings with their history and the artists' history. Job done.'

I'd baulked at the idea. Art has never been my thing. I know little about it and care even less. So I offered an alternative. A spur-of-the-moment decision that seemed wise at the time: investigate some historical markers on the local buildings. Take photos, write about who they commemorate and why, beginning with the blue plaque near the office door, honouring a local architect now long gone. Call it 'Our Hillsbury Heritage'.

It would be the perfect excuse to escape from the office more often, I figured, though I didn't mention that, plus researching in the outdoors is more my specialty.

David had argued at first, saying it wasn't what his readers would want. But I dug in my heels, persisting until he said yes.

And then realised how foolish I'd been.

I've never been interested in history, including my own. Always thought the past didn't matter; it's the future that counts, or the 'here and now'. Too many years travelling maybe, never staying in one place for long enough to create roots or make long-lasting friendships. Even Kilconly, which has been my go-to base for well over two decades, still doesn't feel like home.

Now I'm thirty-three, Dad hopes that will change.

After recent months, I hope it will too.

This article isn't the easiest, I've discovered, as I haven't located many historical plaques. Either very few people living in Hillsbury have ever achieved anything noteworthy or, more likely, very few want to commemorate those who have.

That's why I'd been sitting in the park just now, wondering how I'm going to finish off this article and the rest of the magazine before it goes to press. But I'm not panicking. Not yet anyway. And now I've stumbled across another historical plaque, I'm one step closer to completing this job.

I watch Valerie as she fumbles with her door key. 'Mind if I take a photo?'

'Of what?'

'You and your blue plaque.'

She glances down the street. 'I'm really sorry but not today.'

My eyes follow the direction of hers, inspecting the neat

row of bungalows with their empty, pruned front gardens. 'Today?'

'It's Shabbat. I mean, the Jewish Sabbath. I should be at shul.'

'Shul?' I mull over the word as I say it.

'That's another name for a synagogue, a Jewish place of worship.' Valerie glances at my cheek, purses her lips and shakes her head slowly. 'But it clearly wasn't meant to be.'

The front door swings open and Valerie motions for me to follow her inside.

We walk into a long bright hallway with a large silver-edged mirror reflecting light from the ceiling chandelier along the opposite wall. A rich aroma of meat and spices hangs in the air.

I shut my eyes. Take a deep breath in. It feels warming, inviting and strangely comforting.

'We don't use cameras today, or phones or television or ... well, lots of things. So I'm so sorry but I can't pose for photos.'

Valerie peels off her coat and hangs it on a chrome peg by the front door and takes off her mud-splattered boots, lining them up on the inner doormat. 'We don't drive either, but everyone keeps Shabbat differently. Some Jewish people ... they don't keep it at all.'

She yanks off her beret then scrunches the top of her hair to fluff it back up, but it refuses to cooperate, leaving greying straggles hanging down like the limp branches of a willow tree.

'You use lights though.' I drop my rucksack next to her boots, kick off my trainers and take off my denim jacket, hanging it on the peg adjacent to hers. 'And an oven.'

I inhale, slowly and deeply. 'Something smells good.'

Valerie gives me a broad smile as she places her beret on the marble-topped hall table. 'Thank you.' She straightens her grey knitted dress across her hips and pulls the hem down over her knees. 'Everything's on timers: the lights and the cooker. We set them up before Shabbat comes in and I cook everything in advance. Then we heat up the food on hotplates or use a slow cooker. Bit of a mad rush every week, especially if we have guests, but we get there in the end.'

I'm well aware that every religion has its rules, as I've been exposed to many of them over the years. Catholic school in Ireland – dragged there by my granny. Mosques in Istanbul holding prayers five times a day – watching from afar with Dad. I can't understand why anyone would want to be governed by so many rules and regulations though. Well, maybe once I had, but not now.

'It sounds far more complicated than it is.' Valerie shakes her head. 'Sorry, you're probably not that interested. That looks quite deep.' She points at my cheek, maybe mistaking my silence for disinterest, or possibly pain.

'Of course I am. But about those youths in the park...'

I'm surprised she hasn't mentioned them, the words they used, the hurt they caused her. Pig. Ham. Bacon butty. Foods that Jews are forbidden to eat, thrown as insults. Yid – a derogatory name for Jew, the equivalent of using the N-word or the P-word. Gas chambers... 'How can you ignore it?'

'I...' She shakes her head again. 'Let's get that cut sorted, shall we?'

I open my mouth to say more, but she purses her lips in defiance. So instead I just nod, hoping I won't end up with a scar.

Dad won't be impressed that I've got another injury, especially so soon after the last one. He was so relieved when I said I was ready to settle down, stop the travelling. Less so when he realised I didn't know where. A lump of guilt settles in my throat, but I swallow it away. It's his fault, as he prompted my wanderlust in the first place.

Valerie pulls open the door to a cupboard built under the stairs. As she pokes around inside, I peer through the nearest doorway. Two silver candlesticks with pearly white wax crusted around their base stand on a silver tray on an oak sideboard. The dining table, draped with a cream lace table-cloth, is laid for eight with a cluster of gleaming silver goblets on a matching tray at its centre. Two plaited loaves of bread peep out from under a colourful embroidered silk cloth.

'So, why are you so interested in our plaque?' Valerie's soft voice is muffled by the cupboard door. 'Most people ignore it as they don't seem bothered about history anymore.'

My cheeks grow warm. 'My boss is. Interested in local history, I mean. Our readers too, apparently.'

'Oh, so you're a journalist.' She pauses, like most people when they discover my profession. After politicians, journalists seem to be the most vilified people in the world. 'Which newspaper do you work for?'

'I don't.' I say this a bit too abruptly and stifle a sigh. 'At the moment, I'm working at *Hillsbury Living* magazine.'

Valerie stands up, hugging a green first aid box to her chest, and pushes the cupboard door until it clicks shut. 'Ooh, we get that one.'

Her first aid box is larger than I'd expect in a family home. I've seen lots of trauma kits over the years – Afghanistan, Africa, Iraq – as there's plenty of patching up to do when you're in a war zone or in the back of beyond. But Valerie's first aid supply is the size of a small shoebox.

'I've only been at the magazine a month.' The cut on my cheek stings as I move my mouth. 'It's not a permanent thing.'

'Where were you before?'

'*NewsQuest*, an international news magazine based in London. I started off as a reporter there, then a features writer. But more recently I've been freelance, travelling the world.'

Until the commissions dried up.

Valerie's hazel eyes brighten. 'How exciting.'

I don't want to shatter her illusion, but sometimes my job isn't exciting at all. Most of the time, in fact. Hectic, dangerous, exhausting, even heartbreaking at times. Yet until recently, I hadn't desired anything else.

'Come into the lounge,' Valerie says. 'The natural light's better in there.'

I follow her through a doorway on the right.

'Please, take a seat.' She points at the sofa nearest me. 'Would you like a drink before I start?'

'A glass of water would be great.'

Once Valerie leaves the room I sit down on the sofa, sinking into the plush beige velvet cushions as I take a look around.

It's been a while since I've been in a family home. The furnishings are comfortable and the surfaces sparkle with polish. Photos adorn the sideboard and artwork decorates the walls. Hardback books are stacked in a pile on the coffee table in front of me.

A white earthenware mug on the marble-topped corner table by the sofa catches my eye, just as Valerie walks back into the lounge carrying a glass of water. I peer forwards to read the red words printed on the mug's shiny surface: *KEEP CALM – DON'T KILL THE PATIENTS!*

I look up in surprise.

'My husband Harry's a GP.' Valerie puts the glass down on the corner table and sits down beside me. Gives me a sheepish smile. 'Someone once bought it as a joke. I'd throw it out if he let me.'

'I hope he doesn't take it into work.'

Work.

My mouth suddenly feels dry. I pick up the glass, swirl the water around and take a gulp.

'He wouldn't dare.' Valerie chuckles.

Maybe Harry's job explains the size of the first aid kit. Our house had been jam-packed with medical supplies too, but then I'd been an accident-prone child, always exploring and getting into trouble. Grazed knees. Cuts and bruises. Broken bones. Thinking about it, not much has changed.

'Let's sort out your cheek.' Valerie unfastens the first aid box and lays it flat. It's well stocked with plasters and bandages, sutures and antiseptics, so I assume she knows what to do. When she picks up a pair of sharp scissors and grips them tightly in her fist, I hope she does.

She puts the scissors down, opens a foil packet and pulls out an antiseptic wipe, then begins to clean my cheek with gentle strokes.

'So if you travel a lot, why end up here in Hillsbury?'

She isn't the first person to ask.

'I moved here five weeks ago. I was ... looking for some peace and quiet.' I wince as the antiseptic seeps into the gash and put the glass down on the table.

Valerie chuckles. 'It's not always quiet around here.' She leans forwards, lowers her voice. 'Or peaceful.'

'No, I guess not.' I wince again.

'Sorry.'

'I'm fine.' I clench my fists. *Never show weakness.* 'So that happen a lot? Those youths in the park?'

I wait for her anger, her rant – everything I would be doing and saying if it had been me they were chasing rather than her. Instead, there's just an awkward silence, a clock ticking loudly in the background.

'No,' Valerie says eventually, before biting her lip in concentration as she sticks a narrow white strip across my cheek. 'That's the first time. It's often quiet in the park on a Saturday morning at this time of year so I generally avoid it, but it's a shortcut and I was in a rush.'

'Won't Harry notice you're not at syna ... I mean, shul?'

She shakes her head slowly. 'I don't always go, especially when we have friends over for lunch, though today there's a guest rabbi speaking after the service.'

She glances at the corner table, the silver carriage clock on top, and lets out a sigh. It's eleven-thirty. 'Bit late to go now.' She closes the first aid box and stands up. 'All done. How does your cheek feel?'

'Sore. But it'll be fine, I'm sure.'

'If you want to find another plaque you could try up the road. I think there's one at number twenty-five though I haven't been past there for a while. You should be able to take a photo today as I think it's empty.'

I have a niggling feeling she's trying to get rid of me, but I'm ready to move on anyway. Over the years, I've learnt not to outstay my welcome. And if there's more to this park incident, I'll find out another way. It's what I'm trained to do.

I walk into the hallway and look in the mirror. A heart-shaped face with an olive complexion gazes back at me. My sun-bleached red-brown hair is sticking up at the top, so I lick my palm and smooth it down. I've kept it short for years. Easier to cover with a scarf when I need to, and cooler in the heat. I peer more closely at my reflection. My right cheek is red and blotchy. Hit any higher and I could've lost an eye. Two thin white strips cover the gash and the bleeding has stopped. Valerie has done a good job. I couldn't have done it better myself.

She appears behind me in the mirror as if she heard her name in my thoughts.

And I realise I can't just leave this all alone.

'How can you ignore what happened?' I turn around and glare into her eyes. 'Those thugs ... they were being racist, antisemitic.'

My voice gets louder with every word, with the anger – the indignation – I want, no, *need*, to hear from her. 'It's just not right. They insulted you. Tried to hurt you. You need to report them.'

I put on my trainers while I wait for her answer, seeds of regret slowly sowing in my mind. I always try to linger on the sidelines when I travel. Watching events unfold before me, reporting on them but never getting emotionally involved. It isn't my problem, I constantly have to remind myself, as I did a few months back.

'Report them?' Valerie clasps her hands and squeezes them together, so tightly that her knuckles turn white.

'To the police. If you won't, I will. You can't let them get away with it. Those little shits will do it again.'

Valerie flinches. Probably my swearing. I make a mental note to tone it down. Adapt to your circumstances, adapt to your environment, blend in – the first rules I learnt as I travelled the globe.

'They're just ... just kids. Sometimes kids say things they don't really mean.' She shakes her head in despair, but the quiver in her voice gives her away. She doesn't really believe her words any more than I do.

Another twinge in my shoulder nudges me to back off. Clean slate, I'd told myself. Move forwards, not back. But I need a good story, as I need to find myself a better job.

'Well, give it some thought. If you need a witness, get in

touch.' I reach into the front pocket of my rucksack, pull out my business card and hand it to her, hoping she'll change her mind. 'And thanks for patching me up.'

She shoves my card in the top drawer of the hall table without looking at it. I doubt I'll hear from her again.

CHAPTER THREE

The following morning, I arrive at Valerie's bungalow around eleven. I figure I'll take a photo of the plaque in the daylight, then track down the one further up Campton Avenue. Number twenty-five, Valerie had said. She and Harry live at number three.

I'd considered sneaking a photo yesterday after Valerie had closed her front door, but the rain was chucking it down by the time I left and I hadn't wanted to damage my phone. Plus, it felt wrong as she'd told me not to, and I've always respected different religions even if they're not my own.

Instead, I'd retreated back to my rented apartment. The rush of adrenaline from the park had plummeted by then, leaving me weary and heavy-headed. I'd craved a swig of vodka but settled for a coffee and a cheese sandwich – alcohol at lunchtime had never done me any favours. I'd then spent the afternoon watching random films on Netflix while flicking through media job websites on my laptop, searching for international freelance roles.

Valerie's bungalow looks brighter in the sunlight, calm

after yesterday's storm, with its scrubbed red-brick walls and glossy, white-painted window frames.

I'm calmer too, thanks to a decent night's sleep.

The bungalow's frontage is wrapped in rampant ivy. Evergreen vines cling to the uneven brickwork, creeping in all directions and curling around the window frames, yet they're pruned away from the circular marker embedded beside the front door. Watching the sunlight reflect off the gleaming blue ceramic surface, I can see that this plaque has been cherished and cared for over the years.

I take photos of the plaque, zooming in and out, capturing all angles. Shove my phone in my jacket pocket, pull out my spiral notepad and a black pen from my rucksack. Jot down the words:

GEORGE MASTERS

1880–1942

CAMPAIGNER FOR JUSTICE

LIVED IN A HOUSE ON THIS SITE

1934–1941

Who was George Masters? I scribble a note to do an online search when I get back to the office. Find out what he'd accomplished and why. Write more of this feature to stop David hassling me about deadlines yet again.

As I peer at the plaque, the front door swings open. A man gazes down at me with a bemused smile on his lips and a white plastic bag in his hand. His trimmed salt-and-pepper beard matches the shade of the hair on his head. I assume this is Valerie's husband, Harry. I'm not sure why he looks so surprised as he should be used to everyone gawping at the plaque on his bungalow. Then I remember what Valerie said – that few people are interested in local history these days and most visitors don't even notice what's by their door.

'Can I help you?' His voice is a smooth baritone, clear and calm. His steely eyes pierce mine as he speaks.

'Just looking at your plaque.' I tap my pen against my notepad. 'I met your wife, Valerie, yesterday. I'm writing an article for *Hillsbury Living*.'

A look of affection spreads across his face when I mention her name. His eyes soften as he smiles at me.

'Yesterday? She didn't mention you.' He strokes his beard thoughtfully, then opens the front door more widely to reveal a rugby player's build. Broad shoulders, heavyset but lean and toned. Casual brown trousers with a white shirt. As he looks down, I glimpse the edge of a black crocheted skullcap on his crown.

Harry's eyes wander down from my face, scrutinising my black denim jacket, white jumper, faded grey jeans and red rucksack on my back. I don't need his approval yet I feel a warm flush spread across my cheeks.

I like to blend in when I travel. Sarongs in Indonesia. Saris in India. Headscarves in Morocco. Less hassle from the locals that way. I haven't felt the need to do that here in Hillsbury, which is the nearest I've had to a home for a while. Most of my clothes were bought for hotter climates or are well worn after years of travelling, so I possibly stick out like a camel on an iceberg. Yet I can't, or rather won't, change that right now. The local shops may sell the latest fashions but there's only so much blending in I'm prepared to do on a freelance writer's wage.

'Where did you two meet?' Harry strolls over to the black wheelie bin, lifts up the lid and chucks the bag inside.

I'm surprised he doesn't know, until I remember Valerie said she wouldn't be reporting the youths. Maybe she's gone one step further and told no one at all. Not even about me.

'I knocked on your door.' I'd been taught early on to be selective with the truth. 'I wanted to take a photo but she asked me to come back today. That's okay with you, I assume?'

Harry walks back to the door, brushing past me. 'Absolutely. Take as many pictures as you like.' He jerks his chin up in my direction. 'What happened to your face?'

I put my hand up, press my fingers gently against my skin. My cheek throbs. 'Just stupidity – tripping over my own feet.'

I've left the white strips in place, wanting the wound to heal quickly, but they're like two neon arrows. Yesterday on my walk home, a passing cyclist asked me if I'd been in the wars.

Harry steps forwards and peers at me, so closely that I can feel the warmth of his breath creeping along my skin. His aftershave scent seems familiar, the hint of spice reminding me of Dad, maybe ... of our farm in Kilconly. I clench my fists around my rucksack straps to stop my hands from shaking.

'It shouldn't leave you with a scar.' He flashes a smile, exposing a mouthful of pearly white teeth. Winks at me. 'Don't worry, I'm a doctor.'

'Valerie said.' I take a step back. 'Is she in?'

'No, she's at the synagogue this morning.' His eyes fix on mine. '*Cheder.*' He starts the word with a guttural sound, harsh and throaty like a growl, as in the Scottish word loch. 'Jewish Sunday school,' he adds when I don't respond. 'She works there every Sunday morning. I'll tell her you came by, though. What did you say your name was?'

'I didn't.' I stare back at him. 'But it's Shanna. Shanna Regan.'

'Shanna. Shanna Regan.' He repeats my name slowly, all the while staring directly into my eyes.

I want to remain in control. *Never show weakness.* But I can't stop myself as I look away.

'Enjoy the rest of your day, Shanna.' He dips his head as if he's giving a slight bow. 'I'm Harry ... Dr Harry Lee. Hopefully we'll meet again soon.'

As he closes the front door, a Mexican wave ruffles through the leaves on the surrounding ivy. Church bells chime in the distance, carried by the gentle breeze, as a Sunday-morning welcome to worshippers.

When I gaze at the plaque again, the word JUSTICE glimmers back at me. I pull out my phone and take a close-up shot then zoom out to take another.

As I move off the top step, the left curtain drape quivers. A shadow drifts across the window. I think of knocking on the door again, asking Harry what he knows about George Masters. He likes asking questions, it seems, so I suspect he's the type of man who will know the background to the name by his front door. But I've a niggling feeling the doctor may not be so good at giving answers. He seems friendly enough, but his bemused smile and air of arrogance suggest I've met his type before, several times. I take a step backwards instead, grab my rucksack and head down the path to the pavement.

TWENTY-FIVE CAMPTON AVENUE is also a bungalow, but it couldn't be more different from Valerie and Harry's well-manicured home.

This one looks like it's been neglected for years, with its frontage exposed to the elements, battered by wind and rain, and a faded blue door with paint scraped off around its edges. The front garden is overgrown, with grass stems up to my knees and prickly weeds growing through the crazy-paving cracks. Remnants of yesterday's downpour linger:

small shimmering puddles in the stony earth of the bare flower beds.

I walk up the gravel path to the door, loose stones crunching under my feet. Inspecting every inch of the façade, I feel my heart sinking. Maybe Valerie's wrong – I can't see a plaque. There's a small faded wooden box on the door frame, two-thirds up and not much longer than a matchbox. Maybe it once housed the doorbell as I can't see one of those either, just a large black metal cross beside the front door.

As I wander down the side of the house, a glint of red glaze catches my eye, hidden behind the foliage of a large overgrown bramble bush. I walk over and push the thorny branches away to reveal a black square plaque edged in red and smeared with mud.

I reach into my bag, pull out a white tissue and a bottle of mineral water.

Always be prepared. My grandad's words ring in my ears.

I unscrew the bottle and pour water onto the thin paper. Wipe the plaque gently but firmly, not wanting to damage it but desperate to see what lies beneath the dirt and grime. It feels like rubbing a lottery scratch card with a coin, though I don't expect to win any jackpot.

Gradually I reveal the plaque. Deep scratches run across it as if someone has tried to obliterate the red words in rage. Once I've read them, I turn away. Blink, then look back. Maybe my eyes have deceived me. But no, the words are still there.

Not much fazes me. Over the years I've seen things I wish I could unsee. Lifeless blood-smeared bodies on a Brussels street. Lost teddy bears swept away by Japanese tsunami floods.

But something about these words chills me to the bone.

Maybe I've won the jackpot after all.

CHAPTER FOUR

A shiver inches its way down my spine when I recite the words on the plaque out loud. Maybe I'm hoping someone else will hear me, to reassure me I'm not going crazy, to normalise them in my mind. No chance of that here though, as the street is deserted. There isn't even a hum of traffic at this end of Campton Avenue. It's as if someone has pressed a pause button and the whole world is in silence, listening to me.

PETER STEVENS
BEAT HIS WIFE FOR OVER 30 YEARS
ON THESE PREMISES
REPENT BEFORE YOU DIE
OR MAY YOU NEVER R.I.P.
SEPTEMBER 2015

I pull out my phone, take photos from several angles. Run my fingers around the rough edges of the plaque, then glance around to confirm that there's no one nearby. There isn't, so I try to yank the plaque forwards. It won't budge. It's screwed in firmly to the brickwork.

Why would anyone have put this here? It can't be genuine.

I stroll up to the front door, hoping I'll get some answers from the owners. I rap my fist against the blue panels. No reply. I try again. Still no response. Then I remember Valerie said the house was empty.

The front curtains are closed so I bend down and peek through the letterbox. Envelopes are strewn across the brown doormat and the internal wooden doors are shut, indicating no one has been here for a while.

As I back away, a twitch of the curtain next door catches my eye. This is a quiet road with Neighbourhood Watch stickers on every window, so strangers are probably noticed and logged and monitored. And I want to discover what the neighbours know.

I walk up the driveway of number twenty-seven and press the doorbell. As the shrill ring pierces the silence, a wood pigeon flies off the nearest oak tree, flapping its wings in a frenzy.

The door swings open. A tall, skinny woman stands in front of me, her hands speckled with flour. Her charcoal-grey hair is tied away from her face, emphasising prominent cheek-bones. She wears a red plastic apron that stops at her knees.

'Yeah?' She scowls and puts her hands on her bony hips, leaving white powdery fingerprints on her navy joggers.

From her demeanour I assume this isn't a convenient time but I'm not one to give up easily.

'Do you know when your neighbours are back?' I point towards the house next door.

'Why you want know?' Her accent sounds familiar – somewhere I've visited, but I can't place it.

'There's a plaque on the side of the house. I'm—'

'You come back tomorrow. I busy now.'

As she moves forwards to close the door, I remember where I've heard her accent before. 'You're from Afghanistan? I've been there, travelling with the Red Cross.'

Images of crying children, battered women and injured soldiers flash in front of my eyes. 'Terrible times.'

She wrings her hands together and her dark eyes sadden. Then she sighs. 'Come, I talk for bit. I have family in Kabul. I am Zahra.'

'Shanna.'

She leads me into her kitchen. A large stainless-steel stockpot is bubbling on the stove, a spiral of steam being swallowed up by the noisy extractor fan above it. A wooden chopping board piled with flour and pastry covers a large segment of the grey granite worktop.

'I make beef-and-mushroom soup and chicken pie. My husband love English food.' Zahra picks up a red-and-white checked tea towel and wipes her hands. 'Sit.'

She points towards the pine table in the centre of the room and pulls out one of the four matching chairs, a blue cushion on its seat.

I drop my rucksack on the laminate floor, sit on the chair and lean back against its wooden spindles. 'So, your neighbours...'

'They gone.'

I assume she'll join me at the table, but instead she busies herself at the stove, stirring the stockpot with a long chunky-handled silver spoon.

'There's a plaque on the side of your neighbour's house. Do you know anything about it?'

Zahra stops stirring the soup and turns to look at me, narrowing her eyes. 'He try take away. But it stuck.'

'Who tried to take it away?'

'Mark, their son. After it happen.'

My forehead is beginning to ache. I need to start at the beginning. Take logical steps. Find out what has happened, who to and then why. Get the full story, the whole picture.

Zahra lays the serving spoon down on the wooden board and grabs a small white plastic spoon from an open drawer. 'Want to try?'

I shake my head and thank her for the offer. I've been a vegetarian for years. Dad always said it began as an act of defiance but then became a way of life. Not easy when you travel the world, I've discovered.

'What happened next door?'

'Ruth, my neighbour, fell down stairs one evening.' She wipes a tear from the corner of her eye. 'She was lovely lady. Help me with English.'

'An accident?'

She waves the plastic spoon at me, gripping the handle tightly. 'Of course. What else?'

I don't answer but instead think of the words on the plaque: PETER STEVENS. BEAT HIS WIFE FOR OVER 30 YEARS. Was their marriage an abusive one? Are the words true? There's a story here somehow, whether they are or not.

'Where was her husband at the time?'

Zahra scoops up some soup with her spoon, brings it to her mouth. She blows on it, spattering tiny grey-brown globules over the countertop, then gulps down the liquid. She shakes her head. Tuts under her breath.

'Peter no home when she fell.' She grabs a salt mill from the worktop and grinds some white granules into the stock-pot. 'As I told police, I hear them argue some time. But he no hurt her. He was good man. Go to church.'

Was. Her use of the past tense. The fact she's evaded my

questions. The words on the plaque. 'What happened to him?'

'Peter dead.' She shrugs. No tears this time. 'Someone beat him up, left him to die. No one know who.'

'The police never found out?'

'No, it happen late one night. No one see.'

I lean forwards. 'When was this?'

'Nearly year after Ruth died.'

I think of the plaque's words again. REPENT BEFORE YOU DIE OR MAY YOU NEVER R.I.P. Not the normal words you find on a plaque. But then I'm guessing this isn't a normal plaque at all. Sounds like someone had an axe to grind. Ruth died, then Peter died. Her death was an accident but not his. Maybe my Hillsbury Heritage article is getting more interesting after all.

I take out one of my business cards, leave it on the table. 'My contact details ... if you think of anything else. You mentioned Mark, their son. Where can I find him?'

'At St Luke. He work there every Sunday.'

ST LUKE'S is the main church in Hillsbury, overlooking a busy crossroads at the end of the high street. This tall, majestic building has a stone frontage and fairy-tale turrets on top, reminding me of an ancient Scottish castle. A graveyard at the side backs onto the main road, full of disintegrating headstones leaning over dense patches of grass.

Hillsbury Synagogue stands opposite. It's a modern building with a brown tiled roof and tall black gates guarding the entrance to the car park. Standing at the crossroads, I look from the church to the synagogue then back again. It feels like a stand-off or a choice – which religion do you want to be today?

I cross the road, push open the heavy oak door of the church. A blast of hot air welcomes me in. The Sunday services have finished and there are only a handful of people milling around the oak pews. A good time to visit a church, maybe, though it's been a while since I've been inside one and even longer since I've attended a service.

The vicar is chatting to a couple of parishioners and smiles as I walk in. He grasps my hand and shakes it firmly, the heat of his palm warming my own.

I explain who I'm here to see, though not why. 'Is Mark available?'

The vicar nods and points to a passageway behind the altar. Suggests I come back for a service some time. 'If that interests you, of course.'

I smile and nod, though it doesn't.

I follow the vicar's directions and find a man seated at a desk in a back office, perusing a spreadsheet clipped into a lever arch file. He's a bit older than me. In his late thirties, maybe, wearing a pale blue shirt open casually at the collar.

I watch him for a moment, then knock on the door frame. 'I'm looking for Mark Stevens.'

The man looks up and gives me a welcoming smile. 'That's me. How can I help?'

I walk in and pause in front of his battered ink-stained desk, a dark brown leather writing mat on top. Metal filing cabinets and shelving units are pushed up against the walls, cluttered with an array of leather-bound ledgers, providing some of the modern in with the old.

Mark Stevens leans back in his seat, runs his fingers through his floppy brown fringe.

'I'm researching local plaques for *Hillsbury Living* magazine.' I give him a broad smile. 'Found one on your parents' home.'

His face drains of colour and his intense brown eyes lose

their sparkle, as if I've flicked a switch with my words. 'How did you know it was there?' he whispers. His smile has vanished and now he looks haunted. He grips the rim of his desk as if to steady himself. His eyes flash with anger.

Was he the one who hid the plaque from view? Did he try to scratch out the words in rage?

'One of the neighbours told me.' I decide to keep Valerie out of it. Protect my sources. Figure if she and Zahra have noticed it over the years, others have too. 'It wasn't what I expected.'

'The plaque's not genuine.' He drums his fingers on his desk. 'Just someone's idea of a joke.'

'Why would they do that? Bit odd.'

'I don't know,' he snaps back. 'There are some very odd people around here.' He scrutinises me, clearly figuring I'm one of them. 'Anyway … it's none of your business so please keep your nose out of it.'

He stands up, towering over me, revealing a slim build and faded blue jeans. 'I have work to do so you can see yourself out.' He takes a step forwards as if he's ready to chase me out the office.

I turn towards the door, then gaze back. As Mark Stevens' eyes fix on mine, I look beyond the anger inside them to find signs of hurt and pain.

'If you change your mind, you'll find me at the magazine's office or you can call me on my mobile.' I take out my business card and place it on the nearest filing cabinet. 'Just leave a message if I'm not there.'

No reply.

I leave his office, shuffling my feet as slowly as I can, secretly hoping he'll come running, tell me he's changed his mind and wants to talk. But I reach the outside door without interruption, as even the vicar is now too deep in conversation to see me leave.

Antisemitic yobs in the park.

Fake plaques on someone's home.

I'm onto something, I know it. Valerie is right. It isn't always quiet and peaceful here in Hillsbury.

These are stories waiting to be unravelled. This is my chance to get back into the game.

CHAPTER FIVE

I make sure I look busy on Monday morning in case David saunters into the office. *Hillsbury Living* back issues are stacked up high on my desk and two empty coffee mugs are soaking in the sink. I'd needed a caffeine boost after a broken night's sleep. My phone had rung twice in the early hours, no name or number on the screen and no message.

I can't face more of my boss's quips about slacking on the job, that my fast-paced nomadic lifestyle has come to an end, and that I've given it all up to sit in a tiny windowless office in the heart of Hillsbury.

Even though that's all true.

The office is in a converted listed house on the main road. Black Tudor-style oak beams on the outside, steel and plasterboard inside, creating tiny working spaces with a claustrophobic feel and a perpetual musty odour of rotting plasterboard and mouldy walls. We're currently the only business here. With David barely in the office, this means most of the time it's just me.

He finally materialises at ten-thirty, dressed casually in baggy jeans and a checked shirt. His latest companion is a nervous-looking mutt with a scrawny rust-coloured coat, doleful eyes and strong doggy odour. David is a trustee of the local dog rescue centre and insists on taking its inhabitants out for a stroll. I wish he'd give them a bath once in a while, or at least keep them away from this windowless office. I'll have to spray plenty of air freshener after they leave.

'How are you getting on with that feature – the historical one?' David stares at the plaster strips on my cheek. The dog settles down under my desk, its tail thumping against my leg.

'I've found more plaques.' I point at the photos on my screen while flashing him the sweetest smile I can muster. 'I'm getting the article written, don't panic, but I'll need to be out of the office a bit more. If that's okay with you.'

'Struggling still?' David smirks, then laughs with a cold cackle that makes me want to heave. My glare in response must give away my thoughts as his smug smile slowly transforms into a scowl. 'You would have found it much easier to go with my suggestion,' he continues. 'Hillsbury is well known for its artists, and our readers would have loved it.'

Pinpricks of anger irritate my skin so I count under my breath. *One ... Two ... Three ... Four.* A calming tactic I'd been taught decades ago by my grandad.

David has no idea how to run a magazine, from what I can tell. When I'd applied for the job, I'd asked him about his readers: who they were, their ages, their likes and dislikes. It isn't exactly rocket science – *know your market to tailor your words* is one of the first things I learnt as a journalist – yet he didn't have a clue, just mumbled something about Hillsbury's older population. Any rookie journo would realise the topics in the magazine are too diverse, from teenage beauty treatments and retirement plans to Holocaust survivors and children's toys. They aren't targeted at all, which may explain why advertising seems to be dwindling.

David inherited the magazine from a wealthy uncle who took him in after his parents died, and the freehold of the building along with it. He originally wanted to be an accountant, he told me in a rare conversational moment, but the offer of a magazine seemed too good to refuse. That was nearly thirty years ago, and he's never looked back. The magazine is funded by a family trust as well as advertising, so he just needs a lackey – me – to do the donkey work while he watches his bank balance rise.

David isn't flashy, don't get me wrong. The only hint of money comes from the gold Rolex on his wrist. But he's arrogant, not an easy man to get along with, and prone to tantrums like a teenage boy. From what I can tell, his editors never last long, which works well for me as I don't see *Hillsbury Living* as a long-term prospect. Yet it's a job – and the only job I have, as all my other work has dried up – so for now it will have to do.

David turns my computer screen around to face him, my hackles rising as he does so. His blue eyes widen as he notices my paltry word count – six hundred – just about the equivalent of a page so far.

'Remember I need this issue finished on time.' He runs his stubby fingers through his long strands of white hair, which are draped across his scalp to cover up his bald patches like drizzles of icing on a sponge cake. 'It must *not* be late.'

I notice he emphasises the word 'not'. I wonder why it's so important, then brush the thought from my mind, eager to share what else I've discovered.

'I found another plaque yesterday.' I swivel the screen back around to face me. 'Something very ... different. Be fun to cover that one too. Give the readers a bit of a mystery to solve.'

'How is this one different?' He leans back against the desk opposite mine, officially his desk but I've never seen him use it. Crosses his flabby arms over his slight paunch and narrows his eyes.

'It's not like the others at all. I'm not even sure it's real. I'll show you.' I reach into my bag and pull out my phone. Open up the photo app and wait for it to load. 'It didn't even look like them.'

I click open the first photo of the Peter Stevens plaque.

When I look up, I detect a change in David's demeanour. Back straight, poker stiff, ears pricked up like a bloodhound on the trail.

'That does look very interesting.' Astonishment flashes in his eyes. 'But you're supposed to be looking for genuine plaques – this one just looks like a family joke.'

'It was on a house in Campton Avenue but there's a real plaque just up the road too. In fact, the people in that house told me to—'

'Ah, so you *have* found another real plaque then? That's excellent news.' He gives me a broad grin, but his eyes remain ice cold. 'I assume you've been researching it this morning. Remember you have three pages to fill.'

'Yes, I know but,' I point at the photos on my phone, 'about this other plaque. The words were...' I drum the desk with my fingertips. 'They were odd, weird, I mean. I wondered if they were a joke too at first but now I think—'

'I'm not paying you to *think* in your articles.' David curls his lip. 'We give our *Hillsbury Living* readers facts, not comment, politics or opinion. We had this chat on your first day. I know you're used to traipsing all over the world, finding all manner of complex stories, but you don't need to do that here. In fact, that's *not* what I'm paying you to do.'

A sour taste spills into my mouth and my stomach muscles tighten. *One ... Two ... Three ...* I clench my fists. I don't like being reprimanded like a child or being told how to do my job.

'But—'

'This issue of the magazine is about Hillsbury history. Stories of the locals. *Real. History.*' With each of the last two words, he bangs his fist on my desk. The mutt flinches against my leg, and a waft of doggy odour surges upwards.

'But—'

'Don't complicate matters. Just stick to the facts, and don't waste your time on fake plaques that are probably a family's idea of a joke.' He bangs his fist on my desk again. 'Plus, I still need you to edit other articles that have come in, sort out the letters and find something for the last page. If you're not up to the job, tell me and I'll find someone else. And you can find a job elsewhere. If. You. Can.'

He storms out the room, the mutt trudging behind. Within a few seconds, I hear him slam the front door shut. The building trembles as if in fear. I do too but with anger.

Yet another teenage tantrum.

This reminds me of those two yobs in the park. I flinch as I recall the racist insults they shouted at Valerie. *Pig. Ham. Bacon butty. Jewish bitch.* And worse.

She didn't deserve that.

No one does.

MY THOUGHTS SHOULD BE on my Hillsbury Heritage article for the remainder of the morning, but my mind keeps wandering back to the other plaque, the fake one. The one that seems to have caused Mark Stevens significant distress.

BEAT HIS WIFE FOR OVER 30 YEARS.
MAY HE NEVER R.I.P.

I'm desperate to know the full story. What happened to Mark's parents? He's warned me to stay away yet I'm not sure why. From what Zahra told me, it sounds like the police dismissed the cases. Well, I want to know why this plaque's by their front door.

I print out the photos of the plaque and hold them up to the harsh fluorescent lighting above my desk, squinting to see if there's anything I've missed. After a few minutes, my eyes are beginning to ache – I'll need a magnifying glass to determine more details. I think back to how the plaque looked and felt once I'd removed the mud. The blotches in the glaze. The roughness of its edges. It didn't look professional, nothing like the official ones I've found, but it's still an impressive copy so someone clearly knew what they were doing.

I turn back to the office computer, click open the internet browser and type the name *Peter Stevens* into the search engine. Tens of thousands of entries appear on the screen. How the hell can I narrow this down?

I'm about to try another search when my computer crashes. When I switch it back on, it starts a Windows update, a pop-up indicating there's two hours left. Great timing.

I need computer access for work, even if I abandon my search into this mysterious plaque, and I don't know the password for David's desktop. My phone is fast but the screen is too small. My laptop is back at my rented apartment and I'm too impatient to wait.

I pick up the top copy of *Hillsbury Living* from the pile on my desk. It's an issue from the previous Christmas, covering gift ideas for dog lovers, December walks in Hertfordshire, Holocaust survivor stories, 10 top New Year resolutions...

Flicking through the pages, reaching the local events section, I figure out where I can go.

CHAPTER SIX

illsbury Library is quiet at lunchtime. I'd expected yacking mothers and screaming toddlers or lonely older people looking for a chat. Instead, the front desk is vacant and the library is eerily silent. I follow the sign to the hub of computers, sit down in front of the nearest monitor. The yellowing desktop looks like it's seen better days with sticky fingermarks on its keyboard and grubby smears on its screen. Not that different to the one I've just abandoned at the office.

I type *Ruth Stevens Hillsbury 2015* into the search engine, recalling the year Zahra told me, and find a reference to Ruth in the archives of the local newspaper. It's only a small news story but it's a start.

2nd August 2015. Police report a 67-year-old woman was found dead in her home on Monday evening. Ruth Stevens had fallen down her stairs in Campton Avenue and suffered a fatal blow to her head. She was alone in the house at the time. Her husband Peter and son Mark are distraught. Police have ruled it as accidental death and are not looking for anyone else in connection with the incident.

I type in *Peter Stevens, September 2015* – the date on the plaque – and tap my fingers on the desk as I wait for the results to load.

I've never been the patient type. Always wanting to know what's next, wanting everything now, difficult to surprise. 'Are we nearly there yet' had been my childhood mantra. I guess it's my adult one too. Even though my whole life has been spent waiting. Departure lounges. Customs queues. Taxi ranks. New destinations.

After what seems like ages, several entries appear on the screen, though nothing for 2015. I click on the top one, also from the newspaper archives.

28th March 2016: A 69-year-old Hillsbury man was found beaten to death in a woodland clearing early this morning. Peter Stevens, owner of PRS Clothing, was discovered by a man walking his dog at 5.30 a.m. Mr Stevens' wife Ruth died last year after accidentally falling down their stairs. Police are asking for anyone with information about Peter Stevens' death to come forward.

I witnessed Mark's anger, how he clenched his fists, banged on the desk, asked me to leave. Sadness, I can under-stand. Two deaths in one household, nearly a year apart. Hard for anyone to deal with. Unusual too.

My own mother died when I was seven. I remember little about her and nothing about her death. One day she was there, the next she was gone. I have no photos to prove she once existed, that she's more than just a figment of my imagination, more than a ghost from my past. And because she had no other family, there was no one for me to ask. Dad talks about her sometimes but not often enough. Too painful, I've always assumed so I've never explored her roots. Until a few weeks ago, around twenty-five years on, when I finally demanded some answers from him and no answers came.

Were the words on the plaque true? Did Peter really kill his wife? Did Mark kill his father, taking revenge for his mother's death?

No, that's crazy. Why would he have bothered with a plaque?

The journalist in me is overthinking. And yet more questions play havoc with my mind, bombarding my brain until my forehead aches.

I type Mark's name into the search engine. Scroll down the entries until I find a possible match. Mark Stevens. Chartered Accountants. Hillsbury High Street.

I scribble down the details on my notepad. Then lean back in my chair, feeling the hard fake leather digging into my shoulder blades, and think about the article I still need to write, the one that should be taking up most of my time. I've searched online for more plaques and found very few. I tried the local history society but the archivist is on sick leave and won't be back for several weeks.

I'm relatively new to the town but surely other locals must know where to find them.

I stand up and stretch my legs, feeling a twinge at the back of my thighs, and make a beeline for the front desk. A young woman now sits behind it, chewing the end of her blue biro as she gazes at her computer screen.

I cough to attract her attention.

She looks up and puts the pen down. 'Hi. How can I help?'

'Do you have any books on local commemorative plaques – those historical markers you find on buildings?'

'As in blue plaques, like the official English Heritage ones?'

An image of blank magazine pages thrusts itself into my mind.

I stifle a laugh. 'Right now, any colour will do.'

'Hold on.' She gestures to the chair in front of her, and I plonk myself down in the seat. She clicks her computer mouse until the library's online catalogue pops up on her screen. 'There's Derek Sumeray's *Blue Plaques of London*. It's out on loan at the moment but you can reserve it. There's no queue.'

'I'm trying to find something specific to Hertfordshire. Or even better, Hillsbury.'

She looks back at her screen and types a few words, the keys clicking as her fingers skim across the keyboard. She shakes her head. 'Nothing else, sorry. Are you looking for a particular reason?' Her gaze flickers to the plasters on my cheek.

'I'm writing something for *Hillsbury Living*.'

'I can ask around.' She glances down at her desk, scratches her forehead then looks up again. 'Actually...' She grabs a Post-it pad from beside her computer screen '...I can do better than that. Write down what you're looking for and your contact details and I'll check with my manager. I'm sure we can put it on our noticeboard for a few days.'

'That'll be great, thanks.'

I write down my details as neatly as I can – my handwriting never did win any school prizes.

'You could also pop a few of these into local newsagents. Taylor's on the high street has a noticeboard.' She reaches inside her desk drawer and hands over a pile of blank lined index cards. 'We don't tend to use these. No one will notice they're gone.'

'Thanks so much. Really appreciate it.'

'Anything else I can help you with?'

I think about the fake plaque. How it looks different. Not shoddy, just not professional. I know you can buy fake plaques online for family and friends. I bought one for Dad once – IRELAND'S BEST FARMER LIVES HERE. Is that what someone's done? Ordered a plaque and fixed it to the Stevens' bungalow?

'Does anyone near here make plaques?' I show her the photo on my phone, very quickly so she hasn't enough time to read the words. 'Ceramic or clay ones. Official-looking.'

'You mean a pottery?' The librarian launches her internet browser. 'I can certainly look. Hold on.'

'Thanks.'

She taps away at the computer keys, then looks up. 'I've found one, though it's not very local. I'll write down the details.' She scribbles an address down on another index card and hands it to me.

'Where's Chelsworth? Sorry, I'm new to the area.'

'Not far. It's just past Elmsgrove but you'll need the 239 bus. You can get it from the butchers opposite. Takes around half an hour.'

I leave the library and walk up to Taylor's Newsagents. Business cards and adverts decorate the front window, arranged in neat rows. Cleaners and gardeners and dog walkers, all looking for clients. A Christmas gifts sale to raise funds for the church roof. A Chanukah fete at the synagogue. I glance further down, skimming the words to see if anything grabs my attention, and my eyes latch on to an A5 poster: COFFEE AND CLAY CLASS, EVERY MONDAY EVENING AT ST LUKE'S HALL.

Taylor's is dark and cramped inside with a faint musky odour of days gone by, reminding me of the office. Racks of magazines and newspapers and greetings cards dominate one side of the shop, while rows of sweets and chocolates and crisps crowd the other.

The elderly woman behind the counter smiles broadly as I walk in. She smiles again, revealing yellowing teeth, when I tell her what I want. For five pounds, she says, pointing at a notice on the counter, she'll keep my card up for a week.

I pay her with cash and write out the details.

Urgent. Do you know of any local commemorative plaques? If so, please contact Shanna Regan at Hillsbury Living.

I add my work email address and my mobile number, then stick the card inside the window with the sticky tape the woman supplies.

Now I just need to wait.

And right now, I wish I was better at waiting.

CHAPTER SEVEN

I sit under the sycamore trees, shrouded by low branches above me and piles of brown decaying leaves at my feet. I've sat on this greying wooden bench so many times, it now almost feels like mine. Perfect for watching all areas of the park. The tennis courts, where two tracksuited women are rallying enthusiastically. The children's play area, full of harassed parents and excited toddlers clambering over slides and swings. The grassy slope where those youths were chasing Valerie.

This is more relaxing than sitting in my fully furnished but soulless rented apartment, filled with modern gadgets and pristine furniture, all barely used. Opposite Hillsbury Station, with front windows that rattle when a train thunders by, recommended through one of David's contacts after I'd accepted his job.

Wherever I travel, I try to find an oasis of calm amid all the chaos. A large rock on the side of a mountain. A solitary chair on a back porch. Once, even a low branch hanging precariously over a running stream. I've learnt to ignore noise around me, probably a remnant from my hectic childhood. Sunshine or rain, I don't care, I just hate being hemmed in by four walls.

A teenage girl with dark curls cascading down her back passes by the café, which is shuttered up for the winter. Pulled by five boisterous Labrador puppies, she grasps their leads tightly as she sits down on a bench. She ties the leads around the rusting metal bench legs, reaches into her canvas tote bag, takes out a slim paperback and begins to read. The dogs yap and bounce around her feet until one by one they lie down, side by side, tightly packed like an open box of white and milk chocolates.

I want to run down the hill towards her and find out what she knows. About plaques, real ones and fake ones. About Hillsbury, the church and the synagogue. About Valerie and Harry Lee. About the Stevens family too.

But instead, I lean against the back of the wooden bench, watching my hazy breath spiral into the dusky grey sky. My shoulders relax as if puffs of stress escape every time I breathe. I gaze up at the low-hanging branches where brown and yellow leaves dangle down, twirling in the light breeze like a silent wind chime.

Then I shut my eyes and let the images take over.

A little girl on a swing. Me, aged five or six maybe.

Clutching the ropes. Legs dangling. Giggling with delight. Rising into the air.

'More. More.'

My mother standing behind me. Long auburn hair. Her face hidden by shadows.

Pushing forwards. Gently yet firmly. Again and again.

'Don't let go, Sh—'

A car horn honks in the distance. A screech of brakes. I open my eyes as a deep shout fills the air, followed by a slamming of car doors.

A few minutes later, all is quiet again.

I droop my eyelids back down, but the image of my childhood has shimmered away, once again beyond my reach.

My early memories are scarce. Broken. Shattered. Those of my mother mainly. The 'before' part of my life, hidden behind a stony wall in my brain. But in recent months, some have been breaking through, stirring like ripples in a pond. I just don't know if they're real or a fabrication of my mind. Memories I want, rather than ones I truly had.

I glance towards the café. The bench seat is now empty.

I take my mirror out from my rucksack, hold it in front of me and peer closely at my face. I pull the two thin white strips off my cheek, one by one, taking care not to break the skin. The cut is now a narrow line edged with an angry red flare, surrounded by a burgundy bruise like a red wine kiss.

I put the mirror away, pull out my phone and call the top number in my favourites list.

Dad picks up after the first ring. 'Where are ya?'

I smile at his familiar soft Irish lilt. 'I'm sitting in a park watching the world go by.'

I don't need to ask that same question as I can guess where he is. Sitting in his favourite armchair, as always, with flames licking firewood in the open hearth beside him.

'Outside again? Shoulda guessed so.'

Two little boys run past me, chasing a runaway poodle. The dog pauses and yaps at them frantically before scampering towards the park gate.

'Yeah.' An icy breeze is picking up. Maybe nature has finally remembered that it's autumn, not spring. I shiver and pull my denim jacket around me as if giving myself a comforting embrace.

He coughs down the phone, a harsh rattle that rushes right through me.

'Dad?'

I last saw him nearly six weeks ago after I'd returned to the farm after four months on the road. Worn out and lost and confused, back to the one person I thought I could trust. He asked me not to leave him again, wanting me nearby, to help pack up the farm before it goes on sale. But I've never been able to stay in one place for too long.

'Sorry, still here.' He coughs again.

'Guess you still won't give me some answers.'

Silence in return. I should be angry with him, but I just can't be – because he's all I've got. That's why I've never pressed him about the past.

Until now.

Dad clears his throat as if he's about to give me a lecture, like he's done so many times before. 'Well, wherever ya are, don't get caught up in shit that's nothing to do with ya.' I can picture him shaking his head as he always does when he thinks I'm doing something wrong. 'Sure, not for the first time. But just watch ya'self.'

His words remind me of David and Mark, both warning me away. I remember Valerie's words too. *It's not always quiet around here – or peaceful.*

I press my cheek, feeling the indent of the narrow cut, the aching of the bruise around it. 'I'm fine. I'm always fine.'

'Ya should be resting that shoulder.' He pauses. 'Ya shoulda stayed home.'

I stifle a sigh.

Home.

I've explained countless times but he doesn't get it, or maybe he just doesn't want to. Until my mother died, Dad drifted in and out of my life from one engineering contract to the next. Once she was gone, he took over both parenting roles.

My time in Kilconly was peppered with weeks away. A bag always packed, ready for our next adventure. A granny who ignored me, a constant reminder of the woman who stole her son's heart, maybe. A grandad who wanted to mould me and turn me into the farmer his son never was, so taught me how to shoot and climb and ride, to watch the people around me and to always be prepared. Advice I still carry with me wherever I roam.

Sure, I can picture the river where I dived into the rushing waters. The buttercup meadow where I daydreamed and chased butterflies. The school where I dipped in and out of term time, backed up by lessons with Dad whenever we were on the road. The church that my granny insisted I attended.

But the farm has never felt like home, and now never will be.

At eighteen, I escaped to London to study geography at uni and then a journalism postgrad. By then, Dad had stopped travelling, giving in to duty instead, helping my ailing grandad run the farm. My granny was long gone. After my studies, I found a job on a magazine, writing about adventure holidays and city breaks and remote destinations. And yet again I was back to travelling and broken farm visits.

So, no, the farm doesn't feel like home, and I won't miss it once it's no longer ours. But even if Dad knows that, he doesn't want to hear it.

'I'll be back,' I say to reassure him. 'Soon, I promise.'

'Sure about that?' A cough comes down the phone, muffled as if Dad has put his hand over the receiver. 'See, I worry ya running from me.'

I hear the sadness in his voice, imagine the softness in his dark blue eyes. 'No, Dad. I'm not running from you.'

I gaze into the distance, tears running down my icy cheeks. As I wipe them away with the back of my hand, a salty taste trickles into my mouth.

'Fella called. Andy, he said.'

A shiver runs down my spine, followed by a deep aching pain that stretches from my shoulder to my heart. Those two missed calls on my phone. No name. No number. No message.

'Did he say why?'

'No, but asked where he'd find ya. Persistent fella. Called a few times, he did.'

The trees around me whisper. Just a sudden gust of wind, for sure. But my muscles have tensed, ready to run.

A figure in a coat near the swings catches my eye. Standing still, facing the bench, facing me, even though I'm concealed by foliage. I sit upright, rising on my hackles like a meerkat on guard. I squint, trying to see more detail but the figure disappears behind a tree.

'What did you tell him?'

'Nothing to tell, just ya travelling. He said he'd catch up with ya soon.' He pauses. Coughs again. 'Nadia called too. Ya not been in touch? What's going on, Shan? Who's Andy? What's happened? You and Nadia ... ya've been close for years.'

The figure appears again. I stand up, grab my rucksack and stroll across the grass towards the children's playground.

'I'll call her. I will ... soon.' *Once I decide what to say.* 'And Andy, he's...' I pause. 'He's just someone I worked with. He's nothing.' My skin tingles with memories of hands caressing my back, a flush of warmth down my spine, a sweaty chest pressed against mine and promises whispered in my ear. 'He's ... no one.'

'Something's up.' Dad coughs down the phone. 'Ya don't quit a good job for no reason. Ya no quitter.'

'All's fine, Dad. Really. You worry too much.'

I stumble over a rocky patch of grass, feel my knees

giving way but catch my balance in time. Yet I feel breathless, winded, as if someone has punched me in the gut.

I didn't quit. I was pushed out. The work dried up. A quick word here; a rumour there. Not hard to do.

'Found some things here,' Dad says. 'Sent them on. Ya got them yet?'

'No, but it takes a while for MailReady to forward them.' I stand up and gaze towards the playground. The figure in the coat is still there, further in the distance. A short stocky person stands beside them, pointing at two small boys playing on the swings. I squint but can't see any faces.

'I knows ya won't stop 'til ya find ya answers.' Dad draws in a breath. 'Just come home soon. Please.'

He coughs again, a harsh guttural sound that grates on my ears.

'Dad, is everything okay? Your cough doesn't sound too good.'

We've had this conversation before – many times. That's why I quit the cigarettes a few months back and wish he would too. His cough flares up and down, and he's had several cancer scares over the years, after decades of smoking. False alarms each time, but I worry about the next.

'I'm grand. Tough as old boots, me.' He pauses. 'Don't be worrying. Just miss my little girl, that's all.'

A lump sticks in my throat. 'I'll be in touch.'

I end the call, tears welling up in my eyes again, wanting to go back to Dad, yet wanting – no, needing – some answers. Deciding what's right and wrong. How far I'll take it. How far I'll go.

I think of the plaque on Valerie and Harry's bungalow.

JUSTICE.

My phone rings. No name or number on the screen. I blocked Andy's number but it doesn't take much to get a new SIM and phone. I haven't updated social media for weeks as I'm sure he'll be watching. My Instagram and Twitter and Facebook accounts, all neglected and dormant, no longer the running commentary of my life that they once were. Journalists can be relentless, for sure. He'll find me eventually, I know it. I can't keep running, and at some point, I'll have to take his call.

Just not yet.

I slide my phone into my jeans back pocket, ignoring the persistent vibrations against my skin.

The sun is dipping in the sky as dusk is drawing in, which means the park will soon close. I gaze towards the playground and see the person in the coat drifting towards the car park, this time alone. And yet again I think of that plaque I've found.

MAY HE NEVER R.I.P.

Who put it there, and why?

I'm like a bassett hound following a scent. And I know I won't – can't – stop until I've found the prize.

CHAPTER EIGHT

When I arrive in the office on Tuesday morning, the answerphone blinks at me in greeting. More news of historical plaques, maybe. I should feel enthusiastic yet all I want to do is lay my head down.

Overnight, I'd had three more calls. No name. No number. No message. I'd forgotten to put my mobile on silent and stirred with each one. Finally, after the third call, I threw my phone in the wardrobe and slammed the door shut. I went back to bed with ringing in my ears and the duvet over my head.

Eventually I drifted off but clearly not deep enough. When I woke at six-thirty, my head throbbed as if I had a hangover though not a single drop of alcohol passed my lips last night. My throat felt like it was bursting with bramble bushes, their jagged branches scratching as I swallowed.

I'm used to having little sleep when travelling but I'm now out of practice. Unbroken nights for too long spent in a comfortable bed and a heated apartment, maybe. My fitness levels are dropping too. All that time sitting and not enough moving. My desk-bound lifestyle is taking its toll.

I make myself a coffee. Strong. Black. Plenty of sugar. Down it in one, then close my eyes and wait for the caffeine peak to hit. Forty minutes later I feel ready to get to work. Energy floods through my limbs, my head buzzes with activity and my mind feels alert.

I listen to the answerphone messages, then switch on my computer, ancient and decrepit like everything else in the office. It hums, whirls and chuffs like an overworked steam train until finally the home screen appears. I check for emails. My work inbox is full. Plaques in Hillsbury aren't as scarce as I'd thought, it seems, you just need to know where to look.

I compile a list of places to visit. The Jewish cemetery. St Luke's. Magpie Lane. Butterfly Road. Plus several more. I send emails thanking everyone who has responded so far and tell them to look out for the next issue of *Hillsbury Living*.

Scrolling down my notepad, I sigh with relief. I'm back on track so maybe this article will write itself after all. I locate each suggestion online, then print off a local map to mark my route. Figure I'll need at least two more afternoons to visit all these plaques, especially as I'm travelling on foot. I know how to drive but don't have a car as there's no point leaving it dormant in a garage while I fly the globe.

I sift through the post. Bills for David. Flyers for no one. One letter addressed to me. I flip it around in my hand. Typed. No stamp. Hand-delivered.

All those phone calls. Shit. Has Andy finally tracked me down?

No, that's crazy. He doesn't know I'm in Hillsbury. He doesn't even know I'm in Hertfordshire. Nor does Dad. It can't be Nadia either. I told her I needed time out but didn't say where, just that I'd be in touch.

I take a deep breath, rip the envelope apart with shaking hands. Inside is a white piece of paper, watermarked. Just one line, typed.

GO TO WHOMSOEVER LANE. FIND THE PLAQUE.

Black ink, heavier and darker on each letter *E,* as if typed with an old-fashioned manual typewriter.

I add Whomsoever Lane to my list and check the map. Not far from the centre of town, backing onto mature woodland and a wildflower meadow, with a stream running through it, marked with a thin wavy blue line.

BY THE TIME I leave the office, it's well after three. There'd been more work than I'd estimated. Calls to make. News stories to chase. Pictures to source. David deals with the advertising, but this is far more than one person's job as I seem to be running the whole magazine.

As I close the office door, I welcome the flood of fresh air on my skin, even though it's bitterly cold. I can't wait to be outdoors again. The greying walls have been closing in on me, the yellowing ceiling pressing down on me, cobwebs glistening at me from the corners of the room.

I visit the first three plaques on my printed map. Take photos. Make notes. My usual drill. One plaque is blue, another dusky pink and the final brown. No two plaques are the same but they all have a common bond, commemorating Hillsbury residents' good deeds.

Then finally, around four-thirty, I reach Whomsoever Lane. The narrow entrance is a few paces from Hillsbury High School. The lane backs on to the playing fields on one side. The other side is dominated by oak trees several rows thick, surrounded by colourful mosaics of low-growing shrubs.

I stroll up the lane, slowly and methodically, looking high and low for a plaque, dodging fallen branches and icy patches and brambles stretching out their fierce thorn-covered stems.

Daylight is fading fast. At this time of year, dusk falls quickly, as though an eagle has swooped down shrouding the earth with its broad wings of darkness. I take my torch out from my bag – prepared, as always – using it to light up my way and warn me of hidden dangers under my feet.

Eventually I find a black-and-red square on a lamp post, just like the other fake plaque I found. Similar shape and size and colour. When I shine the torchlight over it, I read similar words too.

GINA ALDERS

PUSHED A CHILD TO HER DEATH

ON THIS BRIDGE

REPENT BEFORE YOU DIE

OR MAY YOU NEVER R.I.P.

MAY 2014

I think of the note with the address. GO TO WHOMSO-EVER LANE. FIND THE PLAQUE. No name or signature. Is someone toying with me, aware I'm searching for local historical markers, adding me to a treasure-hunt game I don't want to play?

MAY YOU NEVER R.I.P.

Those four words haunt me yet again, and invisible fire ants crawl along my arms and down my spine.

Peter Stevens beat his wife, then she fell down the stairs at their home. Accidentally, I assume, until I'm told otherwise. Then Peter died too, nearly a year later. But his death wasn't an accident. Instead, according to Zahra, it was vicious with no culprit found.

If the same pattern applies, should I assume Gina is dead? Did she really push a child to her death? Her child or someone else's? Deliberate or not? And who the hell has sent me this note? So many questions I need to answer, all swirling around in my head.

The lamp lights up the steps to the bridge over the stream. I walk up and stand on the wooden slats.

ON THIS BRIDGE

A muscle twitches at the back of my neck. I grip the metal railing, lean over and gaze into the water churning below. What happened here?

This whirlpool of darkness is like a portal into an unknown world. The more I think about these plaques, the more this sounds like the plot of a movie or an ancient legend. A fairy tale parents tell their kids to keep them in check. Don't hit your little brother or the bogeyman will get you. Don't eat all the sweets or the wicked witch will come. I laugh out loud at the craziness of it all and the sound echoes back at me, as if someone is mocking me, poking fun.

Bile spills into my throat. I wipe my mouth with the back of my hand as I watch eddies of tiny undercurrents below. A crushed beer can bobs about on the surface like a tiny raft. Frothy waves crash against litter and leaves and debris piled up against the banks, unleashing a pungent odour of stagnant water that wafts upwards and makes me gag yet again.

I walk back to the lamp post. Drop my rucksack on a large flat piece of wood, trying to keep it away from the mud and grime on the ground. I pull out my phone and glance at the screen. The 4G sign flickers at me, teasing me. On, then off. On, then off. The close-knit trees are blocking the signal maybe, so that will have to wait.

Instead, I extract my pen and notepad, take photos and scribble down notes. Then I run my hand over and around the plaque. The edges are rough. Yet again, not a perfect finish. Not a perfect square either. Just like the other one.

I walk to the entrance of Whomsoever Lane. The school's black iron gates are bolted shut, the melancholy building looming above me in the darkening sky.

My phone has more signal here so I search online and find a newspaper article mentioning a Gina Alders. She'd been a geography teacher at Hillsbury High and died coming off her bike over the bridge in November 2014, the same bridge that an unnamed twelve-year-old girl had fallen off around six months earlier while in her care. I scroll down the newspaper article for more information. Gina denied all charges, accidental death was ruled, and her death was deemed to be an accident too.

This plaque is in full view of passers-by, but I wonder if everyone ignores it, uninterested in the local history that lies around them, just as Valerie said. I head back towards it for another look.

Rows of trees whisper around me. What secrets can they tell? What have they witnessed? Goosebumps line my arms. A rogue muscle twitches at the back of my neck yet again as if I'm being watched.

'Hello?'

I take a step forwards and shine my torch ahead of me. The beam of light shakes in time with my hand. Bushes rustle in the breeze. Leaves quiver. Shadows dance. I shiver as if an apparition has drifted through me.

'Hello?'

I hear shallow agitated breaths in my ear. Yet when I turn, there's no one there.

I'm not one to scare easily. I've been in some far creepier places in my life. An ancient necropolis near Rome not that long ago, filled with abandoned tombs and disintegrating skulls and mummified remains. But these black-and-red plaques are burrowing deep inside my skin, like a cluster of scabies mites determined to drain my life force.

I hear raised voices from the entrance near the school, then five uniforms come into view. Navy jumpers with a red stripe around the necks, white shirts and dark grey trousers. Three boys, two girls, chatting and swearing and squealing. I recognise two of them and my heart sinks.

I switch off my torch and move nearer the bushes where my black coat blends into the darkness. I pull my hood over my head.

But it's too late...

'It's that fuckin' Yid lover,' the tallest shouts to his companions, his long fringe dangling over his eyes. 'She's spyin' on us. Let's get her.'

They head towards me like a pack of baying dogs.

CHAPTER NINE

The youths obscure the light from the road, with grins on their lips, fire in their eyes and hands clenched into fists.

My legs throb with energy, my body primed to run.

Valerie said they're just kids. But no, I tell myself as I scrutinise them, these are more than just kids. They're on the cusp of adulthood. Taller than me, stronger than me, fitter than me. And while I'm brave, I'm not foolish. Adventurous, but not foolhardy. I know when I'm outnumbered and when the odds are stacked against me.

I search for a gap in the trees, but the shrubbery is packed too close together and the fence on the other side of the path is too high to climb. This means there's only one way to go: over the bridge, into the darkness and whatever lies beyond.

I pull away from the shadows and sling my rucksack over one shoulder. Gripping my torch, I tread over the wooden slats with long slow strides, holding off running until I know the youths' intentions, conserving my energy until I really need it.

When I reach the centre of the bridge, I pause. My stomach is churning and beads of sweat trickle down my forehead.

I figure it's an eight-feet drop, maybe ten. But if I jump, what would break my fall? There are no crocodiles in Hillsbury, for sure. Yet an abandoned shopping trolley under the surface can be lethal; a pile of rocks, too. I think of Gina Alders and the girl who had been in her care, wonder exactly how they died, shake my head and step away from the edge. Even I have my limits sometimes.

A stone whizzes past me, splashing into the stream below. I look up. The youths have now reached the nearest edge of the bridge.

'Come on, get the bitch,' the tallest shouts. His voice brims with excitement, adolescent arrogance etched across his face.

I pull my rucksack over my back, tie the straps securely and start jogging. The bridge leads to a narrow muddy footpath with bushes closing in on me from both sides. Clouds veil the moon so I have to use my torch to light up my way. I stagger over tangled brambles and muddy patches and frozen puddles, stones crunching under my trainers.

A dog barks in the distance. A car hoots. I'm not that far from the road, but I have no idea which way to turn. Stuck in a labyrinth without a map.

Gradually the voices behind me fade. An eerie silence hangs in the air as if I'm the first person to tread these ghostly paths. Though I'm clearly not, judging by the scrunched-up drink cans, crisp packets and sweet wrappers lining my route. My shoulders feel more relaxed yet my pulse is racing. My hands flush with warmth even though my face is ice cold. A toxic cocktail of fear and excitement surges through my veins. I'm beginning to enjoy the chase even though I shouldn't. A reminder of past adventures, maybe, and the life I've put on hold.

The pathway eventually divides into two, with both options looking equally uninviting, dark and muddy and shrouded by undergrowth. I choose the right-hand route for no particular reason; I don't have time to toss a coin.

My jogging rhythm pounds in my ears. *One. Two. One. Two.* A familiar beat, like jungle drums.

I trip and my torch flies out of my hand. Everything goes dark.

Shit.

I kneel down and grope around, sweeping my hands in all directions, but there's no sign of my torch.

Well done, Shanna.

Be prepared. Never panic. My grandad's words. Not such great advice when you're in the thick of it.

I untie my rucksack straps and pull my bag off my back so I can find my phone to provide some light again. I hear footsteps, louder than before, like a herd of wild beasts racing through a jungle. Angry shouts carry along the breeze towards me, followed by peals of laughter.

'Yid lover.'

'Chose the wrong mate, didn't ya?'

Tendrils of fear grip my throat. I grasp my bag to my chest and start sprinting.

My trainers pound over the uneven terrain, dodging more brambles and icy patches. My rucksack weighs heavy in my arms. I'm terrified I'll trip over, all the time glancing around, looking for an opening through the trees, for some-where to go or for somewhere to hide.

In the distance, a flash of light twinkles at me like a beacon of hope. I head towards it, sweeping away obstructing branches with my hands, sharp thorns ripping my skin into shreds. Finally I reach an open area, empty and silent. A solitary wooden bench stands in the centre, bathed with ash-grey light from the lamp post beside it, trees and bushes watching from all sides. It reminds me of a court-room, a place of reckoning, where the one on trial seems to be me.

Five angry faces appear. Their eyes pierce mine, one by one. I was stalked by lions once in Kenya and chased by an angry mob in Kabul. Yet right now I'm more petrified than I've been in a long while. Five strong, hormonal teenagers, unpredictable and aggressive, with chips on their shoulders and clearly something to prove.

The tallest one points to my cheek. Flicks his fringe off his face.

'Healing, innit? Want another?'

He reaches down. Picks up a stone, throws it into the air and catches it, as if he's casually tossing a coin.

'Called the cops yet, ya fucking bitch?' shouts the smallest yob, the one from the park with the gangster moves.

His mates laugh like hyenas.

'Not yet.' I straighten my spine. 'Surely you kids should all be in bed by now.'

The third boy steps forwards. Runs his fingers through his short raven-black hair, then reaches into his trouser pocket.

A glint of metal flashes in the lamplight.

I back away towards the trees, clutching my rucksack to my chest. My heart races, and saliva drains from my mouth.

'Wanna call the cops now?' The youth holds out his fist then opens his palm flat. Another glint of metal. 'Or maybe ya wanna call a friend?' He leers at me. 'Oh, no signal? Shame!' He holds his phone in the air.

I exhale slowly.

Though I wonder who I'd call anyway. No one knows I'm here, no one's expecting me, and no one will notice I'm gone. David, maybe, when he realises his magazine isn't finished, but he won't give a shit. Dad will but only once he realises I haven't called for a while.

The tallest girl hurls a stone towards me. I swerve out the way and trip over a stray piece of wood, landing awkwardly on my shoulder, cushioned slightly by the padding in my coat. My rucksack flies out of my arms. I push myself up and try to stand but end up on my knees, as if I'm facing a firing squad.

The second girl crouches down. Picks up a stone. I see a flash of silver, the sharp edge of a blade. They all saunter towards me, chanting 'Yid lover' again and again.

I've heard this before, decades ago when I was just nine and then again a few months back. I said nothing both times but not now.

This time I'll remain defiant – I won't let them win.

'You're just a bunch of racist thugs,' I shout. 'That Jewish woman in the park did nothing to you.'

Still they keep on walking towards me.

I take a deep breath, count slowly in my head. *One ... Two ... Three ... Four...*

Waiting for them to strike.

CHAPTER TEN

'Hey! Stop! Police!'

The deep voice seems to come from nowhere, until a tall shadow dashes into the clearing. The warm glow of a torch lights up the teenagers' startled faces, before illuminating my own.

My attackers fling their stones on the ground and run back to the path. Laughing and screaming and jostling, until their hazy shapes and youthful voices fade into the distance. All falls silent as if I've imagined it all, but the twinge in my shoulder proves I haven't.

That was close – too close.

Over the years, I've been in precarious situations, but never on my own. Hillsbury seems to make me feel safe, overconfident. I need to keep that in check.

The shadow clears their throat. 'You okay?' The voice is male, strong African accent, booming in the silence.

I press my hand over my eyes to lessen the torch's glare. 'Sure, I'm fine.'

The torch dims and the shadow inches forwards. Light from the lamp post reveals a man with thinning slate-grey hair, wearing a dark suit that stretches tightly across his shoulders and a white shirt that bulges over his belt.

I stand up, slowly so I can assess any damage. 'Police, huh?' Not that I really care who he is, just that he has impeccable timing.

'I'm a criminal lawyer. That's near enough.' The man jangles a lead in his hand. His dark skin, dabbled with sweat, glistens in the brightness of the lamp. 'But I'm currently looking for a cat.'

'With a dog lead?'

'Sheba's a Siamese,' he says, as if that's a valid explanation. I'm not a cat person and I've never really been a dog person either, despite growing up on a farm with both, so that means nothing to me. 'Belongs to my mum,' he continues. 'She doesn't go out much. And when she does, it's on a lead.'

I raise my eyebrows and stifle a cough.

He lets out a deep laugh. 'Sheba, not Mum. The cat escaped from Mum's flat this afternoon and hasn't come home.'

I look down and realise I should try to tidy myself up. As I bend over to wipe mud from my trousers, a sharp pain sweeps through my side. My coat's ripped and my pale blue jumper peeks through the slash. No sign of blood though, so hopefully just a scrape this time.

The man's dark brown eyes scrunch up with concern. 'Are you sure you're okay?' He hands me my rucksack, spattered with mud.

'I will be if you can direct me to the main road. I'll get a bus home.'

He scratches his head. Jangles the lead again. 'Where do you live? Maybe I can give you a lift.'

'It's fine, really. You've a cat to find.'

'True.' He peers into the darkness. 'Though if she was

here, those thugs probably scared her off. She's not good with strangers.' His gaze swivels back to me. 'You'll report them, I assume?'

'For sure.'

I won't, of course. I don't want to do anything that makes me too noticeable, though maybe it's a bit late for that. From now on, I'll just have to be more careful. A stabbing pain in my side reminds me that I sound just like Valerie Lee. Ignoring the racism around here. Sweeping it under the carpet. 'So how do I get back to the road?'

'Through here.' The man directs me to a narrow gap between two hedges, leading to a short alleyway. 'If you report them and need a witness, you'll find me at Parker, Dunham and Co., on Hillsbury Lane, just past the GP surgery. I'm Max Adebayo.'

'Thanks again.'

'Are you sure you're okay?' Max points to my hand. 'You're bleeding.'

I wince as I trace the fresh red scratches on my palm. 'I'll be fine. I've a first aid kit in my bag. Good luck with your search.'

I leave Max standing there calling out Sheba's name, and squeeze through the hedges, following the alleyway to civilisation. I'm not far from the main road, after all. I even recognise where I am, having found a historical plaque here this afternoon. That was only a couple of hours ago yet it seems so much longer. I think of all that's happened since then. Gina Alders' name on that plaque. The bridge. The stream. The teenagers.

Who knew Hillsbury would be such an adventure?

As I'm wandering along the road in the direction of my apartment block, a navy-blue Honda drives past me, slams on the brakes and then edges backwards. The driver's window's open, with loud music blaring from inside.

My heart thumps ominously in my chest as the car inches forwards alongside me.

'Shanna Regan, isn't it?'

I stop walking and peek inside.

Mark Stevens peers at me from the driver's seat, tapping his fingers in time to Freddie Mercury. He gives me the once-over. 'Is everything okay?'

'Sure, I'm fine.' Why's he suddenly being so ... amenable?

'I can give you a lift home. Where do you live?' He picks up two green A4 folders from his front seat and throws them towards the back. They slam down onto the floor. He leans across and opens the passenger door. A strong whiff of fresh, sporty aftershave trails towards me and I catch a glimpse of black gym shorts and a sweat-stained grey T-shirt. 'Or you're welcome to pop back to my place first. I live just over there.' He points to a semi-detached house across the road. 'You look like you could do with a drink.'

Going back to Mark Stevens' place isn't a wise move as I know very little about him. Getting personally involved with work is a bad idea too. Yet this is the perfect opportunity to hear his story, or rather his parents' story, and it's been handed to me on a plate. After our last and only meeting, I'm intrigued about his change of heart. He pretty much chased me off the church premises without even leaving his office.

'A drink would be great.' I sit down in his passenger seat, clutching my rucksack on my lap, and bang the car door shut.

Today seems to be ending better than I thought.

THE FIRST THING I notice about Mark's hallway is my business card, propped up against the letter rack on the white radiator shelf. The second thing is the stack of paint pots beside the front door, all colours of the rainbow, plus blocks of clay and paintbrushes and plastic mats.

Mark leads me into his dining room and offers me a drink. Says it will calm my nerves, even though I insist I feel fine. I stop arguing when he shows me the extensive assortment in his drinks cabinet. Vodka. Gin. Rum. Whisky. I pour myself a generous measure of vodka while he heads off for a shower and a change of clothes.

I glance around the dining room, trying to gain an insight into the man who lives here. But there aren't many clues. The room is tastefully decorated with pale blue walls, natural-looking wooden flooring and modern furniture. Simple yet elegant, uncluttered yet homely. A black wenge sideboard runs along the longest wall, with four deep drawers above four large cupboards, and some bottles of wine, a stack of travel brochures and a digital clock on the flat surface top. All I can tell so far is that Mark likes to drink, has good timekeeping and may be planning a holiday.

Great deductions, Shanna.

I pull at the brass handle of one of the drawers, wincing as it squeaks open, and peek inside. Silver cutlery. I try the next one. Black leather place mats. I open the cupboard below to find cream-coloured altar candles, silver candlesticks and glass dishes in neat stacks. I hear a creak on the landing upstairs, so push the cupboard door shut and creep back to the dining table.

I sit down on the nearest chair, its cold leather seat making me shiver. Put my palms flat down on the black wenge tabletop, scrutinising the pattern of the wood grain, tracing it with my fingers to give me something to do. Now I'm alone, tears well up in my eyes, but I blink them away.

I take out my first aid kit and a small circular mirror from the large pocket of my rucksack. Peering at my reflection, I dab antiseptic on two tiny cuts on my cheeks then on the ones on my hands. I pull up my jumper and use the mirror to check my side. There's nothing to see, just some pain when I move. Next, I find my small sewing kit and repair the rip in my coat, using long uneven stitches.

I shove everything back in my bag and zip it up. Cradle the vodka glass in my hand. Swirl the clear liquid around, then take a swig, faster than I intended. I choke as the vodka burns my palate. I take another swig, smaller and slower this time, lean against the back of the chair and let the drink run smoothly down my throat.

The hatred and ignorance in the teenagers' eyes had been familiar. The first time I saw that expression, I hadn't fought back. I hadn't stood up for what was right. I hadn't the last time either. Not yet, anyway.

A memory shifts into view.

Dad and I were near Dubai, our second time there for one of his longer contracts. I was nine at the time, sitting in a dusty classroom of a multinational school. It was one of the few times I'd managed to make a friend, Lila Benson, and stay for long enough to keep one.

We'd been learning about the Middle East. Iraq. Iran. Syria. Lebanon. The class teacher had left one country off her map, never even mentioned it. Maybe she thought no one would notice but I had and so had someone else.

'Where's Israel?' a quiet voice piped up from beside me. 'My granny lives there.'

I looked at Lila in horror. She clamped her hand over her mouth. I could see the terror in her eyes, and maybe she could see it in mine too.

'Being Jewish isn't bad,' she'd told me when we'd first met. 'But Mummy and Daddy say I have to keep it secret, cos some people here don't like Jews.'

The teacher guessed Lila was Jewish. The other kids did too; some ganged up on her, pinched her and called her names, shouting things I didn't understand.

'Christ-killer.'

'Dirty Jew-girl.'

'Where your Jew-horns?'

I kept silent while Lila cried. I said nothing while she pleaded. And, because the teacher turned a blind eye, I wondered if being Jewish was a bad thing after all.

The Bensons soon returned to their home in New York. By then, Lila wasn't my friend anymore. Shortly after, Dad and I left too, heading back to Ireland for a longer-than-normal break.

A polite cough interrupts my thoughts. Mark stands in the doorway, dressed casually in a pair of blue jeans and a white T-shirt. His damp, tousled hair glistens with copper-coloured hues that catch the light from the ceiling chandelier. He sits down in the chair opposite me, grabs a glass and pours himself a drink from a half-full bottle of whisky. Then points at my hands.

'So what happened to you?'

I weigh the situation in my head. I barely know him so don't know if I can trust him. But then again, I've been on my own for so long, it would be great to have a conversation with someone other than my belligerent boss. And I still want to know more about what happened to Mark's parents.

Decision made, I take a slow swig of vodka.

'It's a long story, for sure.'

CHAPTER ELEVEN

I tell Mark about the plaque and the bridge, the teenagers and the chase, and the barrister looking for a cat, with a dog lead in his hand. He smiles at times; grimaces at others. Makes all the right noises, says all the right things. My heart soars like a swallow in flight as excitement flushes through my veins.

Don't get involved, Shanna, I tell myself, repeating it as a mantra in my head.

I lean back in my chair, take another swig from my glass. My head feels lighter. My shoulders relax. The vodka is clearly working wonders as my bravado is back – though this isn't necessarily a good thing as I've let my guard down. Hopefully though, this means he'll talk too.

Mark swirls his whisky, splinters of reflected light dancing around the spotlight above him. Then he clatters his glass down onto the table.

'So this new plaque is similar to the one on Mum's bungalow.'

I nod. 'They look the same. Even the words are similar.'

He opens his mouth as if to say something, but instead

gazes at the wall behind me, before focusing back on my face.

'So what do you plan to do next?' he asks eventually.

'I'll look into it some more.' David's scowling face pops up in my vision. I blink and it fades away. 'But not at work or my boss may give me the push. He's told me not to spend time on these plaques.'

'That sounds rather drastic.' Mark gives me a sly smile. 'Though you don't strike me as someone who always does what she's told.'

'Maybe.' I smile back, trying to ignore the thumping sensation in my chest. 'But it's got me into trouble before.'

He raises his eyebrows, but I'm not going to elaborate.

'I saw my card in your hallway. Were you going to call me?'

His ears redden. He looks away and tugs at the neck of his T-shirt, stretching it slightly out of shape. 'I was thinking about it.'

'But you told me to keep my nose out of it.'

'Yes, I did ... and I owe you an apology.' His ears are now the colour of beetroot. 'It was just...' He pauses to take another swig of whisky. 'It was just a shock when you turned up and started asking questions.'

'Bit of a shock to me, too. Not often I get asked to leave a church.'

Mark's eyes sparkle with mischief. 'That suggests you have been ... at least once.'

'No comment.'

The temperature in the room shoots up, or maybe it's me. I put my hand to my cheek, hoping it's not turning red.

I've been asked to leave religious venues, of course – churches, synagogues, mosques, and more. Thrown out once, too. From my experience, journalists aren't always welcome, even in a house of worship.

I lean back in my chair. 'So why change your mind about calling me?'

'I was a bit too hasty.' He gives me a sheepish shrug. 'I've been wondering for years about that plaque. I did make some enquiries but, to be honest, I didn't really know where to start. Perhaps you'll have more luck. You *are* a journalist, after all.'

I nod, even though I don't feel like a journalist right now. My work at *Hillsbury Living* is nothing like I'm used to: no digging deep to discover a story, no speaking to the locals to find the truth. Straight facts only, according to David, which is why I'm finding his job mind-numbingly boring.

'No one else took the plaque seriously,' Mark continues, 'until you came along. I didn't think anyone had seen it. I guess the neighbours must have. Now I've let the brambles grow over, it's much less noticeable, but the words *are* bright red. And anyway, now I keep it as a reminder.'

'A reminder of what?'

'That I didn't do enough for her.'

He stands up and walks over to the sideboard. Places his glass down on a small black leather coaster next to the wine bottles. Then opens one of the top drawers, one I hadn't snooped in, and pulls out a creased colour photo.

I push my chair back, stand up and move next to him. My skin tingles at the warmth radiating through his T-shirt. I inch away slightly and glance down at the photo in his hand.

A tall woman gazes at me. Her arms are wrapped around a little boy standing in front of her. Long, honey-brown hair flows down over her shoulders, trailing over a purple dress speckled with tiny white flowers. The boy's hair is cut short. He wears a red jumper and grey trousers – a school uniform, maybe.

I nod slowly. 'You and your mother.' Mark's smile hasn't changed over the decades, and he's inherited Ruth's hair colour and her almond-shaped, chocolate-brown eyes.

A dart rips through my heart, seeing the pride on Ruth's face, the love in her eyes and the grin on young Mark's face that spreads from ear to ear. I don't remember what it's like to feel a mother's love, even though I've tried hard to do so.

As a child, I imagined that my mother didn't really die. That she was somewhere nearby, watching me like a guardian angel, trapped inside a parallel world with a window onto ours. Then as I grew older, I worried that instead she'd run away – from me, from Dad and from the life we had together. That maybe she never really loved me after all.

'I was five.' Mark traces his index finger over his mother's face. 'My first day at primary school. Mum was so excited. Me too.'

'You look like her.'

'I know.' His voice cracks, like a teenage boy's on the cusp of manhood. 'I should have been there for her, when— I didn't do enough.'

With Dad in Ireland, and me here, I understand Mark's regret. I haven't been helping Dad enough either.

'You see' – He takes a deep breath, wipes his eyes with the back of his hand – 'those words on the plaque were true.'

I stifle a gasp and put the glass down next to his. 'So, you're saying ... Peter really *did* beat her?'

Mark nods, the photo trembling in his hand. He swallows sharply, as if a pebble is caught in his throat. 'He hit her. A few times I had to take her to the nurse to get patched up.'

His eyes flash. Even now, all these years on, it seems his anger is still bubbling away inside him like a seething volcano. What would trigger him to erupt? Could he have been responsible for his father's death?

'So what did they argue about?' I'm hesitant to probe but desperate to know more.

'This and that. I'm not entirely sure.'

He turns away, refusing to meet my gaze.

So I wait for the alcohol to talk.

Car headlights flash through the front window, casting ghostly shadows along the wall. I watch them fade into the distance and take a long slug of vodka. No one likes an awkward silence so they usually try to fill it, telling me things they wouldn't usually say.

'I was around six the first time,' Mark continues eventually. 'He smacked her cheek. I cried; Mum cried. And then it happened again and again until it became a habit. I asked her to leave him several times, but she wouldn't.'

'Why not?'

'Because in between ... when he wasn't using her as a punching bag and when he wasn't drunk ... everything was...' He looks down at the photo. 'He bought her things other husbands bought their wives. Flowers. Jewellery. He took her out to nice restaurants and the cinema, even the theatre. As I got older, I realised it was all guilt, but Mum didn't want to know.' His eyes flash with the same look I'd seen in St Luke's, anger combined with regret and hurt. He grips the photo so tightly that his hand shakes.

'But the police looked into her death, I assume?'

'Of course.' He puts the photo down and gazes at me, his eyes intense and narrow. 'They decided it was an accident. Her classic falling-down-the-stairs line, said far too many times, became her epitaph.'

'Did you tell them he hit her?'

'I tried, but I was the only one who'd seen it. To everyone else, they had the perfect marriage. Everyone knew he and I didn't get on, and they thought it was sour grapes. Anyway, he had an alibi that night. His secretary said he'd been at her house, going over some accounts.'

'They were having an affair?'

'Not that I know of.' Mark stares at the photo again. 'Though I've always wondered if Peter bullied her into saying that.'

'And then he was mugged and beaten to death nearly a year later?'

'He was only beaten, not mugged. He had two hundred pounds in his wallet, so robbery can't have been the motive. They left him there like a broken rag doll. I had to identify his body and barely recognised him. Guess someone wanted him dead.' There's no mistaking the grim delight in Mark's chocolate-brown eyes. His hand pulls at the neck of his T-shirt.

'What if someone was avenging your mum's death?' I raise an eyebrow.

An awkward silence hangs in the air.

Mark gives me an indignant look. 'It wasn't me.' His voice rises. 'I was at a conference that evening with plenty of witnesses, and I don't exactly look like a killer, do I?'

I bite my lip. Killers take many shapes and forms, I learnt long ago. I once witnessed a suicide bombing in Iraq. A young woman with explosives strapped to her chest, desperate for public attention, believing she was saving the world. Not every murder, not every death, is straightforward. Most killers, especially those with anger in their hearts, believe their reasoning – even if others don't.

I drain my glass. Mark offers me another, but I decline as my head is beginning to throb. I sit down on the nearest dining chair to steady myself.

'The police never had any suspects?'

Mark sits down beside me. 'They thought it was a

random attack. Wrong place, wrong time. Peter was found in a clearing near some woodland, not far from here, early one morning. The police reckon he'd been there all night. No CCTV so they couldn't check.'

My palms tingle. Is that where I've just been?

'And you told the police about the plaque?'

'Of course I told them, but they thought it was a joke. They weren't going to waste time and public money looking into a fake plaque.'

Thoughts invade my head, like angry bees swarming for attention. I need to figure this out logically. I can't do it any other way.

I unzip my rucksack and pull out my notepad and a black biro. Turn to a fresh page and write down everything I know so far. The names, dates and addresses. Two plaques. Same size, same colour, similar words.

I stare at my scribbled handwriting until my eye sockets ache. There *has* to be a pattern. No way is this a coincidence.

'Look ... I've found two plaques so far. Your dad and Gina Alders. If Peter was responsible for your mum's death, and Gina for this twelve-year-old girl's, then ... then maybe I'm right. Maybe someone in Hillsbury killed them as some sort of revenge.'

Mark gives a deep laugh. 'But that's absurd.'

'Maybe it does sound crazy but hear me out.'

He smiles, leans back in his chair. 'Okay, go on.'

'Peter died in 2016 and Gina died in 2014.' I tap my notepad with my pen. 'Each time, the killer put up a plaque as a reminder of what they did and why they died.' A shiver runs down my spine. 'Maybe there are more of these plaques out there.'

'But if no one knows the plaques are there, why bother?'

'I don't know. Maybe it made the killer feel ... justified?' I drum my fingers on the table and glance down at my notepad. The words swim in front of me, as if I'm trying to decipher an ancient language.

'Anyway, I forgot to mention, the plaque was put up a few weeks *before* he died, not after.' Mark pours himself another whisky, filling the glass to the brim. 'He came back from a business trip and asked if I was making a sick joke. He yanked it off the wall, broke it into pieces and threw it in the bin, but another one appeared a week or so later while he was at work.'

'And no one saw anything – when someone put it up?'

'None of the neighbours said anything.'

'Maybe the plaque was a warning for Peter then. Own up or we kill you.'

'But ... no.' Mark shakes his head. 'If no one else knew he hurt Mum, except me, how did the killer know? And what did they get out of it by killing him?'

He glances at my fingers, still tapping away in rhythm.

I stop and clench my fists. 'I don't know ... Maybe she told someone, or maybe someone saw him do it. I did say it all sounds crazy.'

'Not totally.'

Mark reaches over, picks up the photo. He lays it flat on the table between us, then rests the tips of his fingers on the edge as if he can't bear to let his mother go.

'I do think he killed her, and I think you're right – someone killed him because of it. The plaque proves something was going on.' He gazes into my eyes. 'Though I should have killed Peter years ago myself.'

A shiver rolls down my spine.

CHAPTER TWELVE

We try to leave the conversation there, ignoring it like a treacherous river between us that we're both afraid to cross. We chat until around ten, when our energy levels begin to plummet. Mark cooks scrambled eggs on toast for two. I chop up banana and strawberries into a bowl and drizzle some low-fat vanilla yoghurt over the top. Then we both drink more spirits until way past midnight. Though I add in a mixer of orange juice to try to pace myself.

He describes his experiences as a provincial accountant. Clients committing fraud, now serving inside. Local businesses fighting takeovers. How he'd wanted to travel the world but had felt a need to remain near Ruth instead. Since she's been gone, he's been making plans, which explains the travel brochures, but he's still not yet left the country.

I tell him about my adventures on the road. All the countries I've visited. All the sights I've seen. The trauma. The excitement. The wonders of the world. How writing for *Hillsbury Living* has brought me back down to earth.

But there's no escape for either of us, as our conversation keeps drifting back to the plaques. Eventually we give in to our inquisitive natures, switch on Mark's laptop and search for Gina Alders online. We stumble upon a Hillsbury address for a Mr Robert Alders. Her husband, maybe. And we find the name of the twelve-year-old girl in a newspaper article devoted to the tragic loss of Charlotte Newman. I find an address for her family too, not far from where I live.

By the time we finish talking, it's two-thirty a.m. and I'm struggling to keep my eyes open.

Mark offers me a lift home, then remembers the empty whisky bottle beside him. He offers me his sofa, then his bed.

I call a cab.

I WAKE up the next morning earlier than intended, still thinking about Mark's words, and about my own.

'Just suppose someone in Hillsbury is killing people as some sort of revenge.'

'If you find them, let me know. I'd like to shake their hand.'

I've assumed from Mark's work at the church that he's religious, though I haven't actually asked him. Offering me his bed suggests he isn't, but he may not have intended to join me. I never asked him that either.

Religion has its rules, but rules are made to be broken. Many people I've met over the years seem to tailor their religion to suit themselves. Maybe Mark's one of them. And from the prickling sensation on my skin, it seems my body hopes so.

I don't have a hangover but I feel tired and drained, like I've been tossing and turning all night. I lay back, resting my head against the pillow, and gaze at a black spider hanging down near the wardrobe. It's been hovering there for twenty minutes, suspended by a single delicate silky thread as if, like me, it doesn't know which way to turn.

'Does Mark really believe in an eye for an eye?' I ask the spider. 'Is it wrong to do a bad thing to a bad person for a good reason?'

The spider hoists itself up to the ceiling and stretches out its long spindly legs, exploring its new surroundings. Then it crawls into a dark corner, where it curls up into a tight ball, just a tiny grey smudge, barely noticeable unless you know it's there. Yet watching me from up high, like an all-seeing god.

I don't believe in God myself. But, I wonder, whose role is it to decide what's right or wrong, whether a death is punishment or karma and if anyone should be commended for taking a life.

I won't find the answers in my bedroom, I realise. So I drag myself out of bed, shower and get dressed, then go down to check yesterday's post. The postman has left an official-looking red-and-white card in my mailbox informing me there's a small parcel with my neighbour, Hetty Gordon. I groan with frustration, then annoyance and dread.

Time to knock on the door of number five.

Hetty is in her eighties, slim and elegant. She wears the latest fashions in neon colours with long ginger cat hairs stuck to the fabric, even though pets are officially banned from the apartment block. Every day, she's up early. Useful when you have a parcel to collect before you go to work. Not so useful when she clatters pots and pans at five a.m. and sings at the top of her voice like an off-key Snow White.

'I've a touch of the insomnias,' she said, soon after I moved in.

Touch of something, for sure. She once told me she'd been an opera singer in her younger years – a top West End star. Having heard her massacre Carmen's 'Habanera' at dawn, somehow I doubt it.

Hetty swings her door open straight away, revealing black shiny trousers and a lime-green shirt with ruffles at the collar. She clasps my package for a bit too long before she hands it over.

'Hope it's something nice,' she says in her shrill sing-song voice that grates on my ears.

I snatch the large white Jiffy bag from her grasp. There's a MailReady logo on the front, and the bag has split open slightly at one end.

Hetty shrugs as I stare at her. 'These posties, they can't be trusted. So who's it from? Bet you can't wait to find out. Go on, love, open it.' She hovers in her doorway, a broad grin on her face, leaning against the wooden frame as if she's there for the long haul. Her eyes widen expectantly, bulging out of her wrinkled face, her dark weathered skin reminding me of a shrunken voodoo head. 'I've some scissors if that helps.'

'No, I'm good, but thanks again.' I step back from her door. 'Really appreciate you taking it in. Have a great day.'

Her smile fades, and she shakes her shoulders in a huff. Then she slams her front door shut with more force than I'd expect from a woman of her age.

I shake my head and chuckle to myself. *Nice try yet again, Hetty.* This isn't the first time she's tried to sweet-talk me into revealing something about myself, and I suspect it won't be the last.

Five minutes later, I stand in my kitchen, stacking unwashed plates and coffee-stained mugs into the dishwasher. A job I've been putting off for days. I've never been a domestic goddess and doubt I ever will be.

When I'm done, I feel a sense of achievement, especially as there's now some space on the grey speckled granite counter. I sit down on the kitchen stool and tear open the Jiffy bag at the damaged end, using the red pull tab. There's another package inside. I rip it open and turn it upside down. A bundle of letters drops out onto the surface, held together with a thick brown elastic band. A note in Dad's straggly handwriting lies on top.

Your post. Some been here a while. Sorry.

The farm has always been my official fixed abode, a safe place for letters and bills and other correspondence. When I'm travelling, Dad sends these to a central UK mailbox that forwards post, parcels and packages on to me wherever I am in the world. Though the digital age has largely changed that in recent years. Bank statements and magazine subscriptions, remittance slips and tax returns, all reach me with the touch of a button, so I know whatever remains will be mainly junk.

I rip open the envelope and pull out the letters to discover I'm right on the whole. Credit card companies seeking my business. Supermarket vouchers for me to spend.

But not everything belongs in the trash.

I open my smear test invitation, a reminder from my dentist that my appointment is long overdue, a medical form from the GP surgery to update their records ... I glance down at the latter with tears prickling my eyes, as so many of the questions will remain unanswered.

I'm around three years older than my mother was when she died. I've reached ages she never reached. Visited places she never visited. Maybe I'll have diseases she never had too. Cancers. Glaucoma. Diabetes. Heart disease. Arthritis. And there's no family I can ask.

I push the form to one side, grab a tissue from a white cardboard box on the counter and blow my nose. Then I grab another and wipe the tears that are trickling down my cheeks.

I ARRIVE at work around ten, an hour later than usual. I struggle to open the outside door as the lock is wearing away and my key is stiff to turn. One of the drawbacks of working in a listed building with little renovation for years. I've mentioned my trouble with the lock to David a few times, but he's done nothing about it. Yet another job that's fallen by the wayside.

The door resists as I push it open, its ageing joints creaking with effort like an old man bending his knees. But eventually it gives in.

The doormat is empty, to my relief – no anonymous notes.

I walk up the stairs, taking care not to brush my coat against the mould-ridden wall. I push open the office door, expecting to feel a rush of cold air, but instead the room feels warm and stifling. And it stinks of manky mutt.

A note is stuck to my computer screen. *You're late this morning.*

I slam my bag down on the floor and pull off my coat, then hang it on the back of David's chair. I listen to new messages on the answerphone that he's ignored, check emails with locations of more plaques and write the opening paragraph to my article.

But despite keeping busy, I can't get Gina Alders and Charlotte Newman out of my mind. I still want to know if there's a link with Ruth and Peter Stevens. After my evening with Mark, I feel I need to – for him, as much as for me. I feel like I've found a friend, and I can't believe, or rather don't want to believe, that he's involved in murder.

My mobile rings. I don't recognise the number. A muscle throbs in my shoulder like a nervous pulse. I've already had two missed calls today, and I answered a third one to hear heavy breathing at the other end.

I'm tempted to ignore this call but I've handed my mobile number to loads of people here in Hillsbury and left it on the noticeboards too. It could be about another historical plaque.

'Hello?' My voice shakes when I answer – not sounding like me at all. 'Who is this?' I say, more confidently, more composed.

Deep breaths come down the phone. My finger hovers on the *End Call* button.

'Hello, it's ... it's Valerie Lee.' Her quiet voice sounds even more nervous than mine. 'Is that Shanna? I don't know if you remember me but we ... we met the other day, in the park. You—'

'Sure I do.' I sigh with relief at the familiar voice. As if I could really forget the park ... I still have the fading bruise on my cheek, now a murky shade of brown. 'Great to hear from you.'

'Oh ... well ... I...' More deep breathing down the phone. 'I was wondering if you'd like to come over for something to eat tonight. Nothing fancy,' she says in an apologetic tone. 'Harry wants to meet you. I mean, meet you properly. Not just on our doorstep.'

'Meet me?' I picture her GP husband with his Hollywood smile. 'Why would Harry want to meet me properly?' I grimace when I realise I've said that out loud.

'To talk about your article, of course,' Valerie says. 'The one you're writing for *Hillsbury Living*. He loves history, you see. This way, he can tell you more about the plaque and George Masters, if you're interested, of course.'

I glance at my computer screen, the measly word count glinting back at me, the bare bones of the article I need to write. A meal with strangers, I don't fancy, but I need more information and I've done far worse going in search of a story.

'Sure. What time?' This will be my first social arrangement for months. Apart from the ad hoc drinking session with Mark last night.

'Could you come over around eight? I hope that's not too late. It's just that ... Harry runs a local clinic and—'

'That's perfect for me.' I look at the list on my notepad. That gives me enough time to visit more plaques after work. I turn the page and find the addresses for Gina Alders and Charlotte Newman. I check their locations on the map to discover they're too far away and too far apart, so those house calls will have to wait.

'Is there anything you don't eat?'

Ah ... yes. This could be interesting.

'I'm a vegetarian. No meat or fish. I hope that's not a problem. Happy with a cheese sandwich or scrambled eggs, if that helps.'

Over the years, I've felt like an outsider at times. 'Shanna's the veggie one,' Andy used to say, followed by a series of sniggers. Sometimes on the road I struggled to find suitable food to eat.

I wait for an uncomfortable silence but Valerie answers straightaway.

'Don't be silly.' She lets out a nervous laugh. 'I can't invite you over for a cheese sandwich. That's not how we treat our guests. Just one thing though...'

A thunderous clatter reaches my ears, followed by fumbling sounds.

'Valerie?'

'I dropped ... I dropped the phone. Sorry, I can be a real butterfingers at times.' She clears her throat. 'Harry still doesn't know about what happened with those boys in the park.' She breathes heavily down the phone. 'I decided not to tell him. It's not important, no harm done. They're just kids. Serves me right for walking through the park on Shabbat on my own. So please, if you don't mind ... just don't mention it.'

'Well ... if that's what—'

The line goes dead.

CHAPTER THIRTEEN

GEORGE MASTERS ... CAMPAIGNER FOR JUSTICE

The plaque's blue glaze reflects hazy light from the bronze lantern on the wall beside it. I compare its finish with the black-and-red ones I've found. The writing on this one is clearer, the glaze smoother and the edges cleaner. Those other plaques are poor copies, for sure.

There's a silver-coloured box on the opposite door frame, two-thirds up, slightly slanted. I press my fingers against it, the metal surface cold against my skin. It's shorter than my pen and around the width of my finger, with a screw cap at its base.

'Shanna Regan ... welcome.' I startle at Harry's voice. He's standing in the open doorway less than an arm's length in front of me. 'Come in.'

I stuff my phone into the front pocket of my rucksack and point at the narrow box. 'What's this? A talisman of some sort? I've seen loads of these around Hillsbury.'

'A *mezuzah*.' When I look at him blankly, he continues,

'It designates a household as Jewish – a daily reminder of our faith, to us and everyone walking past.'

I guess that explains why I've seen so many of these around here. Some wooden, some metal, some coloured, some plain. 'Is there something inside it?'

'Yes, a scroll of parchment containing a Jewish prayer, the *Shema*.'

Harry beckons me inside and closes the front door behind me with a forceful shove. Takes my coat and hangs it on an empty metal peg. My quilted parka looks tatty and worn next to Valerie's pristine burgundy felt coat, and I cringe at the white, downy lining peeking out through my jagged stitches. As if he senses my discomfort, Harry straightens the sleeves and pulls the hem of my coat down, his fingers hovering for an instant over the hastily-sewn rip.

'Tripped over again?'

I shrug, then smile. 'I can be a right klutz at times.'

'Somehow I doubt that.' His steely eyes narrow with fatherly concern as he inspects the fading bruise and fresh cuts on my cheek. As his eyes trail up and down me like an airport scanner with X-ray vision, a flicker of surprise passes across his face. Maybe he's noticed that I've spruced myself up for the evening.

I popped into one of the high street boutiques this afternoon, deciding it's time to blend in more with the locals. Realising I need to treat Hillsbury like any other job. Fit in, and the locals will talk. Don't, and they'll be wary. Plus, my wardrobe didn't include anything suitable for dinner with people I don't know. Just fading jeans and scruffy jumpers and trainers in various states of decay.

I wanted to look like I'd made some effort, or at least tried to. So I'd grabbed a knitted dress the colour of burnt caramel off the rack. Checked the size and paid the hefty price, feeling the inquisitive gazes of two women, one blonde and one dark, as I rushed back out the door. The dress is a bit short, but I've paired it with long black boots and hope my hosts won't take offence. Many of the women around here dress this way, but not the more religious members of the Jewish community, I've noticed. They're fashionable but conservative. Hems to the knees. Shoulders covered. No cleavage exposed.

I even applied some brown mascara and plum-coloured lipstick before I left my apartment – not something I usually bother with on a regular basis.

When Harry's eyes reach my face again, he gives a brief nod, as if he's satisfied with the sight in front of him. As if he expects me to care, when I really don't. It's one thing to cover my head in a mosque or my shoulders in a synagogue, out of respect for religion. But here in Hillsbury, dressing to fit in, I feel like an imposter, trying to be something I'm not, someone I'm not. Cinderella at the palace ball. A pauper wearing a princess's gown.

I shiver, despite a blast of warmth from the radiator beside me. Eager to change the focus of attention, I reach into my rucksack and shove a bottle of red wine into Harry's open hand. I bought it in the kosher shop this afternoon, having spent a while Googling 'What do you take as a gift to a kosher home?'

He grips the bottle firmly. 'Thank you, but totally unnecessary.'

'It's good of you to ask me. Hope it's okay.' I point at the wine label. 'I was thinking you'd only drink kosher wine, and the girl in Sammy's Deli said you'd like this one.'

He glances down. 'Merlot. Good choice.'

'She seemed to know you.'

'Well, that's not too surprising. Everyone knows

everyone around here.' He pulls at his beard, gives me a broad grin. 'Not that easy for strangers to escape unnoticed.'

A muscle twinges at the back of my neck and I look away.

A clattering sound from the kitchen breaks through the awkward silence, and a warm spicy aroma drifts through the doorway.

'Mmm, something smells good.' My stomach gurgles in anticipation, reminding me that I've barely filled it all day. 'Need any help?'

'I'm sure Valerie has it covered. Please, come through.'

Harry herds me into the dining room, where the oak table is laid neatly for three: silver cutlery, white plates and blue napkins folded into tall crystal tumblers. The two silver candlesticks I saw on Saturday now sit on the sideboard, cleaned and polished and glistening like new. The silver goblets and tray too. Ready for the next Sabbath, I assume, in the ongoing weekly cycle of religious life.

Watercolour paintings adorn the cream walls. A reminder of the article I was originally asked to write about local artists, the one I refused to do. Considering my run-in with the teenage thugs, maybe that would have been a better option.

'Excuse me for one moment while I make a quick call to a patient.' Harry pulls out the chair at the head of the table. Pats the brown leather seat with the palm of his hand. 'Take a pew. Valerie will be in soon.' He strolls away with long, confident strides.

I watch him turn into another room, then creep to the rear of the dining room, shoving the chair back into place under the table. Mark was right – I rarely do what I'm told.

Books are lined up on two shelving units along the far wall. I move closer to see the spines and maybe find out more about my hosts.

Top shelf. Jewish history and Holocaust history. Crime fiction and historical fiction. Medicine guides and health manuals.

Next shelf. Prayer books with mottled brown leather covers. *The Jewish Book of Why*. *The Children's Jewish History Encyclopaedia*. I run my finger down the spine of that one as it seems out of place, the only kids' book in the room. In fact, it's the only sign of kids in the whole house. I pull the encyclopaedia off the shelf and open the cover. A white label edged with gold is stuck inside, the words printed boldly in black as if trying to attract my attention.

PRESENTED TO SUSAN LEE
BY HILLSBURY UNITED CHEDER
JUNE 2000

Child-like handwriting in a sharp lead pencil is scrawled over the page. I can decipher the name Susie, but only just. There are some symbols squiggled in green felt-tip pen beside it, vaguely familiar. I take a photo of them, out of curiosity, wondering what they mean. Maybe I'll find someone I can ask. Though not my hosts for the evening, as I can't admit that I've been snooping around.

Tucked inside the front flap there's a note. I pull it out and read it.

To our darling Susie. Congratulations. Love Mummy & *Daddy.*

A hand grabs my arm. 'Shanna.'

I startle. The book slips out of my grasp. I bend down and manage to catch it in time, clutching the hard cover as tightly as my fingers will allow.

'Sorry, I was just—'

'You haven't … you haven't reported it, have you?' Valerie whispers, glancing briefly into the hallway. She grabs the encyclopaedia from my hands and shoves it back into the empty space on the shelf.

'Not yet. But I should do...' I explain about the youths chasing me near the bridge, and the plaque I found there. I show her the cuts on my hands and cheeks.

'I'd prefer it if you didn't.' She glances towards the hallway again. 'Or at least ... leave me out of it.'

I take in her tightened lips and her nervous twitch. Picture the first aid kit she showed me and remember what happened to Ruth Stevens. Is Valerie also a battered wife, covering up her bruises and scars?

'But those yobs will do it again.' My voice is gentle, as if I'm speaking to a young child. 'Maybe not to me or you, but to someone else. They shouldn't get away with it. We should do something.' As I say the words, I feel myself cringe inside. Only I know how hypocritical that sounds.

Valerie's eyes flash. She grabs my arm again. 'There is no *we*. I'll deny it all,' she says through gritted teeth. A hint of hardness sets into her eyes.

Footsteps stomp towards us. I hold my breath, my shoulder muscles twinging. Valerie moves closer to me and stands still. The footsteps continue past the dining room and into the kitchen. As I breathe out, I feel my muscles relax. I feel Valerie's do too.

I remember the bookcase behind us, the encyclopaedia I opened. 'Is Susan your daughter?'

Valerie lets go of my arm. 'Yes ... she—'

'Ready to eat?' Harry walks through the doorway carrying a wicker basket filled with small bread rolls. He rolls up his shirt sleeves, neatly and carefully, like a surgeon ready to take control. Adjusts the black knitted skullcap on his head. Gives her a broad grin.

Valerie's eyes soften, all sweetness and light. 'Of course.'

She straightens her long black skirt, gives me a pleading glance and walks briskly into the kitchen.

CHAPTER FOURTEEN

At first I feel hemmed in, with Valerie on one side and Harry on the other. But the more we talk, the more I relax. Valerie makes me feel at home, fussing over me like a mother hen, and I keep my word by not mentioning Saturday morning in the park.

I find myself slowly warming to Harry. He's welcomed me, a total stranger, into his home. He's a natural charmer, full of charisma, but there's a softness in his eyes when he looks at Valerie. Even sometimes when he looks at me.

Dinner is a starter of egg-and-onion mixed with mayonnaise, followed by home-made falafel and hummus in pita bread with salad – a tasty mix of chopped tomato, cucumber, red pepper and red onion in balsamic vinaigrette. A common Jewish supper, they tell me, if they're making a meat-free meal.

They ask me if I've always been veggie and what prompted my decision. I explain it's too long ago for me to remember but Dad said it became a habit that was difficult to break.

They talk to me about Judaism, explaining the dietary

laws and also some of the laws of Shabbat. How they only eat certain animals (no pig, no shellfish), and only if these have been killed in a certain way. They don't serve dairy foods with meat, either. All those laws and regulations sound far too complicated to me. But I guess when you're used to them, they're part of your daily life.

For a while I feel as if I belong – until Harry reminds me I don't.

'I can't place your accent,' he says with a twinkle in his eye, just as I'm scooping my last piece of dessert – apple pie and ice cream – on to my spoon, 'though Valerie tells me you're Irish.'

My fork hovers in the air. 'Yes, that's where my family's from, but I've been told my accent's a bit of mishmash.' He isn't the first to ask and is unlikely to be the last. 'I've travelled all over since I was a child, so it's no surprise.'

'Where's your family based?'

'Kilconly. I'm sure you won't have heard of it. It's a small village near Tuam – in County Galway.'

Harry shakes his head slowly. 'You must pick up accents easily.'

'Guess so.' I stuff the chunk of pie into my mouth, not prepared to skimp on my first proper home-cooked meal for weeks, especially as Valerie's such a fine cook.

'I'm guessing Shanna is short for Shannon? A good Irish name.'

I swallow my mouthful of pie. I haven't used my full name for years and I'm certainly not going to start now.

Harry grabs his napkin, dabs his mouth and coughs as if to clear his throat. 'So, do you plan to stay in Hillsbury for long?'

I put the fork down on my plate and squirm in my seat, feeling like I'm being interviewed for a job. I was right the first time I met him. Harry likes asking questions. Problem is, I don't like answering them.

'Not sure. May need to go back to Ireland for a bit.'

Harry raises his eyebrows but says nothing.

'Dad's clearing out our farm before we sell it.' I wonder if the doctor knows the same tricks as me. I'm filling in a gap, talking when I don't need to, providing information they don't need to know. A lump forms in my throat as I think back to that last phone call and Dad's rattling cough.

I'm worried about his health, I say in my head.

'Just you and your dad, is it?' Harry leans back in his chair and relaxes his shoulders. Open and inviting – clearly his listening-to-a-patient pose. He squeezes his hands together. He's enjoying this, I can tell, trying to learn more about me.

I purse my lips. 'Yes, just the two of us since my mum died, so I should really head back there to—'

'But you can't leave yet.' Valerie slams her cutlery down on the table. 'The plaques, and your article for *Hillsbury Living*.' She nudges her husband's elbow. 'You know ... the reason she's here tonight. Remember?'

'Oh, yes, indeed.' Harry sits up straight, turns to face me. 'I'd totally forgotten. So you want to know more about our plaque?' He relaxes into his chair, stretches out his legs and starts talking.

Harry has clearly done his research over the years, as we spend the next hour discussing George Masters, a prominent 1920s lawyer involved in the English criminal justice system. I scribble down notes, asking how it feels to own a piece of Hillsbury heritage.

I discover more about Valerie and Harry too. He grew up in Hillsbury but she only moved to the area when they married. They fell in love with the bungalow and its plaque as soon as they discovered it, even though it's quite a way from the synagogue. They explained that many Jewish people prefer to live near the shul so it's not so far to walk there on Shabbat and the religious festivals, when they don't use the car.

'Wouldn't it be great if Shanna came to something at shul some time?' Valerie looks at Harry as if seeking his approval. 'To meet some of the local community and learn about Judaism.'

I need to think quickly. Find a valid reason why I can't. I don't do religion but also don't want to offend my hosts. 'Don't I need to be a member?' I pick up my glass and swig back some Diet Coke, 'or,' trying not to smile, 'Jewish?'

'That won't be a problem.' Harry laughs. 'I'm one of the people in charge so I'm sure I can smuggle you in.' He winks at me, then reaches behind him. Picks up a piece of paper from the window ledge, unfolds it carefully and runs his finger over the creases to flatten them. 'Here's our newsletter. Services, obviously. Over-65s club – we're all a bit young for that. Local history club – you should do a talk when your article's finished.' He turns the page. 'We have yoga, a beginners' guide to prayer, Hebrew classes, Jewish learning for women, and even arts and crafts.'

Valerie clasps her hands together in delight. 'I'm sure we can find something for you, Shanna.'

I grimace at the determination in her eyes.

'What do you enjoy, apart from travelling?'

I shrug. 'This and that.' As a child, I played games with Dad on the road. Card games. Board games. Logic puzzles. Word games, too. But most of all I loved watching people, making up stories about them and wondering about their daily lives – a remnant from a childhood spent travelling, meeting different people on the road.

Harry hands me the newsletter. 'We have an interfaith forum meeting next week, in association with the church opposite. We'll be talking about Chanukah and Christmas. You should come along.'

I glance down at the page. 'Not sure my boss would cover it.'

Harry clears his throat. 'I meant for your personal interest. Not for work.'

I look up at him, then at Valerie.

'Amazing how many people have never met a Jew before,' he continues. 'Or don't think they have. But, as you can see, we're just as normal as everyone else. We're not all part of that strictly Orthodox community everyone thinks of. You know, the ones with the black hats and the ringlets. Though I do have this.' He tugs at his short beard and laughs.

I laugh back to be polite. 'I admit they're the ones I thought of when I realised Hillsbury had a big Jewish community.'

Harry gives me a broad grin. 'Jews are far more diverse than people realise. I guess it's harder here to know who's Jewish and who isn't.'

'Please come to the shul some time.' Valerie stands up and leans over me, her finger scrolling down the newsletter page until it stops at a large box of text on the right. 'Here, what about our Chanukah party? I'm helping to organise it. I can introduce you to lots of our friends. The vicar's coming from over the road.' She gives me a nervous smile. 'That would be so much fun ... wouldn't it?'

I fiddle with my napkin.

For you, maybe, I hear in my head.

CHAPTER FIFTEEN

On Friday morning, I decide to have a slightly later start following a busy work-filled Thursday. I take the long route to the office, via the local high street, to buy some breakfast and a new torch, and soon find myself at the heart of the pre-Sabbath rush.

Men and women wrapped up in thick winter coats scurry past me. Most are laden with bulging shopping bags from the kosher butcher and the deli and the bakery. Some huddle together, avoiding the blasts of icy air.

I hover among them, watching the hive of activity and listening to their conversations.

'Fifteen people tonight. It *was* twelve but then I asked the Ginsbergs as their oven isn't working.'

'Shabbat's in so early this week. Three-thirty, can you believe it?'

'Just us for lunch tomorrow. More time to read a book.'

'Sorry, can't stop. Loads to do. But I'll see you in shul tomorrow around ten.'

I wonder what it must be like to lead a life governed by so much routine. Having the stress of Christmas cooking every week. Doing the bakery run every Friday morning. Then cleaning and tidying the house and preparing a three-course meal every Friday afternoon.

Despite some of the panic, I sense frivolity in the air too. That something exciting's coming, something special, more than just a welcome break from the working week.

Not all Jews are religious, Valerie and Harry had told me, but many still follow the Friday night traditions, even if they do nothing more. Lighting two candles, saying blessings over wine and challah bread, and eating together as a family. Some, like Valerie and Harry, do the same on Saturday lunchtimes too, observing all of the Sabbath rules.

This means twenty-five hours without mobile phones and computers and televisions. A day of rest and social media silence – a digital detox – cut off from the rest of the world.

I'm addicted to my technology. My phone is my second brain, my diary, my camera, my address book, and so much more. I can't imagine giving it up for anything or anyone, even for just one day.

A yeasty aroma of fresh bread beckons me from Cohen's Bakery. I follow it across the pavement as if under a witch's spell, and step inside the shop to join the winding customer queue. When I finally reach the counter, I ask for a small challah, pointing to one of the long, plaited loaves. I pronounce it as Valerie taught me last night, beginning with a guttural *ch*.

Twenty minutes later, I'm sitting at my desk, clutching a damp, brown paper bag. I pull out the warm loaf and break off a large chunk. Poppy seeds from the glossy brown top roll onto my desk like tiny black hailstones tumbling off a pitched roof. I stuff the piece of challah into my mouth. It's slightly chewy and eggy, with a sweet flavour similar to brioche. Delicious but filling so I put the rest aside for my lunch.

I settle down to work, replying to emails with details of a few more plaques and writing more of this article.

After lunch, I open up the Facebook app on my mobile and log into my account for the first time in weeks. Scrolling down my feed, I can't say much has changed. It's the same people moaning about the same mundane topics, arguing about politics or boasting about their perfect lives. There are five friend requests from people I don't know, each with over fifty mutual friends and one with the name Huggy Y'Bootie. I delete them all.

I have two messages, both from Andy. I don't open them, but check his profile instead. Like mine, it's been dormant since August.

I find Mark's Facebook account and try to have a nose, but I can't see anything as his privacy settings are too stringent. My finger hovers over the *Send friend request* button but I refrain. Instead, I search for local Hillsbury residents' groups and join the top one in the list, figuring this will be the best way to see what's going on in the area.

Then I check Nadia's profile. Three weeks ago she posted that her father was taken ill but didn't give any details. Thirty-five people commented, expressing their concerns. I feel pangs of guilt – I should have been one of them. Until recently, we knew everything about each other's lives. No wonder she's been trying to track me down.

I can't leave it any longer.

I shut down the office computer and FaceTime her from my laptop. She picks up on the first ring.

'Well ... hello to you, too. About bloody time.'

She blinks at me from the top of the screen, a jade-coloured headscarf covering her jet-black hair, bringing out the green of her eyes.

I cringe at the sarcasm in her voice, the scowl on her face. She's never been one to mince her words.

'Sorry, I've been—'

'Avoiding me?'

'No, I...' I look down. Doodle on my notepad as I think of an excuse but my mind remains blank. 'I've ... I've just been busy, and I—'

'Bullshit. I heard you went AWOL.' She reaches forwards and adjusts the screen. I can see more of her now, slouching on a large well-worn armchair, with colourful wall hangings in the background. 'Still are, I assume, since I haven't heard anything from you in weeks. Where are you? Is that an office?'

I nod. No point lying to her. I hear raised voices speaking in Arabic, the slam of a door, and watch as a dark, hairy arm appears on the side of the screen.

'Hold on.' Nadia stands up, leaving an empty chair in front of me. Two minutes later, she returns. 'Sorry, Dad wanted to know where the TV control was. Effing men. It was right under his nose.'

'How is he? I saw he's been ill ... on your Facebook. I'm so sorry. I haven't been on there for a while.'

'I figured you have your reasons.' She gives a slight shrug of the shoulders. 'He had a minor heart attack but he's on the mend. He's getting on my effing nerves again so nearly back to normal.' She snorts with laughter. Her headscarf falls backwards, revealing more of her glossy hair.

'Don't let him catch you using that language, or he'll have another one.'

'You should see him when I really swear like a trooper.' She scrunches up her face in mock horror, then laughs. 'I mean, he knows I'm no angel. But he isn't impressed if I start effing and blinding. Just as well I do it in English so my *sitto* doesn't understand.'

My turn to laugh, as I try to imagine Nadia, with her vibrant personality and wild streak, dealing with her ninety-year-old grandma watching her every move, trying to live the life of piety in her parents' Egyptian home. She rebelled against her large Muslim family in her youth – drink, drugs, sex, the lot – but then returned back to the fold when a relationship went bad. She lives in London but often visits her parents near Cairo. I've accompanied her a few times.

'Have you heard from Andy?' I stare down at my hands.

'Have you?'

I flex my fingers, curl them into fists. 'I blocked his number. Think he's been calling me from a new phone but can't be sure.'

'I know he's trying to find you – he's called here a few times, which is weird as he's never taken much notice of me before.' She's right. He never gave her the time of day, even though we all worked together, often in the same places. 'I couldn't even send him on a wild goose chase, could I? As I didn't effing well know where you were myself.'

I wince at her raised voice. 'I know. I'm sorry, Nads, but I...'

'Tell me what's happened, Shan. You know you can trust me.'

'I need to sort some things out here, then I'll tell you more.' I know I can trust her, but I just need to get it all straight in my own head first. 'Do you know where Andy is right now?'

'Last I heard he was back in London at the office, bad-mouthing you. I didn't believe anything he said, but some of the others did. That you got too involved in a story and tried to interfere with his reporting. He said it was unprofessional and they shouldn't give you any more work.'

I cringe. 'No wonder I haven't had any new commissions, not just from *NewsQuest*. I've had to find other work. A girl's gotta eat somehow.'

'So where are you?'

'I'll tell you. But no one else. Not even my dad. Please, I—'

'Of course, no one else.' She shuffles forwards. 'So where?'

'I'm in Hertfordshire. A town called Hillsbury. I'm—'

'That makes sense. Paul said someone called him from a local magazine there. Your boss, maybe? David Black. Was asking all sorts of questions about you. Paul wondered if he was giving you a job but he didn't reveal anything. So now, tell me what you're doing there.'

A shout comes from behind her. Nadia yells back. She grimaces and pulls her headscarf forwards.

'Shit, I gotta go.' She glares at me. 'Make sure you keep in touch this time and answer my effing calls in future. I'll be back in London soon. We'd better meet up.'

The laptop screen goes blank.

I lean back in my chair and shut my eyes. My neck muscles feel tight – I need a break from my desk. I call the Alders house on my mobile. An answerphone kicks in.

I consider leaving a message but can't decide what to say. *I'm looking for Robert Alders. I'm interested in his wife's death. And by the way, did she really kill Charlotte Newman?* But I guess that's not the best approach.

When I call the Newman house, a woman answers the phone. Debra Newman, she tells me in a gravelly voice. I explain what I want, and she says to arrive well before three.

I grab my rucksack. Time to get some answers.

CHAPTER SIXTEEN

Debra Newman's short red dress is cinched in at her waist with a narrow silver belt, the hemline lying way above her knees. A streak of rosy blusher emphasises her high cheekbones, and scarlet-coloured lipstick highlights her tight smile. She looks refined and polished, in contrast to her living room, where a faded purple blanket is scrunched up on the floor and wilting flowers are stuffed into a crystal vase in front of the TV. Cardboard boxes are scattered around the room – some empty, others filled to the brim with ornaments and folders, photo albums and crockery.

Debra gathers some paperbacks from the sofa, stuffs them into an empty box and gestures for me to sit down.

'Sorry about the mess. We're...' She pauses, creasing her forehead so much that I can imagine the cogs rotating in her brain. 'We're having a ... a clear out. You said on the phone that you want to talk about what happened to Charlie. Why are you getting in touch now? It's been over five years.'

'I'm writing an article about local plaques for *Hillsbury Living*.' Since she doesn't flinch with disapproval, I pull out my mobile from my rucksack and show her the photo of Gina Alders' plaque. 'I found this by the bridge. I'm so sorry to hear about what happened to your daughter. I've read a couple of the news reports but want to confirm if they're accurate. Did Gina Alders really push Charlotte?'

Debra sits down in the armchair opposite me. Runs her fingers through her short chestnut bob. 'Mind if I smoke?' Her hands shake with nerves, despite her confident tone.

'Doesn't bother me.' Though my mouth goes dry. 'I quit a few months back.'

She pulls out a cigarette from a small packet lying next to a gunmetal ashtray on the coffee table. Marlboro Gold, my favourite brand; Andy's too. She lights the cigarette with a blue Zippo lighter.

'I gave up for years, but started again when...' Her voice trails off. 'Don't want you to get tempted.' She gives a deep, croaky laugh. 'I know it's not easy.' She takes a slow drag, shutting her eyes while her body relaxes.

I taste nicotine as she inhales, craving a cigarette for the first time in months. Then I remember my pack of nicotine gum. I delve into my rucksack, pull out a piece and cram it into my mouth. I chew it slowly, feel the familiar tingle and let the minty flavour seep into my cheeks.

'Benji showed me the plaque.' Debra opens her eyes. 'I don't know who put it there but the words are right, Mrs Alders *did* push Charlie.'

She lets out a slow sigh and looks at the grey wall beside us, where three portraits in square wooden frames are arranged in a row halfway down, none completely straight. In the left one, there's a young girl in a yellow T-shirt. Charlotte, I guess. A young boy in a burgundy jumper peers out from the right frame. Then there's the two of them together in the centre, with matching fair hair, heart-shaped faces and piercing blue eyes.

I take out my notepad and a pen. 'Why do you think Gina pushed Charlotte? Do you—'

A knock on the door interrupts me.

'Mum?' asks a quiet voice. A boy peers into the room. Late teens, I reckon. His fair hair is longer on top than at the sides, spiked up with gel. His eyes widen when he notices me.

'Benji, this is Shanna ... from *Hillsbury Living*.' Debra gestures towards me. 'She's asking about Charlie and that plaque at the bridge. Do you want to come in?'

He shakes his head, a scowl passing across his face. Looks me up and down. 'It can wait.' He backs out of the room. Shortly afterwards, feet stomp up the stairs and music blares out from above.

Debra rests her cigarette on the ashtray. 'That's Benji, Charlie's twin. It's been hard for all of us but hit him the hardest. They were always together, until...' She grabs a tissue from a square blue cardboard box. Wipes the corners of her eyes. Clenches her fists to pull herself together. 'So, where was I?'

I give her an encouraging smile. 'You said Gina Alders pushed Charlotte. Why would she do that?'

'She didn't like her. Because we're Jewish.'

My ears prick up.

'Though not really religious. Friday night dinner together as a family, not much more than that, but Charlie was the only Jewish kid in her class. She stuck out like a sore thumb when she took days off school for the high holy days.'

'High holy days?'

'Two days for Rosh Hashanah, the Jewish New Year, and Yom Kippur, a fast day in September or October. We don't do anything for the other festivals but those, for us, have always been important – traditional, I guess.'

I scribble down some notes. 'So what did Gina Alders do or say to Charlotte?'

'Just little things at first. When Charlie took packed lunch into school, Mrs Alders asked her if the food wasn't good enough.'

'Did other kids take in their own food, or just Charlotte?'

'Just Charlotte in her class. We only eat kosher meat so the school let her bring in her own salami sandwiches sometimes if she wanted to. Mrs Alders knew that but still used to pick on her. Charlie didn't want to make a fuss and told us it was nothing.' Debra wipes her eyes with the back of her hand. 'But she was in a bad mood all the time, so I could see it was bothering her. Then when Charlie said Mrs Alders was deliberately giving her bad marks, we decided to complain. Officially.'

'How did the school respond?'

'They made it seem like they were looking into it, but nothing actually happened. Mrs Alders denied it.'

'That must have been frustrating. Is there a lot of anti-semitism at the school?' I think of those teenage thugs who'd chased me. How they'd called Valerie racist names.

Debra shrugs, picks up her cigarette and takes another drag, blowing smoke into the air. I give my gum another chew, then let it rest against my cheek.

'There's some antisemitism, though no more than anywhere else around here, I assume,' she says in a matter-of-fact tone. 'Most of the kids go to the nearest Jewish secondary school. It's highly sought-after as it's top of the league tables, but there weren't places for Charlie and Benji. So they went to Hillsbury High instead.'

'And Benji? Gina Alders never caused him any problems?'

'The twins were in different classes. We thought it was

better to split them up at school. Charlotte was the confident one, always talking *for* him and *over* him, competitive with her schoolwork and everything else. Benji was the sensitive one.' Debra looks at the ceiling above. Loud music booms back at us. 'He still is. I'm not sure he'd have coped in the same way if Mrs Alders had started on him.'

'And what happened that day? The day...'

'You mean the day Charlie died? It's okay, I can say it now.' She stubs out her cigarette in the ashtray. Grabs a fresh tissue from the box, blows her nose and stuffs the tissue up her sleeve. 'Though it still gets me here,' she presses her hand against her chest, 'every time.'

I nod. It must have been devastating to lose your twelve-year-old daughter, with her whole life ahead of her, especially in such a tragic way.

'They were on a geography field trip, looking at bugs and plants, the usual things I suppose. Benji's class had been the day before.' Debra grabs a fresh tissue from the box to dab the corners of her eyes again. 'The official story is Charlie fell, accidentally, through the bushes at the side of the bridge.'

'But?'

'One of the other girls said she saw Mrs Alders arguing with Charlie before everyone heard a scream and then a splash.' Debra sniffs loudly and stares at the pictures on the wall. Her eyes sparkle with tears and tiny trickles of black mascara run down towards her cheeks. 'Charlie was face down in the water, below the bridge. Another teacher, Mr Cooper, waded in and pulled her out. Charlie could swim but she'd hit her head on some rocks. She wasn't breathing. Mr Cooper did everything he could, but ... but it just wasn't enough.'

I curl my hands into fists, thinking about how close I'd come to jumping from that bridge. I take a tissue from my rucksack, pop the nicotine gum out of my mouth and scrunch it up in the thin paper.

'You said this other girl saw Charlotte and Mrs Alders arguing. Why didn't anyone look into it?'

'There was an enquiry.' Debra plucks a strand of white thread off her lap. 'But the girl who saw it, Tamsin, was a difficult child. Always in trouble with teachers and disruptive in class. So they discounted her story.'

'And you think Mrs Alders deliberately pushed Charlotte over the edge?'

'I guess we'll never know the truth. Mrs Alders didn't own up to anything and there was no evidence to incriminate her. She said Charlie was mucking about and fell. But my daughter was well-behaved, the school knew that. The case was dropped, though Mrs Alders left the school anyway.' Debra looks up at the photos on the wall. 'It's been hard. We've spent five years running to the GP with Benji's mystery ailments. Headaches, tummy aches ... He's missed loads of school and still sees a counsellor. I don't think he'll ever get over it but we've tried to make life as normal as we can.' She gives a sorrowful laugh. 'As if we can.'

'What happened to Gina Alders,' I glance at my notes, 'in November 2014?'

'I'm not sure exactly.' Debra frowns. 'We were away at the time. I heard someone knocked her off her bike one night. She fell into the water and drowned. These things happen, I guess.'

I shake my head as I'm sure they don't. Ruth Stevens was being abused by Peter, then he was beaten to death. Charlotte Newman fell off the bridge, maybe pushed, then Gina did the same. There's definitely a pattern emerging.

'So you don't think anyone would have taken revenge?'

Debra lets out a sorrowful laugh. 'I wanted to kill Gina Alders after Charlie died, we all did. We received so many letters and emails telling us to take revenge, some even offering. But, no, we wanted to go through the courts. Do it properly and get some justice. Though a fat lot of good that did. Tim wanted to ... well, let's just say he was furious.'

Wanted to what? How furious? Enough to kill?

Debra stands up. 'Really sorry, but I must get on. Tim will be back soon and we need to get over to my parents for dinner. Shabbat comes in so early in the winter. They're religious so like to eat early, as soon as my dad gets back from shul. I just need to pack up the chocolate mousse.'

She pops into the kitchen while I collect my coat in the hallway.

A drawer creaks. A cupboard slams.

I glance at the notifications on my phone screen – two missed calls, no numbers – and swipe them away.

The scraping of a key in a lock makes me jump. I turn around just as the front door opens.

'Honey, I'm back.'

A flurry of leaves blows inside, followed by a tall, thin man carrying a well-worn tan briefcase. He brushes past me towards Debra, who's now standing in the kitchen doorway, and gives her a kiss.

A memory ripples through me.

A man in a hallway. Gift-wrapped boxes in his hands. A battered khaki suitcase behind him. Dad. Younger and taller than he is now.

'I'm back. I've presents. Come see.'

A little girl, six or seven maybe, rushes down the stairs into his arms. Me. Laughing and crying with joy.

'Daddy. Daddy.'

Both of us twirling around like a whirlwind until we crash on the carpet, heads dizzy with excitement.

'What time do you call this?' A woman with long auburn hair stands with her hands on her hips, a dark shadow

hovering behind her. I can't see her face. But my mother, I assume. 'You're late. We've all been waiting for you.'

Dad shrugs. 'Plane was delayed. Those damn winds.'

'Well at least now we can eat. It's no good for her. All this waiting. She needs stability.'

'Not now, Lynnie. Treats first for ya. Then we eat, then we talk. Alone.'

A cough brings me back to the present.

'Tim, this is Shanna from *Hillsbury Living*.' Debra gestures towards me. 'She's been asking about the plaque near the bridge. And about Charlie and Mrs Alders.'

Tim gives a brief nod in my direction, his cheeks reddening rapidly. 'Good to meet you, Shanna,' he mumbles, gripping my hand in a clammy handshake while his eyes remain fixed on his wife. 'Honey, we really do need to go.'

'Sorry, I don't want to keep you.' I pull my rucksack straps over my shoulders. 'I know you have things to do.'

As I walk out the house, Tim mutters to Debra: 'Bloody journalists, always sticking their nose in. I hope you didn't tell her anything.'

CHAPTER SEVENTEEN

I walk home via the crossroads, determined to see the hub of Jewish life, the centre of the community, on a Friday evening. The shul lights are on and the front doors are open. Security guards patrol the gates, wearing yellow fluorescent jackets and black stab-proof vests, and carrying walkie-talkies. Scrutinising everyone as they walk by, including me.

I sit down on the bench opposite and pull out my notepad and pen, conscious of the security guards giving me the once-over and glancing at my rucksack. Murmurs of prayer reach me from the shul grounds.

A woman in a woolly cap calls 'Shabbat Shalom' as she passes through the shul gates, and two teenage boys high five each other in the shul car park. A few minutes later, the security guards turn their backs to me, clearly deciding I'm not a threat after all.

An image of Benji Newman's angry face pops into my head. Debra said he'd been having counselling ever since Charlotte died. What must it be like to mourn not just your sibling but also your twin, and at such a young age? Born

113

together but not growing old together, torn apart by tragedy. Was his sullenness earlier just because he's a normal hormonal teenage boy, or could it be something else?

As I mull over everything Debra told me, the questions in my head spill out on to the page. I ponder each one as I write them down, coming up with very few answers. She mentioned that Benji had shown her the plaque. Could he have put it there as a memorial to his sister? Is a twelve-year-old boy capable of taking revenge? And what about Debra? She said she'd seen the plaque but when? Before she nailed it to the post? And then there's Tim too. He behaved like he had something to hide, backed up by the comment I heard as I left. Does he know something about Gina's death?

Darkness has fallen by the time I rise from the bench. I check my watch to discover it's already five o'clock. Shadowy figures cluster inside the shul car park, as men, women and children spill out of the building.

Time for me to head home too.

I left my laptop at the office so I need to pop in there on my way. My stomach rumbles and aches with more than just hunger – a niggling sensation stirring in my gut, a feeling that I'm missing something, something vital to my search. So first, I'm going to take a detour to Peter Stevens' plaque.

As I approach Campton Avenue, I hear footsteps behind me. They speed up when I do. If I slow down, they do the same. Yet when I turn around, there's no one there. My senses heighten as my adrenaline levels rise. My ears and eyes are on alert as if I'm a guard dog on patrol.

I ramp up my pace, taking faster strides to cover more ground with every step. I pass a bungalow with wind chimes dangling by the door, swaying and jingling in the slight breeze. Another has a Chelsea football scarf hanging in a front window, its curtains still open, revealing a television screen flickering in the background.

I stumble over uneven paving stones. Zigzag around overloaded green and brown wheelie bins that litter the pavement, ready for morning collection. Gag at the putrid odour of rotting meat and vegetables that clogs my nostrils.

When I reach Valerie and Harry's bungalow, the familiar sight of George Masters' plaque and the word JUSTICE comforts me, as if I've found a place of sanctuary.

I rap on the front door.

No answer.

As I walk back down the path to the road, I hear footsteps getting closer, so head towards Zahra's house, the next sanctuary I can think of. I pass number twenty-five, where Peter's plaque lies hidden in the darkness, figuring now isn't the best time to stop, despite my original intentions.

A bright security lamp illuminates as I sprint up Zahra's path. Flickering spots of light dance in front of my eyes and I blink rapidly to waft them away.

Zahra peers at me out of her kitchen window. I wave as if I'm an expected guest, just in case someone's watching. As if I do have somewhere to be. As if I'm not always alone.

Zahra opens her front door. 'Yes?'

'Sorry to bother you.' I glance behind me and clear my throat, trying to swallow away my unease. 'Can I ask you a couple more questions?'

'Now?'

'Please.' I take a step towards her.

She peers behind me. Glances both ways down the street. Purses her lips tight.

'Come.' She pulls me inside and closes the door. Presses her index finger firmly against her mouth. There are voices in the other room. 'We have to shush. My husband have busy day at work and now sleep in lounge, in front of news. Again.' She stifles a laugh. 'No surprise he never know what happen in world. Come.'

I follow her into the kitchen. There's another large pot bubbling away on the stove, a meaty aroma in the air. A small, blue light glows from the extractor fan above the cooker.

The outside security lights blink on again. I let out a gasp, clearly louder than intended as Zahra glances at me, her eyes locking with mine. We both peer through the window. Other than a faint breeze ruffling plants in the flower bed, the front garden is eerily still and silent. Then a fox comes into view, his green eyes reflecting light like shards of emerald. He sniffs at a pile of rotting leaves before moving on.

'You find Mark?' Zahra pulls down a floral roller blind, blocking out the outside world, and gestures towards the kitchen chairs. 'The other day?'

'Yes, thanks.' I sit down in the same chair as last time and think about what I've discovered since then. Ruth and Peter Stevens. Gina Alders and Charlotte Newman.

'So you and he talk?'

'Yes, and then again the other night.' Mark's brown eyes hover in front of me. *Stop it, Shanna.*

Zahra smiles as if she can read my mind. 'He nice looking. I think so too.' She glances at my left hand. 'But I married woman, you not.' She winks.

I look away, fiddle with the side of my coat, pulling at the fraying rip. 'Mark said he didn't get on with Peter.'

Zahra shakes her head. 'No, they fight. More after Ruth die.'

'Do you know what about?'

She shakes her head again. Then her eyes drop and she traces lines on the tablecloth with the tip of her index finger.

I wait.

Finally she lets out a deep sigh, like compressed air releasing from a bicycle pump. 'They argue over Ruth. I hear from my garden. It was hot day so windows open.' She grips the tablecloth. 'Mark say Peter push Ruth and...' She pauses.

'And?'

'And Peter, he say nothing at first.' She rubs the corner of her eye. 'Then he say he was there when she fell. They argue and she trip.' Her voice breaks and a tear trickles down her right cheek. 'He say he didn't push her.'

'Did you believe him?'

More importantly, did Mark believe him? Anger crackles inside me. Did he lie to me? Does he *know* that Peter's responsible for Ruth's death? Did he take revenge after all?

I touch the back of her hand. 'You didn't go to the police? The newspaper stated that Ruth was alone at the time, so someone must be lying.'

'My husband say no.' She pulls her hand away. 'No get involved.'

That sounds familiar. Dad's Irish lilt in my head: *Don't get caught up in shit that's nothing to do with ya.* And Valerie's softly-spoken voice: *Leave me out of it. No good will come of it.* And then there's my own voice urging me what to do since a few months back, even though I'm trying to brush it away: *Don't turn a blind eye – you need to do what's right.*

A chair creaks in the other room and the TV voices get louder. Zahra gazes at the wall clock. It's nearly six.

'I'd better go.' I pick up my bag. 'Thanks for your time.'

She moves towards the front window, peers out towards the path.

'You be okay?'

'Sure, I'll be fine.' The security lights are still off. 'It's just dark outside so it feels much later. Going to pop into the office and then I'll head home for something to eat.'

As I walk away from the bungalow, a back gate bangs behind me. I pause, watch and wait but no one appears. The gate bangs again. Probably a gust of wind but my heart somersaults anyway. Then somersaults again when I bump into a brown wheelie bin, which scuttles away from me along the shadowy pavement like a runaway hermit crab.

When I finally reach the office, I put my rucksack down on the front step, pull out my key from my pocket and insert it in the lock. The key turns but the door won't budge. I give it a push but it still doesn't move.

I take the key out and insert it again, give it a firmer twist and a tug. Push at the door again.

Still nothing.

The door must be frozen along its hinges; there's definitely an icy chill in the air tonight. I turn to the side, my shoulder at the ready to give the door a strong shove.

I hear footsteps behind me.

A shadow passes across the door.

A firm hand grabs my right arm. Yanks it back. I grip the office keys tightly in my hand and gasp at the deep pain that plunges towards my elbow.

Someone pushes me, my cheek pressed flat against the grainy wood of the door, tiny splinters scraping against my skin. Warm breath hovers by my ear. A sickly odour of nicotine and mint invades my nostrils, catches in my throat.

I attempt to wriggle out of their grasp, but they grip me so tightly that their fingertips dig through the quilting of my coat. They push me forwards again without hesitation. A man, I'm sure. But too short to be Andy, too stocky to be one of those teenage yobs.

As they lean against me, I groan under their body weight and wriggle again, trying to break free, ignoring the pain shuddering through my elbow.

No luck.

'Leave it alone, you bitch,' whispers a husky voice in my ear. Male. Muffled.

'You've been following me.'

As I turn my head, a deep ache travels down my spine but I fight through it. I want to see him. Yet all I glimpse from the corner of my eye is a dark scarf wrapped around a face.

A car door slams further up the street. My attacker takes a small step back, loosening the pressure on my arm.

Big mistake.

I yank my arm away from him, force myself backwards and shove the office keys into his torso. He bends over, clutching his arms to his chest, hopefully winded. I turn, rush forwards and crash into him, pushing him backwards towards the road. Then I stop abruptly, my trainers digging into the gravel.

He falls over. A dark mound at my feet.

'Not so big now!' I shout.

No reply. Maybe I've done more damage than I think.

I don't hang around. I twist my office key in the lock, grab my rucksack from the top step and fling myself against the wooden door. The door gives up fighting me and swings open. I grab my key, lurch forwards through the open doorway and fall to the floor, letting go of my bag. Then I kick the door shut behind me and lock it from the inside, hoping its hinges will hold.

I crouch down at the base of the staircase. Don't dare turn on the light. Don't even dare to move. A shadow drifts past the window. A distorted face wrapped in a scarf peers inside, broken up by the lead glazing. His eyes stare towards mine. Can he see me in the darkness?

The door handle twists and rattles and shakes. I worry it will break under the pressure.

I hold my breath.

The handle rattles again.

Then nothing.

As the footsteps fade into the distance, I become aware of my thumping heart. I breathe out slowly to stay calm.

One ... Two ... Three ... Four...

My mobile beeps. I startle, pull my phone out of my rucksack pocket and glance at the screen. I have one new message.

I click on it.

Don't look into what you don't understand. Or there will be consequences. Renvok is watching.

Consequences ... Is this about these fake plaques? Is it a genuine threat?

I pull myself up, peer through the mottled glass. Is my attacker still lurking outside? How long has he been watching me – since the park that day? Since I stood near the bridge? Since the first time I saw the Stevens' home, or outside the Newman's house?

Not that easy for strangers to escape unnoticed, Harry had said.

It could be anyone.

I message back. *Who are you?* Then wait.

No reply.

I don't scare easily, and I've been warned off stories before. But here in Hillsbury, my enemy count is stacking up, it seems.

And who the hell is Renvok?

CHAPTER EIGHTEEN

My eyes open to darkness. Goosebumps prickle along my arms. I shiver, wondering why the heating isn't on, as my bedroom usually feels warm. I reach towards my legs to pull the duvet over me but can't find the soft plump cotton fabric.

I stretch my arm towards my bedside table to switch on the lamp. My hand bumps against a stack of papers that wobble then topple, and I startle at a series of gentle thuds on the floor below.

And now I remember ... I'm still in the office.

The previous evening, I huddled at the bottom of the stairs for close to an hour, ready to push against the door if someone tried to break through. But all remained quiet until eventually, bleary-eyed, I headed upstairs to the office and my laptop. I sat down at my desk to conduct some research, not daring to fall asleep, not daring to leave the office, not daring to switch on the light. I was determined to stay vigilant all night long. Except I'd clearly failed.

I unfurl myself, stretch out my legs. Spread my hand towards the middle of my desk, or where I assume it to be, until my index finger hits a plastic key. I press down. My laptop screen springs to life, casting a gentle white glow across the room. Revealing the time, 7.30 a.m., and my last Google search: Renvok. A manufacturing company in Hong Kong – plastics and glass.

What does that have to do with these plaques? Do they produce them?

A glance at my notepad, lying open next to my laptop, provides my response in the early hours. Large black question marks are scrawled across the paper, laced with deep cuts of frustration that remind me of those scratched into Peter Stevens' plaque.

I turn over the page to check for more notes.

Oh.

I shove my chair backwards so I can stand up. I really need to switch on the light.

The front door bangs. My elbow tingles with panic, and my heart pounds. I snap my laptop shut and shove it in my bag, throw my notepad on top, then creep to the light switch by the door, and flip it up. My eyes smart at the harsh overhead lighting.

Footsteps pace up the stairs. I stand behind the door and grab the heaviest item I can find on the nearest metal filing cabinet: a black box file. I raise it, ready. My arms ache from the weight of the file as shudders of adrenaline run up and down my spine.

The office door opens, and someone enters the room. A dog growls.

A strong whiff of aftershave drifts towards me, earthy and woody, stiflingly familiar. I splutter and put the box file on top of the cabinet. Open it and shuffle some papers inside, as if I've been working studiously for a while.

'You're here early.' David glances at my desk, strewn with papers and pens, and then scowls at the blank screen of the idle office computer. The Alsatian by his feet gives a big yawn in agreement, the stench of dog breath pervading the room. 'You look like you've had a rough night. Didn't sleep here, did you? I'll have to start charging you rent.'

I don't bother answering. My eyes are still smarting from the harsh lighting and a muscle is twitching over the bridge of my nose. A headache is brewing, probably from the lack of decent sleep, so I'm certainly not in the mood for his sarcastic tone. Can't say he's scrubbed up well this morning either, with his bloodshot eyes and uncombed strands of hair. Probably been on the booze as usual – he thinks I haven't noticed the faint odour of whisky on his breath. At least his latest companion looks well-groomed, with a sleek fur coat and sharp set of canines.

'Well, it's good you're here early for a change. Even if it *is* a Saturday.' David clips a black lead to the dog's collar and loops the other end around the door handle. 'You do know I don't pay extra for weekends?'

As if.

I take a deep breath to compose myself. *One ... Two ... Stay calm, Shanna ... Three ... Four ... You need this job.* 'Why are *you* here, David?'

'I'm just collecting something I left here yesterday.' He picks up a pile of paperwork from his desk and flicks through it. Looks at me with distrustful eyes. 'You haven't been going through my things, have you?'

'Course not. I totally respect your privacy.'

He glances at the box file next to me, my hand resting on the magazines inside it.

I flick through some papers to prove my point. Look at them more closely in case he starts asking questions. Holocaust survivor stories. Local remembrance events. The local Poppy Appeal.

I smile sweetly. 'Need to track down one or two more news stories and then this issue is ready to go.'

'Not sure you'll find much in there.' He jerks his chin up towards the box file. 'It may help with the next issue though. In the meantime, flick through this for ideas.'

He flings the newspaper down on the filing cabinet, front page facing upwards. It's the latest edition of the local broadsheet, *The Herts Times*.

I read the headlines. 'Outrage over local housing development on green belt land', screams the main one. 'Graffiti daubed on fence of London synagogue', blares another.

'When everything's ready, email it to me.' David glances at the wall clock. 'Then I'll email you about the next issue. I want to focus on local good causes for that one. I'm arranging a fundraiser for the dog rescue centre.'

He unhooks the dog lead and tugs the Alsatian out of the room.

As soon as I hear the downstairs door bang shut, I remove my notepad from my bag. I didn't write anything else in it last night but I did slot something inside. Of course I snooped around on his desk. I'm a journalist. It's what I do.

I pull out a folded piece of paper, one that had caught my eye in the early hours. I'd saved it for a closer look when I was more wide awake. I unfold the page. It's a copy of a letter from the bank to David approving a loan. A large sum of money, which must mean he's finally renovating the building.

I slot the piece of paper back under a pile of books on his desk.

I ARRIVE at Chelsworth just before six o'clock in the evening. The 239 bus ride took longer than I expected. Forty-five minutes, thanks to a burst tyre on the way. I'd spent most of the day on the sofa, trying to catch up on sleep and work out who this Renvok could be. I was more successful with the sleep.

Chelsworth Arts & Crafts Centre is a converted farm guarded by a heavy, green gate with rusting hinges, giving it an authentic rustic feel. Reminds me of our farm in Galway. There are only two cars on the muddy forecourt when I arrive but the trails of tyre tracks and footprints suggest it's been a busy day.

The forecourt is surrounded by several wooden huts, each housing a different business. Similar to a village in Ghana I once visited, except those flimsy shacks were people's homes while here they are people's livelihoods. A picture-framers with multi-coloured wood samples leaning against the door. A florist with a window display of winter-berry trees sprinkled with glitter like a Christmas forest. A small cafe, closed for the evening, with tea, coffee and hot chocolate listed on a black chalkboard in the window. And then there's the pottery, a small stone barn near the farm entrance with a WELCOME sign outside.

The door of the pottery is open so I walk straight in. House numbers and signs are piled up against the stone walls, littered with an occasional BEWARE THE DOG plaque and another with MIND THE CHILDREN. All are black with red trim. Ovals, squares and rectangles. But these look far more professional than the fake ones I've found, with their mottled glaze and less-than-perfect edges.

Shuffling sounds come from the back room. I clear my throat loudly then stomp my feet on the stone floor.

A man walks through the doorway, wiping red glaze off his filthy fingers with a rainbow-speckled rag.

'Can I help?'

He has more bristle on his chin than hair on his head. His curly copper-coloured beard looks like a used scourer, all coiled and matted and flaked with clay and glaze. He's maybe a similar age to me but it's hard to tell under all that facial hair.

'I'm Shanna Regan.' I hold out my hand, then remember the state of his fingers so pull back. 'I spoke to Ray on the phone.'

'Ha, yes. That's me.' He looks at his knuckles, freckled with glaze. 'Sorry, I would shake your hand but I'm a little bit...'

'No worries. What are you making?'

'Christmas decorations. And some shapes for painting – always in demand at this time of year. Come back here and I'll show you.'

I follow him into his workshop. I'm here for information, not pottery, but may as well let him get the sales patter out of his system.

The room is filled with Santas, red ones and green ones, stacked up on shelves and lined up on the floor in neat rows, like an army of winter soldiers. I shiver as their eyes gaze at me. Accusing me, maybe. Knowing full well I've never believed Santa exists, any more than the tooth fairy or the Easter Bunny.

Dad always tried to make Christmas special, buying me presents whenever we were on the road. Beaded bracelets in India. Silken scarves in Indonesia. Wooden nesting dolls in Russia. But back at the farm, it would be business as usual. Getting up early, feeding the cows and the chickens and the goats, then heading off to church. No one at home put up a tree, let alone decorated one.

'She wouldn't appreciate it anyway,' my granny would say.

She was probably right.

Rumours spread quickly at school like wildfire in a drought and stories were shared like Chinese whispers. The other children laughed, poked fun and called me names. *Weirdo. So weird, her mam left her. So weird, Santa never comes to visit.* And each time they did so, it hurt a little bit more.

When I wasn't at the school, they forgot I existed.

I cried myself to sleep every night, wishing I could fit in but not sure how. Dad tried to comfort me, my grandad would watch me, unsure what to say, and my granny closed my bedroom door every time, with a look of resignation on her face and a defeated sigh on her lips.

'Gets busy near Christmas.' Ray's voice snaps me back to the present. 'That's why I asked you after closing hours. Maybe you'd like to buy a Santa for someone?'

I shake my head. 'No one to buy one for.' Though I think of Dad at the farm on his own.

Ray picks up a nail brush with a splintered wooden handle from a ledge behind the sink. Turns on the tap, shoves his hands under the water, one by one, then scrubs under his fingernails.

'So you're here about my plaques,' he says once he's done, drying his hands with a faded blue towel.

'Not exactly. As I mentioned on the phone, I'm looking for someone who makes plaques. Here ... can you take a look at these?' I reach into my rucksack and hand him two photos I printed out this morning. 'Look familiar?'

Ray pushes aside a metal pencil pot and small pad of paper on a table in the corner of the room, then lays the photos flat, side by side. He turns on a black overhead lamp, dangling above the table, fixed to the ceiling.

'Not seen these before. Where are they?' He shuffles to the left to give me standing space.

'In Hillsbury, but I can't remember the names of the roads.' I shrug. 'Sorry, I'm new to the area.'

'Be good to see the real ones but guess this is better than nothing.' He pulls a magnifying glass out from the pencil pot and peers through it. 'Ha, see here?' He points to the edges of the plaques. 'Don't look like a professional job. But I'm no expert on this, so don't quote me in your magazine.'

I laugh, as he's far more of an expert than me. 'If someone's making these at home, what would they need? Would it be possible?'

'If they've got enough knowledge of pottery, then yes. Need clay, glaze, tools, worktop of some sort, though any table would do. And a kiln.'

'Not a normal oven?'

'Not hot enough.'

'So you don't reckon a pottery has made these?'

'Not if they know their stuff. Not if they're any good. See here?' He points at the right edge of one of the photos. Holds the magnifying glass over it so I can peer through. 'Whoever made these plaques knows what they're doing but they haven't smoothed these edges properly. Can't say for certain without seeing the originals though.'

I gather up the photos. 'Well, thanks anyway.'

'Ha, one sec … what was that?' He grabs a photo back from me, the one of Peter Stevens' plaque, raises the magnifying glass over it and points to some squiggles along the edge. 'Here, *you* look. Maybe it's a secret code.'

I can't tell if he's serious or not.

He moves away so I can take his place and hands me the magnifying glass. I lean forwards, squinting at the squiggles.

My stomach lurches. This isn't a secret code. I've seen markings like this before.

It's been worth coming here after all.

CHAPTER NINETEEN

Sunday morning, I wake from my slumber with a start. I hear a faint knock then two dull thuds near my front door. I'd been dreaming of the Rockies, one of my favourite places in the world, relaxing on a daytime safari, watching brown grizzly bears snuffling along the roadside and black-and-white Canada geese skimming across blue lakes.

I reluctantly stumble out of bed and into the hallway. Find two envelopes on the doormat. I pick them up, wander into the kitchen and toss them on to the counter. No point trying to concentrate on anything until I've had my caffeine fix. So I flip the switch on the kettle and make myself a mug of strong black coffee before I sit down.

The first envelope is cheap and white, with *The Occupier* handwritten on the front. The flap's unsealed at the back. I lift it up and pull out a photocopied letter from the proprietor of the apartment block, informing me that the lifts are out of order and someone is on their way to fix them. The repairs will probably take a couple of days. I scrunch the letter up into a ball and toss it into the recycled paper bin by the sink.

I pick up the other envelope. Cream, identical to the one I received at the office, including the typed name on the front, but this one is hand-delivered. Did someone follow me home one night? I think of the man who attacked me outside the office and the email I received afterwards. Renvok can't be leading me to these plaques if he's warning me away from them. So it must be someone else. Does that mean two people are watching me, rather than one?

My hand shakes as I rip open the envelope and pull out the note. Yet again the message is typed on a manual typewriter, with uneven black ink, no name or signature. And yet again, it's leading me to an address.

Go to Stanton Lane. Find the plaque.

It reads like an order. What will happen if I don't follow it – and what will I find if I do?

That man pressing me against the office door, his nicotine breath, that harsh whisper in my ear, and the text afterwards. A shiver inches its way down my spine as I wonder what this mysterious typist wants from me, and how far Renvok will go to carry out his threat. How many more of these plaques are out there waiting to be discovered?

No one can enter this apartment block without a key, but someone found this letter and shoved it through the mail slot in my door. And I can guess which someone that'll be.

I pick up my mug of coffee from the kitchen counter. It's now lukewarm but I lift it to my lips and gulp the bitter liquid down. Then head into the hallway, pull on my white trainers, not worrying about my lack of socks, and grab my coat and the keys to the apartment. Bang my front door shut behind me as I leave.

I bump into Hetty on my way down the stairs. Literally

bump into her. I have to grab her arm to stop her falling. She's wearing a black fur coat – mink, I reckon – with a bunch of red carnations in her hand. Her hair is all coiffed, with a black felt hat perched on her head.

'Where you off to?' I keep hold of her arm to steady her. 'You're all dressed up today.'

'I'm going to the grounds.' Her response is more curt than usual and her voice not quite as sing-song, though the shrillness hasn't gone.

'The grounds?' The grounds of the apartment block are glistening with icy patches and a sprinkling of frost. Not the safest place for a woman in her eighties. I glance towards her feet and grimace. Certainly not one in black high heels.

'The Jewish cemetery.' She tuts under her breath. 'That's what we call it. Don't you know anything?' She gazes at me with dark, suspicious eyes.

Her memory's clearly fading as I've told her before that I know very little about Jewish ways.

'Going to a funeral, are you?'

'No, I'm going there to visit my Solly. Soon be fourteen years gone.' She jerks her arm out of my grasp and clutches the carnations to her chest. 'He was a good man, my Solly. A good man. Wouldn't hurt a fly, he wouldn't. He always used to laugh that he wanted to go first – it would be the only time he'd ever get some peace.' She gives a shrill laugh. 'Said I talked too much, can you believe it?'

I stop myself from nodding.

'So when I visit him, I always make sure I stay there a while, on a bench just by his grave, and tell him all the local gossip. I wouldn't want him to miss out.'

She scrunches up the sleeve of her coat, revealing a dainty silver watch on a wrinkled wrist laced with a map of prominent veins and liver spots. She glances down at it. 'My niece and nephew are picking me up in a few minutes. I don't want to be late. I just need to get down these darn stairs because that darn lift is broken.'

'Need some help?'

'I'm not old, you know.' She puts her hand on her hip. Shakes her shoulders in a huff.

'I'll leave you to it then.' I'm not in the mood to argue. 'By the way, what were you doing up here? Your apartment's on the ground floor.'

'I put a letter through your door.' The sing-song edges back into her voice.

My skin crawls with anticipation.

'About the lift. I hand-delivered one to every flat just now. You found yours?' Hetty tuts and shakes her head. 'Of course you did or you wouldn't be here on these darn stairs.' She looks me up and down. Her eyes widen when she notices my pyjamas peeping through my gaping coat. 'You don't look like you're dressed for the outdoors.'

'That's because I was popping down to see you.' I tug my coat closed. 'There was another letter too. Also hand-delivered.'

'Oh ... yes ... I put that through your door as well.' She pauses for a moment as if to catch her breath. 'Found it on the front mat.'

'Don't suppose you saw anyone hanging around outside?'

Hetty shakes her head slowly. 'Why would I? I don't know everything that goes on here. Or everyone.'

I stifle a laugh. Hetty knows all that and more, we both know it. That's why she lives in that particular apartment, the one nearest the lift but opposite the front door, so she can keep an eye out. There's no escape from Hetty. I've even witnessed her accosting visitors in the downstairs hallway, trying to establish who they're here to see and why.

'You sure you didn't see anyone?'

'When?' Her foot hovers precariously on the edge of the stair below her.

I resist the urge to grab her arm. 'I came home at around nine last night. So between then and this morning.'

'You've been out a lot recently.'

I can't tell if that's an observation or a criticism, though it sounds more like a scolding.

'Sure you don't need any help getting downstairs.'

'None at all.' She folds her hand firmly around the handrail and takes another step, balancing on her narrow shoe-heel.

I avert my eyes. I couldn't bear to watch her tumble down and break her neck, however irritating she can be. 'I'll leave you to it then.'

I turn around and walk back upstairs to my apartment, realising that sometimes ignorance truly *is* blissful.

CHAPTER TWENTY

Stanton Lane is in the posher part of Hillsbury. It feels as if money lines this long, winding road, edged with an eclectic array of detached houses and polished Jaguars and Daimlers parked on sweeping driveways. Each house is set back from the pavement, with a broad approach at the front and carefully manicured gardens disappearing round the sides.

The mid-morning sun is low in the sky. Cotton-wool clouds loom overhead and an occasional flurry of snowflakes drifts down like shaving foam. I shiver under my padded coat. Even my fluffy green mohair jumper isn't warm enough to keep out the bitter chill today.

After twenty minutes or so, searching high and low along the pavements, I finally catch sight of a black square edged with red glaze, on a fence post, just after a sharp bend. Another plaque, just like the others, with bold red lettering.

TERRY MURDOCK

HIT-AND-RUN DRIVER

ON THIS BEND

REPENT BEFORE YOU DIE
OR MAY YOU NEVER R.I.P.
JUNE 1994

I take photos from every angle, write in my notepad. Recall Ray's discovery and check the edges of the plaque. Squint until my eyes ache, noticing some squiggly marks in the glaze.

I read the words on the plaque again.

ON THIS BEND.

The bend certainly looks precarious. One of those sharp ones where you can't tell what's coming round the corner. Someone has stuck a concave mirror to the fence so you can see traffic from all sides, but I doubt it was here over twenty-five years ago. In those days, it would have been a deathtrap if a car was going too fast. Crossing the road equals risking your life. I try it, twice, just to be sure. The second time, a car swerves past me, the driver blaring his horn. He raises a finger. I raise two back.

The plaque looks fairly new – the glaze is barely marked and the writing still clear – which is strange as the date on it certainly isn't a recent one.

I ring the doorbell of the nearest house, a sprawling 1970s mishmash of red bricks and tall glass windows, arranged over three floors. The house overlooks a large circular driveway, edged with mature shrubs. The triple garage door is propped open with a black wheelie bin; a battered dark green J-reg Jaguar in one parking bay, a red roofless MGB in another, and a car jack lying on the concrete floor of the third. A blowtorch is propped up inside, leaning against the wall alongside a paint sprayer. This looks like a used car lot, just with classier offerings. Or maybe someone's doing something decidedly dodgy. If I delve deep enough, there could be a news story in this, for sure. I make a mental note in my head to do some research into the owners sometime.

A man walks around the side of the house, grasping black-and-silver gardening shears. He's older than Dad. In his seventies, I reckon. Slightly stooped, with thinning grey hair and a bronzed face, lined after years spent outside in the sun.

'Can I help you, love?' he calls to me, as he steps carefully over a narrow flower bed, followed by a large Rottweiler.

'I'm interested in this plaque,' I call back. 'It's unusual...'

The man's left green wellie catches the edge of the watering-system tube that dips in and out of the earth like a thin black serpent. He stumbles and wobbles. His canine companion barks. I gasp, take a step forwards, arm outstretched, but the man regains his balance before I reach him.

'Oh that, eh?' He brushes grass off his mud-stained navy jumper with his free hand. 'Been there for years. Can't tell you much.'

'Oh.' The dog growls at me as I take another step forwards. 'Looks fairly new to me. Is this the Murdock house?'

'Yes, but they're away.'

'Shame ... can you help instead?'

'Can't help you, love, sorry.' The man raises the garden shears. 'I've things to do. This place doesn't garden itself ... and the gentleman of the house is very ... particular, you know.'

I pass him my business card. 'Can you give him this when he's back, please?'

He takes my card. Flips it over.

'Shanna Regan. Well, well. A journalist, eh?' He raises his eyebrows.

'I work for *Hillsbury Living* magazine. I'm looking into local plaques.'

He stares at my card for a moment, then pockets it. 'Well, well. I'll pass on your details when Mr Murdock returns, young Shanna Regan.'

Been a while since anyone has called me young but I guess it's all relative.

'And *your* name?'

He looks at the shears, then back at me. 'Jim. Jim the gardener.'

I leave Jim and his Rottweiler in the front garden. Feel their stares following me as I walk away.

My phone rings. I pull it out from my pocket and perch on a nearby wall to check the screen.

It's Mark.

I remember what Zahra told me, about Mark arguing with Peter shortly before he died. My mind is torn in two as my finger hovers over the *End Call* button. Ignore it or answer it? Pretend everything's fine, or admit that it's not? Each time, in my head, the latter option wins.

'Are you free for dinner tonight?' Mark asks straightaway.

'I'm busy.'

'Tomorrow lunch, then?' His voice is laced with disappointment. 'It would be good to catch up and hear how you're getting on with your search into these plaques.'

'Why didn't you tell me you argued with Peter just before he died?'

Silence in return.

'There's no point denying it – Zahra heard you. I popped in there the other evening when someone...' I stop. I don't need to tell Mark about being followed then threatened outside the office. He means nothing to me and I mean nothing to him, though my pounding heart disagrees.

'When someone...?'

'Nothing.' My bruised elbow smarts, reminding me it hadn't been nothing at all. 'Anyway, don't change the subject. Why didn't you mention it?'

'We argued, yes, but it really didn't mean anything.'

Sweat trickles down my back and pools at the base of my spine, even though the rest of my body is shivering. The paint cans and clay near his door, and the alcohol on his sideboard. Did Mark put up those plaques? It's amazing what rage can do, especially when it's fuelled by too much booze. What would drive a churchgoing man to murder his own flesh and blood?

'But Peter admitted he was there when your mum fell. Did you kill him, knowing he was responsible for her death?'

'No, of course not. Why would—'

I press the *End Call* button. Put my phone back in my pocket and stretch my legs as I stand up. Why did I think I could trust him, a man I hardly know? I never learn.

My mobile rings. I ignore it. When it rings a second time, I give in and answer.

'Enough of your bullshit, Mark,' I shout into my phone. 'Is this why you didn't want me looking into these plaques at first?'

A pause. Deep breathing.

I've rattled him.

Good.

'Hello ... sweetheart.'

I can't swallow. I can't breathe. Fog obscures my vision. Images flash in front of my eyes. A hand slamming against my shoulder. A boot kicking a motionless body on the ground.

One ... Two ... Breathe, Shanna ... Three ... Four ... Breathe...

I double over, retch, clutch my stomach as pain rips through me. And then bring the phone back to my ear.

'You're a hard one to track down.' The deep voice I once knew so well now seems to belong to a stranger. 'But you know me, not one to let go that easily.' A deep laugh. 'How's the shoulder? And who the fuck is Mark?'

'Fuck off, Andy. Just leave me alone.'

'What are you doing in Hillsbury?'

Another wave of nausea washes over me.

I end the call. Tears well up in my eyes and pressure builds up in my head, like an atom bomb waiting to explode.

I open the photo app on my phone. Swipe back to a shot of Andy and I outside a bar in Mexico, each holding a beer. Smiling and laughing at the person holding the camera, a random stranger if I remember right. We could be any couple in the first few months of a relationship. Our honeymoon period. Happy and relaxed and relishing each other's company, a look of hunger and lust in our eyes. I swipe forwards to several months later. The backs of four men running up a poorly-lit street. Another shot of them standing around a dark shape on the ground, this time their faces exposed. Finally I click on a selfie, revealing a black eye, bandaged shoulder and an arm in a sling.

I think of Ruth and Peter and the words on the plaque.

BEAT HIS WIFE FOR 30 YEARS.

Not every relationship is what it seems.

CHAPTER TWENTY-ONE

Monday morning, just before ten, I hover outside Hillsbury High. Suspicious, I realise, like a drug dealer, despite wearing my classy caramel-coloured dress and some make-up. Edgy and nervous too, shuffling around as if I'm dancing on an ice rink.

It's decades since I've been inside a school yet the same dread remains. I feel like I'm ten again. Will everyone stare at me? Will they all know I don't belong? Childlike paranoia swoops down on me like an eagle with a field mouse in its view, as I recall the turmoil of my younger years.

Classmates jeering and jostling, making fun of my accent. Fist fights in the playground and shoulder-shoving in the classroom. Me, battered and bruised. Dad called to the school if he was around; my grandad if he wasn't. But not my granny, no, she always stayed home. She probably thought I deserved it each time – that someone would knock some sense into me, maybe. Yet a bruised arm or a black eye was never going to be the answer. We all knew it.

'Never show weakness,' my grandad told me. 'Never let

those bullies win. Insteada fighting with ya fists, learn to fight with ya words. Ya've a good head on those shoulders, so use it. And don't feel ashamed to walk away with ya head held high.'

From then on, I'd sit in the schoolyard playing games in my head, watching classmates play games in the dirt. Responding to the hurtful words that chipped away at my soul with fancy words and fancy phrases. My dictionary became my best friend, my thesaurus became my ally. The foundation for the rest of my life, maybe, as words became my ammunition and pages became my battleground. Bewildering the other children around me, pushing back only when I needed to, and escaping to the farm meadow when it all got too much.

Over twenty years on, my mouth feels like sandpaper as I shuffle through the school gates, push open the front door and cross over the threshold into the reception area.

I'd called the school office at eight-thirty this morning and arranged to see a member of the senior staff. I told the head teacher's PA that I'm writing about religious diversity in education for a national paper and that the meeting couldn't wait.

I just hope no one makes enquiries.

I'd aimed for the head honcho but she's in meetings all morning, so I have to make do with her deputy. I don't really care who I see, though. I just need information. I want to know what really happened between Charlotte Newman and Gina Alders, if I can persuade someone to talk.

I sit in the waiting area, watching kids scurry up and down the corridors, carrying stacks of textbooks and overflowing school bags and grubby PE kits. All seem well-behaved but the navy jumpers with a red stripe send a shudder through my spine, reminding me of the teenagers who chased me and threatened me with stones. I wonder if

I'll see them again. If so, would I even recognise them? The boys, maybe, as I also saw them in the park, but not necessarily the girls. And more worryingly, would they recognise me despite my more upmarket clothes?

When the receptionist calls my name, I swallow back the lump in my throat and put my professional face in place, hiding all signs of the dragonfly sensations in my chest.

The deputy head, Mrs Choudhry, is a petite Asian woman with silky smooth skin and a silky smooth smile to match. Her starched navy pinstriped suit gives her an air of authority. She's friendly and charming yet I still don't warm to her.

She leads me into her office, a small room drenched with a faint sickly-sweet odour of vanilla and honey, like a candy-coated ice cream sundae. The side window overlooks a deserted playground, a prison yard-like area encased with wire fences and laid with grey concrete slabs, a broken basketball net in the far corner. The back wall of the office is crowded with framed hockey match and football team photos, certificates of awards and competition prize winners. My eyes catch on one particular photo, bang in the middle of the wall, featuring eight or nine teenagers lined up in a row. THE SCHOOL ATHLETICS TEAM, states the bronze lettering along the bottom.

As I peer forwards to take a closer look, the deputy head closes the office door behind her with a click, then gestures for me to sit down. I lower myself into the armchair in front of her desk, feeling like a naughty schoolgirl about to get reprimanded, the phrase 'It wasn't me' resonating in my head.

'So, you're here to talk about...'– Mrs Choudry sits in her chair and glances down at a printed sheet of paper – '... diversity and education. Can you explain exactly what you mean by that?'

I take out my notepad and pen. Just as well I've prepared in advance.

'Well, as we all know, it's a time of growing ethnic and religious diversity here in the UK.' I look down at my notes to make sure I get this right. 'Religious tolerance often starts from an early age, at home and in school, and reports show that understanding and respecting other people's faiths help to build it. I'm looking at how secondary schools are educating children about different faiths and also cater for any specific needs. You know, things like assemblies, meals, prayer times ... I'm approaching all of the local schools, but Hillsbury High is first on my list.'

The deputy head pushes the piece of paper away from her. 'Well, we have everything in place here that needs to be.' She relaxes back into her chair. 'My parents were originally from Bangladesh. I was brought up in a large Muslim family but grew up in a multicultural area and went to a multicultural school, so I understand the needs of children from ethnic minorities. And I firmly believe that learning about different faiths makes us all more tolerant.'

She proceeds to tell me about the laws and regulations and current thinking about RE lessons as well as the general running of the school. I try to look interested, nodding and smiling and taking notes, but after a while I move the topic of conversation to the real reason I'm here.

'Do you know the religious and ethnic make-up of Hillsbury High?'

'Hold on.' She shifts forwards, opens the top drawer of her desk and pulls out a wad of papers. 'We did a survey a few years ago to make sure our students' ethnic and religious needs are being met. Early 2014.' *Just after Charlotte Newman died.* 'I can't show you the details but I can give you some idea of the findings. Hillsbury High is around seventy percent white British. Some Christians – Catholic and Protestant – but most aren't practising. Plus, twenty percent black or Asian children, including Muslims, Hindus and Sikhs.' She pauses, runs her finger down to the bottom of the page. 'Oh, and a handful of Jewish children.'

'Just a handful? I'm surprised. It's quite a Jewish area, isn't it?' I don't actually need to ask the question as I'd already looked up the answer. There are over two thousand Jews living in Hillsbury. More Jews live around here and the rest of Hertfordshire than most other places in the country. But I'm interested to hear what she has to say.

'Nothing to do with the school itself.' She frowns. 'Most Jewish children these days go to the local faith schools.'

That's what Debra said too.

'Do you think this could breed a lack of tolerance?'

'What exactly do you mean by that?' Mrs Choudhry stares at me.

'Well, if there aren't many Jewish kids at Hillsbury High, doesn't that mean other kids may be less likely to mix with them? Which brings me to my next question. Have you ever noticed any bullying of the few Jewish kids who *are* here? Or bullying of any other ethnic minority groups?'

Mrs Choudhry picks up a pencil and passes it from hand to hand, left then right, left then right, like a nervous twitch. 'Look, sadly bullying does occur here. It happens in all schools. But we have a strict anti-bullying policy in place and deal with it very quickly. We've never had a case of bullying because of someone's religion or ethnicity.'

'None? What about Charlotte Newman and Mrs Alders? I've spoken to Charlotte's family.'

She flinches. A vein throbs in her neck. 'That was before my time here at the school.' Her friendly tone and smile have vanished. 'It was in all the newspapers so it's not a secret.'

'Well—'

'Nothing was ever proven.' The deputy head raises her voice. 'All I can tell you is that there was an official enquiry. It was just a tragic accident.'

She's practised this press statement before. Several times, I suspect.

'I think we're done.' She stands up rapidly, her chair scraping backwards across the carpet, and offers me her hand. 'Maybe you'd be better off writing about real school news – funding cuts, the recent GCSE marking fiasco and teacher recruitment problems. We don't have a problem with racism, or specifically antisemitism, in our school. If you do write this article, I expect to see a copy of it before it goes to press, to check any quotes or information about Hillsbury High.'

Mrs Choudhry escorts me to the reception area and watches me walk out through the front door. Her way of making sure I leave the premises, I figure. But as soon as she turns her back and trundles off to her office, I press the buzzer and wave at the receptionist to be let back again. I walk over to the noticeboards near the reception desk to investigate the photos of the sports teams. One of the pictures is the same as the one in the office: the athletics team. It caught my eye when I thought I recognised two of the faces. Looking at the photo again, I realise I was right.

The receptionist is on a call, so I wait. After a few minutes, she puts the phone down and smiles at me.

'Can I help?' She peers over her blue-framed glasses.

'Can you tell me who these boys are?' I point at the left corner of the photo. 'I've seen them before but can't remember where. Look like great ambassadors for the school.'

I attempt a straight face.

The woman squints at the board. 'Which photo, did you say?'

'Second one down on the right. The two boys at the front on the left.'

'That's Eddie and Gary Forrester. Best runners in the school.'

I think back to the chase near the bridge. How they caught up with me so easily.

'So they're brothers?'

'Yes, but they look nothing like each other.' She takes her glasses off, holds them at the bridge and picks up a shiny black cloth from her wooden pencil pot. 'Eddie's the older one, the one with the ridiculous haircut.' She lifts her glasses up to her face, breathes on the lenses with a faint 'huh' and cleans them with the cloth, one by one. 'He's in year eleven, GCSEs coming up, and Gary, he's in year ten. Only a year between them. Their father is the local police chief, though you wouldn't believe it. They're always in trouble, those two, always at the centre of it all. But obviously the parents think the sun shines out of...'

She looks up at me, her cheeks glowing pink. 'Well, where it certainly doesn't shine. Eddie looks like his dad, he's often in the local papers, so maybe that's why you recognise him.'

I'm surprised she's being so indiscreet. Maybe she knows more than she's letting on.

I think back to how Eddie Forrester flinched in the park when I voiced my threat. No wonder he hadn't wanted me to call the police.

CHAPTER TWENTY-TWO

S t Luke's Hall is tucked away behind the church – a squat stone building overlooking the graveyard. As I push open its heavy oak door, a blast of warm air caresses my icy cheeks. I follow the babble of voices along a short corridor into a large rectangular room, with chunky burgundy curtains draped across three floor-to-ceiling windows on both sides.

At the centre of the room, four long trellis tables are arranged in a square, each covered with a white plastic cloth, topped with plastic pots, paintbrushes and clay shapes. Twenty or so people are milling around, some stacking chairs, some clearing tables and others deep in conversation.

As I bang the door behind me, several pairs of eyes swivel towards me. Even the wooden effigy of Jesus, nailed to a cross on the back wall, gives me a curious look. I inhale slowly, compose myself and feel a flush spreading across my cheeks. Nothing like being the centre of attention when you're trying to lie low.

A young woman wearing a red-and-green striped jumper and blue jeans grins at me. Pushes her long strawberry blonde hair away from her face to reveal rosy cheeks and a flawless complexion. I figure she's in her early twenties – oversmiley and overenthusiastic, two traits that tend to make me cringe.

'Hi, I'm Lou,' she says in a bubbly voice, followed by a fleeting giggle. Her silver nose ring glints at me under the harsh fluorescent lighting. 'You must be Shanna. I'm so glad you've made it.'

'Sorry, I thought you'd be finished by now.'

'We started late. It's such a shame you couldn't join us.' She bounces up and down in her shiny silver trainers, like Tigger on hot coals. 'Come on, I'll show you what we've been doing.'

Lou pulls me over to the nearest table, arm linked through mine as if we're long-lost friends, pointing at some familiar clay shapes that have been decorated with glaze. Some look fairly professional but others not so much. A star with wonky rainbow stripes and a hole at the top for a ribbon. A round bauble daubed with red and silver glitter.

'Christmas tree decorations,' she says proudly. 'Aren't they fab.'

I treat that as a statement rather than a question. 'From Ray at Chelsworth Pottery, aren't they?'

As I reach forwards, Lou pulls on my sleeve and yanks me back.

'Don't touch them yet!' she squeals. 'They'll be wet for a while.'

I shake her off. 'I wasn't going to.' I pick up one of the plastic pots beside the clay shapes and peer at the glaze inside. It's a deep red, very similar to the shade on the plaques. I swivel the pot around in my hands. There's no label so it could have been sourced from anywhere.

I glance around the room, sure that the person who made the plaques is here, right now.

'Did Ray supply the glaze too?'

'You'll have to ask Mark over there.' Lou points towards a group of men hovering around the next table. 'The one in green. He buys everything we need.'

I follow the direction of her hand. Spot a large man with thinning brown hair leaning against a black plastic chair. He's wearing a bright green lumberjack shirt, buttons popping out over his bulging belly. He looks over at me and grins, his top lip leering upwards, exposing a mouthful of chipped teeth. I take a reluctant step towards him.

Lou grabs my arm. 'Not him,' she says with a giggle. 'The one behind him.'

She pulls me to the left. A whirlpool of dread swirls inside me when I spot a familiar face. I prefer lumberjack man after all.

Mark, in a khaki green T-shirt, is packing up pots of glaze into a large brown cardboard box. He looks up, catches my eye and gives me a hesitant smile. A faint aroma of his aftershave drifts towards me, as he walks in our direction.

My pulse races.

Steady, Shanna.

'You know each other?' Lou gazes up at Mark with adoration, like a loyal spaniel puppy. As she puts her arm through his, he flinches.

'Yes, Shanna's a friend of mine.' Mark winks at me. 'An old friend.'

I recall our first meeting at St Luke's when he sent me packing. Our late-night drinking session before I went home. And our last phone call, when I pressed the *End Call* button.

Slight exaggeration, Mark.

'Small world.' Lou's sweet smile contrasts with her voice, now laced with venom.

'Known each other for years.' I smile back just as sweetly. 'Family friends. I—'

A crashing sound in the far corner of the room interrupts me, followed by a gruff voice shouting Lou's name. She glares at me as she walks past.

'She seems nice,' I say to Mark, trying hard not to grit my teeth. 'Close, are you?'

'Not as close as she'd like.' Mark's cheeks flush. 'She's far too young for me. So what are you doing here? You've missed the class.'

'That was my plan.' I fail to hide my wicked grin. 'Art really isn't my thing.' I look at the box in front of him, then at the pot of blue glaze in his hand. 'Lou says you're in charge of supplies.'

Mark nods. 'Mum was an artist. She used to run this class and a few others locally, including one over the road at the shul, so I still help out when I can.'

'Where'd you get the glaze?'

'I bought it online. Why?'

My phone pings. I slide it out of my back pocket and glance at the screen.

One message.

We've warned you. Don't look into what you don't understand. Or there will be consequences. Renvok is watching.

A cold shudder works its way down my spine. I swipe the message away.

'You okay?' Mark cocks his head, eyes wide with concern. 'You look a bit pale. Do you want to grab a coffee up the road?'

'I should head home. It's been a busy day.'

As I slide my phone back into my pocket, Mark grasps my arm, gently but firmly.

'Shanna, about our phone call. You rang off before I had

a chance to explain, and you've ignored my calls ever since. I'd like to talk to you about something.'

My head tells me to refuse – *he'll just tell you what you want to hear, and you don't know if you can trust him.* Yet my heart disagrees – *let's see how honest he can be.*

My heart wins.

FIFTEEN MINUTES LATER, we're sitting in a booth of the local café, each of us cradling a mug of frothy cappuccino to warm up our icy hands. Two young teenagers are sitting opposite one another at the next table, leaning forwards with their fingers lovingly intertwined. They spring apart when the waitress brings over two hot chocolates in tall glasses, topped with whipped cream. The boy runs his fingers through his ginger hair. The girl bites her lip.

I smile to myself, recalling my first date when I was fifteen, leaning against the farm gate while Tom Flanagan was leaning against me. His warm body and a slight bulge in his crotch. A long slow kiss with tongues. He wanted more. So did I, but I said no, like the good Catholic girl my granny wanted me to be. He ditched me a week later and told all his friends I was frigid, so I didn't follow Catholic ways after that.

'How's your search going?' Mark's voice pulls me back to the café. 'Have you found something? Is that why you went to the craft session tonight?'

'Something like that.' I gaze at his friendly smile and eager eyes. I still don't know if I can trust him but I need to run some ideas off someone and right now he's all I have. 'Whoever's making these plaques may be involved in the church,' I continue. 'The words on them feel religious, obsessive even. The art class seemed a good place to start.'

'Have you found any more plaques?'

'Yes, one more.' I tell him about Terry Murdock, the hit-and-run, my visit to the pottery and the symbols Ray noticed around the edges. 'They look like Hebrew letters.'

'Hebrew? So maybe the plaques are made by someone Jewish.' His voice gets louder with excitement. 'Can you show me?'

I look up, glance around and check no one heard him. The teenagers are all loved up, heads pressed tightly together, and the waitress behind the counter is busy drying cutlery with a red tea towel.

I pull out the photos and lay them on the table. Point out the symbols. 'What do you reckon?'

'I think you're right. It does look like Hebrew.'

'Not much use though if I don't know what it means.' I pick up my mug and take a sip of cappuccino. Lick the sweet milky froth off my lips. 'And it doesn't mean they're definitely made by someone Jewish. Just someone who knows Hebrew.'

'Maybe it's something to do with the Bible.' Mark cradles his coffee mug in his hands. 'Have you spoken to the vicar about the wording?'

'No, not yet.' I eyeball him as I put my mug back down on the table. 'You're the churchgoer though, so you should know more than me, shouldn't you? "Repent before you die. Or may you never R.I.P." Do you recognise it?'

'No, I don't.' He clatters his mug down next to mine and tugs at his shirt collar. Shifts in his seat. 'And I'm not *that* religious.'

I eyeball him again. He recognises the Hebrew, goes to church and helps to run an art class, so he could be making the plaques, after all. Or maybe he knows who is. I shake my head. No, he's just trying to help me look into these plaques, isn't he? Just a nice guy wondering how his parents died. I decide to go with that and push all other thoughts out of my mind.

'I need to figure what to do next.' I drum my fingers on the table. 'You must have some ideas, surely? I need all the help I can get. I've left three messages for Robert Alders but he hasn't called me back.'

'Well, we assume the plaques are made by the same person who killed Peter and Gina Alders.' Mark scratches his chin. 'And Terry Murdock, assuming he's dead too. All three of them allegedly killed someone, yes?'

'But why put Hebrew on the plaques? None of the victims were Jewish.' I look down at the photos on the table. 'Well, not as far as I know.'

'Ah, but what about the original victims?'

'Only Charlotte Newman so far. I don't yet know the name of the woman in the hit-and-run.' I shake my head. 'But that doesn't work anyway, as whoever's doing the killing isn't targeting them.'

'I guess not.' Mark takes a sip of his coffee, swirls it around in his mouth, then swallows. 'If there's Hebrew lettering, there's likely to be a Jewish link, yes? Otherwise what would be the point in putting it on there? I guess finding the original hit-and-run victim may help.'

'I've tried, but it's too long ago, before internet records. But anyway, that still leaves your mum, so they *weren't* all Jewish. It doesn't work.'

Mark takes another gulp of coffee and gazes at the table. Eventually he looks up. 'This is what I wanted to talk to you about.' He pauses. 'You see, Mum was.'

'Sorry?'

'My mum, Ruth...' he tugs at his collar and clears his throat '...she *was* Jewish. My dad was too.'

My hand shakes. I put my coffee down with a clatter.

Milky brown droplets spring over the sides onto the table, like Atlantic salmon leaping upstream.

Ruth? Peter? I think of the large black cross by the front door of their bungalow. *What the...?*

'But Peter was heavily involved in the church.' I press my shaking hands flat against the tabletop to steady them. 'You said so yourself.'

'He was, yes, but Peter wasn't my dad.'

What?

Mark leans forwards. 'He was my step-dad and insisted I took his surname, but I could never think of him as *Dad*.'

'You asked me what they argued about,' Mark continues. 'Well, it started when Peter became more involved in the church, St Luke's. At first it was just *him* getting involved but then he insisted we go as a family.'

'Surely he knew you were both Jewish when he and your mum met?' I'd brushed up on the rules of the religion a while back. Orthodox Judaism traditionally follows the mother's line. So if Ruth was Jewish, that means Mark is too.

'Of course he did.' Mark nods. 'My real dad died of cancer soon after I was born. Mum met Peter when I was two. She lost interest in Judaism for a while but she always kept the traditions going and eventually her interest came back.' He leans back in his chair. 'She wanted me to know my roots, she always told me. I never had a bar mitzvah at thirteen – Peter wouldn't allow it. But Mum taught me how to light candles on a Friday night to welcome in the Sabbath and say the prayer. At first, we used to do it when Peter was around.'

'At first? What changed?'

Mark grimaces. 'Peter went a bit crazy, obsessed, demanding Mum turned her back on her religion and her culture.'

'But obviously she wasn't prepared to do that.'

'No, she wasn't.' His voice brims with pride. 'But she tried to tone it down when he was around. Peter was a bully. It wasn't even about religion; it was about her. He liked to be in control, and that meant taking away the one thing that kept her going – her love for Judaism. Sometimes she'd still light candles on a Friday night with me when he was at the pub. Though that's when the trouble started.'

As he's talking, some things start to make sense. 'It was a Friday night when he first hit her, wasn't it?'

'Yes. He came back from the pub early, I can't remember why, but the candles were still lit and he went crazy. She didn't give in though.' His eyes glaze over for a moment and he gives a small laugh. 'She *never* gave in. Mum was far more resourceful than he realised. After that, she still lit the candles every week, just earlier, and I'd act as lookout, watching for him walking down the road. As soon as I saw him, she'd douse the candles with water if they were still lit. We threw them in the bin, stuffing them near the bottom where he wouldn't find them.'

I pick up my spoon from the saucer, stir the remainder of my cappuccino and watch the individual swirls of froth merge into one. I look up at Mark, as so many questions bubble inside me. 'So how come you're so involved with St Luke's if you're Jewish?'

'I started doing odd jobs for the church when I was a teenager. Peter arranged the work, ironically, and now I do their accounts and quite a lot of their admin.'

'But do you still *feel* Jewish? Inside, I mean. Do you do anything Jewish at all?'

Mark's eyebrows twitch, wrinkling his forehead. 'You really want to know?'

'For sure.'

'Well, some weekends I go to shul services over the road

on a Saturday. And then on a Sunday I sit at the back of the church and listen to the sermon there too.' He gives a sad laugh. 'I don't eat bacon, ham, pork or shellfish, foods forbidden to Jews. Mum never let me and I've never done it, maybe out of respect for her, I don't know. But I do eat non-kosher meat – *traif*, as Rabbi Dov calls it. Beef, chicken, lamb ... I celebrate Christmas and Easter but none of the Jewish festivals. And I still light the candles on a Friday night ... when I remember.' He laughs again. 'I guess I am a bit confused.'

An image pops into my head of the synagogue and the church, Mark standing at the crossroads, torn between the two. 'Guess that's religion for you.' I give a small laugh.

'You should speak to Rabbi Dov at Hillsbury Shul.'

My skin tingles with invisible fire ants. 'Why?'

'He'll be able to tell you what that Hebrew means.'

My shoulder twinges as if I need a reminder of Brussels. I shrug it away. He's right, though – I should. But how can I stand in front of a rabbi, knowing what Andy did and what I didn't do. What I need to do.

Then I remember Renvok's message: *Don't look into what you don't understand. Or there will be consequences.* If that isn't a reason to continue, I don't know what is.

I won't let them win. Renvok *or* Andy. I'm stronger than this. I'm stronger than them. Words are my super-power, that's what my grandad taught me, so I've an article to write.

Which means it's time to face things I can no longer ignore.

CHAPTER TWENTY-THREE

A bald man in a yellow hi-vis jacket and dark blue jeans is sitting on a chair in the synagogue security hut. He's holding a mug of hot, murky brown liquid and watching TV. One of those crummy US sitcoms, judging by the New York accents and canned laughter drifting through the open doorway.

'Hi, is the rabbi in?' I call to him, inhaling the aroma of strong coffee drifting towards me, wondering if this will satisfy my Tuesday-morning caffeine craving. I woke up late and didn't get a chance to switch the kettle on before rushing to work. I've worked diligently all morning and now I'm here in my lunch break, plagued by the deep ache of an empty stomach.

Baldo peers out of the hut. The security light reflects off his shiny head. 'Do you have an appointment?'

'No, I—'

'You will need to make one.' He pauses, shakes his head. 'I cannot let you in.' His voice is gruff and husky, with an Eastern European accent. Russian, maybe.

'Well, can I make one *now* for later then?'

He laughs, walks back into the hut and sits down. 'You will need to call office.' He swivels his chair back round to face the TV screen. 'The phone number is on shul website. We have strict security. These are rules from top.'

I reach into my coat pocket. Figure I may as well make that call. As I pull out my mobile, I glance towards the synagogue car park. A short stocky figure in a long-sleeved, white shirt, bright blue tie and black trousers staggers out of the building. He's carrying a large brown cardboard box with black files peeping out the top. He unlocks a silver estate car, shoves the box on the back seat, then looks towards the gate.

He nods at me. 'Vad?' The man has a deep voice, English with a hint of northern.

'Yes? Coming, Rabbi.' A shattering sound comes from inside the security hut. I peer inside. Baldo, or rather Vad, as it transpires, is sitting motionless with a spark of anger in his eyes, a smashed mug at his feet and splatters of steaming coffee all over his lap.

I try not to smile but fail, so cover my mouth with my hand and fake a cough. 'Need some help?'

Vad scowls at me.

I shrug. Next time I won't even try to be polite.

'There's a young lady at the gate.' The rabbi grins at me, with a twinkle in his warm blue eyes. 'She looks like she needs assistance.'

I grin back. I like him already. He's not much older than me, with a short, trimmed beard, greying in the corners, light brown hair and a black skullcap on the top of his crown.

Vad stands up and peers out the doorway, his cheeks flushed and his right hand covering up the wet patch spreading across his crotch. 'She says she want see you, but I told her she must make appointment like everybody else.'

'Well, sure, that's true usually.' The rabbi pushes up his

sleeve and checks his watch. 'But I'm free right now for a while and it would be rude to leave her on my doorstep.' He speaks quickly, barely taking a breath.

'I cannot just let her in. She could be anybody.' Vad inspects me, top to toe, eyes narrow, as if viewing me through a camera lens. 'These are security rules.'

'Well, let's find out who she is and what she wants, shall we?' The rabbi peers at me through the gate. 'Hello ... mind telling us your name?'

'Shanna Regan.'

'Hello, Shanna. Why do you want to see me?'

'I work for *Hillsbury Living* magazine. I'm writing about some local plaques and have some Hebrew I need to check out. Mark Stevens suggested you.'

'Ah, Mark.' The rabbi glances across the road towards the church. 'Sounds like you come highly recommended then.'

I smile. Mark took his mother back to her roots after she died, he'd told me. Ruth is buried in the Jewish cemetery, in a reserved plot next to his real dad. Rabbi Dov helped him organise the funeral and mourning prayers.

The rabbi whispers to Vad, who leans over and presses a button at the side of the pedestrian gate. The gate clicks. I give it a sharp shove with my hands and stroll into the synagogue car park.

Vad points to my rucksack, mumbling something under his breath. I unzip the bag and hold it open. He puts his hand inside and shuffles around, unzips the inner pockets, then nods and gestures me forwards.

I offer my hand to the rabbi, then realise my mistake when he doesn't take it. Orthodox Jewish men don't shake hands with women for religious reasons, just as Orthodox Jewish women don't shake hands with men, I learnt a while back. They avoid any possible signs of affection with the opposite sex, outside of marriage.

He gives me a warm smile. 'Please ... come inside to my office.'

Vad takes a step forwards as if to intervene.

'We'll be fine.' The rabbi waves him away. 'You worry too much.'

THE RABBI'S office is filled with steel filing cabinets, with barely enough room for his desk. Prayer books are piled high on every surface, alongside stacks of papers and folders. He sits down on a black plastic chair behind the table, then gestures towards the matching chair in front.

'Sit, sit. Let me introduce myself properly. I'm the rabbi here, though you've probably guessed that. My official name is Rabbi Eli Dovetsky, but most people call me Rabbi Dov.' He puts his elbows on the table, steeples his hands as if he's in prayer. 'So, now tell me about these plaques.'

I tell him about everything I've found and everyone I've met. It takes a while, and all the while he listens carefully. Mark, he knows anyway, and he nods when I mention the Newman family. Then I hand over the photos.

Rabbi Dov reaches inside the top drawer of his desk and removes a small, black rectangular case. He opens it, takes out a pair of silver wire-rimmed glasses and puts them on, balancing them at the end of his nose. He hums as he peers at the photos. It's a familiar tune but I can't place it. Then he puts the photos down flat on the desk and looks up at me.

'You clearly recognise the Hebrew. I'm impressed. Not many people would. And you think these plaques are linked with Hillsbury Jewish community?' He studies the photo of the Terry Murdock plaque again.

'I don't know for sure, but the Hebrew suggests there could be a connection. I don't know the name of the last victim though, the one linked to Terry Murdock.' I point at the photo on the desk. 'Can't guarantee anything until I do.'

He strokes his beard.

I stay quiet.

Eventually he speaks again. 'Have you tried the local papers to find out more about this particular plaque?'

'The online records don't go far back enough so I need to get to the newspaper library.' I point to the edge of the photo. 'About the Hebrew though. What does it say?'

'Ah, yes, of course.' He picks up the photo again and studies it, first with his glasses on and then with them off. 'These are a bit too fuzzy. I can make out some letters but not all of them.' He scrunches up his eyes, moves the photo towards his face, then back again. 'No, I definitely can't read them.' He shakes his head. 'Can you take some closer shots, perhaps, so I can see the full shape of them? If I get one of the letters wrong, it could be a whole different word with a whole different meaning. Hebrew's complicated in that way.'

'I can try.'

'Excellent, just pop back whenever you're ready.' He hands the photos back to me.

I stuff them in my bag. 'You have good security in place. Bit like Fort Knox. Is antisemitism much of a problem around here?'

'We have our fair share but no many major issues, *Baruch HaShem*.' He shuts his eyes for a moment as if in prayer, then opens them. 'It's more of a latent antisemitic sentiment. Disputes between neighbours, words muttered under people's breaths, posts and comments in the local Facebook group, that sort of thing. But we're always vigilant. I assume you're aware of what's been happening in

Europe recently? Terrorist attacks at shuls, kosher supermarkets, primary schools and shops, in Paris, Brussels, Nice, Rome, to name but a few.'

I nod, make a fist around my rucksack strap, swallow the lump in my throat. Blink rapidly to waft away the image that hangs there, of an elderly man on the ground and a young boy hovering over him. I shiver. Some images will never leave me, long after the photos are gone.

'Does it bother the locals? Having all that security?'

'They're used to it, or they certainly should be. Never had any official complaints that I know of. Our security is both a precaution and a deterrent. Any gathering of Jews is a potential target.'

'Are you at any more risk than, say, the local mosque?'

'That's a difficult one to answer. There've been attacks at mosques too, and no doubt you'll have seen them in the press, though nothing specific has happened around here. That doesn't mean it won't happen, obviously. I think we're all at risk from extremists. But now let *me* ask *you* a question. Do you know who Zac Wagner is?'

'No ... should I?'

'He's twelve years old. He was attacked on Saturday afternoon – on Shabbat – in the park just because he was Jewish, wearing a kippah, a skullcap, on his head. A group of boys threw stones at him and said he should die in the gas chambers with the rest of his people. They punched and kicked him, then ran off, leaving him lying there until a passer-by found him and called an ambulance. I visited him in the hospital yesterday. He's not in a good way – in intensive care, with a blood clot on his brain.'

I think back to the boys in Hillsbury Park and near the bridge. Would they have gone that far? Not just throwing those stones at me – but worse. Would they have hurt Valerie if they'd caught her? Would they beat up a younger child? I recall the newspaper David left me at the office, the headlines on the front page.

'Why haven't I heard about him? There was nothing in the latest *Hillsbury Times*.'

'And it's unlikely you *will* hear about him.' Rabbi Dov grimaces. 'People think antisemitism hardly exists because these incidents are brushed under the carpet. But things happen all the time, every week, up and down the country. Last month, a sixty-year-old Jewish woman was pushed and shoved on the street in Manchester late one night. Her attacker called her a filthy Jew. I could go on but we would be here for a long, long time.'

MY PHONE RINGS as I walk out of the shul gate.

Number withheld.

Feeling bold, I answer it.

'Hello again, sweetheart.'

I lean forwards and take deep breaths to stop myself retching into the dirt by my feet.

CHAPTER TWENTY-FOUR

I hold my mobile against my ear, hand shaking. 'What do you want, Andy?'

'Anyone would think you've been avoiding me.' Andy laughs, harshly and deeply. 'But then you've always liked playing hard to get.'

Before we became lovers, Andy hounded me with WhatsApp messages and phone calls and late-night visits – even following me to Africa on one of my work assignments. I'd been reluctant to get involved with not just a colleague but my boss – features editor at *NewsQuest*. Eventually I gave in, won over by his persistent charm. And now he's chasing me yet again but for very different reasons.

'Is this your apology? Because you've fucked everything up so I can't get work.'

He snickers. 'Apology? I warned you things would get tough unless you gave me those photos.'

'Fuck you, Andy.' I walk to the side of the shul gates and lean against the brick wall. I want to terminate the call but also want to know what he's going to say. Find out what else he's done.

'I just want those photos, Shan, then I'll leave you alone.'

I imagine him pushing his long wavy hair away from his eyes, as he always does when he's perturbed.

'Which photos?'

'Don't play games with me.' His voice drops. 'And I know where you are. In fact, I'm watching you right now.'

A fire engine thunders past, lights flashing and sirens blaring. Another follows, then a police car. The sounds echo at me down the phone. I glance at the church, up the street, across the pavement. An elderly woman perches on the bench at the crossroads with a little boy, her grandson maybe, bouncing on her lap. A man in a pinstriped suit, carrying a battered tan briefcase in one hand and leaning on a grey crutch, hobbles into the church.

'Where are you?' I clench my phone. 'How did you find me?'

'You joined a new Facebook group for local residents. Showed up in my feed.' His snicker sends an icy ripple down my spine. 'So it wasn't exactly hard to track you down. Then I found Shanna Regan written on a postcard in a newsagent window, asking for information.' He laughs. 'Can't be too many Shanna Regans around here ... with *your* phone number. I always said you were one in a trillion.'

'You're not getting the photos. They're in a safe place.'

'I'll find them somehow. Don't underestimate me. I've found *you*, haven't I?' He goes silent for a moment, then continues, 'So what were you doing in the synagogue just now, Shanna?' He hisses my name, a reminder of the snake he's become. 'What are you getting involved in?'

'It's none of your business.'

'Are you sure about that? I still don't get why it mattered to you that much. Me and the lads, we'd had too much to drink. And it's not like he didn't deserve it.'

'Deserve it? What's wrong with you, you bastard?' My voice rises as I recall the thug he turned out to be.

'Going soft in your old age?' Andy rasps at me. 'Or are you just a Jew-lover after all. You like those filthy rich bastards then? Prefer them to me? Think they'll—'

A press of the *End Call* button and he's gone. My hands shake and a warm flush spreads over me, as if my blood is boiling inside.

That phrase. *Jew-lover.* I've heard it so many times, too many times. I'm no Jew-lover. And now I need to prove it.

I turn back, rattle the gate.

Vad peers out of the security hut. 'What?'

'I just need to pop back in. Left my notepad in the rabbi's office.'

He looks at me with suspicious eyes.

'Please?' I ask politely, digging my nails into my palm. If I don't do this now, I know I never will. 'I can always call him.' I hold up my mobile.

Vad sighs dramatically and presses the button on the wall. The black pedestrian gate clicks. I shove it forwards and saunter through with my head held high.

I find my way back to the office. Knock on the door.

'Come in.' Rabbi Dov looks up as I walk over to his desk. 'Back so soon?'

'I need your help.' I grab the empty chair and clutch the back of it. Millions of words stumble around my head yet I'm struggling to find the right ones.

'Oh?' Rabbi Dov peers at me over his glasses. Then he takes them off, folds them and places them carefully down on his desk.

'I've waited a long time for this.' A sharp pain stabs the back of my throat. Nine-year-old Lila Benson hadn't been the only one with secrets all those years ago. When her secrets became mine, my secrets became hers.

'Go on...'

'My mother ... she...' – the words cling to my mouth – '...she died when I was seven, though I can't remember much about her.'

'I'm sorry to hear that.' The rabbi's eyes crinkle with kindness. 'But I still don't understand how I can help you?'

'She lived here in Hillsbury.' I take a deep breath. Buzzing fills my ears, like a swarm of bees leaving their hive. 'And she was Jewish, which makes me Jewish too.'

As I say the words out loud, my stomach churns.

Because now I feel like a traitor and a fraud.

CHAPTER TWENTY-FIVE

I shift the red folio back on the trolley. Grab the next one off the pile and lower it on to the wooden table. Each hardback volume contains at least twelve newspaper broadsheets, heavier and bulkier than I expected.

I've spent an hour in the newspaper archive so far. Taken a full day off work, figuring I'm owed a break once in a while. I massage the knotted muscles at the back of my neck, trying to unravel them with my fingers. A gritty dryness stings the corners of my eyes every time I blink.

I turn the pages slowly and carefully, skimming the text. So much detail to take in from the tiny, fading newsprint – feature articles and job advertisements, properties for sale, though it's the news stories I'm here to scrutinise.

On the table opposite, a man with vintage John Lennon glasses is flicking through a colourful illustrated journal. Every few pages, he scribbles on a notepad, then sticks his pencil back behind his ear. In the far corner of the room, a woman wearing a smart navy trouser suit is standing in front of a microfilm reader. She scans down each page with a frown on her face as she flicks her fringe away from her eyes.

What are their stories? Why are they here? Researching their family history or a novel, maybe. What would I say if someone asked me that question? Looking into other people's lives when it's none of my business? Researching a good story to sell so I can get my career back on track? Or following a treasure hunt without a prize?

Finally, the phrase 'hit-and-run' grabs my attention in the June 1994 issue of *The Hillsbury Times*.

A 22-year-old man was killed by a suspected hit-and-run drink driver in Stanton Lane, Hillsbury, in the early hours of Saturday morning. Terry Murdock was taken to Watford General Hospital but died soon after. Police officers and an ambulance were called to reports of an incident just after 2 a.m. There were no witnesses. 'We are devastated by our loss,' said his father, James. Police are urging the driver to come forward.

I write down the details in my notepad. Figure I'll find the original incident if I keep going backwards in time. I'm right – though it takes me another hour to find it, in October 1993.

Police are still searching for the hit-and-run driver who failed to stop at the scene of an incident in Stanton Lane last month. Detective Chief Inspector Keith Fields is urging anyone who witnessed the accident or has any relevant information to contact Hillsbury police station.

I carefully flip the pages back to September 1993.

Police are hunting a hit-and-run driver who left a 30-year-old mother with life-threatening injuries late Thursday evening … in Stanton Lane, Hillsbury, shortly after 11.00 p.m. An ambulance arrived but she died at the scene. Police are calling for witnesses to come forward … the driver … who failed to stop …. Her father … paid tribute to her as a 'wonderful, caring loving daughter …'. Anyone with any information is urged to get in touch with Detective Chief Inspector Keith Fields at Hillsbury police station.

The page is torn and some of the text is missing, rubbed off over the years. I note down what I can, then clench and flex my hands – I still don't know the name of the victim or if there's a Jewish link.

Yesterday, a weight had been lifted from my shoulders. The lid of a pressure cooker finally being released. I've always known I'm Jewish but until recently it meant little to me.

I explained to Rabbi Dov about my past. Life on the road, and what Dad had told me all those years ago, just as Lila Benson had been told by her parents.

Don't tell them ya Jewish, Shanna. It's our secret, remember that.

But Mama always said—

I knows that, Shanna. But it's safer that way here. And some lies are okay, for sure.

So I became Shanna Regan, Irish through and through, and pushed my mother's traditions to the back of my mind. Lila Benson made me think being Jewish was a bad thing or something to be ashamed of, especially as Dad also made me hide my roots. My granny would drag me to church, desperate for me to fit in and relieved when I did. For a while, anyway.

Over the years, I witnessed racism from the sidelines. Antisemitism on the campus. Snide remarks towards Miriam, an Orthodox Jewish girl from Manchester, when she first joined our university course. Students egged as they left Jewish Society events. Yet I ignored the nagging feeling at the back of my mind – that I should be doing something, taking action, getting involved.

Until I met Andy.

Until I witnessed his hate and anger.

Until I began to question everything I'd believed for twenty-five years.

Until I realised that I shouldn't be embarrassed or afraid.

When Dad and I were travelling, very few Jews had been living in Arab countries for decades. Those who remained hid their background or just lay low. In Egypt, there's a small group of mainly elderly women still clinging on to their Jewish past. Nadia interviewed them for *NewsQuest* a short while ago. In Dubai, times are now changing. A Jewish community has founded its first synagogue there, though the location is still a secret. I visited a few months back – before I went to Brussels and realised it was time to go in search of my own Jewish roots.

I know I was right to come back to Hillsbury. Finding these plaques has been timely, for sure, and this search now feels personal. Two out of three victims were definitely Jewish, Charlotte Newman and Ruth Stevens, so just one more to go. Could these deaths have been hate crimes with antisemitism at the heart of them? But if so, why did someone create these plaques?

I wander over to the library counter and chat to the man behind the desk. He checks his computer, tells me another copy of the newspaper is in storage and he'll need to order it in, but it could take a couple of days.

That suits me just fine, as right now I've somewhere else to be.

Robert Alders just doesn't know it yet.

CHAPTER TWENTY-SIX

Robert Alders reminds me of a scarecrow toy Dad once bought me in Ireland. Long straw-coloured hair, with a loose, yellow jumper and brown, brushed cotton trousers at least a size too big. His hands tremble when he speaks. He's reluctant to help me at first but eventually invites me inside, once I've taken drastic measures and informed him that I'm searching for Gina's killer.

When Robert offers me a coffee, I accept. Gives me a good excuse to look around his cluttered living room while he shuffles around the kitchen. Three armchairs face a small TV on a black corner stand. A jade chiffon scarf hangs over the back of one of them and there's a faded 'Happy Birthday To My Wife' card on the window ledge. Two tall bookcases lean against the left wall, opposite the front window. They're stacked haphazardly and precariously with books of various sizes, ages and genres, from battered leather-bound classics to chick-lit paperbacks and recent glossy hardback bestsellers.

An upright piano separates the bookcases, with a cluster of photo frames resting on its flat polished surface. I pick up a large silver filigree frame for a closer look at the photo inside it. Gina stands next to a group of children dressed in Hillsbury High uniforms. She's wearing a short green-and-white checked dress, black tights and black patent knee-length boots. Her small round face is dominated by large square glasses and a broad warm smile. I spot Charlotte Newman at the front of the photo, with a scowl on her face as if she'd rather be somewhere else. In another photo, in a glossy white plastic frame, a little boy crouches between Gina and Robert, his arms wrapped around a cocker spaniel puppy.

'She adored kids, you know ... whatever the rumours say. That's why she was a teacher.'

I turn around to find Robert staring at me. He's holding a white melamine tray with two mugs on top, steam rising like they're Icelandic hot springs. His hands shake as he puts the tray down on the glass coffee table, reminding me of Andy when he's had too much to drink. Is Robert slurring his words a little? Did I smell whisky on his breath? I look around and notice a half-empty bottle on the bookcase, third shelf down.

Robert gestures for me to sit in the nearest armchair. I try not to lean backwards against the jade scarf. I've seen no signs of another woman here and he hasn't mentioned one. Maybe I'm sitting in the place of a ghost.

'That's us in that photo ... with Cooper, my nephew in Miami ... and Scratch, his dog.' Robert stares at the photos with a wistful expression in his eyes. 'Cooper's turning thirteen this year, you know. We used to visit there ... every summer.' His voice catches. 'I ... I haven't been there since ... since I lost Gina.'

I pick up my mug. Blow gently on the coffee inside. The surface ripples like the dark water below the bridge where both Charlotte and Gina fell to their deaths. I look back at the school photo. Did Gina really hate Charlotte Newman that much?

Robert clears his throat. 'So, you said you wanted to talk … about the plaque.'

'Yes, I—'

'It's all lies, you know.' His voice drops until it's quiet and serious. 'All lies. Gina never … never pushed anyone. She loved all the kids.' He crosses his legs slowly and clasps his hands together on his knee.

'Even Charlotte?'

He gives a sorrowful laugh. 'Not sure about that, though she certainly wouldn't have pushed her. Charlotte wasn't a nice girl, you know.' His sallow cheeks redden.

'Oh?'

'Gina always said she was a difficult child … with a chip on her shoulder. She tried to get to know her … and look where that got her.' He shakes his head slowly. 'Gina was always trying to … to do the right thing, you know. But it's hard being a teacher when certain kids … don't like you.'

He speaks with authority, like he knows what he's talking about. And then I realise he does when I look back at the photos on the piano.

Robert, standing at the front of a classroom, holding a whiteboard pen. Wearing a light blue shirt, red striped tie and blue jeans, like an eccentric professor. He looks younger, plumper maybe, happier for sure.

'You're a teacher?'

'I was.' He gives me a half-hearted smile. 'English, at an all-boys secondary school in South London.' He unclasps his hands, the right one shaking as he points at the photo. 'I gave it up … three years ago.'

'How come?'

'Early-onset Parkinson's,' he says slowly. 'I didn't *have* to stop, but I was constantly exhausted. Too tired for a full day's work, couldn't talk for long periods, and the *kids* ... they started to notice my tremor and called me an alcoholic so I...' His voice fades away. 'You know what kids are like...'

My cheeks flush with warmth as I glance at that half-empty whisky bottle on the bookcase shelf. I take a gulp of coffee, trying to wash down the pangs of guilt in my throat, ignoring the temptation to kick myself. It's all too easy to jump to conclusions without the full facts. I should know that in my line of work. And now I can see the signs. The tremor in his hand, the way he speaks slowly and pauses often, his shuffling gait. Nadia's mum has Parkinson's too, though she's had it for decades and her tremor's much worse.

'I know what they say.' Robert's right hand shakes as his voice rises, so much that it catches the corner of his mug on the tray and coffee slops out. He mops it up with the edge of his jumper sleeve. 'That Charlotte died because of something Gina did ... or didn't do. That Gina didn't like Charlotte because ... because she was Jewish. But I've never believed that. *Not* my Gina. One of her oldest friends was Jewish, you know. She didn't have an antisemitic bone in her body.'

'But I heard Charlotte's friends backed up her story.'

'Teenagers.' His eyes flash with anger. 'They'll say anything, you know. Pack mentality ... sadly. I spent long enough teaching them. If one of them has it in for a teacher, they ... they all follow.'

'So who do you think put up the plaque, then? Could it have been one of the kids, or maybe even one of the parents?'

'Clearly someone with a sick mind ... whoever it was.

One of the kids, we always assumed. But ... thinking about it, it could ... it could have been a parent.' He picks up his coffee, gulps some, then carefully puts the mug down. 'Charlotte's parents led a witch-hunt against Gina through the school's Facebook groups. Disgusting ... disgusting comments.'

'You saw them?'

'One of the groups was open to anyone associated with the school. Well, only adults. Parents, teachers ... you know. I think they forgot Gina was in there. We received notes through our door too. Including one telling us about the plaque.'

A wave of excitement spreads through me. I place my mug down on the tray. 'What did this note look like?'

'It was typed ... on white paper. I remember Gina commenting that it looked a bit ... a bit old-fashioned.'

'Old-fashioned?'

'Typed, with a typewriter. One of those ribbon and ink ones, you know. My grandparents used to have one.'

I gaze at the clutter around the room, the jade scarf and the anniversary card, memories of Gina still seeming sacred. 'Do you still have the note?'

He shakes his head slowly. 'No. Gina chucked it out the same day it arrived.'

'Shame.' I pull out the note from my rucksack. 'But was it a bit like this one?'

Robert takes the piece of paper. His hand trembles as he grasps it tightly and looks at the typed words. 'Yes, though ... though the wording was different, obviously. Ours was more, you know ... more threatening. It said if Gina didn't admit what she'd done, she'd pay. They gave us six months, you know.' His voice breaks as he hands the note back. 'We thought it was a hoax. And then six months later, Gina, she...'

'So it was warning you, giving you a get-out clause? A chance to make amends?'

He eyeballs me, the tremor in his hand more prominent now. 'Except. Gina. Wasn't. Guilty.'

'No, no, of course not.' I shake my head rapidly to placate him. 'Did anyone else see the plaque?'

'They didn't mention it if they did.' He shrugs. 'Whoever put it there ... they can't have had any evidence. Otherwise ... they would have gone to the police. I destroyed the plaque, you know. This one isn't even the original.'

'Oh?'

'I managed to prise it off the post and smash it to pieces. But then, two days later, there was another plaque ... exactly the same ... in exactly the same place. And then Gina died, or rather was killed, just as the note said.'

'Did you tell the police?'

'Of course.' He wrings his hands together. 'I told the police and I showed them the plaque.'

'And what did they say?'

'They said it was just teenagers playing games ... and Gina's death was ... was an accident. They didn't have time to look into fake plaques.'

My eyes latch onto a wedding photo on the piano: Gina in a white lace dress; Robert in a black tux. Of course he'd believe his wife was innocent, wouldn't he? For better, for worse, that's how traditional marriage vows go.

'How long had you been married?'

'Five years, but we'd known each other for ... for over fifteen.' He looks towards the photos and smiles, his eyes glowing with warmth. 'We met as teenagers, you know. We were each other's firsts. First date, first love...'

I stare at the photo of the two of them, holding hands and gazing into each other's eyes. Was she really as gentle as he says? People don't always see what they should see.

Don't always see loved ones for who or what they really are.

I should know.

'Did Gina notice anyone following her before she died?'

'Everyone was.'

I raise my eyebrows. 'Sorry?'

'Well not everyone, obviously, but she became ... paranoid. Not surprising with what ... what everyone was saying. The charges were dropped but she didn't want to go back to teaching. She thought it was the end of her career, yet teaching was all she knew.'

'So no one in particular was following her?' I pick up my mug.

'We saw Charlotte Newman's brother in the bushes ... outside the house ... a couple of times.'

'Benji? Are you sure?'

'Yes, definitely him. Gina knew him from school. It was strange though, as he was just ... just watching us. Except one time when he walked up to our front door and then turned back ... as if he wanted to speak to us but changed his mind. He did the same after Gina died.'

'Why would he want to speak to you?'

'I have no idea.' He shakes his head. 'I certainly wasn't going to talk to a teenage boy who thought my wife had ... had killed his sister.'

We sit in silence for a moment. I gaze into my coffee while he gazes into his. I watch the slight tremor of his hand.

'Did Gina know about the Parkinson's?'

Robert nods. 'I was diagnosed a few weeks before, you know ... before she died. Sixteenth of November twenty-fourteen.'

'You've a good memory.'

He nods, gazes back into his coffee mug, his eyes glistening. 'It was the same day she discovered she was pregnant.'

'Pregnant?' My own hands start shaking so I put my coffee down. That wasn't mentioned in the newspaper story.

'Yes, pregnant. So whoever killed my Gina,' Robert says slowly, 'they killed our baby too.'

CHAPTER TWENTY-SEVEN

After a busy morning on Thursday, including visits to three more plaques for *Hillsbury Living*, I pop home at lunchtime, wet and bedraggled thanks to angry rain clouds emptying their wares. It's hard to believe that less than a year ago I was living in sunshine and tropical heat without a care in the world. Now I'm living under a shadow of grey skies with the heavy weight of guilt on my shoulders.

At the front entrance to the apartment block, a young man is taking photos with a digital compact camera. Slightly built, fresh-faced and clean-shaven, he looks like he's only just left school, despite his formal grey suit, orange tie and pressed white shirt. An estate agent, I guess, from the shiny new property brochures stacked up by the front door and the crisp business cards on the window ledge beside them.

I scurry up the stairs, desperate for dry clothes and a strong black coffee to warm me up from inside. But when I reach my apartment, I draw to a halt.

My door is slightly ajar.

I'm sure I closed it and locked it this morning. I've no

cleaner or expected guests – I don't even have anyone to expect.

On closer inspection, the lock has been damaged. I nudge the door open with my foot. Grip my rucksack tightly, preparing to swing it if I need to. Prepare for the worst, as my grandad used to say.

I wait another moment.

So far, so good. No signs of life.

I tiptoe inside.

The hallway is empty. I stand still, listen carefully and hold my breath. No sounds. I scrutinise shadows on the floor. No signs of movement. I lower my rucksack slowly onto the cream rug, then creep along the hallway, conscious of the creaky floorboards beneath my feet.

The kitchen door is ajar. Did I leave it that way?

I creep closer.

Peer round.

Breathe a sigh of relief when I see the room is empty, but grab a large bread knife from the wooden block on the granite counter anyway. Holding the knife close to my chest, blade facing away from me, I creep towards my bedroom.

I peer through the crack down the side of the open door. My bed is just as I left it, messy and unmade; my purple paisley duvet is scrunched up, exposing the lavender-coloured sheet, still with my moulded dent from last night.

So I creep in. Check under the bed, then tiptoe over to the pine wardrobe.

Holding the knife in the air, gripping it tightly so it's facing upwards, my hand shakes more and more.

Is this really a good idea? What if...

I fling open the panelled doors, left one first, then the right. My meagre collection of clothes gazes back at me. Pairs of ripped jeans. Caramel-coloured dress. Black jumper. A few white T shirts.

I check the other rooms. The bathroom. The kitchen. The living room – and discover that this is where the intruder's made their presence known.

The chrome bookcase is bare, hardbacks and paperbacks emptied out onto the wooden floor. And the desk has been ransacked, pens and pencils and papers strewn across the rug.

At first glance, nothing seems to be missing, though anything of any value is with me in my rucksack: my laptop and my phone and all my notes. If someone means to unnerve me or warn me, they've certainly done so. This, combined with those texts from Renvok, makes my skin tingle and my stomach churn.

Who would take the risk of ransacking my apartment during the day when neighbours are still milling around? And how did they get inside? Someone must have seen something. Hetty, I figure, as she misses very little that goes on in the block.

I leave the knife on the kitchen counter – I don't want to panic her – and exit my apartment. Pull the front door towards me, though the busted lock means I have to leave it slightly ajar. Take the stairs down to the ground floor and knock on her front door – twice. Knocking gently at first, then banging with my fist.

No answer.

There's a light on inside. Maybe she's having a nap. Or maybe she just can't hear me. I'm not convinced her hearing is at full whack.

A thump and a crash of crockery comes from behind her front door. Now I wish I'd brought the knife.

I reach under her brown WELCOME mat where I know she keeps a spare key.

'In case I have a senile moment,' she once told me. I've

noticed she has them more often than not. And this is certainly an emergency.

I open the door, then pause and listen and wait. No more noise, and no one rushes at me, so I tiptoe inside. Her apartment is a similar layout to mine. A long corridor with the kitchen and living room on the left, bathroom and bedroom on the right. But while mine is modern and bright, hers is dark and dingy, with a faint musty odour of cat pee and cigarettes.

I creep into her kitchen first. Fragments of white china are scattered over the floor tiles. A brown earthenware mug, half-filled with black coffee, lies neglected on the counter, next to a milk carton tipped on its side, its white frothy contents dripping into a puddle on the floor.

I touch the outside of the mug. It's slightly warm.

'Hetty?'

I try the living room next. It's empty, except for Hetty's fat ginger-and-white moggy sleeping on a dusty-pink velvet armchair. It lifts up its head, opens one eye then closes it. I catch a glimpse of white, milky froth around its mouth before it curls up into a ball, as if it's trying to pretend it's not there.

Hetty's bedroom is in darkness, with its long floral curtains still closed. I flick the main light switch down.

Nothing happens.

Laundry is piled up on the floor by her divan bed. I nudge it with my foot as I push past to open the curtains; it hardly budges. I'm astonished Hetty lives in such chaos as she's always looked so well-turned-out to me.

I drag the curtains across the chrome rail at the top, flushing light into the room, then look back down at the pile of clothes. A bunch of thin brown twigs is sticking out from a cerise jumper sleeve. As I bend down to push the washing out of my way with my hand, nausea rises in my throat and bile spills into my mouth.

Hetty lies by her bed like a broken rag doll: lifeless eyes, arms stretched out at odd angles, thin spindly fingers at the ends of wrinkled hands. Her floral bed cover is hanging down, her right hand clutching the fabric in one corner as if she tried to stop herself from falling.

I press my fingers against her wrist: no pulse. I rest the back of my hand against her nose and mouth: no breath. Calling for an ambulance will probably be a wasted effort. But I make the call just in case I'm wrong.

I call the police too. Hetty was in her eighties so this could be natural causes, but I want to be sure.

I back out of the bedroom, turn around, stumble to the bathroom and vomit into the sink. Splash cold water on my face. Dry it with a towel. Catch a glimpse of myself in the mirror, my face drained of all colour other than a green tinge.

My front door ajar; Hetty's closed. My apartment ransacked; hers untouched. No similarities, it seems. But a burglary and a death in one apartment block on the same day, possibly just minutes apart?

I don't believe in coincidences.

CHAPTER TWENTY-EIGHT

Three hours later, the police have vacated the premises (they haven't ruled out foul play) and a locksmith has fitted a new lock to my front door. I'm finally sitting down at my kitchen table, cradling a steaming cup of coffee, when a rogue thought pops into my mind. Hetty's mug had still been warm when I looked around her kitchen.

I wander downstairs and pick up one of the estate agent's business cards: white edged with red, and a black outline of a house in a magnifying glass in the top right corner; MARTIN SNARKS, HILLSBURY HOUSE HUNTERS, printed in block capitals on the left. Maybe Martin witnessed my intruder leaving the building or, even better still, captured them on camera.

I call him on his mobile. When he answers, the line is crackly and his deep voice fades in and out, as if he's in Africa rather than just up the road. Eventually I give up trying to make sense of the conversation, end the call and walk through the driving rain to his office on the high street.

MARTIN'S NOT BACK YET, his colleague tells me, as she fetches some paper towels from a bathroom at the rear of the agency so I can dry my soggy hair and wipe moisture off my face.

'Perhaps I can help you instead. I'm Sharon Bloom, the senior negotiator.' Her posture's stiff and upright, alert to the possibility of a new client. 'I don't know how long he'll be, and I'm sure you're in a rush – who isn't these days?'

Looking around, I'm not certain I'm the one who needs help. The inside of the estate agency looks like an artist's palette, as if someone was on acid when they furnished it. Black metal desks, plastic chairs in all colours of the rainbow and psychedelic abstract art hanging on yellow-painted walls. Even the carpet is a not-very-subtle bright shade of royal blue. I wish I'd brought my sunglasses to soften the glare.

Someone sure has idiosyncratic taste. I wonder if it's Sharon, watching her rest her hefty backside on a turquoise chair and smooth down the hem of her black-and-purple striped shift dress.

'Do you have any specific requirements?' She points at a large blue-and-white printed map on the opposite wall. 'Did you want to be near any of the local schools, the shops, the synagogue...?'

'An apartment, maybe, or a maisonette, or even a small house.' Figure I may as well play along with her neediness. 'To be honest, I'm not sure. But two maybe three bedrooms, a good-size kitchen and living room, not too far from the shops.'

'Do you have a particular budget?'

'Not really.' I think of my measly bank balance and

focus on keeping a straight face. 'Just checking what's around.'

'New to the area, are you?'

'Not exactly. I grew up here ... for a while anyway.' *Though it still feels very new to me.*

'It's a lovely area you've chosen.' Sharon stands up, opens the top drawer of a neon green metal filing cabinet, pulls out a wad of papers and hands them over. 'Please do take a seat while you look at these.' She gestures towards the orange chair in front of her desk. 'They'll give you an idea of prices and what you can get for your money.'

I sit down on the hard seat and flick through the pile of papers while Sharon watches me like a hawk.

If I was looking for a property, none of these would be right, though. I dream of a character cottage, wooden beams and an open-tread staircase, beside vibrant green meadows or a cool blue river. Something that reminds me of my childhood, maybe. Though the first part of my life was spent here, in Hillsbury, and I still don't know exactly where. I look down at the papers in my hands; one of these could have been my first home.

The third property in the pile looks familiar. I pull it out.

Sharon's eyes light up and she takes a deep breath before she speaks. 'That one is bigger and more expensive than the others but a much better investment in the long term.' She leans forwards, ready to give me the hard sell. 'Three bedrooms and two reception rooms, so ideal for a family.' She glances at my naked ring finger and clears her throat. 'Or if it's just for you, you could use the extra space for an office, or for laundry or—'

'Do you know why they're selling up?' I stare at the photo of the living room with its three family portraits on the wall. A blonde girl in yellow, a blond boy in burgundy, and the photo in between of the two children together before they were so cruelly torn apart.

Sharon glances at the door leading to the street, then leans towards me. 'Downsizing for financial reasons, I think,' she says in hushed tones. 'Their daughter died a few years ago. Very tragic, it was. They remortgaged the house to pay the legal bills.' She shuffles further forwards as if the walls are listening. 'The husband then lost his job, putting them in debt, so they've had to move. It was under offer but that fell through so they're now desperate for a quick sale.'

Five minutes later, Martin Snarks walks into the estate agency. He takes off his sodden raincoat, hangs it on a rack at the back of the office and sits down in the lime green chair behind the desk next to Sharon's. I pick up the pile of property details and move across to the pink chair in front of him.

I explain about the break-in at my rented apartment, give him the address and ask him if he saw anyone lurking. I've omitted Hetty's demise from my story for now. If the police find anything, they can investigate that themselves; I'm not doing their job for them, even if there *is* a link.

'I saw a few people leaving the building.' Martin opens his briefcase. 'But I wasn't really paying attention, sorry. I was taking photos of a couple of the flats and the grounds outside. We're selling number twelve and may have another couple on the market soon, if you're interested.' He pulls out his camera. 'I'll take a look at my photos though.'

He plugs his camera into his computer, presses a few keys on the keyboard and we both drum our fingers on his desk while waiting for the photos to download. All two hundred of them.

We wait.

And we wait.

'Sorry.' He taps his keyboard. 'The computer's slow

today so this looks like it's going to take a while. Maybe you could come back later?'

'You could just download them onto a USB for me.' I unzip my rucksack. 'I've got a spare. I don't have time to wait as I need to get back to my office – before my boss gives me the sack.'

Martin glances over at Sharon. She's on a call, talking animatedly with her hands, but looks up at him, gives him a broad grin and a thumbs up. If she's relying on me for a property sale, she'll be sorely disappointed.

Martin picks up a black fountain pen from a pot on his desk and twiddles it with his fingers. 'Tell you what, I'll call you when I've been through them.'

I look at his computer, still downloading photo number ten. 'Sure ... that works for me.' I reach into my rucksack and pull out a business card.

This reminds me ... I need to take some close-up photos for the rabbi. Figure I'll do that on route to the office as I'm heading that way anyway.

Twenty minutes later, as I approach Gina's plaque through the alleyway, shouts fill the air.

Fuck ... not again.

CHAPTER TWENTY-NINE

My legs throb, as if remembering the last time I was here, already primed to run. But I don't want to run this time so head towards the noise.

Another shout, then another – young, male, enraged – from near the plaque, near the bridge.

'Fuck you, Gina Alders, for not watching my sister. Fuck you, Charlie, for being such a bitch. Fuck everyone.'

My body relaxes like a cadet told to stand down.

A dark figure stands in front of the plaque. A grey ribbed beanie hat is pulled down low over his ears, a shock of blond hair spilling out. A black leather-looking biker jacket is zipped up high around his neck. His white high-top trainers are scuffed at the front.

He kicks the post. Once. Twice. Three times. The post wobbles, the plaque does too, but they both hold their own.

I take a step closer. 'Hey, what are you doing?'

Benji Newman looks up at me. Anger flares in his eyes. 'Fuck you too.' He bares his teeth at me like a rabid dog. 'It's your fault. You brought it all up again. Mum keeps crying now. I hate you and I hate this plaque.'

He kicks the post again but it still doesn't budge. He gives it another kick, more half-hearted this time, then slumps down on the rain-glistened gravel. Leaning forwards, he puts his head in his hands, his chest shuddering with sobs.

I sit down beside him, trying to ignore the sodden ground beneath me. Pull my hood over my head to keep out the sleety rain. 'What do you know about the plaque?'

'N-nothing,' he stammers through his tears. When he looks up, he won't meet my gaze.

'Tell me, and it'll go no further.'

Benji eyeballs me, sits up straight. 'You ... you sure?' His beanie has fallen down over his brow. He pushes it up with a quivering hand.

'Sure I'm sure.' With the icy rain coating my skin, I welcome the warm flush of a lie in my cheeks.

'Dad says not to trust journos.' He kicks at a mound of drenched gravel near his feet. The dark grey stones reflect light from the lamp above us, like glittering panther eyes. 'He's always swearing at them. Says they're all liars, bit like politicians, can't be trusted.'

'We're not all bad.' My skin crawls as I see Andy's face in a puddle nearby. I pick up a stone and chuck it into the rain-water, creating a tiny swirling whirlpool, and the image shimmers away. 'So ... about the plaque?'

'Saw it just before Mrs Alders died. Used to come here lots, now I try not to.' Benji turns and glances at the bridge, wipes his eyes with the back of his hand.

'What you said before...' – I wipe water away from my eyes too, but sleet, not tears – '...about Charlie ... about her being a bitch. What did you mean?'

Benji's eyes flare with fury. 'She *was* a bitch. To me and most of the kids in our year, like, everyone, the teachers too. Mrs Alders did nothing to her.'

'Really? How do you know?'

'Cos Charlie lied about what Mrs Alders said. Her mates did too. She didn't like Mrs Alders cos she gave her bad marks, so she spread rumours.'

'But Mrs Alders was on the bridge when Charlotte died?'

He kicks at the gravel again. 'Yes,' he whispers, 'but Tamsin lied. She didn't see Mrs Alders push Charlie. She told me afterwards. Charlie was mucking about on the edge, and Mrs Alders tried to save her.'

Gina Alders' face appears in front of me, kindness and enthusiasm shining in her eyes. 'Why did Tamsin do that?'

'Because one of Charlie's mates told her to, probs. Maybe they even threatened her. I heard some of them talking after. Wanted Mrs Alders to pay.' He reaches down, picks up a long twig from the gravel near his shoe. 'And whatever Charlie and her mates said, everyone did.'

'Did you tell your mum and dad? The police?'

'Why bother? Charlie was their favourite. Better at school, better at making friends. Never thought she did anything wrong.' He scratches the twig into the gravel, creating angry zigzag lines – if Sigmund Freud were here, he'd be having a field day right now. 'Not sure Dad believed it all. But after I saw the plaque and Mrs Alders died, he told me to keep, like, quiet. So I did.'

Why would Tim have done that? I look up at the plaque. The words MAY SHE NEVER R.I.P. glint at me in the rain.

'You saw who put it up, didn't you?'

Benji keeps grating the tip of the twig into the gravel.

'Well?' I nudge his arm gently.

He grips the twig tightly, digs it into the ground, grinding it round and round. 'I was in the bushes when they did it. Then I saw them walking away.'

'Man or woman?'

'Dunno. Couldn't tell. It was, like, dark already.'

'My height? Taller? Shorter? Your height?'

'Don't remember.'

'What were they wearing? Coat? Jacket? Colour?'

'Why the fuck should I remember?' He jumps up, throws the twig down and pushes his beanie back towards his eyes. 'Stop asking. Just, like, leave me alone.'

He scampers off down the path, reminding me of my run-in with the teenagers, and also of my adolescent self: angry, lost and alone.

Did Benji see who put up the plaque? I'm not sure Debra's tall enough to hammer in those nails, not just once but twice, according to Robert. What about Tim though? He seemed to be hiding something. Did he put up the plaque before killing Gina?

And then there's Peter ... At first Mark suspected he'd killed Ruth, and then he knew for sure. So is Mark the one I should be watching? Is there a connection between them all? Or maybe there's a puppet master behind them, pulling their strings – forcing resentful family members to make someone else pay.

I reflect on Benji's words. Gina Alders hadn't been bullying Charlotte, he said. It was all lies, just as Robert Alders told me. That really puts a spanner in the works. If this is a killer with a conscience, targeting those who wouldn't own up to a crime, how would they feel if they knew they got one wrong – and that she was pregnant? Does this make them no better than their victims – killing someone who didn't deserve to die?

I stand up, gaze at the plaque. Read the words again.

MAY SHE NEVER R.I.P.

Raindrops trickle down the glistening red words like tiny blood-filled tears.

CHAPTER THIRTY

I haven't chosen the most convenient time to visit the synagogue unannounced – certainly not for a confidential chat – with its hallway full of nattering adults and squealing children. But it's too late to turn back as Rabbi Dov has already spotted me and called out my name.

I should have realised a Sunday wouldn't be ideal, but I'd had no time in the week to visit him, instead concentrating on finishing off the issue of *Hillsbury Living* and then celebrating alone when it was done.

I walk over to the rabbi reluctantly, sure that everyone is scrutinising the stranger in the room. He's sitting on a black plastic chair behind a grey table, a metal cash box in front of him. He introduces the woman at his side as Tova, his 'best friend, wife and boss, though not necessarily in that order'. Her thick dark wavy hair, parted neatly down the centre, stops at her shoulders with an outwards flick at its base.

'I've printed off a new photo with the blown-up writing.' I raise my rucksack in front of me. 'But I guess now isn't a good time. I should have called first to check.'

'This is as good a time as any. Tova's in charge – she

always is.' He winks at her. 'Show it to me over there. I can spare a few minutes.'

He stands up and leads me to a large noticeboard on the wall with community announcements pinned haphazardly behind the glass. I dump my rucksack on the mottled brown carpet and unzip the front pocket of my bag. Pull out one of the photos.

'Let's have a look.' He removes his glasses from his shirt pocket and puts them on. Then takes the photo from my hands and peers closely at the blown-up letters.

'Can you read the Hebrew now?'

He nods. 'It's definitely Hebrew. It says *Nokmim*.'

'What does that mean?' I pull out my notepad and pen from my bag. Find a blank page.

'It stems from the Hebrew word *Nakam*, which means revenge.'

I scribble down some notes, my heart pumping so furiously that I hear blood pulsating in my ears.

'The *Nokmim* were Jewish assassins who targeted Nazi war criminals after the war.' Rabbi Dov looks at me with concern etched in his eyes. 'What have you found, Shanna?'

The treasure-hunt notes and the warning emails. The boys in the park. The man pushing me against the office door. The burglary at my apartment.

Hetty, dead by her bed.

Sharp brambles scrape my throat as I answer quietly, 'I don't yet know.'

'Have you thought about taking all this to the police so they can look into it instead?'

'I will do, when...' – I pause and wonder if it's wrong to lie to a rabbi – '...when I get the chance.' I figure I'm not lying if I simply stretch the truth.

'Please be careful,' Rabbi Dov says in an apprehensive tone.

'Is everything all right?' A dark shadow casts itself across the carpet, reflecting our change in mood.

'Glad you've made it.' The rabbi envelops Harry in a warm embrace, then steps back and gestures towards me. 'You know Shanna, I believe?'

'I certainly do.' Harry greets me with a bemused smile. 'So you made it then?'

'Made it?'

'We mentioned the Chanukah party to you when you came over for dinner.'

'Oh ... yes ... so you did. I forgot.' Another potential lie in front of the rabbi, though not *to* him so guess that doesn't count either. 'I popped by on the off-chance the rabbi was here.'

'Good timing then.'

'Sure is ... though I wasn't expecting *quite* so many people to be around.'

I wonder if Harry can sense my sarcasm. Possibly not, as his expression turns serious when he twists back round to Rabbi Dov. 'You mentioned the police? Has something happened?'

'No. No. Not at all. Nothing you need to worry about. Just some strange plaques with Hebrew writing on them that Shanna found.' Rabbi Dov points at the photo in his hand. 'We're wondering if she should report them to the police, just in case there's something untoward going on.'

'This sounds very intriguing.' Harry takes the photo from the rabbi and scrutinises the Hebrew letters. 'I see what you mean by strange. It says *Nokmim*.' He turns to me. 'Is this something for work?'

I nod. Seems like I'm on a lying spree tonight.

Rabbi Dov steeples his fingers, interlocks them and squeezes his hands together. 'Maybe you can give Shanna some background, Harry, since you're one of our Jewish history experts.'

Harry laughs. 'Well, I wouldn't say I'm an expert, and I don't know much about the *Nokmim*.' He hands the photo back to me, slides his mobile out from his trouser's back pocket and presses a few keys. 'Here you go. "The *Nokmim* were a secret group of Nazi hunters, Jewish assassins, formed in nineteen forty-five",' he reads from the screen. '"They wanted to make the Nazis pay for the mass murder of all the men, women and children during the Holocaust."' He gives me a quizzical look. 'How is this relevant to your article?'

'I'm not sure yet.' I stuff the photo, notepad and pen back in my rucksack. 'Valerie with you?'

'She's here already, helping with the children. She'll be desperate for a break by now, I expect.' He brushes past me towards an open doorway on the right. 'You coming in?'

'No, I wasn't—'

'Why don't you go in for a while, Shanna?' Rabbi Dov gives me a knowing look. 'No pressure to stay but you may find it interesting.'

He's right. If I want to remember more about my child-hood, this may be a good way to start.

A piece of card on Tova's table states the entry fee is a fiver so I pop a note into the cash box. The rabbi tries to hand it back to me, mouthing 'no need'. But I ignore him and follow Harry, pausing for a moment in the doorway before I cross into an unknown world.

I find myself in a large square room decorated with a blue-and-white theme. 'Happy Chanukah' banners are taped to the walls; clusters of pearly balloons are tied to the chandeliers. Music blares from the far corner – a man singing, and playing a keyboard. I assume it's Hebrew but I can barely hear him, thanks to the thunderous whoosh of air from three large inflatables – an assault course, bouncy castle and bungee run – and thirty or so kids and adults shouting, climbing, jumping, racing, laughing and lolling about all over them.

I'm relieved when Harry leads me into yet another – quieter – room. In here, around twenty kids are clustered around five small tables. Some are playing with colourful plastic spinning tops. Dreidels, Harry explains, with a different Hebrew letter on each of their four sides. The kids are playing for chocolate coins covered in gold foil, and handfuls of jellybeans, popping these in and out of white plastic cups.

'It's a game of chance,' Harry explains. 'Each letter means something different: skip your turn, take the whole pot, take half the pot or add something into the pot, until you've won.'

As if on cue, a little boy wearing a Mickey Mouse-themed skullcap squeals loudly and stuffs sweets into his mouth.

Other kids are painting flat candle-shaped clay pieces with chunky paintbrushes and poster paints. Adults are hovering around the perimeter, pretending they're watching their kids but really more engrossed in their own conversations. A few are drinking from small plastic shot glasses (whisky, I assume, from the liquid's golden shade), which could explain some of the raucous tones.

Valerie sits at a small wooden table in the corner of the room, holding a palette of face paints in one hand and a thin paintbrush in the other. In front of her, a fidgeting toddler on a small plastic chair clutches the hem of her blue satin Disney princess dress. Valerie seems far more relaxed than when I saw her last, brushing her hair away from her face with the back of her hand, taking care not to splash paint on her skin. Maybe it's because she's doing something she enjoys in a place where she belongs.

Glad one of us feels that way. My guts are churning inside as I have no idea what I'm doing here, and I'm worried I'll look like a fool if anyone asks.

Valerie finishes off the girl's orange-and-white tiger face with a brown painted nose. Then leans back and picks up a mirror. Shows her artwork to the little girl, who shifts off her chair and skips in our direction towards the clay-painting table, shouting out 'Mummy' at the top of her voice.

Valerie watches her leave with a wistful expression in her eyes. Then a grin stretches across her face when she catches sight of us. 'Shanna! You're here! What a lovely surprise!' She stands up, marches over and gives me a welcoming hug.

'I came to—'

'She was talking to Rabbi Dov about some strange plaques she's found.' There's no mistaking the serious tone in Harry's words. 'The rabbi seemed concerned.'

'Concerned?' Valerie scrapes a fleck of orange paint off the cuff of her navy dress. 'In what way? Is everything alright, Shanna?'

'It's nothing.'

I shuffle my feet. Why are these strangers so worried about me? Only Dad's allowed to be worried – if or when I let him – which isn't very often as I don't tell him much.

'Nothing? Are you ... are you sure?' Valerie asks. 'Still writing that article?'

'Yes, I'm nearly done.' I point at her last client, now smearing her hands with orange and black poster paints, matching the pattern on her face. 'Great artwork, by the way.'

Harry puffs out his chest like a proud peacock and squeezes Valerie's shoulder with affection. 'My wife is a very talented painter.'

'She sure is.' That reminds me. 'Valerie, do you know

where the clay shapes come from? The ones the kids are painting.'

'The clay shapes?' She scratches the side of her nose, then shrugs. 'The *rebbetzin* organised all of this. She does it every year.'

'*Rebbetzin*?'

'The rabbi's wife, Tova.' Valerie glances at her watch. 'She was going home at four to feed the baby. It's twenty past so you'll have missed her.'

Damn. 'I met her but only briefly. I should probably go too.'

'But you've only just got here.' Valerie nudges my arm. 'You must try a latke. You can't leave without one, I won't let you.'

'A latke?'

'It's a bit like a potato rösti, but *so* much better. I'm sure there'll be some veggie burgers too. And doughnuts, of course.' Her hazel eyes light up. 'Yes, you *must* have a doughnut. The jam ones are the best. Come on.'

She grabs my hand and drags me across the room.

CHAPTER THIRTY-ONE

I sit on my usual bench, with a brown paper bag on my lap and an open can of Diet Coke beside me. I'd made my excuses soon after Valerie led me over to the food table. No veggie burgers left, but she made sure I didn't leave empty-handed.

I reach into the bag, pull out the last latke and take a bite. It's soft and gooey on the inside – a deep-fried golden cloud of grated potato and onion, dripping with oil. A heart attack in the making but delicious all the same. I take another bite, then another and another until the last morsel is gone.

My fingers feel greasy so I grope inside my pocket for an old paper tissue and give my hands a wipe. Then I lean against the back of the bench and shut my eyes, enjoying the lull of the park after the clamour of the shul hall. All I can hear is a faint purr of traffic in the distance. I'm back in my oasis of calm.

Harry gave me a running commentary as Rabbi Dov lit five candles on the large nine-branched menorah, a golden candelabra.

'Chanukah is the Festival of Lights,' he explained. 'Commemorates the Jewish battle to reclaim the Holy Temple in Jerusalem from the Syrian-Greeks, more than two thousand years ago. The Jews only had enough olive oil in the Temple to last for one night but miraculously the oil lasted for eight nights. That's why we celebrate Chanukah by lighting candles and eating oily foods.'

A memory stirs.

My mother holding a silver menorah. She has her back to me, but I recognise her long auburn hair. *She places the menorah down on a table, slots five candles in, one for each night of Chanukah.*

A flare of a match. Five candles lit, glimmering in a row, dancing in a gentle draught from a nearby window. My mother says a prayer in Hebrew, then we sing in unison, clapping our hands in rhythm.

I feel a tightness in my chest.

Ma'oz tzur yeshu'ati.

This is the same Hebrew song I've just heard at the synagogue, Harry and Valerie singing it loudly beside me.

A man stands in the corner, hovering in the shadows. Watching us. Watching me. Now he's joining in, clapping and stomping his feet.

I'm *sure* this is a real memory, or at least I hope so, from the way my skin prickles and stirs. Maybe Dad knows more about Judaism than he's told me. Maybe he can remember things I can't.

I pull my notepad out from my bag and switch on my phone light, shining it over the pages to find my most recent scribblings: everything Harry told me about the *Nokmim*.

A nicotine odour wafts towards me, mixed with a light scent of sweat. Nearby, the soft orange glow of a cigarette tip dances in the darkness like a solitary firefly.

The bench creaks as someone sits down.

They blow smoke into my eyes.

'Hey,' I shout, turning towards them. Then I halt.

An invisible hand clamps my mouth shut.

My cheeks turn ice cold.

My shoulder throbs as if it's being crushed.

The last time I saw Andy was in June, with fury burning in his eyes. Today he looks tired, older even, his blond hair speckled with silver flecks and his brow more creased. I shine my phone light upwards and take a closer look at the greyness of his face and the contours of guilt around his eyes. The last few months haven't treated him well at all. I see the anger on the surface but also the desperation behind it, as if I'm the one holding his holy grail.

Maybe I am.

We both know why he's here in Hillsbury.

'Miss me?' He stubs out his cigarette on the wooden slats between us and grabs my notepad from my hand. Leans forwards and stares at my notes. '*Nokmim*. Holocaust. Jewish Avengers. What you up to, Shanna?'

I lean over to snatch my notes back but he grabs my elbow, draws me close. I sink into his chest as if my body's on autopilot. Hunger pangs call me from deep inside as he bends down and his mouth rests on mine.

That bitter nicotine taste. That smoky odour.

So familiar.

Too familiar.

'Get the fuck off me.' I pull away, wincing with pain as I make the sudden move. My body may want him but my head doesn't. 'You've done enough damage.'

'Shoulder still bothering you, is it?' Andy snickers. 'Teach you to mess with me.'

'Was it you outside the office? Did you chase me there?'

'I don't know what you mean.' Despite his denial, I can

hear the truth in his voice. 'And what's with you and these fucking Jews. Got a taste for them, have you?'

I picture that elderly man again, lying battered on the ground, then shake my head to waft away the memory.

'Stood up for them in Brussels, and now here,' Andy whispers in my face, his stale nicotine breath warming my skin. 'What's with you these days? We were good together, Shan.'

I say nothing, though he's right – we were ... for a while.

'Do their black hats, long coats and twisty sidelocks turn you on? Just like I used to?'

I clench my hands into fists. *One ... Two ... Three ... Four...*

'They don't look like that here. Look no different to you or ... *me*.'

Of course they don't look any different, as they *are* no different – and *definitely* not to me. Okay, so they follow rules I don't, but maybe once I did. My memories certainly suggest so. Maybe if my mother hadn't died, if Dad hadn't taken me to Kilconly, I'd still be here now, living among them, belonging here. Though with no family, who would have taken me in?

'Why do you hate Jews so much?' Anger bubbles away inside me. 'What have they ever done to you?'

'They're filthy rich, aren't they.' A statement, not a question. 'Those blokes were right, in Brussels, when they said Jews are taking over the world, ruining it. 9/11. Brexit. All down to the Jews.' He raises his voice. 'Think they're high and mighty, lording it over the rest of us.'

'That's a load of rubbish. And they're not all rich.' I think of the Newmans with their house for sale, trying to keep a semblance of the money they don't have. I think of Valerie and Harry. And I think of me. I suspect trying to argue with Andy will be a waste of time, though. It always was.

I take deep breaths, trying to get more oxygen into my lungs. *Don't rise to the bait, Shanna.*

I snatch my notepad out of his hands. 'What if *I* was Jewish? How would that make you feel?'

'As if. You're not exactly rolling in it.' Andy laughs, a hollow sound echoing into the darkness. 'And you're Irish anyway.'

'Never heard of Irish Jews?'

He stares at me, stumped. 'No ... no ...' he says in a devastated tone, as if I've told him he has only twenty-four hours to live. 'No way you're Jewish.' He looks me up and down. 'You're fucking kidding, right?'

'For fuck's sake.' I shove my notepad back in my bag, safe, secure, away from prying eyes. I'm torn between telling him the truth – that he's slept with Jewish blood – and keeping it *my* secret, letting him fester for longer. I opt for the latter. 'Have you even had a proper conversation with any Jews? There's no such thing as "looking Jewish". Not all Jews look the same.'

Andy stares at me.

'But, yes, I'm just kidding – as if *I* could be Jewish. Ha fucking ha.'

As Andy sighs with relief, I wish I was brave enough to thump him.

'Where are those photos?' he growls. 'The ones you took in Brussels.'

'As if I'd tell you.'

'Maybe you don't need to.' Andy grabs my rucksack and yanks it open.

'Give that back!' I try to snatch the bag from him but he pushes me aside, stands up and walks away across the grass. 'They're not in there,' I call after him.

I'm no fool, he should know that. I wouldn't carry those photos with me knowing he's nearby. They're hidden on three different USB sticks in three different locations, not just in Hillsbury. I know how the world works and I know how people behave. I've seen some of the worst of it over the years, after all.

But I still need my bag back. That rucksack has been my trusted companion through the continents – Africa, Asia, Europe – through good times and bad, and I'm not going to abandon it now. Plus, I need what's inside.

I stand up and pace after him, me picking up speed, then him too, until we're both sprinting.

Andy is faster and more sure-footed than I am, but I know the terrain better than he does. He lurches where Valerie stumbled, a dip in the icy grass. My rucksack flies out of his hand, landing in a heap further ahead. My notepad and some photos spill out from the open pocket.

Ignoring Andy, I run to my belongings, bend down and pick them up. One photo is smeared with mud across a top corner but they're otherwise undamaged.

Andy grabs my foot. I kick him away.

'Stay. Away. From. Me.' I march across the grass towards the park exit.

'Hey.' A familiar male voice, deep, African accent. 'You okay, Shanna?'

The last time I heard it, a man had been standing in front of me with a cat lead in his hand. Now, a little girl in a purple duffel coat clutches his arm. She smiles at me shyly and looks nervously at Andy.

I'm surprised Max remembers me, let alone recalls my name. 'Sure, I'm fine.'

I smile my thanks to him, then look down towards the ground. 'Andy, I'd like you to meet Max. He's a criminal lawyer and has a copy of everything safely stored away.' I glance at Max with pleading eyes, hoping he'll go along with my ad hoc plan. When he nods, I continue. 'If anything happens to me...'

I don't finish the sentence as I don't need to. Andy glares – at me, then at Max and then at the little girl still holding Max's hand. His body shakes but he keeps his anger in check. Maybe he's learnt some self-control since we last met, though somehow I doubt it.

Andy stands up, brushes mud off his jeans and walks back across the grass. 'I'll be in touch, Shanna,' he shouts. 'Don't think this is over.'

Max picks up the little girl and hugs her in his arms. 'Trouble again?'

'Guess trouble seems to follow me.'

I watch Andy disappear into the distance. He's right. It isn't over.

'Don't suppose you'll need a lawyer this time?' Max puts the little girl back down on the grass. She sticks her tongue out in Andy's direction – clearly a good judge of character.

'Funnily enough, I think I will.' I glance down at my rucksack containing photos of the plaques and all my notes. 'Just not quite yet.'

CHAPTER THIRTY-TWO

The newspaper library feels less oppressive second time around, maybe because I know what I want and what to expect. I'd emailed David and told him I was taking another day off. I never heard back but assumed it was fine, following my rules of 'no news is good news' and 'no reply means yes'.

Lucy-the-librarian, as printed on her badge, leads me to an empty table in the corner of the reading room. She huffs and puffs as she pulls a red folio off the trolley and lays it down on the desk in front of us. I offer to help but she shrugs her broad shoulders and tells me that library rules mean I can't handle this folio myself, as it's a highly fragile document. I let her get on with it without arguing. Sometimes I have to accept that there really *are* rules that can't be broken or bent.

Lucy-the-librarian turns the pages slowly with her short stubby fingers until she finds the right one. She shifts to the side so I can have a look, but warns me – in a bossy tone – not to touch the pages, her beady eyes watching my every move.

This time, the news story is intact.

Police are hunting a hit-and-run driver who left a 30-year-old mother with life-threatening injuries late Thursday evening, 9th September. Eve Lee was knocked over by the car in Stanton Lane, Hillsbury, shortly after 11.00 p.m. An ambulance arrived but she died at the scene. Police are calling for witnesses to come forward and are trying to trace the driver of a dark blue Jaguar who failed to stop. There is no evidence that the car was damaged in the collision. Floral tributes have been left at the scene of the crash. Eve Lee leaves a husband and young daughter. Her father Izzy paid tribute to her as a 'wonderful, caring loving daughter, wife and mother'. Anyone with any information is urged to get in touch with Detective Chief Inspector Keith Fields at Hillsbury police station.

I take a photo of the page and scribble down some notes as a backup. The librarian closes the folio carefully, making sure no pages get creased, and returns it to the trolley, huffing and puffing again so loudly that I worry she'll collapse.

Twenty minutes later, I'm sitting in the library café sipping a steaming espresso when a delayed flush of excitement spreads over me. I now know the name of the woman who died and a few scant details about her. Eve Lee had a family: a husband, a daughter, a father.

I switch on my laptop and search online for the word combination of Lee and Hillsbury. Dr Harry Lee, GP, comes up first – obviously I know him – followed by another thirty entries, including: Ben Lee, retired lawyer; Lee Sugarcraft Supplies; Jessica Lee, nutritionist; and Adam

Lee, children's balloonist. I'll ask Valerie first, and make a note to check out the others.

Mark calls my mobile as I walk down the library steps towards the pavement. I explain what I've discovered about Eve Lee and the word *Nokmim* on the plaques, deliberately omitting all mention of Andy as though I can wipe him out of my life – if only it was that easy.

'I still don't know if Eve Lee is Jewish.' I watch the hustle and bustle of London street life around me. Tourists wander past in both directions: some, old-fashioned traditionalists clutching London A-Zs; and others, hi-tech modernists browsing Google Maps on their mobiles. 'Lee's a popular Jewish name. But it's also a popular name all over the world.' I think of Mina Lee, the photographer I worked with for a while in China when we were in our early twenties.

'What about trying Hillsbury Jewish Cemetery?' Mark asks. 'If this Eve *is* Jewish, she's likely to be buried there.'

'That's a great idea.' A middle-aged woman in a grey suit dashes past me, a magazine tucked under her arm, talking rapidly in Spanish into her mobile. 'Where's the cemetery, though? I haven't seen it.'

'It's just outside the ... town, near ... motorway,' Mark's voice sputters. 'Hello? Can you hear ... you're cracking ... can you ... me?'

'You're cracking up too. It's noisy round here,' I shout into my phone, as a young pizza delivery guy zooms past on a motorbike, revving his engine and careening round the cars as if he has a death wish.

'Tell you what ... I don't have any ... this afternoon,' Mark shouts back at me. 'You can't get ... without a car, so I'll pick ... from the station, if that works ... you?'

The line goes dead.

I send him a text. *See you at Hillsbury Station in an hour.*

Hillsbury Jewish Cemetery is a vast sprawling desolate area of greyness surrounded by main roads. The only sounds are murmurs of the mourners and humming of light aircraft from a nearby airfield.

Despite the rain, the cemetery is teeming with people, clustered around rows of granite and marble headstones, many with their heads bowed. Most look bedraggled, even those holding open umbrellas, as rain spatters them from all sides.

Our first destination is the cemetery office. A young woman slouches behind the information desk, flicking through a battered copy of *Cosmo*. She tugs at her long streak-dyed hair: black around her crown graduating to fuchsia at the ends, as if it's been dipped into a vat of bubble gum.

I cough to attract her attention.

She looks up, her dark brown eyes drowsy with boredom, and closes her magazine.

'I'm looking for someone who may be buried here.' I point towards the door, in the vague direction of the graves. 'The name's Lee. Eve Lee. She died on the ninth of September 1993 but I'm not sure when she was buried.'

'I'll have a look for you,' the woman says in a nasal voice as she presses a few keys on her keyboard. 'Yes, she's here. Jews are usually buried within twenty-four hours of their death, but there's been a couple of extra days on this one. Probably means a coroner was involved. Unexpected, was it?'

I shrug my shoulders.

She tears off a scrap of yellow paper from a notepad on her desk, scribbles on it with a blue ballpoint pen and hands it to me along with a black-and-white cemetery map. 'You'll find her in block J, row sixty-five, plot four. Walk down the right-hand side of the cemetery all the way to the end and take a left.'

According to the map, the cemetery is divided into identical uniform blocks, each containing hundreds of headstones arranged in neat rows with clay pathways between them. Mark and I soon find out it's not quite up to date. The cemetery's recently been extended, with an extra row added at the front and a few graves added to the ends of each row, right next to the path.

In some places it's a squeeze to walk between the graves, especially with older headstones leaning backwards with advancing age. But eventually we find the right one. A shiver streaks its way down my spine as I read the words, knowing Eve Lee's remains are buried here, beneath this stone.

EVE LEE

9TH SEPTEMBER 1993

SORELY MISSED BY HER HUSBAND, FATHER AND

DAUGHTER

MAY SHE REST IN PEACE

ALWAYS IN OUR MEMORIES AND IN OUR HEARTS

Some Hebrew writing is engraved into the top of the headstone. I take a photo and point it out to Mark. He shrugs so I glance round to see if someone else can help.

An elderly man is walking up a nearby path, leaning on a woman's arm for support. She looks too spritely to be his wife, with her short leopard-print skirt and thigh-length boots, though these days I know you can't be sure. I wander over to them, show them my phone with the picture of the Hebrew words.

'It says *Eve bat Yitzchak*. Eve, daughter of Yitzchak,' the woman says in a high-pitched voice. 'Is that right, Pops?'

Close up, I can now see she's barely more than a teenager.

Her grandfather holds my phone close to his face, stares at the screen for a moment, then nods.

'Thanks.' I think of the Izzy mentioned in the newspaper article. Could Izzy be short for Yitzchak? If so, this may be the right Eve Lee.

When I return to Mark at the graveside, I notice small stones scattered at the side of the grave. I assume it's random until I realise they're arranged in the shape of the letter E.

I nudge his arm. 'What are those for?'

'People put them here as a sign they've visited.' He bends down, picks up a small speckled grey stone and hands it to me. 'It's a common Jewish custom – a way of showing the dead that they're still remembered.'

'Can anyone put a stone down?'

'Yes, of course.'

I place the stone next to the others at the end of one line, retaining the E formation as it feels like it's the right thing to do.

We visit Ruth's grave next. She's buried in a newer part of the cemetery.

RUTH STEVENS NÉE NATHAN
22ND JULY 2015
REUNITED WITH BERNIE, THE LOVE OF HER LIFE
MOURNED BY HER SON MARK
TRAGICALLY LOST TOO SOON

No mention of Peter.

Mark pulls out a navy crocheted skullcap from his jacket pocket and pops it on his head. Then takes out a small thick book from the same pocket: green leather cover with

Hebrew words on the front, beige pages, yellowing round the edges.

'It's a *siddur*,' he explains to me. 'Mum's Jewish prayer book. I can't read much of the Hebrew so I read most of it in English, but Rabbi Dov taught me the main mourner's prayer.'

I stand beside him and listen carefully as he recites the Hebrew. He stumbles over several of the longer words, some sounding like a tongue-twister with their guttural sounds. I find myself shutting my eyes as I realise how familiar the words are.

'*Baruch ata adonai Elo-kenu melech ha-olam.*'

When Mark has finished, he bends down and picks up a brown mottled stone and murmurs something under his breath, then places it on the graveside. He stands there silently, staring at the headstone with a teary glint in his eyes.

Mark and I return to the prayer halls on our way back to the car park. The rain has subsided, leaving a fresh earthy smell in the air and muddy footprints all over the paths.

A dozen or so men and women are streaming out of the nearest building. Harry and Valerie are standing by the door talking to the rabbi. They glance in our direction as we walk towards them. Rabbi Dov nods at us before going inside the prayer hall.

'Shanna?' Valerie pushes her black beret upwards, revealing red-rimmed eyes.

I pause. 'Sorry to … to see you here.' I stumble over my words, unsure of the right thing to say.

'My … my auntie,' Valerie clutches the black chiffon scarf around her neck, 'she died … a couple of weeks ago.'

'I wish you and your family long life,' Mark says. At least one of us knows the Jewish traditions and what to say.

'Auntie didn't have any family of her own.' Valerie's

hand trembles. 'Her husband died years ago, so ... it's been up to us to look after her.'

'Sorry to hear that. Was it sudden?'

'Yes, she was found ... in her ... in her bedroom,' Valerie stutters. 'In her eighties but in pretty good shape for her age, so ... we're not really sure what happened ... exactly.' She reaches into her coat pocket and brings out a scrunched-up paper tissue, uses it to dab her eyes. 'But the police ... they're looking into it.'

Police? Investigating her aunt's death? Two elderly women found dead in their bedrooms under suspicious circumstances in Hillsbury in the same week?

'Not Hetty Gordon?' My voice echoes, and Rabbi Dov peers out of the prayer hall, stares at us, then disappears again. Valerie nods. 'I'm in the apartment upstairs. She often brought in my post.' *And tried to open it.*

Harry grasps his wife's hand, protective and caring. 'Hetty *did* talk about her Irish neighbour, the journalist. We just never put it all together.'

'So you're the neighbour who found her?' Valerie holds a tissue to her mouth with her free hand, stifles a sob. 'I'm so glad it was you ... that feels ... that feels right somehow.'

'Have the police found out what happened?' I think back to the other day, when Hetty was on the staircase. They must be the niece and nephew she mentioned. Seems like I'm discovering all the local connections and what a small Jewish world it is. 'They're looking into a break-in at my apartment on the same day but there's been no news.'

'The police think someone else may have been in her flat when she fell.' Valerie wipes her eyes with a corner of the tissue. 'But there were no signs of any struggle.'

'Sorry to hear that.' I make a mental note to chase up Martin Snarks for those photos.

Harry lets go of Valerie's hand. 'So what are *you* doing here?'

'We went to visit my mum's grave.' Mark puts his cold hand on mine, I suspect to steady his emotions. Can't say mine feel very steady either.

'And you are?' Harry looks Mark up and down, in the same suspicious way he looked at me when we first met.

'He's an old friend.'

Harry raises his eyebrows, a quizzical expression in his eyes.

I don't elaborate.

After a brief chat about the inclement weather (how British of us), Valerie nudges her husband. 'We need to visit Auntie before the rain gets any worse.'

As I watch them wander off into the distance, I realise I forgot to ask if they knew Eve Lee and her father Izzy. Though I guess maybe this wouldn't have been the best time.

I follow Mark towards his car, with the names bouncing around in my head like random balls in a lottery machine – as if they're trying to attract my attention, tell me something I should already know.

Eve and Izzy. Izzy and Eve. Izzy, short for Yitzchak. The names in the newspaper article.

'Of course,' I exclaim, as I slide into the passenger seat of Mark's car. 'I need to head over to Stanton Lane. Now.'

CHAPTER THIRTY-THREE

I ring the doorbell. No answer, though I'm sure I see a downstairs curtain twitch. I ring again, and again.

Still no answer.

I turn round, walk back to Mark's car and open his front passenger door. Slide into the seat, pull the door shut and punch the dashboard in frustration.

I need to speak to James Murdock, and I want to speak to him now.

I slump down, staring at the carefully manicured gardens. How did it take so long for my brain to kick into gear? Who pays a gardener to work in this icy weather? The frozen grass is too stiff to mow, and you can't dig a spade into the compacted soil.

'You okay?' Mark asks, worry creasing his brow.

I glance back at the Murdock house, with its lights off, downstairs curtains closed. The left drape twitches. I wonder if it's a draught at first but then it happens again, followed by the right one for marginally longer.

I open the car door and swing my legs round onto the pavement. 'Sure I am. Be right back.'

I march up to the front door, crouch down and nudge the letterbox open with the tips of my fingers. 'I know you're in there, James Murdock,' I shout through the gap. 'I'll wait on the doorstep till you answer. I know who you are.'

The letterbox snaps shut when I pull my fingers back.

I stand up and tap my feet on the ground.

Within seconds, Jim-the-gardener, aka James Murdock, opens the door. 'I have nothing to say to you, Shanna Regan.'

'Terry was your son. Why didn't you admit it the first time?'

'There's been enough blame round here all them years ago, there has.' He glares at me. 'My Terry did nothing wrong. So leave me alone.'

I take a step towards him. 'Are you saying the words on the plaque aren't true? That Terry didn't kill Eve Lee?'

He flinches. 'I've nothing more to say.'

He begins to push the door shut but I'm one step ahead of him ... literally. 'Move your foot, girl,' he growls like a disgruntled bear, nudging at the door that's pushing against my trainer. 'Or I'll call the police, I will.'

'Go ahead.' I fold my arms. 'But first, you tell me why Terry's name was on the plaque and why you're so sure he didn't do it.'

A car door slams. Footsteps head towards us.

'Everything okay, Shanna?' Mark calls.

I gaze at James, holding my ground and keeping my foot in place. Then I gesture towards Mark behind me. 'Last chance to let me in so we can talk in private ... or he comes too.'

James glances at Mark, who's now standing beside me, tall, broad and straight like a bodyguard, then he nods and fully opens the door. 'Just you, it is then.'

'Everything's fine, Mark.' I give him a nod. 'I'll be out in a bit.'

'If you're sure.' Mark takes a step back. 'I'll wait here. Holler loudly if you need me.'

I follow James inside, through his hallway, past open doorways leading into his kitchen, lounge and dining room, until we reach a large room at the back of the house. I'd been expecting another lounge but instead we're in what seems to be a workshop, with a grimy beige tiled floor and tall metal shelving units, two along each side, stuffed with car parts, tools and grubby cleaning cloths. Car magazines and repair manuals are stacked up in two neat piles on the flat surface of a wooden workbench along the opposite wall, with a few coiled springs, pliers, spanners and a wrench scattered around them.

His Rottweiler is stretched out on a mat in the middle of the room. It raises its head, licks its paws, then goes back to sleep.

Despite a small convector heater blowing out warm air, there's a chill in the room, thanks to the open doorway next to the workbench. I peer through into the garden. Like the front of the house, it's well-tended, with neat flower beds, sculpted edging and a pristine striped lawn. The only sign of mess is a half-polished car radiator grille and a rusty car bumper on the patio's crazy paving slabs.

'You're a car mechanic?' I'm hoping some small talk may break the silence; encourage him to talk.

'No, I'm not a bloody mechanic. I renovate classic cars and sell them to top collectors here and abroad. Anyway, you're not here to talk about that ... or me.' James pulls out two battered folding metal chairs from a gap between the shelving units on the left. 'Here.' He hands one to me. 'We'll sit on these.'

I look down at the hard chair. 'You don't want to sit

somewhere more ... comfy?' I picture the large plush floral sofa I noticed in the lounge.

James opens his chair, puts it flat on the tiled floor facing the garden and sits down, so I have no choice but to follow his lead. As I perch on the chilly seat, a shiver runs upwards from my butt towards my spine.

'Why didn't you tell me who you were the first time we met?' I try to keep my voice as amiable as possible.

'Didn't need to, did I? Nothing to say. Someone killed my Terry and blamed him for something he never did.' He points at a photo pinned to a large corkboard beside the workbench, of a big bloke with small piggy eyes, cheeks puffed out like a chipmunk.

'How can you be so sure Terry didn't do it?'

'Because I was his dad.' James glances outside, his eyes catching on a small robin that's landed on the car bumper on the patio. 'My Terry weren't no angel but he was no killer either.' He waves his hands in a shooing motion and the bird flies off.

I glance down at the dog, which is now snoring and drooling. 'So who do you think ran down Eve Lee that night?'

'She and her husband were at one of them parties, I was told by the police, so it could have been *any* of them people there. They was always having parties along here, they were. Loud music, every,' he bangs his hand against the chair seat, 'every Saturday night. My poor Rose was sick in bed with cancer in her bowel. She couldn't take all that noise. I told them people to turn it down time and time again, but they never took no notice.'

'Them people?'

'Them Jews.' He waggles his index finger at me. 'Taking over the area, even then they were. Big houses, big cars, big mouths...'

I flinch. 'Jews?' *One ... Two ...* I count slowly under my breath to stop myself saying something I'll regret.

'Yeah, loads of them round here. I don't have a problem with them, of course, as long as they keep to themselves and don't impose their religious nonsense on anyone else. But they seem to be in control of everything.'

'Everything?' I nudge my chair forwards. 'Like what?'

'You seen all them Jewish shops on the high street?' James scowls. 'Selling kosher goods? Our butcher closed down but not theirs. And have you seen any Christmas decorations round here this year? No? Well, there you go, must be them stopping us from keeping our traditions.'

'I read that was local budget cuts.' I've seen several posts about this in the local Facebook group. 'And maybe the non-kosher butcher just couldn't get enough custom, with everyone buying their meat from the big supermarkets instead.'

'Yeah, well ... don't believe everything you read,' he mutters.

'Do you have Jewish neighbours now?'

'There's a few. As I said, no problem with them as long as they leave me alone.'

I suspect that's his attitude to people in general, especially if his idea of entertaining is sitting on a hard seat in a chilly room. But it's time to move swiftly on before he gets more agitated, the dog stirs and I don't get the information I'm after.

'The plaque on the fence ... did it go up before or after Terry died?'

He sniggers. 'It's only been there two weeks.'

'So you lied to me the other day? Are you sure?'

If this plaque wasn't put up before Terry died, like the others, why put it up now? I shiver as I realise what this may mean – that someone put it up just for me.

'Course I am. I may be getting on a bit but I'm not doolally. It appeared overnight last week. I prised it off and left it by the bins. Weren't easy, let me tell you. Just as well I have my tools.' He points at a crowbar propped up against the back door. 'Then the next day, it was back there in the same place.'

'Another plaque?'

'No ... the same one,' he says in an irritated tone. 'I should've smashed it up with that crowbar in the first place.'

'And you didn't see anyone?'

'No, didn't hear anyone either. Happened while I was sleeping, it did. Though my Rose always did say I'd sleep through the bombing of the Blitz if I had to.' He leans towards me, his sour breath wafting up my nostrils. 'So are you saying the person who killed my Terry is the same person who put up this plaque?'

'No idea. But could be.' I shuffle back in my chair and glance at the photo of Terry on the pinboard. 'Where was he that night ... the night Eve Lee died?'

'Can't remember, was years ago, but don't matter anyway. He said he didn't do it and I believed him.'

A gust of wind blows a handful of yellowing leaves through the open doorway. James bends down and picks them up. 'Police did too. They came round a few days later to check our cars, just to be sure, but none of them was damaged.'

He clenches his fist, the leaf fragments still inside, scrunching them up in his hand until they're as fine as grains of rice. 'And we hadn't taken them to any garage either.'

Looking at the radiator grille and car bumper in the garden, I figure it's easy to fix a car when you renovate them for a living. Sand down a bumper, smooth away a few scratches, give it a respray. Not hard to do, especially if you're a pro – and he clearly is, whatever he might say.

'What made the police look at *your* cars?'

'Someone said they saw my Terry in my Jag.'

'Do you know who?'

'No.' James stands up and walks over to the workbench. Drops the leaf debris on the surface and picks up the wrench in his right hand. 'But they were lying, they was.' He thumps the wrench against his left palm, reddening his skin. The dog opens its eyes and hoists itself up, wobbling on its legs.

I flinch, swallowing sharply. James doesn't strike me as a man who would think twice before hitting someone if he felt he'd been aggrieved, and I suspect he would relish the opportunity to avenge his son's death.

Terry Murdock liked his drink, was out that night, seen driving a car that fit the description, lived in the same road ... no wonder someone else thought he was to blame.

'So what happened the night Terry died?'

James puts the wrench down. Glances at the photo of his son. 'He was at The Wild Horseman till closing time – pub used to be up the road – then wandered off. No idea where, before you ask. He was old enough to do whatever he wanted. Was trying to save up enough money to move out and buy a place of his own.'

'What did he do ... for a job?'

'Worked for me, he did. I paid him a good wage, but he kept spending it on drink.'

I raise my eyebrows.

'Well, not that much, he weren't ... weren't an alkie,' James splutters. 'If you can't have fun when you're young ... He were a hard worker and a dab hand at bodywork.'

I gaze at the car bumper in the garden. 'So no one saw what happened that night? No witnesses?'

'None. Police knocked on the door to say my Terry'd been knocked over. Was early morning. Still don't know who did it. A neighbour thought they saw a large black estate car driving away, but it were never found. And whoever the bastard was, he never came forward.'

'Sounds a lot like what happened to Eve Lee.' Anger is again bubbling away inside me. 'No one found that dark blue Jag or knows who did that either. Coincidence?'

James tenses his hand into a fist and slams it down on the workbench. The stack of car manuals wobbles.

'We're done, we are.' His dog growls in agreement. 'You can show yourself out. I got things to do.'

I glance at the wrench that's a bit too close to his fist, and then at his irate eyes. Yes, it's time for me to leave.

CHAPTER THIRTY-FOUR

Rabbi Dov is sitting behind his desk reading through a hefty A4 document when I knock on his office door and peer round it. I'd called him first to check he was free for a chat, and waited until lunchtime to visit him so David couldn't complain that I was shirking my work duties – at least, not today.

'Good to see you, Shanna. Come in ... sit down.' I turn to close the door but the rabbi holds his palm up. 'It's fine to leave it open. It gets stuffy in here.'

I do as instructed, drop my rucksack on the floor and sit down on the chair in front of him.

'How can I help you on this fine Wednesday?' He places the document down on his desk and shoves it away from him, then takes his glasses off and sticks them in the breast pocket of his white shirt.

'I've been thinking about those plaques and the writing on them. There's a Jewish link, for sure, but I can't work out why.'

'Have you been to the police?'

I flex my fingers. 'Not yet.'

He raises his eyebrows, followed by a slight frown. 'Why do I suspect you're not going to?'

I shift in my seat. This 'lying to a rabbi' isn't coming easily to me at all. 'Are you going to if I don't?' Figure it's always worth throwing a question back when you don't have an answer.

He leans against the back of his chair, steeples his fingers together to form a bridge and presses them towards his mouth. Stares me in the eyes. 'I trust you to make the right call so I'm leaving it with you. In fact, you should also report it to the CST.'

'CST?'

'Community Security Trust. It's a Jewish security organisation monitoring antisemitism.' He opens his desk drawer, pulls out a business card and hands it to me. 'Shanna, they should be told so they can keep an eye on things round here, just in case there *is* a Jewish link.'

I look down at the card in my hand. COMMUNITY SECURITY TRUST is printed in blue lettering at the top with a list of contact numbers below it. I slip the card into the front pocket of my rucksack and glance at the bookshelves beside me, the spines of prayer books and Jewish law tomes and Jewish encyclopaedias. A large Hebrew calendar with all of the festival dates highlighted in red is sellotaped to the wall. Here in this office is everything I could possibly want to know about Judaism, I figure, if I decide to find out more about my heritage. But right now, I can only focus on finding who put up these plaques – and why.

REPENT BEFORE YOU DIE is probably the best place to start.

I look across the table at the rabbi. 'What's the Jewish stance on repentance and forgiveness after killing someone?'

'Intention is a major factor there.' Rabbi Dov pulls a chunky brown leather book off the shelf next to him. 'It's not God's role to forgive what man has done to man. It's for that person to find their own way, beg for forgiveness. You can't repair what damage has been done, and you can't erase the past.'

'So what can they do? Or rather, what *should* they do?'

The rabbi pulls his glasses out of his shirt pocket and places them, still folded, on his desk. 'Change their future. Determine to be a different person, a better one.'

'And the Jewish stance on revenge?' I reach down, take my notepad and pen out from my rucksack and rest them on my lap.

'How long have you got?' Rabbi Dov smiles at me. 'I expect you've heard the phrase "an eye for an eye"?'

I nod. 'I remember that from Sunday school, along with "two wrongs don't make a right", but that's about it. I wasn't that interested, to be honest.' Maybe I should have taken more notice, I realise now, rather than scowl at the back of the classroom, wishing I was somewhere else instead.

'Well in Judaism we don't believe in it,' Rabbi Dov continues. 'Never take a life to replace a life. We're not God. It's not our place to decide who dies and when.' He opens up the leather tome and turns to a page near the back. Picks up his glasses and puts them on. 'Although ... have you heard of the Redeemer of Blood?'

I shake my head.

'An ancient concept from biblical times. *Go'el ha-dam*. If someone killed someone through negligence or intent, a relative – a kinsman – of the victim had the right to take revenge.'

I lean forwards, open up my notepad and grasp my pen tightly in my right hand.

'In biblical times, anyone who had committed murder with intent would typically have a trial first,' the rabbi continues. 'They would face the court's justice. Our Torah created the rules of law.'

'And if someone was found guilty?'

'They were sentenced to death, to be carried out by the court executioner.' He looks down at the book. Flips the page over.

'And if not?' I scribble down some notes, thinking of Gina Alders and Charlotte Newman. What if Gina had pushed Charlotte without meaning to while she was trying to save her? 'I mean, if they killed someone accidentally with no intention, no negligence? Manslaughter, we'd call it now.'

'Then they were at risk from this blood-redeemer, this *go'el ha-dam*, who had the divine right to avenge the wrong in a way that society and the courts couldn't. In fact, six cities were created out of necessity for this doomed person to flee to for protection.'

'So why was this blood-redeemer permitted to take a life but no one else could, even in the case of murder? If it's so wrong to murder, I mean.' I stare at my notes. *Go'el ha-dam.* Could this be it – a blood-redeemer taking revenge, thinking they're doing God's will?

'Judaism doesn't believe in revenge, but it does believe in justice.' Rabbi Dov looks down at his leather-covered book. 'The blood-redeemer in this sense represented the quest to have a just world. But without this divine appointment, we would consider the same act to be wanton bloodshed and not permitted.'

Surely this killer can't believe they're the blood-redeemer. 'And now? Does the concept of the blood-redeemer exist?'

The rabbi shakes his head. 'No, we would need a Jewish court system that has the ability to give the death penalty to have the blood-redeemer and,' he chuckles softly, 'obviously we don't.'

'But what about after the Holocaust? You're saying revenge killings wouldn't have been permitted under Jewish law?'

Rabbi Dov shuts his book. 'Exactly that. The world needed warriors to take up the cause but to seek justice, not revenge. Think of Simon Wiesenthal, often called the Nazi hunter. For decades he made sure Nazi war criminals were brought to justice, that they were held accountable for their crimes. But through the courts, not through more killing.'

'But what about the *Nokmim*? It doesn't sound like they believed in that approach?'

'Ah, well...' He grabs an A4 pad of lined paper from a shelf behind him. 'I've been doing some reading since we met last.' He opens the pad flat on the table, revealing a page of neat writing. 'The *Nokmim* wanted justice too but emotions were high at that time, as you'd expect. So they took revenge on the Nazis for spilling Jewish blood. But it wasn't *all* about justice for them.'

'Really? I assumed it was.'

'No, the *Nokmim* wanted to make a stand.' Rabbi Dov reads from his A4 pad: '"They wanted to send a message not to mess with the Jews and that they wouldn't stand by and let the Holocaust happen again."'

'So what did they actually do? The *Nokmim*, I mean.'

'Well, first of all, they tried to poison the water supply in Nuremberg, but the authorities discovered their plans and the plot was abandoned.'

'I assume they didn't give up.'

'Not at all. In fact, it made them even more determined. Some of them managed to get jobs in bakeries near an Allied prisoner of war camp, planning to poison the bread supply and kill all the German inmates.'

'And did they?'

'Well, they *did* try but it wasn't successful. In fact, quite a few of the inmates became very sick but – *Baruch HaShem* – no one actually died.'

I detect a sparkle of relief in his eyes. 'You make that sound like a good thing.'

'As I've already said, we don't believe in revenge in Judaism, and nor did most Holocaust survivors. After the war, they wanted to rebuild their lives, find lost family members if they could and settle somewhere they could feel safe.'

He puts the leather-covered book back on the shelf beside him, slotting it carefully into place.

'You have many survivors in Hillsbury?'

'Unfortunately not anymore.' He shakes his head slowly. 'We've lost most of them over the years, and those who are still with us are very elderly now ... In fact, soon there will be none left at all.'

I think back to the notes I've received, and the two messages to my phone. There's still another avenue to explore.

'Does the name Renvok mean anything to you?'

'How do you spell that?'

'Here.' I write the word down in my notepad in large capital letters so he doesn't have to decipher my messy writing, turning it round so he can see it.

The rabbi traces the letters with his right index finger while humming quietly to himself. After a while, he looks up and shakes his head. 'No, it doesn't look familiar. Should it?'

'I don't know. Someone's been sending me messages using this name, trying to warn me off the story, so it *must* mean something to someone.'

Rabbi Dov stares at the word again. 'Hold on.' He picks

up a blue biro from his desk, scribbles down a few letters followed by combinations of letters, then dramatically slams his biro down on the paper. 'Bingo.' His eyes light up. 'I thought it might be an anagram but it's not. It's just spelt backwards ... Kovner.'

'What's Kovner?'

'Not what, but who.' He turns back a couple of pages in his A4 pad. 'Abba Kovner was the Jewish resistance fighter who started the *Nokmim*. The partisan who set it all off.'

I lean forwards, feeling my veins surge with excitement.

'What can you tell me about him?'

'Hold on.' The rabbi swivels round to his computer, opens up the internet browser and types a few words on the keyboard. 'He was a leader of the resistance and urged the Vilna Ghetto to revolt. Here you go.' He turns the screen towards me. 'Abba Kovner said, "We will not be led like sheep to the slaughter." This became the motto of the United Partisan Organisation he helped form.'

I try to imagine it – not just being persecuted for their religion but dying for it too. All those Jews sent or led to their deaths, and those who weren't, wanting to fight against it. Not willing to give in. What courage and determination they must have had. What strength this Kovner must have had.

'Could Kovner be sending me these messages?'

Rabbi Dov shakes his head. 'I hope not. He died over thirty years ago.'

'Okay...' – I tap my fingers on the desk – '...so if Kovner's dead, what about his family? Children? Grandchildren? Other members of the *Nokmim*?'

Rabbi Dov glances back at his computer screen. After a few seconds, he shakes his head again. 'It's unlikely to be someone from his family. He moved to Israel after the war and remained there, although it's possible that members of his family came back here. It looks as though most of the other *Nokmim* members settled in Israel as well.'

'But not all of them?'

'I have no idea.' He shrugs. 'No one knew exactly who was part of the *Nokmim* – it was all very hush-hush. Not all of them were Holocaust survivors, by the way. Some were from the Jewish Brigade, part of the British army. But if Kovner's contemporaries were still alive, they would be very elderly now.' He chuckles. 'In fact, I can't see them being physically able to kill anyone.'

'But they may have had families.' I drum my pen against the desk. 'Do you have a list of local survivors and their relatives?'

'The best person to speak to is Valerie.' The rabbi takes off his glasses, folds them and places them in his shirt pocket. 'Valerie Lee. Maybe she can put people in touch with you ... if they're interested ... rather than the other way round. She does a lot of work with local schools.' He stares at me, rubs his forehead and swallows. 'And your own journey? The reason you're here in Hillsbury. Have you made any progress?'

I flinch. 'Not yet.'

So far I've put off doing any research into my mother's family. That fine line between knowing too little and knowing too much. What will I find? Who will I find? There's so much Dad hasn't told me. What if I still *do* have family here but they didn't want me then? Maybe I'll find out that's why he took me away. And what if they don't want me now?

'You *will* do when you're ready; when the time is right.' Rabbi Dov smiles. 'Every soul comes into this world with a mission, Shanna, and it's God's job to help that soul fulfil that mission.' He steeples his fingers. 'Perhaps now you're just beginning to understand what your soul's mission might be. That your mission involves Hillsbury, which is why you're here, right now.'

Trickles of guilt pervade my pores as I think back to that night in Brussels. What if somehow the rabbi knows? What if he knows more about my recent past than he's letting on?

That reminds me...

I open up the photo app on my mobile. 'Can you tell me what this says?' I scroll down until I reach the photo I took in the Lees' house, of the Hebrew writing inside that children's encyclopaedia.

The rabbi takes out his glasses, puts them on, then squints at my phone screen. 'Where did you find this? Is it to do with the plaques?'

'I just found it in a book ... in the apartment I'm renting.' I feel myself flushing. 'Nothing to do with the plaques at all. Just my natural inquisitive self.'

He hands my mobile back to me. 'It's a popular Jewish name, the name of my youngest.' He points at a photo in a wooden frame on the window ledge behind him, of a pretty blonde-haired baby. 'Shoshana, meaning rose.'

A bitter taste rises in my throat.

CHAPTER THIRTY-FIVE

A square yellow Post-it note is stuck to my computer when I get back to the office. Bang in the middle of the screen so I can't miss it. The room stinks of dog.

Gone to bank. Back at 5. Be here.

It's brief and to the point, even by David's standards. Has Andy discovered where I work and been in touch with him? Has he told more of his lies? Okay, this isn't the best job in the world, far from it, but I can't afford to lose it right now. I shake off the shroud of dread clinging to my shoulders.

The next issue will be Holocaust themed, to tie in with Holocaust Memorial Day at the end of January, and will also cover this dog rescue centre fundraiser he mentioned the other day. He's emailed a list of topics, tasks and demands and left some further instructions on my desk. At least this will be relevant to my research.

I grab the black filing box, the one I nearly used to bash David's head in, off the shelf by the door. Inside are old *Hillsbury Living* articles: interviews with Holocaust survivors, coverage of Holocaust Remembrance Day activities at the synagogue ... I make notes of names and places and dates in messy handwriting scrawled all over my notepad page.

I think over my conversation with the rabbi. What Kovner and the *Nokmim* did, or tried to do, taking revenge for the millions of Jews who died ... Was it that simple? *Is* revenge that simple? What kind of person would do this? A brave one? A foolish one? One with nothing to lose?

I conduct a Google search for Abba Kovner. Find more news stories about the *Nokmim* and scroll down each one. After the war, it was estimated that over thirteen million West German men were eligible for arrest but only 300 Nazis paid the price, with many of the guilty left unpunished. The *Nokmim* was created in Bucharest in 1945. The details vary in each report but I gradually get the gist of it. Before the large-scale operations involving the poisoning of water and bread, the *Nokmim* targeted individuals – punishing former Nazis who had eluded justice due to a lack of evidence.

The more I read, the more my gut churns. Deaths caused by faulty car brakes, hangings portrayed as suicides and one German ex-officer dying in hospital after minor surgery, with kerosene found in his blood. All revenge killings, all sounding so familiar – too familiar.

At the bottom of the black box file, I find some old cassette tapes, labelled neatly in block capitals with names and dates. There's also an old white Sony Walkman, yellowing on top and battered around the edges. I check there are batteries inside, then shove one of the cassettes into the Walkman and shut the lid. Grab my headphones from my bag, plug them in and press the *Play* button.

The machine whirrs but the tape doesn't move. I press *Stop*, open the hatch and pull the cassette out. Insert another. Press *Play* and wait. This tape scrolls forwards and I hear faint voices in my ear. I make a note of the name and date on the cassette label.

Miriam. 12 December 1988.

I boost up the volume until I can hear the voices clearly, almost as if they're in the room beside me.

'Can you remember arriving at Birkenau?' A woman's voice. Squeaky and high-pitched, as if she'd been on too much helium.

'I will never forget.' An elderly voice. Female. Croaky and frail. Hint of a Polish accent. 'I wish I could but it is branded in my memory forever. I remember the acrid smell of burning flesh, stinging my nostrils as we stepped off the train. The taste of burning ashes hovering in the air, souring my tongue.' Silence, then a faint sob. 'I remember it as if it were yesterday.'

I press *Pause*. Flick through the back issues of *Hillsbury Times* until I come across the February 1989 issue, an interview with Miriam Steinberg, Holocaust survivor. The article was published two months after the date on the cassette, so maybe these tapes were created by previous editors of the magazine during their research. Could one of them be taking revenge after hearing these harrowing stories?

I press *Play* again.

'What happened after you arrived?'

'We lined up. They shaved off my long blonde curls. Forced me to remove my clothes. Then they tattooed this number on my arm.'

Eventually the recording crackles and Miriam's voice fades away. I press *Stop*. Pull out another cassette from the box file.

Rifka. 20 October 2000. I look through the stack of magazines to find an article about her. I'd expect it to be in the December 2000 issue, two months after the date on the cassette, but it's not there.

'Why is it so important that you keep talking about the Holocaust?' A man's voice, deep and slow.

'My mother made me promise that if I survived, I would make sure the world...' Another woman's voice. A strong German accent, her voice wavering as she speaks with faltering English.

'What would you make sure?' The recording crackles.

'That the world remembered those Jews murdered by the Nazis.'

'Were you afraid when the Nazis came?' The interviewer speaks gently, quietly.

'Not until...' Rifka pauses. I hear tapping, followed by the faint sound of a nose being blown. 'I could tell you so many stories, but this one ... this one was the start of them all.' She pauses again. 'When the soldiers came, my mother made me hide in our barn ... under the hay ... but I was a rebellious child. I had chutzpah as they used to say, so I raised the hatch ... and watched. I watched as the soldier lifted his rifle, aimed it at my mother and shot her ... in the back of the head. I watched her blood spill ... out on the ground.'

'Did you cry out?' The interviewer's voice is fading so I turn up the volume.

'I wanted to, but how could I? I knew if I did, they would come for me. I closed the hatch and buried myself in a mound of hay ... for hours, maybe even days ... until I heard my father call my name. I remembered that promise to my mother ... all my life ... to stay alive and tell the world. I have not let her down.'

'Could you ever forgive them?'

'Never can I forgive.' Rifka's voice rises. 'How can you

forgive the unforgivable? How can I look at the past and say I understand why?'

'Why what?'

'Why they murdered so many innocents. All these years on, I can still hear my mother's scream. I still see her blood. And I still feel my silent sobs.'

'Would you consider taking revenge?'

I lean towards the cassette player. Turn the volume up to maximum. The recording crackles again and I hope it doesn't fail ... not now.

'If the soldiers were here ... in front of me ... if someone handed me a gun ... I would shoot every one of them ... Does that answer your question?'

I wonder if Rifka had family in Hillsbury. Would they want to follow her last wishes, avenging murders from the past, finding people who've murdered Jews? There's no surname on the cassette box and I didn't hear one at the start of the recording. Maybe David will know.

When the tape ends, I play another tape, then another. Leaning back in my chair, I shut my eyes until I can feel the tears running down my cheeks and my eyes stinging with sorrow.

'People can never be replaced.' Isaac, an elderly man with a strong Polish accent. 'There vill always be a hole in my heart. My little sister was murdered in the woods near our shtetl. But my granddaughter fills the gap somehow – my daughter named her after my sister, so she vill never be forgotten.'

Yet another survivor. 'I owe it ... to my family ... to my mother ... to talk of what happened.' This woman sounds frail, taking long pauses after every few words as if she's close to her last breath. I realise it's Rifka again, just five years later, her health now in serious decline. 'I owe it to myself ... my children ... my grandchildren ... and to future generations ... to make sure it cannot ... and will not ... happen again.'

'I was born a Jew; I knew I would die a Jew.' Polish accent – Isaac again, maybe. The cassette tape label is torn and the recording is old and scratchy and well-worn so it's hard to tell. 'The Nazis could not take that from me. I can and never vill forgive them for what they did.'

The front door rattles. The letterbox snaps. I leave the tape running, rush down the stairs two at a time, and open the outside door. Two puddles of sleet shimmer at me from the mat like marshmallow droppings. I step forwards, peer to the left then the right. Screw up my eyes into the distance. No signs of life.

An envelope has been stuffed through the letterbox. My name, typed in black, on the front. No stamp.

As I pull it out, I think back to all of the notes I've received. Three envelopes, all hand-delivered: two to the office; one to the apartment block. So whoever it is knows where I work and where I live.

Back at my desk, my hand shakes with a mixture of excitement and dread as my fingers scramble to open the envelope flap. The cassette tape has ended and now the room seems eerily silent, a sense of anticipation in the air.

I pull out another typed note, just as I expect, but unlike the others this time there's a full address: 125 Hillsbury High Road. That's right near the kosher bakery. Saves me the trouble of looking for it, for sure, but I wonder why they've suddenly changed the rules of the game, speeding up my search.

I glance at the pile of magazines on my desk, the list of work on my notepad, my computer screen blinking at me, urging me to settle down. Then I stare at the note in my hand. It's just a ten-minute walk up the road; David won't be here until five and it's currently only three.

My thoughts swing one way then another, as if clinging to a pendulum. *Do I? Don't I? Do I? Don't I?* As if I really have a choice.

I can't leave this. Not now. Not ever, maybe.

I need to find this next plaque.

CHAPTER THIRTY-SIX

The plaque is secured to the side of Ming Palace, the local Chinese restaurant, opposite the entrance to the apartments above Hillsbury Pharmacy. It's down a narrow pathway, steep and slippery, with icy patches down the centre and mounds of greying slush piled up against the sides. A cluster of green, brown and black wheelie bins crowd the bottom of the slope in front of two closed filthy white garage doors.

I hold my palms flat against the jagged brickwork, clinging like Spiderman to a skyscraper, and inch my way down until I reach the plaque. My tatty trainers have lost their grip so I'm sliding with every step. I lean against the wall to keep myself steady while I take some photos with my phone.

Yet again, the plaque is black and red with a slightly mottled glaze. And yet again someone has tried to hide it. This one's been here for a while, judging by the surface build-up of dirt and grime, unlike the spanking-new one put up for Terry Murdock. Someone has splashed the plaque with black paint to hide the raised red words, but I can still see a faint outline so I trace each letter with my finger.

BILLY PEARSON
KILLED A CUSTOMER
FROM THESE PREMISES
REPENT BEFORE YOU DIE
OR MAY YOU NEVER R.I.P.
APRIL 2001

As I read it for a second time, questions buzz about in my head like fireflies around a streetlight. Who can be sending me on this quest? Someone who knows all these plaques exist, for sure, but do they also know the truth behind them?

Each plaque has been strategically placed out in the open yet obscured from view: Peter Stevens, under brambles at the side of his house; Gina Alders, on a tall lamp post where she cycled regularly; Terry Murdock, on a fence just around a bend near his home; and now this one, Billy Pearson, down a side alley. Why would it be here, in this exact spot? Someone who worked in the restaurant, maybe, who was always putting out the rubbish? Mark and Robert both said that someone warned the recipients about the plaques, giving them around six months' notice. Why? To give them a chance to make amends, I've assumed. *Own up or you'll pay.* But what if the intention was to also make sure they saw the plaque and lived with the guilt for a while?

I pull out my phone to take some photos, and then retrieve my notepad and pen. As I copy down the words, I wonder how Billy Pearson killed a customer. Did he stab them with a chopstick in an argument over chow mein? Did he poison them with contaminated pork or magic mushrooms? Whatever it was, I suspect it's not as straightforward as it sounds – not if his name is on one of these plaques.

I think back to the revenge killings by the *Nokmim* – hit-and-run, hanging, car accident, poisoning ... Could Hillsbury's vigilante assassin be following in their footsteps?

I stagger back up the path, stepping carefully over the icy patches, yet again clinging to the wall to keep my balance. Ming Palace opens for dinner at six o'clock according to a wooden sign in the window just above their impressive five-star hygiene rating.

I check my watch. It's only three-thirty. Well ... I don't like waiting.

I rap my fist against the main restaurant door. The lights are on inside. On the third rap, I hear the sound of a key turning in a lock. A Chinese woman opens the door. She's holding a mop in one hand. There's a full red bucket of soapy water behind her, foam bubbling on the surface. The chemical stench of bleach clears my sinuses as I peer past her into the restaurant, noting the glistening tables and floor.

'Can I help you?' The woman speaks with a strong Chinese accent.

'Know anything about that plaque?' I point down the pathway towards the garages below.

'Plaque?'

'Here, I'll show you.' I gesture for her to follow me.

She props her mop up against the door, drizzling soapy suds along the wooden flooring. Dries her hands on her white long-sleeved T-shirt, pushes two wayward strands of shiny black hair off her cheeks and follows me down the path. She pads gingerly over the icy pavement, sliding around more than I do. I look down at her feet and shiver, realising she's wearing flimsy grey Converse with no grip at all.

I point out the plaque when we reach it.

She peers forwards. Shakes her head. 'Know nothing, sorry.'

'It's been here since 2001 so it's not new.'

She shakes her head again. 'Was Jewish owner then. Not us.'

'Would anyone else know?'

She shivers and wraps her arms around her. Pangs of guilt prod me for bringing her out into the cold. 'Maybe my husband.' She begins to inch her way back up the path. 'He is busy now but if you come back tonight you can ask.'

When we reach the restaurant, she rushes inside and bangs the door shut without a goodbye. I hear a key turn in a lock. Guess she's taking no chances, not wanting to get involved. These plaques are none of my business either. Yet I know it's far too late for me. Someone has sucked me into this quagmire of intrigue and I couldn't claw my way out now if I tried.

I'm determined to find out the history of this plaque, so I wander three shops along to Cohen's Bakery and ask to speak to the owner. A man with a black-and-white crocheted skullcap on his head confirms that Ming's Palace was once a kosher restaurant, but he can't remember who owned it at the time. Suggests I search online. I buy myself a bagel filled with a thick layer of cream cheese and sliced tomato and head back to the office for a very late lunch.

BACK AT MY LAPTOP, I search for kosher restaurant + Hillsbury + death and find a short newspaper article in a February 2001 edition of *The Hillsbury Times*. In a Persian restaurant called Ko-Sha on Hillsbury High Road, a customer had a severe allergic reaction and died at the scene. None of the staff accepted responsibility but the owner,

Tony Mayer, was quoted as 'being devastated'. A full investigation was taking place. No name; no other details. The death fits the time frame but I have a niggling feeling that it doesn't quite fit the pattern. Would someone have deliberately triggered that allergic reaction? More importantly, there's no mention of Billy Pearson.

My phone rings and I answer it. It's Andy. I shout at him to leave me alone. He shouts back, telling me he wants the photos and he'll be coming to get them very soon. I hear traffic in the background and wonder if he's still in Hillsbury, still watching me.

My mouth feels parched. I'm craving a *real* drink but the vodka bottle in my desk drawer won't aid my concentration. I wander over to the kettle and flick down the switch. Unscrew the lid of the coffee jar, grab a teaspoon from the wooden cutlery rack and dump two spoonfuls of coffee into a purple mug.

The downstairs door creaks, footsteps stomp up the stairs and a few seconds later David saunters into the office with a laptop bag under his arm.

'Slacking on the job?' He points at my coffee mug. 'I don't expect you to spend all day eating and drinking. This isn't a bleeding cafe, you know.' He points at the half-eaten bagel on my desk. 'I hope you clear up the crumbs as the last thing I need is an infestation of rats.'

I count silently in my head before I respond. He's the only rat I've seen in this office. 'I'm entitled to a lunch break.'

'You are, you're right, but you seem to have *far* too many breaks. And it's not even lunchtime – it's five o'clock. You think I haven't noticed you're never here when I call or come by? Do you spend *any* time in this office at all?'

I'm not really cut out for a full-time office job but I'm not going to tell him that … at least, not yet.

'How did the bank appointment go?' I pour boiling water into my mug and watch granules of coffee rise to the surface then sink back down again. I'm feeling generous, so add, 'Want one?'

'No, I don't ... and it's none of your bleeding business,' David snaps back. 'So where are you up to with this next issue? Have you found a Holocaust survivor yet?'

I grab my mug and take it back to my desk. 'I'm working on it.' I sit down. 'You only told me about it this morning. Rabbi Dov at Hillsbury Synagogue suggested I speak to Valerie Lee. You know her?'

David narrows his eyes. 'Any relative of Harry? He's a local GP.'

'Yes, his wife.' My tummy rumbles. I glance at the rest of my lunch. 'Did you want to speak to me about something? You left a note to—'

'It can wait. I have another meeting.' He grabs some papers from under his desk and a bulging red folder from the ledge near the door. 'I'll be back on Monday morning. Make sure you're here...' – he jerks his head towards the bagel – '...and make sure you're working, not eating.'

He exits the room, leaving a faint whiff of nicotine in the air. The door below slams and I'm alone again. I look at my pile of work.

Fuck this.

He wants me to find a Holocaust survivor? Well, that can be easily arranged ... just not from my desk.

TWENTY MINUTES LATER, I'm sitting at a small table at the back of the kosher café, facing the door. I take out my phone and call Valerie. No answer so I text, asking if she's free for a chat. I don't tell her what I want – just where I am.

Soon after, the café door slams open. A burst of icy air rushes inside, rippling the wooden shutters, followed by Valerie, with her coat hood pulled over her head, the fake fur edging sprinkled with sleet like a bad case of dandruff.

She spies me at the back and makes her way towards me until she stands shivering by my table, her hands trembling from the cold. 'It's freezing out there – stupidly forgot my gloves.' She peels off her coat and drapes it over the back of the white chair. Her cheeks are flushed like someone's slapped her, leaving two red flares against her pale skin.

'I saw your message.' She rubs her hands together to warm them up as she sits down. Pushes up the cuff of her blouse sleeve and looks at her watch. 'I only have twenty minutes, sorry. I help the teachers clear up at the shul nursery in the afternoons. I've been doing that ever since Susan was...' – she picks up the menu and opens it – '...was small.'

The waitress totters over to us, balancing on black heels like a circus stilt act. 'Ready to order?'

'What're you drinking? It's on me.' I order a hot chocolate and apple crumble.

'Just a peppermint tea, please.' Valerie glances up at the waitress. 'Fresh leaves, if you've got them.'

'Nothing to eat?' The waitress taps her pen against her notepad.

Valerie shakes her head. 'Not for me.'

We both watch the waitress head off to the kitchen with our order. 'So what did you want to discuss? Your message was very vague.'

'I need to speak to a Holocaust survivor for my next *Hillsbury Living* article. Can you help?'

'We don't have many left in the community. Miriam, Solomon and Jakob were some of the last ones. I'll try to find you someone though. How quickly do you need to speak to them?'

'In the next week or so. I could always speak to a family member instead and write the article from a different angle.'

The waitress arrives with our order on a wooden tray. My hot chocolate fills a tall glass topped with a thick layer of whipped cream and a sprinkling of chocolate flakes. Valerie's glass matches mine but contains fresh mint leaves swirling around in hot water like newly hatched tadpoles. The apple crumble sits in a small ramekin on a large square white plate, with a dollop of vanilla ice cream on the side, gradually melting in the heat of the restaurant's strip lighting.

'I'm not sure I should give you the list.' She stirs her tea with the long metal spoon. The tea-leaf-tadpoles race around in the water. 'But I'll ... I'll ask a couple of people to get in touch with you instead. That may be better.' She nods rapidly. 'I assume this is for the next issue?'

'Yes, it is. Though there's one more thing. I forgot to ask you the other day: does the name Eve Lee sound familiar?'

Valerie picks up her glass, her pale hands still shaking from the cold. 'No, I don't know her. Should I?'

'She died a long time ago. I'm trying to find her daughter.' I scroll down the photos on my phone and show her the image of the newspaper article. 'I thought she may be a relative of Harry's. A cousin, maybe?'

'No ... definitely not a cousin. He only has two and I've met them both.'

'I guess Lee's a common name.'

She takes another sip of her drink. 'I'll ask him tonight and get back to you.'

We both look up at the sound of loud voices at the front of the café. The waitress is directing three young women to the table near ours. They're in their mid-twenties, I reckon, all wearing knee-length skirts, thick tights and ankle boots.

Two of them have a hairstyle similar to Tova's with a flick at the base. I wonder if they're wearing wigs that religious Jewish women often wear to cover their hair. I saw quite a few women wearing them in Brussels.

The fourth woman wears a purple headscarf, dark brown curly fringe peeking out at the front. She recognises Valerie and waves at her. Valerie gives her a hesitant smile. When headscarf woman passes our table, she leans forwards and envelops Valerie in a warm hug. I guess she must be a similar age to Susan.

Valerie looks at her watch and turns back to me. 'I'm so sorry, Shanna, I'm going to have to go or I'll be late for work. Sorry I can't chat for longer.'

She grabs her coat, bag and umbrella. Glances behind her when she reaches the door. She pauses, gives me a nervous smile and walks briskly into the sleety rain.

Fifteen minutes later, my phone buzzes. I open it to find a list of names and phone numbers and a brief message from Valerie.

This is what you need. Keep it quiet. You didn't get it from me.

CHAPTER THIRTY-SEVEN

aturday afternoon, I'm sitting on the floor in my living room, leaning against the sofa. I've spent the last few days at work, leaving little time for anything else, and now I'm desperate to get back to my search. I scribble names and dates on small square Post-it notes and line them up on the rug like a pink, green and yellow patchwork quilt. Add more dates, names, ages and locations. Examine them, contemplate, trying to connect together all the facts and read between the lines like a Bletchley codebreaker.

A buzz on the entry phone disturbs me. I get up, press the speaker button and ask who it is. No answer. I'd better go down to check before I buzz them in. Since Hetty died, we've had no unofficial neighbourhood watch at the block.

I grab my black jumper from the sofa, pull it on over my head and drag my arms through the sleeves. I've been sitting in a white ribbed vest top with the heating turned up high, pretending this mustard-coloured rug is a sandy beach and the blue walls are my sea view. I didn't expect to miss travelling so much. Maybe it's the cold weather or being stuck in one place for so long. Being indoors too frequently. Or not appreciating life's pleasures until they're gone.

Downstairs, I find a white envelope sticking out through the flap in the outer door. It's addressed to me, with smudges of ink framing each letter like a halo.

I rip the envelope open straightaway, rather than wait until I get upstairs. Pull out a typed note as expected.

Go to 22 Cavendish Road. Find the plaque.

Another full address. I look up Cavendish Road on Google Maps and discover it's near the cemetery. Cavernous houses with large gardens. A good neighbourhood, it seems.

I arrive there around six. A flurry of icy white flakes swirls in the evening sky like polystyrene balls in a shaken snow globe.

I find the plaque on the front gate of a large semi-detached house. It's glazed in black and red like the others, but seems far more slapdash, with bubbling around its edges and the red lettering slightly smeared.

Once I read the words, I know exactly who lives in this house.

EDDIE AND GARY FORRESTER

BEAT A BOY TO DEATH

REPENT BEFORE YOU DIE

OR MAY YOU NEVER R.I.P.

DECEMBER 2019

I pull my phone out of my coat pocket and do a quick Google search, looking for news stories in the past few weeks. Zac Wagner, the boy who was beaten in the park, died three days ago. The perpetrators still haven't been identified. But someone – the person who put up this plaque – must suspect these two youths.

I take a photo, then pocket my mobile as the snow flurries begin to escalate into a blizzard. Pull my hood over my head. The front door of the house opens and a blonde woman strolls out. Stands in the porch.

'You,' she hollers. Her loud, screechy voice contrasts with her neat petite frame, clad in a smart lavender-coloured shirt and shiny black trousers. 'Yes, you,' she shouts again, fixing her beady eyes on me. 'What do you know about this?' She jabs her index finger towards the plaque, gold polish glistening on her well-manicured nail. Her hand shakes with fury.

'Nothing. Just noticed it.'

She glares at me. 'What's your name?'

'Sorry?' I wipe icy snow crystals off my cheeks. 'My name? Why?'

'Well, you're standing outside my house and gawping at this plaque, so I assume you must know something about it.' She looks up and down the street, then back at me. 'I can't see anyone else here, can you?' She wrinkles her pointy nose as if there's an unpleasant odour in the air. 'Are you one of those effing press?'

Can't see the point in lying. 'Sure. Shanna Regan from *Hillsbury Times*.'

'Mum,' whines a tall shadow behind her, 'why can't Dad get it taken away?'

A teenage boy peers over her shoulder, rubbing his eyes with the back of his hand as if he's just woken from a long sleep. Standing behind his mother, Gary Forrester looks like he's sprouted upwards since I saw him last. Longer and lankier in the body, thinner in the face, yet somehow he also looks younger. His white T-shirt hangs awkwardly as if he's yet to fill it. His voice isn't the voice of the boy I heard in the park or near the bridge – no gangster tones now. His eyes flicker in my direction, then widen with fright.

I give him the broadest smile I can muster under my current circumstances – cold, snowy and bedraggled.

He gulps, his prominent Adam's apple rising in his throat.

'He's sorting it, Gary. Get back inside.' His mother grabs his arm and shoves him through the doorway, the way people stuff coats into a hall cupboard. 'Tell your dad the press is here already. That's all he needs.' She grimaces and turns back to me. 'You keep out of it. Shitty press, always sticking their noses in. Don't you know who my husband is?'

'Nope, who is he?'

She exhales deeply, with puffs of steam rising in the air, like a dragon about to spurt fire. 'No one. Keep your nose out of it. And if we see anything in the papers, we'll sue your shitty arse off.'

'I heard your sons chased a Jewish woman in the park.' I can't help myself. 'Then lynched a young boy to death.'

The woman mumbles something.

'Sorry, I didn't quite hear you.'

'No comment.' She bangs her front door shut.

Of course I heard exactly what she said: 'Those fucking Jews probably deserved it.' I suspect Eddie and Gary learnt their antisemitic views at home.

When I reach the pavement, a muscle twitches at the back of my neck. I turn around and glance back at the house. A pale net curtain quivers in an upstairs window, a shock of blond hair behind it, a face peering out towards me.

CHAPTER THIRTY-EIGHT

Two teenagers may die but I could stop it. Two teenagers may die but I could stop it.

This mantra hums in my head, giving me a sense of urgency while I'm sitting cross-legged on the floor, Carrie Underwood's 'Love Wins' playing in the background.

Eddie and Gary Forrester called Valerie names and tried to hurt her, then targeted their threats towards me. Yet they still don't deserve to die. No one should have the power to take a life in revenge.

I pick up the open bottle of Smirnoff from my lap and stare at the names scribbled on the Post-it notes in front of me.

Ruth and Peter Stevens. One swig of vodka.

Charlotte Newman and Gina Alders. Another swig.

Eve Lee and Terry Murdock. And another.

Billy Pearson alongside a question mark, a name I don't yet know. One more swig for luck.

I screw the cap back on the vodka bottle. Prop it upright

against the sofa behind me so I can write three more names on a pale green Post-it.

Valerie Lee and Eddie and Gary Forrester.

Ironically, these two boys are the reason I have the list in the first place, the reason I met Valerie in the park and discovered the Stevens plaque. What's the connection? What, or who, ties all these names together? How can I find this missing link? Who could, in theory, know what happened in the park that day – that those two teenagers chased Valerie and called her names?

My skin crawls as I think of their words. *Pig. Bacon butty. Jewish bitch.* Did the same person also witness the attack on Zac Wagner – assuming, of course, that those Forrester brothers are to blame?

I pick up my notepad and scribble down a list of people who know I'm investigating local plaques or what happened in the park.

Valerie and Harry, though Valerie never told him about the boys.

Mark, but I gave him no descriptions and didn't yet know the boys' names.

David, who told me to focus on my work instead, real plaques not fake ones.

Zahra, who knows about my interest in the Stevens plaque.

Rabbi Dov and Tova, with links to the Jewish community.

I pause, lean back against the sofa. Shake my head in despair as I realise there are more.

The woman in the library.

The woman in Taylor's Newsagent.

Ray, the potter.

There's everyone in the park that day who saw the

Forrester boys chasing Valerie across the grass. That young man with the baseball cap. The young mother at the swings.

And then there's Max, who chased off the teenage thugs at the clearing. The school receptionist, who seemed to know more than she was letting on. And anyone Valerie's told, despite her insistence that I keep it to myself. I know little about her, her friends, the people she mixes with. Valerie could have confided in anyone ... at synagogue, the nursery ... And what about Susan, living away from home? She must have friends here in Hillsbury – that young woman in the café, maybe? It could be any of them.

I think of the *Nokmim* and the families of these local Holocaust survivors. I try to recall some of the names: Rifka, Hannah, Isaac, Jakob ... I feel like I'm going in circles, like a German shepherd chasing its tail.

I stand up and stretch my legs, aching and cramping after sitting curled up for too long. Walk into the kitchen and open the fridge to reveal five empty shelves. I grab a can of Diet Coke from inside the door, pull open the tab and gulp down a couple of mouthfuls. Then go back into the other room and grab my notepad from the floor. Pull out a dining chair and sit down at the table to read through the names again.

Whoever this killer is, they have to be linked to everyone, somehow. I glance down at the patchwork of Post-its on the mustard-coloured rug. Someone had to know about Ruth and Peter's abuse, and about Charlotte being bullied by Mrs Alders, even though I now know that's not true.

I dial the Newman house. Debra answers the phone.

'It's Shanna Regan. Can I speak to Benji?'

'We're running late. He's going to a party.'

'Please. I'll only be quick.'

She tuts, sighs, then I hear a muffled shout. A gruff

teenage voice responds. I hear fumbling sounds and muttered words and raised voices.

'What?' Angry breaths in my ear.

'Benji?'

'What do you want? Mum's told me to talk to you.'

'Who did Charlotte tell about the bullying?' I tap the pen gently against my knee.

'No one.' He pauses. 'Just us.'

'So, no one else? You sure? A rabbi? A doctor? A teacher? Another adult, maybe?' I stab my pen tip into the notepad. 'Did she go to a youth club? After-school club? Anything or anyone? Please, Benji.'

I hear the begging tone in my voice, sounding like lives depend on it. Then think of Eddie and Gary Forrester and the plaque I saw, and realise they possibly do. 'Please, think.' I stab the page again, ripping a tiny hole in the thin lined paper. 'Is there anything else? It's important.'

'Charlie, she...' Benji breathes heavily down the phone.

'Yes?' I hold my breath.

'She didn't tell anyone. She knew she'd be found out if she did.'

I exhale slowly and shake my head. Stab the paper again. I was so sure...

Silence down the phone. Then a cough.

'But it was me,' he whispers. '*I* did. *I* told someone. Before Charlie said she lied. I saw the nurse about my asthma and told her why I was so angry.'

My neck muscle throbs. 'Which GP surgery?'

'Hilltop.'

'And the nurse? Do you remember her name?'

'No, but ... but she was nice to me, not like Doc Jackson.'

'Doc Jackson?'

'The doctor I always saw. She was a bitch. I told *her* too but she wasn't interested. Don't think she liked kids much.'

As soon as I end the call, I switch on my laptop, search for the Hilltop Surgery website and find a staff list. There are three nurses but I have no idea which one it could be.

I call Mark. 'You said your mum saw a nurse once or twice to patch her up after Peter hurt her, is that right?'

'Yes, why?' Music blares in the background. 'It was years ago.'

'Well ... which GP practice, and who did she see?'

'She was registered at Hilltop.' A car hoots. 'Hold on, I'll need to check my phone. Just pulling over.' Fumbling sounds. 'I went with her once when she'd fractured her wrist. Still have the appointment in my diary. Jane Hatchett, that's it.' Mark laughs. 'Mum said she hoped Jane wouldn't chop her up with an axe but she'd happily give her Peter's details if she wanted them.'

I try to ignore the thumping sensation in my chest. 'She actually *told* the nurse that?'

'No, she just said that to me, as far as I know. But then again, someone *must* have known about Peter.'

'Why?' I gaze at the names of the three nurses on my laptop screen. There's no Jane listed.

'Because a few weeks before Peter died, I received a letter asking me if I wanted to take revenge for Mum's death. If I wanted to kill him myself.'

A letter? Debra had mentioned one too, in passing, but I'd ignored it.

'Who was the letter from?' What if I've been right all along; what if the families did take revenge with someone else's help? 'And why didn't you tell me?'

'It was from someone called Renvok.'

My elbow begins to throb.

'I ignored it at the time and then forgot about it. Only

just thought of it now. After Mum saw Jane the second time, I pleaded with her to get help from the nurse or her GP ... so maybe she *did* tell someone. Because someone *had* to know.'

'Who was your mum's GP?'

'Dr Jackson. Carol Jackson, I think. She was quite old, if I remember correctly, close to retirement. Never liked her much myself but Mum seemed happy. Why?'

I look back at the staff list. No Dr Jackson either, but she's now been mentioned twice too. 'Can't explain. Gotta go.'

I end the call and stare at the list of names. Jane Hatchett and Dr Jackson are linked to two of the original victims.

This is no coincidence.

CHAPTER THIRTY-NINE

The postman shoves a package into my hands as I'm closing the door to the apartment block on Monday morning. It's been sent by MailReady. I rip it open. Inside are two envelopes, both A5, rectangular and brown, bound together with a thick elastic band, my name and the MailReady address written in black biro on the top in Dad's scrawled handwriting.

I pull off the elastic, catching my fingers as the rubber twangs, shove the envelopes in my rucksack and jog to the office – or rather, skate on the icy pavements – as I'm already running late. By the time I arrive, I'm hot and sweaty, despite the cold, crisp air outside. I peel off my coat, throw it over the back of David's chair and stuff my bag under my desk. Then collapse in my own chair to settle down to work.

I've decided it's time to move on and go back to travelling once I've solved the mystery of these plaques. Not until I've finished this issue of the magazine though – partly as I hate to leave jobs half-finished and partly because I may need David as a reference.

I print off the list that Valerie messaged to my phone, with the names of phone numbers of local Holocaust survivors. I recognise some of the names from the tapes – Miriam, Rifka, Isaac – all with one word beside them: *Deceased.* I'm surprised she hasn't sent me an up-to-date list. Maybe finding a survivor to interview for the next issue won't be so easy after all.

By lunchtime, I need to take a breather. Six phone numbers were unobtainable, two rang and rang until I gave up and hung up, and I've left messages on four answer-phones. I've edited three articles that have come in, called the dog rescue centre to arrange a visit to discuss David's fundraiser, and chased photos for a 'precious pets' competition that should have been in the last issue but he forgot to mention – until I asked him why the inbox was littered with details of ten dogs, twelve cats, five rabbits, two lizards and one chinchilla.

Now I'm ahead in my job, I have some spare time to research these plaques. First, I make myself a strong black coffee. Then I sit back down, open my rucksack and take out my laptop. I notice the two envelopes from Dad, pull them out one by one and lay them side by side. One has *Open first* scrawled in the top right corner. The other one is labelled *Open second.* I'm tempted to do the opposite but figure Dad must have labelled them for a reason.

I tear open the first envelope at one end and pull out a wad of photos. The top one is faded, sepia toned and frayed around the edges as if it's been handled repeatedly over the years. A young girl sitting between two adults. I turn the photo over.

Hannah and Isaac Stein with Evelyn aged twelve.

My hands shake as I gaze at the image. This is the woman I've been dreaming of. Evelyn, my mother ... Or

Lynnie, as Dad called her. Here, barely more than a child but with a face that could almost be my own. Eyes slightly rounder, maybe, a mouth just slightly thinner, but the same auburn hair, hers long, as mine used to be.

I pick up my phone and call Dad.

'Why send these now? You told me there weren't any more photos.' I want to bombard him with more questions but I'm not sure where to start.

'Found them while I was clearing my room, in back of the wardrobe,' he says. 'Must have shoved them there years back. Ya want to know more about ya mam. Follow my instructions, didn't ya?'

I nod. Then say, 'Yes,' when I remember he can't see me. Though I haven't followed his instructions at all. He told me not to come back to Hillsbury, as there was no point in researching my mother's past with all her relatives long gone.

I look at the next photo in the stack. My mother again, older now, with her arms wrapped around a little girl. Me, aged around three, I reckon, wearing denim dungarees over a pink T-shirt. We're both laughing, comfortable and happy and natural, as if we belong together.

The third is of the three of us. My mother, Dad, and me, sitting between them, each arm linked through one of theirs as if I was the glue holding them together. I must have been about five. I flick through the other photos and see people I don't recognise, socialising at birthday parties, playing in a garden, lined up at a family wedding...

I switch on my phone speaker and trail my finger over my parents' faces. 'Why did you two never marry?'

Dad was a handsome man. Still is. Never short of female attention, for sure, with his boyish good looks and soft Irish lilt. I always wondered why he never found someone in all these years, or maybe there was someone once, maybe there have been several. I know only too well that relationships on the road don't always last.

'Isaac, Lynnie's dad, wouldn't let us. I weren't Jewish, as ya know. He hoped Lynnie would have grown tired of me and...' he coughs, 'find a nice Jewish boy, settle down. Guess he hoped ya mam would do better. Guess she did so. Plus, I was nearly ten years older and my life was spent travelling.' His voice catches. 'That's how Lynnie and I met ... in Paris.'

'Was I happy? Happy, I mean, in Hillsbury.'

'So happy,' he pauses, 'but I couldn't leave ya after ya mam died ... not with him.' He pauses again, as if he's waiting for cogs to turn, for my memories to fall into place.

If only they would.

'I don't remember Isaac.' I pick up the first photo and stare into my grandfather's dark eyes, wondering about the man my father wouldn't leave me with, the man he took me away from when my mother died.

'*Zeida*, ya called him. Yiddish for granddad.'

Zeida. I feel light-headed and a pain pierces my chest, as if that name has ripped a hole through my heart.

'*Zeida? Why you crying?*'

'*Because vunce I knew another little girl called Shoshie. And today was her birthday.*'

'*She had my name?*'

'*No ... you have* her *name, my little* bubala. *Shoshana. It means rose, a rose among thorns. My little sister, just ten when she died.*'

'*Ten? That's ... one, two, three, four years more than me. Why did she die,* Zeida?'

'*Because the Nazis murdered her. Shot her in the street.*'

'*Dad, you'll frighten her.*'

'*Ach. This* bubala *does not scare so easily. She is a strong one.*'

'Shan?' Dad's voice sounds so distant. 'Still there?'

I grip the phone tightly as the memory fades. I feel like I've found something yet lost it again – something important, something I should know. A cool draught ripples over my skin, when I realise Isaac's voice sounds familiar, one I last heard not so long ago.

'Isaac, was he...' – I stare into my grandfather's eyes as I whisper the words – '...was he a Holocaust survivor?'

'He was. Told everyone stories about surviving the camps, he did so, even to ya – to ya mam's horror.'

I look down at the list from Valerie and see the name Isaac next to the word 'Deceased'. 'If I had a grandfather here in Hillsbury, why did you take me away when Lynnie...' – I swallow, feel the dryness in my throat and take a gulp of coffee, now bitter, cold and stagnant – '...when my mum died?'

'When she died, I wanted ya to stay here at the farm ... with me.' Dad's voice crackles, fading in and out, as if he's on the cusp of tears. 'Go to school ... make friends ... have a happy life ... a settled one.'

'Well, that worked out just fine.' Bitterness swirls inside me. 'Feels like I've been travelling, running maybe, since I was eight.'

'I tried to get ya settled ... but ya screamed for days when we got here, ya did. Wouldn't eat. Only kosher meat, ya said. First time ya saw ya granny slaughter a pig, ya shut ya'self in your room for hours. Went from my bubbly little girl to a quiet shadow. Only way I could keep ya happy was to take ya travelling with me when I could.'

'You always said I'd stopped eating meat as an act of defiance.' I think back to what Valerie and Harry told me about kosher meat: how the animals have to be killed in a special way, then the blood drained a special way, the meat salted in a special way. No pork, no bacon, no ham, no shellfish.

Can't have been easy sticking to this on a fairly remote Irish farm.

'T'was an act of defiance, just aimed at me, hoping I'd take ya back to Hillsbury, to what ya knew. Nothing kosher round here to get.' Dad pauses. 'Ya granny made vegetable stew every day, hoping ya'd eat something, and eventually ya did so. But ya was stubborn – still are – and refused to eat meat again.'

I think back to my grandmother's scowls, her silences and her glares. 'Granny hated me from the moment I arrived.'

'No, she didn't. She thought ya were...' Dad pauses. 'She thought ya were ... different. She'd never met Jews before. Didn't understand ya ways. Lighting candles on a Friday night, saying a prayer in a language she didn't know. Refused to celebrate Christmas, ya did. Wouldn't eat the food she cooked. Tried so hard, ya granny did, but ya pushed her away. So much so, she soon kept her distance. Left it to me and ya granddad instead.'

I sense he's not telling me something, I just wish I knew what. As my eyes fix on the table, a sour taste splurges into my mouth.

'What's in the other envelope?' I pick it up and hold it towards the light. It's too opaque to see inside.

Dad coughs nervously into the phone. 'Guess ya'd better open it. Said ya need them answers.'

I rip open the envelope and reach in. Pull out two smaller brown envelopes, again labelled *One* and *Two*. Dad has spent time putting this together, like a game of pass the parcel. What's with everyone and these party games? Yet again, I don't know if I want to play.

'Open the first one,' Dad says quietly.

I follow his instructions and pull out a piece of paper. Crisp and new, just one fold down the centre.

I take a deep breath, unfold it to reveal a marriage certificate.

'You never married.' I shake my head. 'I don't understand.'

But when I read the names, I realise I do.

CHAPTER FORTY

Evelyn Stein (29) married Harry Lee (30) on 20 August 1992 at Hillsbury United Synagogue, Hertfordshire.

I rip apart the second envelope to reveal another official-looking document, again crisp and new and neatly folded once down the centre. But this one is a death certificate. I unfold it and read it, tears welling up in the corners of my eyes. Dad's lied to me for all these years. My mother's life *was* snatched away, but not by a car accident, not an accident at all.

Eve Lee, daughter of Yitzchak Stein, also known as Izzy or Isaac, and wife of Harry Lee, was hit by a young hit-and-run driver called Terry Murdock.

'Dad, I'm here in Hillsbury,' I whisper. 'I've been here for a while. I needed to know what happened to her, where I've come from. I've met Harry, his wife Valerie, and I—'

'Ya lied to me?' Dad raises his voice. 'I told ya not to—'

'And *you* lied to me ... I found Lynnie's grave at the cemetery,' I whisper, wiping tears off my face with the back of my hand. 'I knew her full name was Evelyn but you've always called her Lynnie and this said Eve. I didn't even know her married name. Never realised it was her. Harry, Valerie – they didn't say.'

But did I sense it somehow?

I recall the emotion I felt in front of her grave as if something was calling to me. Leaving the stone because it felt right, as if somehow it belonged there, as if *I* belonged there. I could have ordered my mother's death certificate in all these years but I kept putting it off. Was it because I'd believed Dad for so long and didn't want to hurt him? Or was it because I was too scared to find out – or to remember – the truth?

I swallow back the bitter taste in my mouth and lay the two certificates on the table, side by side. Read the names again.

'Harry Lee,' I say slowly with a mixture of wonder and disbelief.

'Her and Harry, they'd known each other as kids,' Dad says in a quiet voice. 'I were always a spare part. He thought I took her away from him, yet really he took her away from me ... from us.'

'Why can't I remember they married?'

'Ya didn't know. Harry were always hanging round the house anyway, so guess ya didn't think much of it. Ya never liked him, ya see. Wanted to come live with me, *with* ya mam, so Lynnie didn't tell you. When time was right, they were going to. But then...'

But then...

A dark car, Terry Murdock in the driving seat.

I pick up the photo of my mother, my eyes blurring as tears flood down my cheeks.

'I couldn't stay after ya mam died.' Dad's voice catches in his throat. 'But I also couldn't leave ya with *him*.'

That mysterious 'him' again. Isaac?

No.

I look down at the marriage certificate.

'Harry,' I murmur.

'Yes ... Harry Lee.' I hear the bitterness in Dad's voice as he spits out the name. 'Golden boy in Isaac's eyes. Ideal husband for his little girl, maybe.' Dad snorts with laughter, then coughs. 'But not the ideal father for mine.'

HALF AN HOUR LATER, I'm sitting on the sofa back at the apartment, staring at the photos and the certificates, cradling a large glass of vodka in my hand. After Dad rang off, I couldn't stay at the office. I needed to be somewhere else, somewhere I could think. I would've gone to the park but it's chucking it down outside. And I needed a drink, a strong one.

Lynnie Stein.

Evelyn Stein.

Evelyn Lee.

Eve Lee.

My mother.

It reads like a bad word chain game. Knowing it's her name on the green square Post-it note on the rug in front of me means I'm more determined than ever to find this missing link, discover the identities of the killer and this mysterious Renvok.

And then there's Harry. The man who brought me up when Dad wasn't around. The man who was almost my father. The man who must have known all along who I am – that tender look in his eyes. But why hasn't he told me? And why can't I remember?

The jigsaw pieces are gradually slotting together, but I still need the other name linked to Billy Pearson. I don't like leaving loose ends. I reach for my computer and perch it on my lap. Search online again for deaths at the kosher restaurant but find nothing that feels right, so I expand my search to other variants of the name Billy Pearson in Hillsbury. Eventually I find a news story in the archives of *Hillsbury Times* in October 2001. My gut feeling tells me this is right – it fits the pattern.

William Pearson, a former pharmacist, was found dead in his apartment above his pharmacy on the high street. This means his front door would have been opposite the plaque on the wall, positioned exactly where he'd see it whenever he left the building.

I read more of the news story, discovering that William – Billy – called in sick, with a bad case of flu according to the doctor who visited him. A week later, Billy was found by his cleaner, dead on the floor in his dining room, flies buzzing around his decomposing body. With his body was a letter of confession and three empty syringes of insulin. The coroner recorded a verdict of suicide and the cause of death as an overdose.

A confession? To what?

I search for more stories in the months earlier and find reports of a pharmacist called William Pearson investigated for supplying counterfeit medicines, cheap from India and China, some five times stronger than they should have been, others contaminated with harmful illegal drugs. He denied the charges in early 2001 and blamed a member of staff. Two customers had died: a woman in her seventies after taking fake fentanyl tablets, and a six-year-old girl after taking adult-strength fake penicillin.

Valerie stands in her hallway, running her fingers through her wispy locks, flustered and perplexed at the unexpected interruption as I hang my coat on the peg next to hers.

'Would you like a coffee?' She wanders into her kitchen and clatters the cupboard doors. 'Or maybe some tea? Or a cold drink? I've made a marble cake if you want it.' She's rambling, stalling maybe.

I get straight to the point. Two boys' lives may be at stake so I don't have time to waste.

'Tell me about Susan.'

Valerie pauses, leaving a cupboard door swinging on its hinges, exposing the mugs on the shelves, her hand hovering over the white one with red writing.

'Where's she living, since she's clearly not living here?'

Valerie slams the cupboard door shut. I take a step towards her, grab her wrist, gently but firmly, enough to make her startle and try to wriggle from my grasp. 'I think it's time you explained, don't you? I know what happened. I know where she is.'

Valerie's mobile buzzes on the counter. *Shul office* flashes up on the screen. She looks at me, panic in her eyes, then down at her phone. I let go of her wrist so she can answer it.

'Hi, Mandy,' she says in a fake chirpy voice. 'How can I help?' She leans against the counter.

I back into the hallway and sprint up the stairs, two steps at a time. Pause on the landing at the top for a moment to get my bearings and my breath back, then peer through the doorway on my left. It's a large bathroom with a black-and-white tiled splashback, a white enamel bath and sink and black and purple 'his and hers' towels – clean, fresh, smelling of lavender.

To my right, there's a bedroom door with a pink glazed name plaque, five black letters: S. U. S. A. N. Like the plaque beside the front door, it's been treasured for years, polished and glistening like new.

I give the bedroom door a sharp shove. It swings open with a faint squeak of hinges. I walk inside to find a shrine to a little girl who left home one day and never came back. Dusky pink carpet, white wallpaper dotted with powder-pink hearts, a plush brown teddy bear with a silver bow, and a white unicorn with a golden horn waiting patiently on the neatly made bed.

On the left, there's a pink wooden dressing table with a shiny mirror and four little trinket boxes on the back ledge. I open the nearest one to reveal three glistening white milk teeth. Another contains a selection of small hair scrunchies in a rainbow of colours. I spot a ballerina treasure chest on the window ledge. When I open it, classical music fills the air. There's a dainty silver necklace inside, with five Hebrew letters – a name I now know as Shoshana.

Susan's Hebrew name.

The rabbi's baby's name.

My true name.

I pull out the necklace and grip it in my hand. I edge around the bed to the pine wardrobes and open the doors of the nearest one. Inside, on the left, pink, blue and lavender clothes hang down from the metal rail. A denim skirt edged with embroidered white flowers. A burgundy corduroy winter coat. On the top right, shelves are stacked with story-books and jigsaws, a Lego set, a toy stethoscope ... relics of a life tragically lost but never forgotten.

As I reach for one of the drawers below the shelves, a floorboard creaks behind me. I pull my hand back and turn round.

Valerie stands in the doorway. 'What are you doing up here? I never said you could—'

'I never thought to ask.' I unfurl my hand to reveal the

necklace. 'I just assumed Susan was all grown up and didn't live here anymore. Until I recognised her name linked to Billy Pearson.'

Valerie stifles a sob. 'She was our little girl, my baby, taken too soon.' Her voice breaks. 'I wanted to see her grow up, see what she'd become, like any mum would. She wanted to be a doctor like her daddy.' She slumps down on the bed and picks up the unicorn. Clutches it close to her chest. 'Billy Pearson snatched that away from us.'

I stay quiet – this is her time to talk, not mine.

'She had a bad cough and fever so I took her to the GP, not Harry as he wasn't allowed to treat family members. The doctor said it was a chest infection and prescribed antibiotics. I got the medicines from Billy Pearson's pharmacy just like I always did when one of us was ill. How could I have possibly known it was an adult dose in a child's bottle when I gave it to her?'

She holds the unicorn up to her face and inhales deeply. 'I couldn't wake her in the morning. I shook her and shook her, shouted and shouted, but she still didn't wake. I called an ambulance ... we went to the hospital. My poor, poor baby, my little Susie, fell into a coma...' – Valerie's body shakes as tears stream from her eyes and snot dribbles down from her nose – '... and she died three days later.'

I walk over to the window, feeling Valerie's grief, her anguish, seeping through me. Nothing I could say will help.

I clutch the curtain drape and push it away from the window, staring out into the garden. A robin sits on the roof of a large studio at the far end – a speck of red in the greyness of a sullen winter sky.

I turn back into the room, tread carefully to the other pine wardrobe and clasp my fingers around the wooden handle.

'No, don't.'

Valerie's now beside me. She grabs my arm. 'Please. That's my stuff for work, for the nursery.'

I shake her off. Pull open the cupboard and peer inside.

An old typewriter sits on the middle shelf; reams of paper stacked up on the lowest. I pull out the typewriter and place it carefully on the bed, slot a piece of paper in and scroll to the top. Press the first six letters – Q W E R T Y – again and again until I've filled a line in black ink.

I pull out the paper. When I hold it up to the light, my suspicions are confirmed. The letter E is sticking each time, darker and more smudged than the other letters.

Valerie begins to sob.

CHAPTER FORTY-ONE

A toddler crouches on the tatty brown carpet in front of me. She zooms her police car across my white trainer for the third time in ten minutes. I move my foot away as I watch the TV screen, willing a specific name to appear.

The little girl bum-shuffles sideways and zooms her car across my foot again, making sounds of revving engines and car horns and screechy brakes. My foot throbs a warning but I resist the urge to kick her away.

Twenty minutes later, the name I've been waiting for blinks at me in yellow lettering on the black screen.

Finally.

I watch Mrs Sylvia Cohen limp towards room five, pushing her Zimmer frame in front of her. Arthritis? Gout? A sprained ankle? I hope she doesn't have too many aches and pains as I've waited long enough already.

Soon after, she limps back to reception, clutching a green prescription in her shaky hand, and waves goodbye to the receptionist, a plump beady-eyed woman who's been watching me for thirty minutes. The same receptionist who told me which GP took over Carol Jackson's patients when she retired, after Hilltop merged with Trenton Surgery next door – this surgery – not long after Charlotte died.

I stand up and follow the signs to room five, ignoring persistent calls from the receptionist. The grey door is ajar, the doctor inside expecting his next patient.

Guess that's me then.

As I step into the consultation room, he looks up. His eyes scrunch in confusion then widen. I feel a sharp tug on my coat sleeve and the receptionist yanks me to one side.

'Stop right there,' she hisses at me. I try to squirm out of her grasp but she's stronger than she looks. 'Sorry, Dr Lee,' she calls into the room, 'this woman just walked straight through.'

Harry peers at her over a pair of reading glasses. Then he peers at me.

'It's fine, Judy.'

'You sure?' The receptionist lets go of my sleeve. 'She doesn't have an appointment. Should be Mr Ahmed next, at ten-twenty.'

Harry takes off his reading glasses and puts them down on his desk. Glances into my eyes with the bemused smile I've come to know so well. I don't smile back. 'Is Mr Ahmed here yet?'

'No.' The receptionist clears her throat in annoyance.

'So when he arrives, delay him for a few minutes.'

'But...'

'Ask how his son is. He'll talk for hours. That should work.'

Judy looks me up and down, narrows her eyes in full glare, then slams the door shut behind her as she leaves.

I turn to face Harry's desk, gearing up to say the speech I've rehearsed in my head. But he gets there first.

'Good morning ... Shoshana.'

I flinch at my name, one I haven't used for years, the one on my birth certificate. The one my mother gave me, naming me after my great-aunt, a little girl shot by the Nazis all those years ago. The name Dad officially changed to Shanna when he took me away from Hillsbury. *Less Jewish, more Irish*, he said, while we were on the road.

'How long have you known who I am?'

Harry gestures to the empty chair beside his desk. 'Take a pew.'

I walk over but stand behind the chair instead.

'You weren't very co-operative even then.' Harry scowls. 'Must take after your father.'

A growl rises in my throat. 'How long have you known who I am?' I grip the back of the chair.

'Ever since you arrived in Hillsbury.' Harry inspects my face as if he's seeing me for the first time. 'I warned you it's a small community. You may behave like ... *him*.' He spits out the last word, then clenches his fists as if he's trying to stay in control. 'But you look just like *her*. I'm not the only one to notice.'

'Who's noticed?'

Silence.

I yank open my rucksack and grab the marriage certificate and photos. Throw them on the desk in front of him.

'You married my own mother, and didn't think to tell me?'

Harry raises his eyebrows, his bemused expression back, then laughs. 'It's not like you were open about who *you* were.'

'I didn't think I needed to be. I didn't realise anyone knew her. Dad said she had no family left.'

'I was so sure you'd remember us eventually.' He shrugs with disappointment. 'I waited all these years for you to come back here. We all did. Your mother would have been so proud of her little Shoshie.'

'Don't call me that.' Tears of frustration sting my eyes. 'I don't remember any of it. I barely remember her, and I don't remember you at all.'

Or do I?

That shadowy man in my memories – when lighting the candles, when Dad came back to see me, singing songs at Chanukah ... Maybe Harry's always been there, lurking in the background. I just couldn't see him, or maybe I didn't want to.

'Evie and I once made a promise.' Harry puts on his reading glasses. 'We were about fifteen. We said we'd be together forever.'

He picks up the marriage certificate and peers down at the paper, pursing his lips with regret. 'It didn't quite happen that way though.'

'Why not?'

'Joe. Bloody. Regan.' Harry clenches the certificate so tightly that I worry he'll rip it. 'If he hadn't got her pregnant ... if you hadn't come along ... the Irish fool.'

'Dad's no fool.'

'Fool enough not to marry her.' His face reddens, his anger gushing across his skin. 'Fool enough to travel the world and leave you both here for weeks at a time. If I'd—'

'He said Isaac wouldn't let them get married.' I'm determined to defend Dad, to tell the whole story, or at least the parts I know. 'Lynnie stuck to her father's wishes.'

Harry's eyes darken. 'Don't call her that.' He lays the marriage certificate flat on the table. 'That's what the fool called her. She was always Evie – Eve – to me.'

His voice softens as he says her name, and his eyes light up. 'Isaac wanted us to get married.'

'But she didn't want to?'

'Of course she bloody did. It was because of you. Or rather you and Joe Regan.' He picks up the photo of me and my parents, traces his finger around my mother's face, then mine. 'Little Shoshie. I loved you like my own but it still wasn't enough. Evie was worried it would ruin your relationship with ... *him*.' He jabs his finger towards Dad's face.

'But you did get married eventually,' I point at the marriage certificate, 'so what changed her mind?'

'Joe did.' Harry laughs. 'Ironic, isn't it? He was offered a big project in the Middle East. Good money but it meant being away from you for a long time. I finally persuaded Evie that you needed a father here: a family, security.' He swallows sharply. 'So we got married, quietly, without any fuss. Just Yitzchak there, the rabbi, a couple of old friends and neighbours.'

'And me?'

Harry shakes his head slowly. 'Evie didn't want you there as she worried how you'd respond. You were such a daddy's girl, ignoring me, especially when the fool was around. We were going to tell you when we felt the time was right. But then...'

'She died.' My words hang in the air between us. 'And you were with her that night.'

He nods and slumps back in his chair, his eyes clouding over as if he's in another place, at another time. 'We were coming back from a party. It was a lovely evening, unusually warm and dry, so your mum ... she wanted to walk.' His hands are shaking. 'She always loved being outside.' He smiles at the memory. 'It was hard to keep Evie indoors for long.'

Just like me.

'And then?'

Harry shakes his head slowly, grimacing. 'The car seemed to come from nowhere. That drunken fool didn't see us. We were at the side of a narrow road and it was dark, but there was nowhere else to walk. I jumped out of the way in time, but Evie, she...' He stifles a sob.

I want to push him for more about that night but Mr Ahmed could come in at any time. 'And then six months later you killed the driver, taking revenge for Evie's death. You ran down Terry Murdock late one night, just like he did to my mother.'

'No, I bloody well didn't run him over.' Harry picks up his pen and grips it tightly. 'I wasn't driving that car.'

'You're lying, Harry. I know what's been going on around here. You're the link between all of them.' I take a deep breath as I finally launch into the speech I'd prepared. 'You took over Carol Jackson's patients when the surgeries merged. So you read all her notes: what Benji told her about Gina Alders and what happened with Charlotte. Did Jane Hatchett come to you with her concerns about Ruth Stevens and domestic abuse? And what about Isaac, Yitzchak? He was a Holocaust survivor. Did you listen to his stories of the *Nokmim*? Take his lead, killing people who've killed someone Jewish and didn't own up to it, as some sort of twisted revenge? And then there's Susan, your own daughter. Billy Pearson was visited by a doctor just before he died. Was it you? Did you inject him with his own dodgy insulin?'

'Susie should never have died.' Harry's eyes flash with anger and sorrow. 'Billy had apparently been stocking counterfeit medicines for years, and no one took any notice of the occasional drug overdoses or deaths until there were several in a short space of time. He claimed it was a member of staff who conveniently then disappeared.'

'But you knew it was him? So you went to see him while he was ill?'

'I wasn't one hundred percent certain he was responsible for Susie's death, no. But, yes, I did go and see him in an official capacity. He called the surgery to say he was too unwell to attend an appointment but needed a doctor because he was wheezing. One of the other doctors was on home visits that day but she was delayed with a patient, so I visited Billy instead.'

'And then you went back again. What did you do? Force him to write a suicide note, then inject him? Did it give you satisfaction to avenge your daughter's death, just as you did after Evie's ... my mother's—'

'No!' Harry stands up and leans towards me, his eyes burning bright with rage.

'So why do this? Why kill all these people?'

Silence.

I think of George Masters' plaque and the word JUSTICE glimmering in the sunlight. Maybe that's why Harry chose to live in his bungalow with that constant reminder of the *Nokmim* by his front door. Does he believe he's the Redeemer of Death – the *ga'ol ha-adam*?

'Gina Alders was innocent.' I fix my eyes on him. 'She should never have died. Charlotte lied about it all. What happened on the bridge was an accident.'

Harry's mouth twitches and he pulls at his beard. 'I don't know what you're talking about.'

'You're lying, Harry. Of course you know. And she was twelve weeks pregnant so that makes you a baby killer too.'

His face drains of colour. 'I've. Killed. No one.' He speaks slowly as if I'm a child, the innocent child he once knew maybe, but that child's now grown up.

His hands shake, the knuckles stained white with rage.

'I'll give you twenty-four hours.' I grab the marriage certificate and photos. 'If you don't go to the police and tell them, I'll do it for you. Those two brothers ... whatever they did ... that's no reason for them to die.'

'Sounds like you're warning me.' Harry isn't asking who those youths are – *he knows*. 'If you go to the police, I'll deny it all and push the blame on others. I don't think you'd like that.' He tugs his beard again. 'My wife isn't just talented with a brush, you know.'

A muscle at the back of my neck twinges. Those notes Valerie's been sending me, leading me to these plaques...

I grasp the door handle. 'I won't let you get away with this.'

'If you want the truth about Terry Murdock, maybe you're looking in the wrong place. Where was Joe Regan the night Terry Murdock died? What would he do for his sweet little girl, his darling little Shanna?' Harry walks around the side of his desk. 'Go ask him. Ask him why he really took you away.'

Dad? Has he been telling me more lies for all these years – even when we last spoke? No, all the clues pointed to Harry ... it *has* to be Harry. He's just messing with my head ... isn't he?

The consulting room door creaks open. Judy peers round it. 'Mr Ahmed's here. Thought his appointment was ten-forty.' She rolls her eyes in disbelief, then swings them in my direction. 'You still here?' She pulls the door fully open and stands to one side. 'Well, now you need to go.'

An Indian man hovers behind her, in a smart navy tweed suit and a travel brochure under his arm.

I brush past Judy, then stop and turn. 'I haven't finished, Harry. I'll be back.'

'Oh, I think we *have* finished.' He gives me a smug smile. 'Go ask him, Shoshana. Go ask your fool of a father about that night.'

CHAPTER FORTY-TWO

I stumble out of the surgery and head towards the park. Slump down on my bench in my usual place. Pull my mobile out from my jeans pocket, scroll down the names until I find the right one and press the *Call* button.

I hold my breath until I hear his voice and then launch straight in.

'Did you come back to Hillsbury after you took me away?' Silence at the other end. 'For fuck's sake, Dad, just tell me the truth. I'm sick of asking you. Enough lies already.'

A slow sigh down the phone. 'Once,' he whispers.

'When?'

'Few months after ya mam died. Had a letter from Isaac, asking me back. Wanted me to do something for him.'

'What?' Though I've already guessed.

'Wanted revenge, he did. Wanted me to kill the man who'd killed Lynnie. But I couldn't do it, I swear over ya mam's grave.'

'But *someone* ran over Terry Murdock and killed him.' I lean back against the bench, the chill from the wooden slats seeping through my coat, the winter sun warming my face. 'Can you prove it *wasn't* you driving that car?'

'Course not but it weren't.' He raises his voice. 'Asked Harry about that night, have ya? Harry Lee?'

'He told me to ask *you*.' My voice catches in my throat. 'Said you were going to leave me.'

I watch the children in the playground, faint shadows stalking them as they dart around on the gravel. Did I once play on those swings? Did I once climb up that slide? I wish I could remember. I wish Dad hadn't snatched my Hillsbury childhood away.

'That's true.' Dad coughs down the phone. 'A job came up. Long-term one I couldn't afford to lose. I wasn't going to take it but Lynnie told me to. Said what we'd both known for years; that she and I would never be together, that she was going to marry Harry. To leave ya with them. Safe, I thought. Then Isaac wrote and told me about Evie. I hadn't gone anywhere yet. Was packing my bags and trying to work out how to tell ya, my little girl.'

'So you came back for me, then took me travelling instead.' I think about Lila Benson and the secret we shared. 'You told me to forget I was Jewish as you didn't want anyone to know. Changed my name. Why? To stop Harry from finding me?'

Silence.

'Dad?'

'Wanted to keep ya safe, that's all. They didn't like Jews in some places we visited. Not sure they do now much, either. And I surely weren't going to leave ya with Harry Lee or anyone else.'

'You think Harry killed Terry Murdock? And the others?'

'Isaac asked all of us.'

'All of you?' I sit up straight. 'Who else?

'Lynnie had other friends who came round a lot. Isaac did too.'

I realise something that's been bugging me ever since I opened those two certificates. 'Why did you call her Lynnie when she was Evie to everyone round here?'

'When your mam and I met, we were in Paris. I was working there. She was with friends, just for a week or so. Lynnie was a nickname, that's all. How she introduced herself. Maybe she liked being someone else for a while – and then ya came along, we were linked for life. But leave it now, Shanna. Ya know how she died. It's time to come home.'

Home.

'I can't.' I watch a little boy bum-shuffling down the slide and think of the childhood I could've had. 'There are some loose ends I need to tie.'

'And then ya going travelling?' I sense the defeat in Dad's voice.

'Not yet. I need to stop it happening again. You see, there's these two youths. They're trouble, for sure, but I think they may be in danger. I can't leave it alone.' I tell him about the new plaque, what happened with Valerie in the park, about Zac Wagner. 'If it's not Harry, then who could it be?'

'Ya shoulda told me bout them lads.' Dad coughs. 'There was someone. Never knew his name. Came round a lot, doing odd jobs. Isaac was a jeweller, ya know, and this fella used to do his accounts. Gave him money too, bought ya and Lynnie presents. Maybe ya can find him.'

An accountant? I think of Mark, the clay and paints by his door, his words to me about taking revenge for Ruth's death. But no, he's too young – he's not much older than me.

Soon after I end the call, I hear a nervous cough and

twist round to find Valerie standing by the bench. I shuffle up and offer her a seat.

Leaving a small space between us, she sits down, her back as stiff as the wooden slats behind us. She's clutching a black leather bag tightly in her arms as if cradling a baby, her hands shaking, just as they did the first time I saw her running away from the yobs, willing myself not to get involved. Running towards me...

Another jigsaw piece clicks into place.

'You knew it was me in the park that day.'

I see the truth in her forlorn hazel eyes. Coincidences don't exist.

'Yes,' she whispers. 'Harry told me ... he told me to find you ... befriend you.' She grasps my arm. 'I'd seen you here a few times.'

Her cold hand trembles against my skin. 'But that day ... those boys ... I didn't...' She looks at my cheek, the bruising now long gone, just a faded memory, one that we share.

'That's why you begged me not to report them. You didn't want Harry to know ... in case it happened again ... in case he found them ... in case he killed them.' I push her hand off my arm. 'But now it's too late. They're in danger anyway. He found out.'

Valerie sniffs loudly. She reaches into her coat pocket, pulls out a paper tissue and wipes her nose. 'Harry called to say you'd been to his surgery. He told me to show you this.'

She unzips the front pocket of her bag, pulls out a package wrapped in brown paper and hands it to me.

I unwrap it carefully to reveal a square piece of clay glazed in black with a red rim. I flip the plaque on its back then on its front.

'I make them in my studio in the garden and fire them up in a kiln.'

I trace my fingers around the plaque's rough edges.

'Harry was right when he said you weren't just talented with a brush.'

'Making the plaques was his idea.' Valerie takes the plaque from me, wraps it safely in the brown paper and rests it on her lap. 'The first one was for Billy Pearson. We wanted Billy to know we were watching him, that we were on to him, after Susie died. We hoped he would hand himself in. Admit what he'd done.'

'How did you make sure no one saw you put the plaques up?'

'We just waited for the right time, watching people's patterns and asking around.'

'Never had you down as a stalker.'

Valerie gives me a sheepish smile. 'I then sent a note telling them where to find the plaque, to make sure they saw it each time. We wanted them *all* to own up, to admit to what they'd done. We tried to give them a chance before...' – she rubs her nose with the scrunched-up tissue and stuffs it in her coat pocket – '...before bad things happened. We didn't want them to die.'

I gaze down at the package on her lap. 'And the one for Terry Murdock? That looked like new.'

'I put that one up a couple of weeks after we met. I thought it was time for you to know the truth about your mum. I wanted to lead the trail back to when all this started.'

'Why now? Why me?'

'Because it ... it needs to stop,' she whispers. Tears spring into her eyes. 'It all needs to stop. I needed someone to find the plaques and start looking into them. Discover the truth about what's been going on here in Hillsbury.'

'So why not do something yourself? Go to the police?'

'I ... I can't. I'm not brave enough, you see. All those things you've done. All those places you've been to. The way you stood up to those boys here, in this park. I needed someone who … someone who wouldn't give up … someone brave, like you.'

Brave.

If only she knew what demons I'm battling … what happened that night in Brussels … what led me here to Hillsbury.

'This plaque … it's empty. Whose name were you going to put on it?'

Her mouth quivers.

Mine.

'But you sent me those notes.' I shake my head slowly, confusion rattling around my brain. 'Why would you do that if you're the one making the plaques? Why would you threaten me?'

'Brussels,' she whispers. 'He knows.'

A shiver inches its way down my spine. Andy, here in Hillsbury searching for me and those photos. Speaking to the locals. Speaking to Harry.

'After that day in the park, Harry made me invite you over.' Valerie gazes across the grass. 'He wanted to see the daughter he'd wanted but never had. I thought I'd hate you. But you helped me and … and you seemed so nice.'

'But why would Harry care about me being back here? My mother died over twenty-five years ago, and I left soon after. I don't even remember him.'

Valerie shoves the brown-paper package into her bag. 'He married me because of you, you know.'

'Because of me?'

'Well, your mother, Evie. My dad … he was a survivor too, like Yitzchak. Harry looked after Yitzchak until he died, then met me. We married two months later, and Susie was our honeymoon baby. I was the substitute, a poor one maybe. He had wanted Evie but he lost her, and he had wanted you but couldn't have you. So when we had Susie...'

She dabs the corners of her eyes, looks up and gazes longingly at a little girl dangling her legs on a swing. 'When we had Susie, he wanted to name her after you: Shoshana. But I ... I wouldn't let him, so we compromised on Susan, an English version. He still insisted on Shoshana as her Hebrew name though, and I often heard him call her that when he thought I wasn't around.'

She turns to me and gazes into my eyes, her cheeks shining with tears. 'I spent all those years hating you, jealous of the daughter he almost had.'

I grasp her icy hand. 'Did Harry kill them all? Billy Pearson? Terry Murdock? Gina Alders?'

'I don't know,' she says softly.

'Valerie, for fuck's sake, just tell me. Was it all down to Harry?'

She flinches, at my swearing maybe or at my raised voice but it doesn't matter which, as I need to know the truth – and I need to know now.

Enough games.

She stares into the distance. 'When Susie died, Harry couldn't deal with it. It was like he had lost you and Evie all over again.'

'So he killed her killer in revenge?'

'Harry said Billy got what was coming to him.' Her voice is now barely more than a whisper.

I recall that mug in their living room. KEEP CALM – DON'T KILL THE PATIENTS. Maybe that's what he's been doing for years.

Or has he?

By putting up the plaques *before* they died, he's been giving everyone a chance. Would he do that if he was the killer? Why not just kill them straightaway? Except for Terry

Murdock, whose father didn't mention any warning. What makes *him* so different? He was the first one so maybe Harry thought of the plaques afterwards, once he'd met Valerie with her artistic talents. But he and Dad have been so cagey, blaming each other ... and Dad mentioned this man who helped my grandfather, listened to his words and did his accounts. Am I right – has someone else been pulling their strings?

I stare across the grass towards the playground. 'If it's not Harry, then who? Is someone making you do all this?'

Valerie's hand tightens around mine, tears welling up again. 'He—'

A shadow passes in front of the sun. I look up to find David standing in front of the bench, a scruffy Alsatian by his side. The dog growls and bares its teeth. Valerie shuffles backwards on the bench, her knuckles turning white.

'Not in the office?' He sneers at me and glances at Valerie. 'I expected you to come in this morning.'

'I needed some air. Had something to do.'

'You seem to need a lot of air, I've noticed.'

He looks Valerie up and down, then turns back to me. 'I didn't expect to find you socialising when you should be working.' A faint scowl touches his lips. 'I'll give you until one-thirty. Otherwise you're fired.'

The Alsatian lurches forwards, saliva dripping from its mouth. Valerie shrieks. The dog stops just before it reaches us, and David gives me a twisted smile.

I stand up. 'Then I quit.'

'What?' The scowl spreads across David's face, furrowing his brow. 'You can't do that. The next issue needs to be finished.'

'So go find some other slave. I'll drop by to collect my things.'

'Over. My. Dead. Body.'

He turns round and stomps off across the grass, like an angry adolescent, followed by his canine companion.

'I ... I should go,' Valerie stutters, her hands shaking as she watches David and the dog heading for the park gates. 'Wouldn't want to get you into trouble.'

'Don't worry about that. That's just David, my boss ... or rather, he *was* my boss. He can be a bit...' – I struggle to find the right words – '...a bit full on. I suspect his bark is worse than his bite. Same with the dog.'

She lets out a small laugh, then a sob. 'Please, Shanna, I need your help ... before it's too late ... for all of us.'

I think back to Harry's words. He said if he goes down, others do too. I look at her shaking hands, her pale face, the tears on her cheeks. Think about her notes and her plaques. I can't do it to her, she's not strong enough for this. And what about Dad – is he also involved? If he is, how can I do that to him?

I sit back down. 'There's nothing I can do.'

'Please...'

I think back to that night in Brussels and the guilt I've felt ever since. This could be my chance for redemption; my chance to repent and make amends. Maybe it *should* be my name on the blank plaque in her bag, or maybe it should be Andy's. And maybe the rabbi's right. Maybe some things *do* happen for a reason and that's why I'm here in Hillsbury – right now.

Yet still my stomach churns.

CHAPTER FORTY-THREE

Nadia FaceTimes me. Her sleek black hair hangs down over her face and she's cradling a steaming purple mug in her hands.

I must look a fright, as she raises her eyebrows and stifles a snigger. I'm sprawled on the sofa, wearing an old bra, faded navy joggers and a yellow towel draped around my shoulders. To be fair, she'd seen me like this before, and worse.

My phone is propped up against a pile of books on the coffee table, and I'm grasping a full glass in my hand, a bit too tightly maybe.

'Bit early for that.' Nadia points at the glass, then at the vodka bottle leaning against my side. Gives me a disapproving stare.

Midday is too early by my standards too, but it's just yet another rule to be broken.

'Been a bad morning.'

'Clearly.' She grins at me. 'Well, I have something to cheer you up. There's a job going. Want it? I think you'll like this one.'

She pans her phone camera out so I can see where she is. Somewhere I used to know well, popping in there between my travels for occasional meetings and drinking sessions. She gestures at the bare desk behind her. The last time I saw it, it was covered in newspapers, empty Stella bottles and packs of Marlboro Gold.

'Where is he?' I duck down so no one at *NewsQuest* can see me in my semi-clothed alcohol-fuelled state. I've just come out the shower and haven't even bothered to brush my hair. My curls are beginning to grow out but I'm still at that halfway looks-like-a-scarecrow stage. No point getting my hair coiffed at a salon until there's enough to cut and style.

'Gone.' Nadia gives me a triumphant look. 'Paul gave Andy the boot three weeks ago apparently. But I only found out when I came in today.'

'Really? Why?'

Paul Mack, head honcho of *NewsQuest*, doesn't fire people without good reason.

'The police are looking for Andy. He's been a naughty boy, even by his standards. He's been going to fascist meetings, taking part in neo-Nazi demos, that sort of thing.'

Nadia glances around, then leans forwards and whispers, 'The neo-Nazi group had been plotting something, apparently. Not sure what, as Paul didn't say, but it's big. They're looking for more evidence, and they're now looking for Andy. Have you seen his tweets recently?'

I shake my head.

'All full of racist shit. Don't suppose you can shed any light on what's going on?'

She gives me a hard stare, then pans her phone camera down towards her hand, unfurling her fingers slowly to reveal a blue rectangular USB in her palm.

'Well?'

I take a deep breath. 'Have you looked at it?'

'Of course I have. I'm a nosy journalist, just like you.' She narrows her eyes. 'Why didn't you tell someone, Shan?'

'I...' I pause as I don't have an answer – or rather, not an answer she'd understand. 'Andy was here in Hillsbury but I haven't heard from him in days. I don't know where he is.'

Now I think about it, I wonder if I scared him off in the park when I involved Max.

'He found you?' Nadia takes a gulp of coffee and scrunches up her nose in disgust. Guess the *NewsQuest* blend hasn't improved in these past few months.

'He saw I'd joined a local Facebook group, so he followed me here.' I point at the screen in the direction of her hand. 'Wanted the photos and video on that USB.'

'Tell me exactly what happened in Brussels, Shan, the parts the photos don't show.'

'Not if everyone will hear me.' I gesture with my finger, indicating the bustle of activity behind her. I know all these people. They know me. I used to be one of them.

'Hold on.' Nadia puts her coffee cup down on her desk. The screen jiggles around as she stands up, saunters along a narrow corridor, opens a door and slots herself into a small cubicle.

'Nads, I know we're good friends but do I need to see you take a—?'

'I'm not here to pee, you idiot.' She sits down on the loo seat. 'Figured we need some privacy. So tell me what happened and then we can decide what you're going to do next.'

And so I tell her. And as I do, a silent movie plays in my head, with deep voices shouting and a kaleidoscope of images I've been trying to forget. A religious Jew, black suit, white shirt, grey side curls, black hat perched on his head, being chased by four men, three of them in black T-shirts and jeans with shaved heads and swastika tattoos.

'We were there to report on the neo-Nazi demos. You know the drill; the usual stuff we do. Watch. Listen. Don't get involved, emotionally or otherwise.' I slug back some vodka, the only way I'm going to get through this.

'But Andy *did* get involved? And then you?'

I nod and close my eyes for a moment. Then take a deep breath, filling my lungs with air. 'He got chatting to them in a café, then got pissed with them in a bar. And started agreeing with things they said. Showed interest.' I shake my head in despair. 'I thought maybe he was just doing it for the story, listening and going along for the ride, you know, the things we usually do to get people to talk. But it wasn't. I soon realised he believed all their shit, everything they said. That blacks were...' I stumble over the words, struggling to say them out loud, 'were scum, and Jews were ... taking over the world.'

I swig more of my drink. 'They all left the bar and started walking the streets, shouting, singing abusive songs I'd prefer to forget. Chasing any Jews they could find. I followed them. I didn't want to be part of it but I was worried about Andy. I still thought he was putting it on, trying to get a good story. But then they found *him* down a quiet side street.'

'Found who?'

Tears spring into my eyes as I recall what happened next. 'An old Jewish man carrying some books, one of those white tasselled prayer shawls around his shoulders. The neo-Nazis took the first slugs. Knocked him to the ground. One of them grabbed his hat, perched it on his own head and started taking the piss out of Jewish ways. I couldn't even...'

I let out a sob, remembering that's when Andy crossed the line and I learnt a lot about the man I thought I loved.

'Andy kicked him in the ribs,' I continue once I've composed myself. 'The Jewish man, I mean, not the neo-

Nazi as I wished he would. "You fucking Yid," he shouted, and kept kicking him. I stayed in the shadows, taking photos and video, everything you saw on that USB. I wanted to help that poor man but knew I had no chance against the four men. I was worried they'd hurt me too.'

I hear a clamour of voices. A door bangs. Nadia puts her finger to her lips and glances to her left. I hear a trickle, then a flush. A door bangs again, then silence.

'Go on,' she says.

'After a while, Andy and the three yobs stumbled off, leaving the Jewish man lying in the street. A little boy ran over to him. Crouched down on the ground.' My phone buzzes. Emails have come in. 'I don't know where he'd been hiding. I thought it would be better if I just slipped away back to the hotel. I don't know what happened to the man after that.'

'Effing hell.' Nadia's voice echoes in the confined space. 'Never really liked Andy but assumed he must be a decent enough bloke if you were with him. And then you flew back to London?'

My shoulder twinges. 'Not exactly. Andy got back to the hotel around five a.m. I couldn't sleep so sat in the armchair in the corner of the bedroom, lights off. As soon as he came in, I snapped. Told him he was a bastard, a fascist.'

'Bet that went down well.'

Tears spill into my eyes. 'He laid into me. Hit me and yanked my shoulder. Kicked me in the ribs. "Since when did you become a Yid lover?" he was asking me, and he just kept punching me. When he finally went into the bathroom for a piss, I grabbed my stuff and ran out the room. I made it down the stairs, no sign of him behind me, and out the hotel. I took a cab to the airport and booked myself onto the next flight to Ireland.'

'What did your dad say?'

'I didn't tell him. He knew not to ask – thought I'd tell him when the time was right.'

'Does he know now?'

I shake my head.

'So how did Andy know about the photos and video?'

'I sent him a text when I landed.' Tears are now streaming down my cheeks. I try to wipe them away with the back of my hand but there's an endless supply. 'Stupid, I know, but I wasn't thinking straight. I was angry ... upset.'

That's an understatement. What Andy had done felt personal. Until that moment, until I saw him kick that man on the ground, until I heard the words coming out of his mouth, my Jewish background had never seemed important to me.

And that's when things changed.

'I told him I had evidence. If he didn't own up, I'd do something about it. I gave him six months.'

Ironically, just like Valerie and Harry had done with these Hillsbury plaques. I'd always believed coincidences don't exist but maybe occasionally – very occasionally – they do. 'I copied the photos on to three USB sticks and kept one with me, left another hidden at the farm, planning to tell Dad about it at some point, and sent that one to you.'

'But why haven't you done something with them?'

Good question. Why haven't I? How do I explain?

'Because I kept – no, keep – hoping Andy didn't know what he was doing, maybe it was the alcohol. I don't want to ruin his career.'

'Like he's ruined yours?' Nadia sneers. 'Listen to me ... Andy's not owning up. He's on the run now. You need to tell the police where to find him.'

'They'll think I was involved. They'll come for me.' My heart beats furiously. 'I don't even think he's still in Hillsbury. And maybe he'll see the light. There's still time. The six months aren't up yet.'

'Shan, you have concrete evidence that can help put Andy and the others away.'

She's right. Though I would still have some explaining to do – why I didn't intervene and why I didn't report it. Am I any different to Valerie – watching from the outside but not getting involved? I've given Andy a chance but he hasn't taken it. I'm no murderer, but I can ruin his career just as he's tried to ruin mine.

'I'd better get back to work. Can't sit on the loo for much longer or they'll call an ambulance.' Nadia stands up, flushes and opens the cubicle door. 'Well, there's a job here if you want it. You'd be great. Less travelling involved too. Let me know as they haven't advertised it yet. I think Andy's sacking has been a shock for everyone. Oh, and do something about this.' She reaches her hand into her jeans pocket, pulls out the USB and waggles it in front of her. 'Just speak to a lawyer first, maybe, to check your rights.'

'I'll be in touch.'

'You'd better.' She reaches towards the screen and ends the call.

I open the email app on my phone to check my inbox.

The name Martin Snarks is at the top. He's emailed me the photos he took at the apartment block on the day Hetty died. Andy, in his black leather jacket, talking to her outside my door. Another photo shows him rushing out the apartment block, a worried expression on his face.

Maybe Hetty found him in my apartment. Maybe he chased her and she'd tried to hide. It makes sense for him to be the one who ripped my apartment apart, looking for those photos, safely hidden, somewhere he couldn't access without a key. Guess I'll have to hand these over to the police. Maybe they've found some DNA evidence by now.

I call Max, tell him what I've discovered, then forward him the photos from Martin Snarks. And I tell him about the USB, the photos and videos and Andy, everything I've just told Nadia. I ask if he can do some digging to find out where the police are in their investigation, and say I'll pop by his office soon to go into more detail. I'll pay him, I add, not wanting him to think I'm after a freebie.

Now I just need to collect my belongings from the office. And then I'll be on my way.

CHAPTER FORTY-FOUR

F ive o'clock shadows dance across the pavement in front of me, their long stems trapped by flickering street lamps. I turn my key in the office lock. To my surprise, it swivels without much effort.

I pause, moving the door backwards then forwards, backwards then forwards, confirming what I've just heard ... or rather, haven't heard. No rattling or squeaking or creaking of the hinges – finally.

Once upstairs, I empty my desk. A few pens, notepads, a red USB stick, nicotine gum, emergency chocolate bars and a large Smirnoff bottle and plastic shot glasses, also for emergencies.

There's a faint sickly odour in the air, like rotting meat. I check the office bin for leftover dog food but it's empty. Must be something I've stepped in. Dog shit left outside by one of David's strays, no doubt.

I open the black box file, riffle through it and pull out a few old *Hillsbury Living* magazine articles, realising that once I leave this office, I'm on my own without these extra resources. My own grandfather was a Holocaust survivor, living here in Hillsbury. I don't want this to be a wasted opportunity to discover more about my family's past.

I check through the pile of cassette tapes until I find him. Isaac. Yitzchak. I'd already listened to all of his interview the other day, not realising who he was. Now I want to listen to him again.

I push the tape into the cassette player, press *Rewind* for a while and then *Play*.

A whirr of the tape, white noise of interference, then voices.

'*Show me your arm,* Zeida. *I want to see your numbers again.*' A young girl's voice. Me.

'*Not now, Shoshie.* Zeida'*s busy.*' A woman's voice, soft and mellow. It sends a shiver down my spine.

'*But Mummy...*'

'*Ach, it is fine, leave her. We finished the interview.*' A man's voice. Old and croaky. Polish accent. Isaac. '*She is just inquisitive. Children should be. That is how they learn. Come here,* bubala. *Sit down next to me and I vill show you again.*'

'*1 ... 8 ... 3 ... I don't have numbers on my arms. Look,* Zeida.' I hear a swish of clothing as if I'm pulling up my sleeve. '*Why do* you *have them?*'

'*Because bad people, the Nazis, put them there. Like I vas cattle. Taking away my identity. As if I no longer had a name.*'

'*Dad ... not now. She's too young to know these things.*' My mother again.

'*Ach, the* bubala *should know them. You vorry too much.*'

'*She's only six.*'

'*So she is old enough to know right from wrong and ven people should pay for their crimes.*'

'*You're right. It's never too early for Shoshana to learn*

how to stand up for herself.' Another man's voice. Much younger than Isaac. English accent. *'We can't let people get away with it, can we, Yitzchak? Not if they've done something wrong but don't take responsibility for their own actions. Someone has to make them pay.'*

Harry?

Then I hear the familiar tone in his voice.

'No, not Harry,' I whisper.

I pull out Dad's old photos from my rucksack and flick through them until I find one featuring a birthday party, a pink-and-white castle-shaped cake with six candles, all lit. I'm wearing a long floral short-sleeve dress, a purple Alice band keeping my long, unruly curls off my face. I'm surrounded by family and friends and neighbours. A familiar face catches my eye.

The answer's been here all along – I just couldn't see it.

At six-thirty, I pick up the office phone and make a call.

'Meet me at the bench at the crossroads between the synagogue and the church. I'll be there at eight-thirty.' I look down at a newspaper article on the table, one about the *Nokmim*. 'I know what you've been doing. I know who you are. I just don't understand why.'

At seven o'clock, I make myself a strong black coffee. I've scanned some documents and made some notes. Sent emails to Dad, Max, Mark, and Paul at *NewsQuest*. Time for a caffeine fix so I can stay awake, remain on the ball, before I set off for the crossroads. I lean back in my chair and shut my eyes. Think about what I'm about to do; what I'm about to say.

At eight o'clock, it's time for me to leave. I stand in the doorway and gaze into the room to check I haven't left anything of mine, with Freya Ridings' 'Lost Without You' blaring through my headphones.

Pain at the back of my head – a blow from behind.
I fall, whacking my elbow on the door frame.
The lights dim.
Everything fades into darkness.

CHAPTER FORTY-FIVE

I open my eyes. Squint to let my vision adjust to the harsh lighting. But the brightness is too much to bear so I snap my eyes shut. My head throbs, my elbow twinges and my hands ache behind my back. I've no idea how long I've been unconscious. When I wiggle my fingers, they don't feel stiff, so more likely minutes than hours.

It feels like I'm strapped to a chair, duct tape tying my wrists together. I hear deep agitated breaths so open my eyes again. As I twist my neck, a shadow appears in the left corner of my vision.

I part my lips, ready to break the silence, but someone else gets there first.

'I wouldn't bother if I were you.'

My nose twitches at the stench of cigarettes wafting towards me. 'Bother to what?' My voice sounds husky. When I swallow, my throat feels dry and prickly.

'Scream.' Footsteps pad towards me, along with a creaking of floorboards. 'No one will hear you. The walls are well-insulated, as you know, the downstairs door is shut and the lock's sturdy so no one's coming in. Why would I meet you at the crossroads in public when we could do this in private?'

I inhale slowly and will my muscles to relax.

One ... Two ... Three.

I'm not going to cry. I'm not going to show weakness.

Not in front of him.

David is leaning against his desk, watching me, with his chubby arms folded against his blue striped shirt. The contents of my rucksack are arranged neatly on the wooden surface behind him. Smirnoff bottle and plastic shot glasses. Notepad and pens. Laptop. Mobile phone.

'It's just you and me ... *Shoshana.*' A smug smile flickers across his face when he sees me flinch, and his eyes flash with triumph.

Has he always known who I am? Or did Harry tell him? I add these questions to a list whirling about in my head.

He steps forwards, cups my chin and squeezes it firmly. I try to squirm out of his grasp but his hand is clamped tight. 'Always wondered what happened to you, sweet little Shoshie. And now you're all grown up.'

His eyes crinkle with affection for an instant, then snap back to their usual ice-cold. He leans forwards as he talks, his warm breath souring my nostrils.

'Harry and I knew it was you when you turned up in Hillsbury. You look like her – same colour hair, same eyes – though with your father's stubborn chin. That's why I gave you this job when you applied, to keep an eye on you, and because Evie would have wanted me to.'

My skin crawls under his touch. My nostrils flare at the whiff of cigarettes and mint emanating from his mouth, and bile spills into my throat as I put the pieces together.

'It was you ... you followed me through the streets. Attacked me outside the office.' Hot anger surges through my veins like lava from an erupting volcano. I want to thump him but can't move my arms, and resist the urge to groan with frustration instead.

David's mouth curls into a smirk. 'I wanted to stop you sticking your beak in where it wasn't wanted. You just don't know when to give up. You always were an inquisitive one, mind. Liked asking questions, even then.'

He strokes my cheek with his fingers. I will myself not to heave. 'Stubborn too. You should have taken more notice of my texts, warning you off looking into these plaques. Then we wouldn't be here now ... like this.' He takes a step backwards.

Those texts.

'*You're* Renvok?' My head throbs. The room spins.

David beams. 'And did you work out what that means?'

'It's Kovner backwards – a reference to the *Nokmim*.'

My hands are beginning to ache and tingle so I wriggle them, one by one, to keep my circulation flowing. 'So why not come in that night and finish off the job?' I jiggle my wrists. The tape around them loosens slightly. 'Perfect opportunity.'

'I'd left my office keys at home when I went to the pub. I saw you wandering around so followed you, to see what you were up to. And then you locked me out.'

He opens up the black box file, grabs some papers from inside, scrunches them up and tosses them around on the floor. 'I only wanted to scare you off anyway ... until now. Good idea of mine to fix the lock.' He scrunches up more papers. 'Made it much easier for me to sneak in.'

'Now I know why you never wanted me to write about local plaques. You didn't want me to find the fake ones Valerie made. Didn't want me to discover you'd killed all these people, starting with Terry Murdock.'

He sniggers. 'Yet you're so perfect yourself, are you?' He reaches inside his jeans pocket and pulls out a red USB – the one I'd stored in my desk drawer concealed under a stack of papers, figuring it would be safer in a locked office than at my apartment. Away from Andy, for sure, but, now I realise, not away from other prying eyes.

David gives me a sinister smile. 'Yes, that's right. You should have helped that old man in Brussels rather than leave him there. I made enquiries. He died three days later from his injuries.' He jerks the USB in my face. 'And as for these photos ... you have poor taste in men, don't you, just like your mother did. Joe. Bloody. Regan. I had a long chat with that ex of yours, mind. He was begging me for forgiveness eventually, but by then it was too late.'

My skin smarts. I feel dizzy and faint. I recall the sickly odour when I first came into the office. Nadia told me Andy's on the run from the police, lying low probably. But what if—?

'You're lying.'

'Am I really? Wouldn't be the first ... as you know.' He jerks his head towards the tall walk-in cupboard in the corner of the room. 'So tell me how you guessed it's all down to me.' He tosses more scrunched-up papers on the floor.

I think carefully before I answer. 'I saw how Valerie looked at you in the park.' I don't want him to know everything I've found – not yet anyway. 'She was afraid of you. I thought it was just because your snarling dog scared her, but now I realise it was more than that. It wasn't the dog – it was you.'

'Valerie.' He spits out her name. 'Spineless tart. Guess she's told you everything. About making those plaques to warn them, and how the good doctor put them up each time. Not that it did anything, of course. Murderers, the lot of them, even if they didn't think so. Though after a while I liked the idea of having those plaques out there, a written record of injustice, so I didn't bother to stop them. It made me feel better – justified – if these dregs of society had a chance to repent for their sins and didn't take it. Anyway, I'm safe enough as she's not going to say anything to incriminate her old man, is she?'

I smile with satisfaction. Hopefully Valerie and Max have had a long chat by now. 'I found you in some old photos. Dad mentioned a family friend who prepared Isaac's accounts. Helped around the house. You knew him, my mother, Harry, me...'

David scrunches up more magazine pages and throws them towards my feet, then around the base of my chair.

'Just let me go, David. People will be looking for me.'

'Really? Who's going to be looking for Shanna Regan?' He sniggers. 'Can't say I've noticed you having much of a social life.' He reaches into his shirt pocket and plucks out a matchbox. Places it on the desk in front of him. Then opens the top drawer and pulls out a pack of Marlboro Gold. 'You used to smoke these too, I heard from Andy. Poor Shanna, under all that stress, all alone, missing her poor old dad, left without a job. She just couldn't help but fall back into her old ways and have a smoke and a drink.'

He walks back over to me, kicks at the papers by my feet to clump them together, then scrunches up some more and adds them to the pile. 'Guess this isn't quite the showdown you'd planned when you called me earlier. So tell me more. It's not like you'll be going anywhere any time soon.'

He's right, it isn't as I'd planned. I'd wanted my Miss Marple moment at the crossroads – my big reveal. And as for not going anywhere – I know I need to keep him talking, stall him. 'David, just let me go. I'll be quiet. I'll forget about all of this, that we ever met. I'll leave Hillsbury.'

'Leave? You've only just arrived, Shoshana. Surely you're here to learn more about your mother and what happened to Terry Murdock?' He picks up my Smirnoff, unscrews the lid and sniffs the contents. 'I *did* run him down, by the way, but I wasn't alone. Made them all come in Harry's car with me, witness what the three of them weren't brave enough to do themselves.'

'Three of them?'

'Everyone who loved Evie. Yitzchak, Harry...' David pauses. Gives me a cruel smile. 'I assume you can work out the third? Guess he's never told you ... in all these years.'

I flinch. Is that why Dad was in a rush to get me away from Hillsbury? Trying to keep me safe from the truth, what he'd witnessed ... maybe even what he'd done.

'How did you force them?'

'I didn't force them. I was paying Yitzchak's household bills and helping Evie with the cost of bringing up a young child ... The old man was getting too frail to work and the house needed maintaining. Evie wasn't earning enough with just a part-time secretarial job. Harry helped, of course, but I made sure you never wanted for anything. They needed me. I was always in control.'

'So you blackmailed them?'

'Something like that. And afterwards, when Yitzchak called me the blood-redeemer – the ancient vigilante – I liked it. I felt powerful, able to change lives, avenge injustice, stick up for the wronged, the underdogs.'

I want to butt in – tell him this wasn't an act of vigilantism at all, just murder – but instead I let him continue, trying to justify his past.

'It didn't matter that I wasn't Jewish, that I wasn't family. I'd done the right thing, Yitzchak said, avenging Evie's death.'

'Is this why you're a trustee of the rescue centre – dogs who've been abandoned and abused, mistreated? And is this why you carried on murdering people?'

'Murdering?' David thumps the table with his fist. 'No, this isn't murder. I'm no murderer.' He thumps the table again. 'I offered every family the chance to take revenge themselves, be the *go'el ha-adam*. But they refused. So I had no choice but to kill Peter Stevens and Gina Alders on their behalf. I *am* the blood-redeemer. Though I didn't touch Billy Pearson.' David gives me a satisfied smile. 'That was all down to the good doctor, Harry. Billy Pearson killed his daughter so I told him he had to do it himself. Restore the balance. He refused at first, just like the other families, but I soon changed his mind. We'd always been in this together, ever since Evie died.'

'You threatened him?'

'Of course.' David smirks. 'I said I'd make sure the police got him for Terry Murdock all those years ago. We'd used his car that night. I'd arranged for a mechanic to fix it on the quiet afterwards to destroy any evidence – but I took a few photos and I'm sure just a few words to the police now would get him arrested. Anyway, Harry's a doctor so knows more about injecting insulin than I do. Dodgy insulin at that, thanks to the dodgy pharmacist.'

David steps in front of me, holding the open vodka bottle close to my face. 'And now, as we're talking about medicines, open wide.'

He should know by now that I rarely do what I'm told. I shut my mouth and press my lips together as tightly as I can.

But this doesn't stop him. He pulls my head back until I feel a deep ache at the rear of my neck. He yanks open my jaw. Pours vodka inside. I wriggle, attempting to free myself from his grasp, trying to spit out the burning liquid in my mouth. But he clamps my jaw tight and holds my head back until gravity takes over. I gag and cough as the alcohol runs down my throat, a stray trickle running down my chin.

David opens the matchbox and pulls out a long match. 'So where were we?'

He scrapes the match tip rapidly along the brown sand-paper on the side of the box. A yellow flame appears, dancing like a ballerina on a pedestal, tendrils of smoke trailing towards the ceiling. 'Oh, yes. So tell me more. What else have you found?'

I clear my throat, trying to ignore the raw pain inside it. I eye the match in David's hand as it flickers and flares. 'No, *you* tell me more.'

David sits back in his chair, holding the match away from his face, gazing into the flame. 'I had Harry over a barrel. I'd taken photos of him sticking the syringe into Billy Pearson. I had proof he was a murderer. So he told me lots of useful things about his patients – especially after a shot or three of whisky at the pub. Peter Stevens beat his wife and threw her down the stairs, he said. Gina Alders knocked that poor child off the bridge, after months of antisemitic abuse. These people deserved to die.'

The flame gets closer to his fingers and then dies out. 'Now *your* turn again.' He laughs. 'This is fun, isn't it?'

I glare at him, then glance down at the papers near my feet. Notice an article with Isaac's name near the top, David Black as the byline. Think back to the cassette tape I listened to last night. 'I found the Hebrew for *Nokmim* around the edge of the plaques. You've written all these articles on the Holocaust over the years. You've interviewed all these survivors. You listened to Yitzchak. You're obsessed.'

'Obsessed?' David snorts with laughter. 'If people have murdered others, they need to be punished. Simple as that. Valerie added the word *Nokmim* to the plaques. Maybe it made her feel better about what I – what *we* – were doing. Seemed to justify it for her.'

'But if all of the original victims were Jewish, it *does* make sense in a twisted way. To her, I mean. That you were acting like the *Nokmim*. Avenging the murders of innocent Jews. Not that this makes it right though.' I narrow my eyes. 'And anyway, if people who murder innocents deserve to be punished, you do too. Gina Alders was pregnant when you killed her, and Charlotte Newman's brother told me that she was innocent anyway.'

David raises his hand. Slaps me around the face. I gasp with pain and my cheek throbs. 'I'm doing what's right,' he shouts. 'I'm the blood-redeemer. Yitzchak told me so.'

I flinch and push back in the chair. 'But why do this? What gives you that power?'

'I used to run errands for Yitzchak, or Isaac as he liked to be known by the locals, and help him with his accounts.' David lights another match. 'I was originally the boy next door but my father lost his accountancy job when I was twelve. His boss wrongly accused him of embezzling funds. No one else would employ him and his debts built up. The bailiffs came and took everything we had, other than the house. You must understand that my old man was desperate. He needed money. His boss had ruined his life. He wouldn't have done it otherwise.'

'Done what?'

'He and my mother set fire to our house while I was at school, expecting to put the fire out before it did too much damage and then pocket the insurance money. But the fire spread too quickly and they were caught inside.'

The flame is approaching his fingers now. I stare at it, willing it to spread further, but he blows out the match in time.

'My father's brother took me in and paid for private education, and left me all this.' David waves his hand in the air. 'The building, the magazine, his house...'

'If your uncle was so rich, why didn't he help your parents out?'

'He offered, but my father was a stubborn man.'

Just like you, I want to say. Instead, I let him continue talking.

'I'd grown up listening to everything Yitzchak said about the Holocaust. Evie needed me. *They* needed me. I couldn't stay away so I kept coming back. As I got older, I recorded every word he said – all the horrors, the abuse, the brutal murders, and the revenge of the *Nokmim*. The world needed to know.'

'Was Isaac one of them? One of the *Nokmim*?'

'He never said, but I did wonder.' He leans back against his desk. 'Sometimes you would sit with us, taking it all in. Remember?'

I shake my head.

'Shame.' His eyes crinkle with pity. 'Broke your grandfather's heart when you left. Mine and Harry's too. It was like losing Evie all over again, though it was worse for Yitzchak. Second time he'd lost a beloved Shoshie. His sister, then you.' He shakes his head. 'He asked me – no ... begged me – to kill Terry Murdock after our Evie died. Harry and Joe were too spineless to do it. Yet if I'd had the chance to kill my father's boss ... the man who spread those lies ... who made my father...'

David pauses to wipe his eyes. 'If I'd had that chance, I would have grabbed it. But I was just twelve. I didn't even know where to find him.'

'I won't let you get away with this, David.'

'Bit late now, don't you think? It's an old building so it won't take much to burn it down. Just one match – and I have plenty in here.' He picks up the matchbox and shakes it. 'Kill two birds with one stone, I reckon, as the magazine has been draining my bank account for years.'

'Is that why you've never fixed the building?' My eyes flicker to the Rolex on his wrist. 'I've always assumed you were just a stingy bastard.'

David laughs. 'It's been a struggle to get advertising in so I've had to dip into my own funds. The bank has finally given me a loan but insurance money would be useful too. My old man didn't have such a bad idea – though I'll do it properly.'

He lights another match and throws it towards my feet. A scrunched-up piece of paper begins to smoulder. I kick at it. Stomp the flame out.

'You bitch.' David lights yet another match and tosses it somewhere behind me. I catch a whiff of smoke. 'Now let me make sure you can't get out and then I'll leave you to it.'

'David, put the fucking fire out.' Pain rips through my throat as I shout the words. 'Even if you kill me now, people will know. Everything I've found is with someone ... a lawyer. If I don't get back to him, he'll take it all to the police.'

'You're bluffing.'

'Am I? Are you prepared to take that risk?'

David pulls some duct tape out from his top drawer, bends down and holds it towards my ankles. 'Poor David, should never have taken on that Shanna Regan, they'll say. Trouble from the start. Andy told me about the rumours he spread. Handy for me.'

I lift up my leg. Kick him in the face.

'You bitch.' He leans forwards, clutching his nose, blood pouring down towards his chin.

I kick him again, this time directed at his forehead.

'Come on!' I scream. Surely my time is up. 'Come on!'

I wriggle my wrists, feeling my joints click and the duct tape loosen. I keep on wriggling, my arms aching so much that I worry I'll pass out. The chair digs into my back. Tears flow down my cheeks, from pain, smoke or anger, I'm not sure which, but I have to keep going. I can't let him beat me. I won't let him win.

The fire is inching closer to my trainers. I stand up slowly, lifting the chair up behind me with all my strength, my adrenaline levels at an all-time high, and stomp on the flames.

But the flames are too stubborn to comply and my energy levels begin to plummet. So I put the chair back down and slump in my seat.

David stirs. Lifts his head. Pulls himself up. Grabs hold of my trainer.

I try to kick him away but he holds on tight.

The flames are travelling towards the door, blocking our path to safety.

Soon, neither of us will be going anywhere other than the morgue.

David reaches up and grabs the Smirnoff. 'I'm punishing *you* for what you ignored in Brussels; what *you* let your ex get away with.'

I wriggle my hands again. The tape loosens and I pull one wrist free.

As David glances towards the cupboard door with a big grin on his face, I make my move and kick him in the balls. He drops the bottle and clasps his hand to his groin. Glass smashes on the table. Vodka spills out over the surface, trickling towards the table edge. If it lands on the floor, it'll be right in the path of the flames.

I yank off the rest of the tape to free my other wrist and stumble to the door, leaving David writhing on the floor.

I hear banging downstairs, then a splintering of wood. Heavy boots stomp towards me. The office door swings open. A policewoman stands in the doorway, a familiar tall figure behind her.

I slump against the wall as my final ounce of adrenaline fades. Feel the tiny voice recorder tucked into my bra. The cavalry has arrived.

Always be prepared.

If my grandad taught me one useful life skill, it was definitely this.

CHAPTER FORTY-SIX

Rain pounds down onto the pavement, like a firing squad aiming a barrage of water bullets at the ground. Yet bad weather hasn't kept the neighbours at bay. I've never seen Campton Avenue so full of life. People peering through windows, around open curtains, over their garden gates. Others standing in their doorways or crouching under large golfing umbrellas, watching the two police cars parked in front of us.

I stand under a small poplar tree, shielding my bandaged head from the rain with my hood.

Harry walks out of his bungalow, head held high. His narrow eyes lock onto mine. His stony gaze pierces me like a heat-seeking missile finding its target. There's a stillness inside him. Cool hatred, maybe, judging by his clenched jaw. No bemused expression now, just a hardness I haven't seen before. A confident smile spreads across his face as he's marched to the waiting police car.

I don't need to imagine what he's thinking.

I know.

I'm the enemy, the cause of his anger and the reason for his arrest.

Harry was a father figure to me when Dad was on the road, and my mother must have loved him, so he can't be all bad. David admitted that Valerie and Harry helped him reluctantly and they both tried to give everyone a chance.

So have I done the right thing, giving their names to the police? My heart and brain say *yes* but the lump of uncertainty in my throat says otherwise. I silently beg my churning stomach to settle.

The police questioned me at the hospital, and also quizzed Mark who refused to leave my side after he rescued me. He'd waited at the crossroads, where we were going to meet David together. When I didn't turn up, he called the police. I showed them my notes and the photos and told them everything I know. Ruth and Peter Stevens. Gina Alders and Charlotte Newman. Terry Murdock and my mother – Evie, Lynnie, Mum, whatever I want her to be. Billy Pearson and Susan Lee. I directed them to the plaques and told them about Harry and Valerie and David and the parts they played. And about Andy, Brussels and everything that had happened in Hillsbury, and that I hadn't seen him for days.

I left nothing out. No more lies.

The police said they'd be in touch. Then Max called me to confirm that David was remaining in custody and the police had found Andy's body in the office cupboard, kicked in the head and stabbed through the heart. Andy's fingerprints were found in Hetty's flat.

A murmur spreads through the crowd. A small figure walks through the doorway of number three, wearing a burgundy felt coat. Her eyes meet mine but no steely gaze here. Instead, she seems soft and mellow.

Thank you, she mouths as the police lead her past me.

She gives me a gentle smile, with a look of relief and a brightness in her eyes that I haven't seen before.

Valerie was right when she said Hillsbury isn't always quiet and peaceful. Maybe even then she was trying to give me a clue.

I walk forwards a few paces to the front police car. Harry sits upright on the back seat, confident and composed. He looks at me through the window then turns to look at his wife climbing into the car behind him. He clenches his fists, as if he wishes he could punch something – or someone.

I understand his pain – their pain. How they suffered with Susan's killer going unpunished, until David offered them a way to take revenge. But that doesn't mean it's right, any more than it was right to murder Terry Murdock for running down my mother late one night.

I gaze back at Harry, defiant, the image of Valerie's relief fuelling my bravado.

His smile drops off his face.

The lump of uncertainty in my throat fades away. The churning in my stomach has gone.

I know I've done the right thing. Chosen the right path.

A folded piece of paper is shoved into my hand. I look up and see someone with a purple headscarf scurrying away from me, the young woman Valerie and I saw in the café that day. I unfold the paper and gaze at the words, typed with an old-fashioned typewriter, harder on the letter E.

You're not alone. Find Evie's sister. V

CHAPTER FORTY-SEVEN

It's Sunday morning and I'm standing at the crossroads facing the synagogue, peering through the black gates. Watching children in the car park, wrapped up in thick coats and woollen hats, colourful scarves woven around their necks. Some are playing with skipping ropes and footballs and hula hoops; others are huddled together, telling stories or singing songs. Tinkles of laughter fill the air.

It's a frosty day, with a sprinkling of icing sugar on the cars and pavements. Yet the sun is shining down on us as if spring isn't too far away.

When the rabbi sees me, a smile stretches across his face and his eyes light up. He waves and calls to me but his words are lost in a sudden gust of wind.

Other than one. My full name. Shoshana.

My mother's face swims in front of me. I hear her voice, and tears well in my eyes.

Shoshie. Shoshie. Come quick.

And I hear my grandfather, my *zeida*.

Never forget who you are. Where you've come from.

Then someone behind me shouts out 'Shanna' so I swivel around.

Mark is standing in the church doorway, wearing a woolly beanie hat and clutching a blue folder in his hand.

'How's your head?'

'Fine.' I rub it gently. 'Just a bit sore.'

'Maybe later you'll come over for lunch?'

I look at the front of the church with its open door and welcome sign, Christmas lights draped around the door frame and the wreath hanging at the centre.

I think of Dad. He'll be at church already, just up the road from the farm, the place he still calls home, the place waiting for my visit before it's sold.

Don't tell them ya Jewish, Shanna. It's our secret, remember that.

But Mama always said...

I knows that, Shanna. But it's safer that way here. And some lies are okay, for sure.

I think of David, all those lies he told, covering up his crimes. His urge to take revenge, taking matters into his own hands, to become the blood-redeemer.

'It has to stop,' Valerie had whispered to me on the bench under the sycamore trees after David had gone. 'I want it to stop and only you can do it. I love my husband, Shanna. The truth when it comes out will destroy him, destroy my marriage and destroy me. But I can't let those two boys die. They're just kids ... And you ... you're on the outside but you're still involved. This is personal to you. You can set everything in motion. Help me ... please.'

I think of Andy in Brussels and the hatred I saw in his eyes that day – and the ultimate price he paid.

I look at the synagogue and the children and the rabbi, then at the church and Mark waiting for an answer.

At this crossroads, my present and my past collide. But which way should I turn?

I never thought my own past mattered, until I realised how much my family history shapes me, my own history too. My resulting wanderlust. My search for the truth. My nomadic lifestyle. Always running away. Never truly giving myself to anyone. Afraid to reveal too much.

But my memories are beginning to surface, like canaries in a cage finally being set free, and I am no longer prepared to hide.

I think of Mark, so close to the church but also with ties across the road. Someone split in two, a bit like me.

Maybe I'm ready to settle down, give up travelling, find a place on a local newspaper or magazine, create long-lasting friendships. But to decide where that will be and how to live my life, I need to understand more about my past.

You're not alone. Find Evie's sister.

'Lunch will be great,' I shout to Mark. 'But right now, there's somewhere I need to be. Someone I need to see.'

Life is a crossroads. A series of pathways for us to choose from. A constant decision-making process.

Where should I be?

Who should I be?

And why?

Well, now it's time for me to find out.

I pick up my trusty red rucksack, sling the fraying black straps over my shoulders and start walking.

ENJOYED THE REDEEMER?

IT'S TIME TO MEET THE ASSOCIATE

Thank you so much for choosing to read *The Redeemer*. I hope you enjoyed it. If you have time, I would be very grateful if you could leave a rating and/or short, honest, spoiler-free review of *The Redeemer* on Amazon, Goodreads or wherever you bought this book. Your ratings and reviews help me reach new readers. And please recommend my book to your family and friends.

Now it's time to meet *THE ASSOCIATE*, the next book in my Shanna Regan Mysteries series.

A missing architect. An interfaith charity project. Vandalism and online threats. Can racist slogans lead to kidnap – or even murder?

When an architect vanishes in East London, her concerned fiancé asks journalist Shanna Regan to find her. The missing woman has been leading an interfaith Jewish-Muslim charity project that's become the target of malicious damage and racist threats.

After Shanna witnesses a teenage girl fall to her death,

she's convinced the architect's disappearance is also linked to a local youth outreach project. And then another woman is reported missing.

Amid rising local tensions, danger appears to be lurking around every corner. Even the safest sanctuaries seem to be hiding the darkest secrets. As Shanna uncovers a tangled web of lies, she puts her own life on the line. Will she find the missing architect before it's too late?

PLEASE KEEP IN TOUCH!

I'm a freelance journalist, editor and proofreader. *The Redeemer* was shortlisted for Best Debut Crime Novel of 2022 in the Crime Fiction Lover Awards 2022 and was given an honourable mention in the Capital Crime/DHH Literary Agency New Voices Award 2019. I live in Hertfordshire with my husband and two sons.

If you would like to keep up to date with my latest book releases, you can join my Readers' Club for occasional news and exclusive giveaways. It's completely free, your email address will never be shared, and you can unsubscribe at any time.

vgoldmanbooks.com/join-my-readers-club/

You can also follow me on Amazon to be notified about my next book. To do this, find one of my books on Amazon. Click on my name to arrive on my Amazon page and then click the Follow button.

It's always lovely to hear from readers. You can connect with me in various ways:

Website: vgoldmanbooks.com
Twitter: @VictoriaGoldma2
Facebook: www.facebook.com/VictoriaGoldmanBooks

AFTERWORD

All of the anti-Jewish hate (antisemitic) incidents in *The Redeemer* are based on real-life events that took place in the UK while I was writing the book in 2018 and 2019. According to the Community Security Trust (CST)'s Antisemitic Incidents Report 2019, published in February 2020, CST received notifications of 1,805 antisemitic incidents in the UK during 2019, which was seven percent higher than the total for 2018.

One hundred and fifty-seven antisemitic assaults were recorded nationally in 2019; 105 of these assaults were random attacks on Jewish people in public places, and 64 of these were reported to the CST as being on people who were visibly Jewish, usually because of religious symbols, Jewish school uniforms or traditional clothing. There were 24 assaults on Jewish schoolchildren, of which 14 took place away from school premises.

Antisemitism in the UK continues to rise. According to the CST's Antisemitic Incidents Report 2021, published in February 2022, 2,255 anti-Jewish hate incidents were reported nationwide in 2021.

If you witness an anti-Jewish hate incident in the UK, this can be reported to the CST.

- In an emergency, always call the police first on 999, then call CST's 24-hour National Emergency Number on 0800 032 3263.

- Non-urgent incidents can be reported: online at https://cst.org.uk/report-incident; by emailing incidents@cst.org.uk; or calling the CST Psychological Support Helpline on 0800 032 8477.

ACKNOWLEDGMENTS

Hillsbury is a fictional town loosely based on where I live in Hertfordshire. If you know the area, some of the locations in this book may seem familiar. But I'd like to reassure everyone who lives nearby that none of you have been immortalised as a character in this book!

The Redeemer hasn't reached its readers without some help. Firstly, thank you to my editors, Sara Starbuck and Louise Voss, and to my proofreader, Kate Noble (who also provides general cheerleading support). To logo designer Paul Sandler, Design for Writers for the cover, and Alexandra Amor for formatting and typesetting.

Thank you also to Kate Moloney, for her suggestion of Kilconly as Shanna's Irish hometown and for fixing Joe's dialogue, and to Rabbi Elchonon Feldman for taking the time to discuss the concept of Judaism and revenge. Any errors in this book are mine alone.

I have so many other people to thank for giving me advice and support during my writing journey. I can't mention everyone, or these acknowledgments would spread across several pages. But here are a few of them, in no particular order: Stephanie Rothwell, Liz Barnsley, Joy Kluver, Alex Caan, Jen Lucas, Liz Robinson and Susi Holliday. Also, thank you to Lynne Milford and Miranda Boers for their advice on getting *The Redeemer* out into the world, and to the Waterstones Piccadilly Writing Group (now on WhatsApp) and the Crime Fiction Coach Facebook group. I would also like to thank the authors, bloggers and reviewers who have been cheerleading me on social media, and all of my family and friends who have been cheerleading me from behind the scenes.

Finally, to Richard, Samuel and Adam, thank you for being there – always and forever.